Praise for *Hot Flashes a*

"Hilarious doesn't begin to describe Diann H *ot Flashes and Cold Cream*! The truth and wisdom layered with the humor will make you realize the best is yet to come and that it's not time to sit in a rocker on the porch and watch life pass us by. Now where did I put those old Donny Osmond records?"

—Colleen Coble, author of *Black Sands*

"Fresh, witty, and brimming with giggles from start to finish."

—Linda Windsor, award-winning author of *Paper Moon* and *Fiesta Moon*

"*Hot Flashes and Cold Cream* delivers a fun experience with sparkling prose, sharp wit, and genuine characters. Diann Hunt takes us through the treacherous territory of aging with delight and divine grace. Even if you're not yet flashing hot or smearing on wrinkle cream, this book is still for you! Read it and weep and laugh—and laugh some more."

—Kathryn Mackel, author of *The Surrogate* and *Outriders*

"*Hot Flashes and Cold Cream* could coax the giggles out of a bristling porcupine, but the real appeal of Diann Hunt's novel lies in its proficient blend of truth and honesty. Another delicious treat from an author not afraid to let us see inside ourselves."

—Lois Richer, author of *Past Secrets, Present Love*

"Diann Hunt skillfully immerses her characters into the murky waters of middle age and requires them to sink or swim—no treading water permitted! Grab a latte and settle in for a lighthearted read with a compelling midlife message."

—Judith Miller, author of *First Dawn*

"This book had me laughing aloud and left me with an uplifting feeling! The characterization is BEYOND excellent. GET THE BOOK! I give it my highest rating!"

—www.book-reviews.ws

"This is a warm and wonderful story for every woman who's ever felt she's had too many birthdays and every woman who's ever felt insecure and vulnerable. It is a book that will show all of us what's really important as the years pile up, and how to live them with joy and thankfulness."

—Lorena McCourtney, author of the Ivy Malone Mysteries series

"Diann Hunt has touched my heart—and my funny bone—with multiple peals of laughter and some satisfying tears. *Hot Flashes and Cold Cream* is a must read for anyone who has ever known anyone who hit the wall of menopause and anyone who loves to laugh."

—Hannah Alexander, author of *Last Resort* and *Note of Peril*

"Diann Hunt's *Hot Flashes and Cold Cream* is a story every woman 'of a certain age' can identify with. And you've got to love a heroine whose toy Chihuahua is named Crusher!"

—Lyn Cote, author of The Women of Ivy Manor series

"What a hoot! *Hot Flashes and Cold Cream* had me laughing out loud and staying up late. I instantly fell in love with Maggie, whose flaws are as endearing as her sense of humor."

—Denise Hunter, author of *Saving Grace*

"Diann Hunt is a hilarious new voice in women's fiction. *Hot Flashes and Cold Cream* will make you laugh out loud and laugh with Maggie for all her loveable foibles. Diann has created a character that all women can identify with!"

—Kristin Billerbeck, author of *What a Girl Wants* and *She's All That*

"Join Diann Hunt's hilarious character as she sorts through her life crisis, not one event at a time, but all muddled together. Laugh out loud laughter is guaranteed between the covers of this book."

—roadtoromance.ca

"Hot Flashes and Cold Cream is a hold-your-sides, laugh-out-loud book! [It] leads readers through the mines of midlife to a wonderful place of rest and refuge!"

—www.inthelibraryreview.com

Hot Flashes & Cold Cream

a novel by

DIANN HUNT

WestBow Press
A Division of Thomas Nelson Publishers
Since 1798

visit us at www.westbowpress.com

Published in Nashville, Tennessee, by WestBow Press, a division of Thomas Nelson, Inc.

WestBow Press books may be purchased in bulk for educational, business, fundraising, or sales promotional use. For information, please e-mail: SpecialMarkets@ThomasNelson.com.

Publisher's Note: This novel is a work of fiction. Names, characters, places, and incidents are either products of the author's imagination or used fictitiously. All characters are fictional, and any similarity to people living or dead is purely coincidental.

Library of Congress Cataloging-in-Publication Data

Hunt, Diann.
Hot flashes and cold cream / Diann Hunt.
p. cm.
ISBN 1-59554-069-5 (pbk.)
1. Middle aged women—Fiction. 2. Married people—Fiction. I. Title.

PS3608.U573H68 2005
813'.6—dc22

2005024773

Printed in the United States of America

06 07 08 09 RRD 9 8 7 6 5 4 3 2

To all the boomer ladies
who suffer in silence.
I feel your pain.

1

With one glance at my body in the bedroom mirror, my suspicions are confirmed. Everything has gone south—and I didn't make a reservation.

"Gordon!" I scream for my husband like a deprived woman at a sidewalk sale. "Come quick! I've been kidnapped!"

Without a moment to lose, I try to reverse the aging process by shooting determined arms into the air. I'm reaching for the ceiling as if my life depends on it, and jogging in place. Immediately thinking my waist needs it most of all, I clasp my fingers overhead and plunge sideways in one dramatic swoop. Denise Austin would be proud.

My husband dashes around the corner, heaving gulps of air, panic on his face. "Maggie, what the—"

Suddenly my hands wallop the side of Gordon's nightstand lamp and send it crashing against the wall, narrowly missing his head. The shade flies across the room, sparks scatter with bulb pieces, and the remains sizzle like a steak on the grill.

One look at Gordon's face, and I'm thinking my days of worrying about this age thing are over.

I may not live to see breakfast.

"I thought you screamed"—he's bending over now and gasping for breath—"that you were being kidnapped." Pulling a handkerchief from his pocket, he wipes his forehead. I feel bad that I've caused him to sweat when he's already dressed for work. He stuffs the hankie back in place. "Well?"

Okay, so my body wasn't kidnapped, but somehow this doesn't seem like the time to tell him that Grandma borrowed it. Can we say *Freaky Friday* moment here? I'm walking around in Grandma's skin, and somewhere in heaven Grandma is walking around in mine. No, that can't be right. Grandma now has a heavenly body, and I know my body is anything but heavenly.

"Maggie?"

I avoid the issue. "I'm sorry about the lamp, Gordon." We stoop down to pick up the broken pieces.

"That was a close one. If I didn't know better, I might think you were trying to get rid of me. What's going on, Maggie?"

Okay, I'm a klutz. So rub it in my face, why don't you. Next time, maybe I won't miss. Whoa, Maggie. Down, girl.

"I'm waiting." Gordon steps behind me, his heavy breathing sounding a lot like Darth Vader.

Scooping the last bit of bulb into the trash, I put the lamp back on the stand, hoping that if I stall long enough, he'll go away.

He doesn't.

I take a deep breath and turn to him.

"Well, see, I ran into Debra Stiffler—or whatever her married name is now—at the store yesterday . . ."

"What does that have to do with you screaming? I thought you hurt yourself or someone was hurting you." He doesn't bother to hide his irritation.

"Okay, so sometimes I overreact." A fact he still struggles with after almost thirty years of marriage, I might add.

"Sometimes?" He's peering over his glasses the way he used to do to our kids, Heather and Nick, when they were in trouble.

"Most times?"

"You ever heard of the 'Little Boy Who Cried Wolf'?"

With a lift of my chin, I walk over to the dresser, pick up my brush, and run it through my hair, all the while staring at Gordon through the mirror.

His breathing quiets and now his eyes turn soft as his reflection looks back at me. "Look, Maggie, you scared me, that's all." His Tommy scent soothes me. I put the brush down, and he wraps his arms around my waist. "I don't want anything to happen to you."

"I'm sorry, Gordon."

"Now, what about Debra whoever?" he asks, resting his chin on the top of my head.

"Stiffler. You remember her," I prompt, "the high-school cheerleader, homecoming queen, girl-that-every-guy-wanted-to-date, Debra Stiffler."

His face brightens. He lifts his head and stares at my reflection. "Oh, *that* Debra Stiffler."

I think I might have to hurt him.

"What is she doing in Charming? Indiana doesn't seem to fit her. Anyway, I thought she had moved to Colorado."

"Probably came home to visit her parents. Who knows?" My hand brushes the comment aside. "Anyway, we served on student council together for four years," I say, as if this should mean something to him.

"She married that football jock, Greg somebody, didn't she?"

"I don't remember who she married. Could we move on here?"

"That guy had an ego the size of Texas."

Staring at him a moment, I mentally shake myself. "Whatever. Look, Gordon, the point is—"

"Yeah?" He nuzzles his face in my neck. I have to wonder if he's paying attention.

"—I told her how good she looked, how great it was to see her, when it suddenly dawned on me that she didn't have a clue who I was." His breath is warm against my skin, and his whiskers tickle. At this point it becomes obvious to me that Gordon cannot nuzzle and listen at the same time, so I pull free from his grasp and turn around to face him.

He frowns.

"It's like this. I knew her at once with her upturned nose, crisp, snappy cheerleader walk, and size 6 body." Okay, so there's a bitter edge to my voice here. The only thing size 6 on me is my wedding ring.

I haven't been able to take it off in years.

"How could she not have recognized me, Gordon?"

"Honey, it has been, well—" I do not miss the fact that he backs away, slowly, "—over, um, thirty years," he says with great caution, as if we've had this discussion before. My eyebrow is raised, and he knows better than to finish.

"Have I changed that much?"

"You're beautiful as always, my love." And without so much as taking a breath, he adds, "How about some coffee?"

"Don't think I didn't notice how you changed the subject, Gordon Paul Hayden."

He winks, then darts down the hallway like a gangster in a getaway car, leaving me to the mercy of our mirror, which by now I'm thinking must have been previously owned by the wicked witch in *Snow White.*

Forcing myself to take another glimpse, it's as though I'm seeing myself for the first time in twenty—would you believe thirty?—years. Transfixed by the wrinkled, soon-to-be-fifty-year-old frowning back at me from the mirror, I pinch my cheeks to add some color. Pale and dry, my skin just sort of lies there like old leather. If I didn't smell coffee coming from the kitchen, I'd think I was dead.

Though not exactly homecoming queen material, I looked pretty good back in the day. Not that I want to be twenty again, but, well, being young has its merits.

My thoughts flit to Gordon's new paralegal who could pass for Paris Hilton's twin—maybe with a bit more meat on her bones. Maybe that's why I'm noticing the changes in me all of a sudden. Meeting her at our daughter Heather's wedding last weekend and then seeing Debra Stiffler at the store was obviously more than my sagging self could handle.

Daring another look at my reflection, I raise an eyebrow, suck my cheeks in with my teeth, and pull on a sexy look. With all the confidence of Pamela Anderson—well, her mother, anyway—I think to myself: *Paris Paralegal can move those baby thighs right on over, 'cause a real woman is a-comin' through*!

My husband enters the room again. "Are you okay?" he asks, looking at me strangely as he walks over to his dresser.

I let my cheeks fall back into place and sigh. "I'm fine," I say, thinking I'll break that mirror when he leaves.

Gordon continues to look at me for a moment, then shakes his head, shrugs, and roots around the top drawer for socks. I watch him through the mirror. What does he really think of me? He says all the right things, but what lurks in the hidden corners of his mind? When we gather for office parties, does he compare me to the younger women? Does he prefer their company to mine? Is that why he stays at work so late into the evenings?

Have I let myself go? There's no question that Gordon brightened at the memory of Debra Stiffler. Do I have that same effect on him?

A sock drops from his grasp, and he picks it up with his toes. What a guy. I call him Claw Foot. My toes just sort of stand there like chubby little soldiers, never really amounting to anything. Gordon, on the other hand, scrunches his toes together and, in one quick swoop, goes in for the kill. I tell you, the man is amazing.

I'm sure Gordon is surrounded by temptation. He is handsome, after all. True, his sandy-colored hair is starting to thin a bit, but his goatee makes up for it. All right, so there's a streak of gray in his facial hair, but men look more distinguished with gray. Why is that? I look at his body. The low-carb diet is kicking in big time, and his pounds are melting away as fast as my memory.

He puts on his socks and shoes, then turns to me. "Let's go have that coffee, Gorgeous."

I perk up. It doesn't matter if his glasses do need a change in prescription, he thinks I'm gorgeous. The thought warms me like an electric blanket—or is it just a hot flash?

Gordon walks over and pulls me into his arms. Sucking in my stomach, I throw out my chest. He looks down into my wrinkled face. "I love you," he says tenderly, and for that instant, all is right with my world.

"I love you too," I say, meaning it with my whole heart.

He releases his hold and walks out the door. Like a baby duck, I follow him into the kitchen where he pours the steaming brew into our cups.

"Here you go," he says in a chipper voice. He extends the mug toward me and all but skips to his chair.

How can anyone be that happy in the morning? *Anytime* for that matter? It isn't normal. I should have him committed.

Coffee in hand, I slip over to the sofa.

Gordon pulls open the newspaper and soon wanders into the world of finance. A place of fascination for lawyers, accountants, and financial advisors. A place of sheer boredom for me.

With a glance at the area around his chair, I'm reminded of Gordon's love for stacks. A stack of magazines, stack of laundry, stack of pancakes, it doesn't matter. He's into it. His desk at his office is the worst. He insists the stacks are organized, but when I go through them at home, I'm thinking there's no correlation whatsoever between bank brochures for home equity loans and low-carb candy wrappers. He must have struggled with that "Which one does not belong in this group?" question in school testing.

While I'm staring at his ever-growing stacks, Gordon starts to whistle. We're not talking a one-note deal, but a whole song, a Bing Crosby–type whistle—cheerful, carefree. He turns the page of his newspaper and peeks around the side to wink at me.

"Are you sure you're all right? I mean, you didn't hurt yourself when you were doing that *Incredible Hulk* thing in the bedroom, did you?" he asks with a grin.

"Oh, that's cute, Gordon."

He shrugs.

I'm walking around with Grandma's body, our kids have moved out of the house, and he's okay with this? The man is clueless. Completely clueless.

"I'm just tired." I don't want to get into a big discussion over my self-worth. *Who am I without the children? When did my body fall apart?* It sounds petty even to my ears. Still, I can't help the way I feel.

He puts the paper down and smiles at me before he takes another drink of his coffee. Studying him, I wonder how he can just cruise through life without a care in the world.

He picks up his Bible, opens it, and reads our Scripture for the day, along with the devotional; then he prays. His words ride along the fringes of my consciousness as my mind wanders to my ever-changing body, our "empty nest," and Gordon's new paralegal.

I need to pull myself out of this mood. Maybe go shopping or call Lily. Lily Newgent is the kind of friend who listens to your problems and then offers a chocolate truffle.

No one could ask for a better friend than that.

• • •

I roll down my car window and allow the crisp, fall air to chase away my menopausal mood as I make my way to The New Brew, Charming's recently opened coffee shop. Along the way, several Amish buggies pass by, a sight I always enjoy.

By the time I arrive, I'm feeling pretty good. Warmth hits me the moment I enter The New Brew. Have I mentioned I'm into this whole coffee-shop thing? The scent of rich coffee beans, the whir of the cappuccino machine, the soft chatter coming from cozy tables where friends gather to talk about nothing in particular, there's nothing like it.

Standing in line at the counter, Lily sees me and waves. I walk over to her.

"Hi, Maggie." We hug like we haven't seen each other in years, but of course it's only been four days.

Lily is my best friend and has been since that fateful day in first grade when Ritchie Wallace stepped on Lily's yellow crayon and broke it. I could tell Lily was trying desperately not to cry, so I gave her my yellow crayon to make her feel better. We connected that day. She says only a kindred spirit would do such an unselfish thing. It's not like she had to know I don't like yellow.

"Hi, Lily. That's cute, is it new?" I point to her yellow knit top. It's still her favorite color.

She grins and nods. Even her bobbed hair is yellow—well, bottled yellow now, but it was a striking blond all on its own before her husband, Bob, died six years ago.

"May I help you?" the small voice behind the counter asks. I turn to the girl to place my order. She has dark, pixie-cut hair and droopy brown eyes, similar to Bambi's after his mother died; but what I struggle to get past is the silver ring in her nose. To keep from staring, I rummage through my purse for my coffee card. I'm almost sure I've already accumulated enough stamps to have a freebie coming this time.

"Yes, I'll take a hot, single-shot, tall, nonfat caramel latte with whipped cream, please," Lily says without skipping a beat.

I'm downright proud that Lily can remember a name that long. Every time she orders it, I think she's christening her drink. I stop rooting through my purse long enough to give her the respect she deserves.

My order sounds so plain next to hers. "Skinny mocha, please." It's the best I can do without ginkgo biloba. Resuming my search in the last pocket of my purse for the coffee card, I discover it's not there. I collect the receipts, gum wrappers, and eyebrow pencil shavings that have spilled onto the counter. Stuffing the papers back inside my bag, I smile at the cashier, whose name tag says "Jade."

She rings up the sale, stamps a new card, and gives it to me, then takes my five-dollar bill.

"Does that hurt?" I hear myself say.

She looks up in surprise. "What?"

I point to her nose.

"Oh, this?" She beams. "Nope. Isn't it cool?"

Cool? A ring in her nose? I want to say, "Maybe, if it's a tribal custom," but I don't. I lift a tentative smile. "With all these piercings nowadays, it's a wonder you kids don't leak when you drink water." Uh-oh, now I look and sound like Grandma, and it's scaring me. Not wanting to offend Jade, I give a generous laugh.

It takes a minute for her to digest my comment and then she laughs along.

My kids are gone a week, and already I'm disconnected from the younger generation.

She gives me my change, her hand hovering a little too long near the "Thanks a Latte" tip cup. Taking the change from her, I add two quarters to the cup, hoping all the while that I'm not contributing to another piercing.

The sun is streaming through the front window, and I want to sit at the table perched next to it. Unfortunately, it has a used cup and some coffee spills on it. Lily starts to move elsewhere.

"No, wait. I want to sit here. Be right back." Placing my drink on the table, I walk to the counter. "Hi, Jade," I say, like we're old friends now. "Could I have a cloth to clean that table?" I point toward where Lily is sitting.

"Oh, I'm sorry," she says. "I'll get right to it."

"You have customers. I'm glad to do it."

She shrugs and hands me the cloth. After cleaning the table, I return the cloth to the counter. Jade and I exchange a smile and then I walk back and settle into my chair by Lily. We talk about Heather's wedding, the ceremony, Heather's moving away. Gloom settles over me at the thought of my empty nest.

Lily picks up on my mood and stares at me. "You okay?"

"I'm having a pity party and can't seem to snap out of it."

Lily lifts the lid from her coffee, stirs the whipped cream into the hot liquid, and licks the coffee stick clean. "Someone once told me there are two things wrong with a pity party," she says as she snaps the lid back into place. "Number one, you're the only one invited. Number two, they don't serve refreshments."

I chuckle. "How did you get so wise?" No matter how dark my mood, Lily can always make me smile.

She shrugs. "You know, you should try some Siberian ginseng."

"Oh, here we go." I roll my eyes. "Dr. Lily has joined us once again." I grin and take a drink.

"Well, you can make fun all you want. Plenty of people ask my advice on such things." She hikes up her nose a bit.

Swallowing my chuckle, I put my cup down. "Okay, Lil, tell me about Siberian ginseng. Does it help with hot flashes?"

She blinks.

"You know, the Siberian part. Siberian, as in cold. Get it?"

She must not. She's not laughing. "It helps calm the changing moods," she says in her most professional, doctor's voice. A voice I'm sure she learned to emulate by watching *ER* reruns. "Why are you having mood swings?"

"I think it's my age, the kids leaving home, all that."

Lily looks a little perplexed. "You still have Nick at home—well, sort of."

"Not really. He is in college during the school year, then he travels in the summer with his singing group. We don't get to see him much."

"You know, maybe you just need something to do. Get a part-time job or volunteer for something," Lily says cheerfully.

"A job? Easy for you to say. Your mom told me you've been cutting hair since you were in second grade."

"It was *my* hair I cut at that age. She didn't bother to tell you that I made such a mess of things that she had to give me a perm to hide the uneven spots. I'll never forget it. All the boys in my class made fun of me when the teacher passed around our school pictures. Very traumatic," Lily says, shaking her head as though she means it.

All these years I've known Lily, and I didn't know that story. You think you know a person.

"At least you can do something, Lily. I haven't taught school since the kids were born. I'd probably have to take some classes before going back into teaching."

"Well, if you don't want to go to school, do something else. The possibilities are endless, Maggie." She drops her chin in her hand and stares at the ceiling. "Let's see, there's secretarial—"

"Hip expansion," I cut her off like I'm blazing a trail.

"Excuse me?"

"You know, sitting all day? Hip expansion."

Not one to be easily deterred, Lily continues. "How about waitressing?"

"Varicose veins."

She stares at me. "You're pathetic."

"I know." I drum my fingers on the table. "Hey, I've got it. How about you teach me how to do hair?" I like Lily's schedule; I'm thinking this could work.

She shakes her head. "I've seen how you do Crusher's hair," she says, referring to our Chihuahua.

"What? Crusher doesn't have any hair to speak of."

"Exactly." Her eyes sparkle with an ornery glint.

"Ha, ha."

Lily taps her finger against her temple. "There must be something—" One look at my face and her enthusiasm fades. Now she gets it. I just need a pout fest, a pity party, a look-at-me-my-life-is-empty sympathy session. "Okay, maybe not."

"Have you noticed how much I've changed?" I ask abruptly.

She takes a drink, wipes her mouth with a napkin, and places her cup on the table. "How do you mean?"

"Well—" I glance around the room. There is no one over thirty. "I look"—My cheeks feel warm. I feel silly talking about it—"old."

Lily tries, but fails, to hide her amusement. "Oh, is that all? Good grief, Maggie, all of us look older. We're not twenty anymore. It happens." She takes another drink.

"But Debra Stiffler—"

"Oh, puh-lease!" She sets her cup back on the table with a thunk, causing some coffee to slosh out. "She's had more nips and tucks than a wedding dress passed down three generations." She wipes up the coffee with a napkin.

Okay, I'm liking this conversation. "Really?"

"Girl, if she were any tighter, she'd be a corset."

"Doggone it. If that's the case, I should have ordered a mocha with whole milk, slathered in whipped cream."

We look at each other and start laughing.

Lily looks me straight in the eyes. I laugh harder. Then all of a sudden my laughter turns to hiccupy sobs. You know how sometimes you're so emotional that when you laugh, you cry? Well, that's what happens here.

Lily laughs with me, then stops when she sees me crying. "Okay, you're scaring me."

A couple more chuckles and sobs, then I dab at my face with a napkin and blow my nose. "You know me, Lil. I cry at everything from greeting card commercials to *Little House on the Prairie* reruns."

Compassion fills her eyes. "Now, you listen to me, Margaret Lynn Hayden: you look wonderful. Do you hear me? You're being too hard on yourself."

I groan. "My mother named me after Princess Margaret. Did you know that?"

Lily nods.

"Do you know how hard it is to live in the shadow of a princess?"

"Maggie, I'm named after a flower. Do you know how many people at church think they're so clever when they tell me to bloom where I'm planted? If I were a weed, I'd choke 'em."

We giggle again.

"I think you could pass for a princess," Lily says sweetly.

"More like the fairy godmother in Disney's version of *Cinderella,*" I say, thinking: *A princess is petite, graceful, and elegant. Remind you of anyone? Um, no.*

"How about Gordon? Is he missing the kids too?"

"Humph. Gordon is too busy with legal work and the cars he tinkers with to notice that they're even gone."

"I think that's normal. Dads aren't hit nearly as hard by the empty nest. I think it's kind of cute. He's excited to have you to him-self—but then Gordon has always been a romantic."

Lily's right. Gordon is a romantic.

I look at her hard, wondering why she doesn't seem to be dealing with all these issues. "Have you had any of these kinds of feelings, Lil?"

She shakes her head. "A few headaches here and there, but not much else. Not everyone experiences the same symptoms in menopause."

I nod, thinking I'll try Siberian ginseng or maybe see the doctor.

"You know, Maggie, these are the best years of our lives. We have a handle on what we want out of life, your kids are raised, and we're better off financially than we were at twenty. Come on, it's time to enjoy life, girlfriend." She smiles brightly.

"Easy for you to say, Miss I've-Only-Had-A-Few-Headaches," I say, trying to recapture my lighthearted self.

Lily giggles. "What can I say? I live right."

My mood shifts upward again, rising and falling like the ocean's tides. "Hey, want to go shopping? There's a new dress I want to try on at the boutique down the road."

Lily nods eagerly, and we finish our coffees. Tossing our cups, we wave good-bye to Jade and bop out of the shop with all the energy of a couple of overgrown kids.

2

"Well, somebody's feeling better today," Gordon says with a smile as I join him the next morning on the deck for coffee.

I settle across from him at the table. "Yeah, so far so good." I'm still leery of my ever-changing mood swings. One minute I feel like gutter clutter, the next, I'm soaring like a jet. I definitely plan to check out the Siberian ginseng. "If I don't get my body figured out soon, we'll have to buy stock in the drug companies."

"Looks like you're doing your research. I saw the computer printouts."

"There's a lot to learn. But when I land upon the right combo, look out." I wiggle my eyebrows.

"Oh, I like the sound of that."

"You ain't seen nothing yet, baby." I smile sweetly.

Gordon laughs. "So what's on your agenda today?" He flips to the next page of his newspaper, then looks into my face and waits for my answer.

It still gives me goose bumps when he looks at me that way, as though he's ready to hang on my every word. "I thought I would get out the kids' old toys from the attic, sort through them, save the things they might want, give the other stuff away."

Gordon appears surprised.

"I know. I need a real life."

He shrugs. "Doesn't sound like much fun." He turns the page of his paper.

"All that junk in the attic bothers me. It's just sitting there collecting dust. Remind you of anyone?"

He looks up as though he didn't hear me. "What?"

"Me, dust, rust. Notice the similarities?"

Gordon stares at me a little too long. "You really do have too much time on your hands."

I shrug.

He goes back to his paper. Guess I can't blame him.

Gordon is a smorgasbord-type attorney. Meaning, although he concentrates his legal work on estates and some personal injury cases, he will handle other matters if friends come to him with legal problems and want his representation.

I, on the other hand, clean attics. What else is there to do with no kids to run after, nurture, and otherwise raise into respectable, godly citizens? At least I accomplished the task of raising good kids. Well, other than TP'ing a few houses here and there, our children are law-abiding citizens.

A slight autumn breeze rustles through the colored leaves on the maple, oak, and elm trees clustered in our backyard, and I drink deeply of the morning air, crisp with the scent of turning leaves. I do love our home. I love Charming with its rolling meadows, colored leaves, Amish community, quaint little shops, and cobbled streets. The fact that there are only about ten thousand residents—and that's if you count when everyone comes home at Thanksgiving—adds immensely to its small-town charm.

Crusher, our toy Chihuahua, jumps up on my lap. His scrawny

body circles a couple of times and finally falls into a heap. I stroke his nearly bald head and wonder how we got stuck with Crusher when he really belongs to our son. Little surprise that Nick named a toy Chihuahua "Crusher." It's such a junior-high thing to do. I smile.

A vision of a pudgy junior-high Nicholas, otherwise known as Nick to all who love him, appears in my mind. "Watch this, Mom." I can see him throwing Crusher's toy hot dog across the room. Nick watches with delight as his puppy scampers after the toy, grabs it between his teeth—he had a mouthful then—and returns to him. Nick lifts a triumphant grin my way.

The vision evaporates.

My boy is all grown up now. Nearly a man. I swallow hard and turn my attention to rubbing Crusher's back.

Why couldn't Crusher be the Taco Bell dog and make us a lot of money?

Yo quiero Taco Bell.

I sigh. No Taco Bell dog here. Instead, we have this bony little bald thing that looks suspiciously like a chicken and *so* does not live up to his name. If anyone talks to him, if he hears a loud noise, or if he is feeling the least bit, well, emotional, his hind legs shake, and he wets a river right then and there as big as you please. I suppose it's his way of coping.

I wonder if I'll do that someday.

"Well, I guess it's time for me to head for work," Gordon says, folding his paper and laying it neatly on the table. He downs the last bit of his coffee.

"Do you have to work late again tonight?" We rise from our chairs and step into the kitchen. Crusher follows.

"Afraid so, honey." He puts his mug in the sink, then walks over and gives me a peck on the cheek.

Though I'm hesitant to ask, I decide to risk it. "How is Paris working out?"

"Who?"

I clear my throat. "I mean—" I search for the paralegal's real name.

Gordon chuckles. "Oh, you mean Celine Loveland? She's working out great. Best paralegal I've ever had." Gordon flashes a grin, causing his blue eyes to crinkle.

My stomach starts churning like I'm the whale that swallowed Jonah.

"Don't wait up for me, hon," he calls over his shoulder as he ambles with his briefcase and laptop into the garage.

I see Crusher. "Don't slam—" I call out, but it's too late. Gordon yanks the door closed behind him with a bang.

When I turn around, my eyes lock with Crusher's. He's looking a little insecure. *Please don't.* His hind legs start to shake. I wince. He looks away as if he's, well, embarrassed. The hallway clock ticks. I barely breathe. We both know it's coming. We're right. A puddle forms upon the hardwood floor.

This *is* going to be a good day. Right?

• • •

I've purchased the new shampoo that was advertised on TV a couple of days ago. It's supposed to give thin hair added fullness and shine. After my shower, I dry my hair and look in the mirror.

They lied.

Shrugging on my jeans and a T-shirt, I then apply my makeup, deciding to take another morning trip to the coffee shop. My emotions have been so up and down lately, I can use this little pick-me-up. Besides, the stuff in the attic isn't going anywhere.

Crusher is lying in his warm doggie bed but still shivering slightly. Little wonder, he has less hair than Gordon. Poor thing.

Crusher's seen better days in his fourteen years. Right now he's looking for all he's worth like he could use a hot water bottle. Come to think of it, that does sound pretty good. He looks up at me. I think we're bonding. Knowing that he is feeling a little "fragile" this morning, I quickly look away before it's too late.

Grabbing my handbag, I head out the door.

Once inside Gordon's navy SUV, I start the engine and slowly back out of the garage. Gordon drove my Volkswagen Beetle today so he could have a problem window checked. I love Beetles. Not the singing group, the cars. The first car I ever owned was a red Beetle. What great news when they brought them back into production. Gordon bought me a brand-new Beetle three months ago. It's red, compact, and perfect. Now Gordon doesn't buy the most expensive cars, but he does prefer to drive newer models—well, except for the old cars he repairs, drives for a while, then sells at a profit. We're not rich, mind you, but we live comfortably. There are quite a few law firms in Rosetown where Gordon works (twelve miles from Charming), which keeps our income at a level below snooty. It's probably a good thing, considering how I'm prone to shop—especially now that I have extra time on my hands.

A few Amish buggies pass me. Living in the midst of an Amish community may require dodging certain elements on the road, but it's worth the effort. The people are hardworking, talented in woodworking and quilting, and their home-cooking can't be beat. Charming is a lovely town, and the Amish add to its appeal.

Still, lately, I've been wondering if I'm missing out on something by living here. You know, like a life. After all, there's not a whole lot to do for fun around a small town. Oh, we have the local mom-and-pop stores for Friday night entertainment, but can we talk here? Charming is not exactly a happening place, you know what I mean? In the fall we have the usual corn and harvest parties, but somehow I don't think that compares to what, say, New York City has to offer.

I do love the new coffee shop, though. Maybe there's still hope for Charming. Spotting The New Brew, I drive into the parking lot and cut the engine. One step into the sunshine, and I take a huge breath. The air smells sweet with autumn, like fresh apples.

It is a beautiful day, and I determine to enjoy every minute of it. There is practically a bounce in my step as I throw my purse strap over my shoulder and head for the shop. The bell over the door jangles when I enter. Jade sees me and waves. We're bonding too.

It's midmorning with few customers. I step up to the counter. "I think I'll be adventurous today." I stare at the choices. "So many different drinks, how do people decide?"

"You should try something new every day, see which ones you like best," Jade says with a grin.

Not only pretty, but she's smart too. "I love chocolate, so that's a given. Hmm, caramel sounds good too. Let's see, a skinny mocha—no, wait—make that a mocha with whole milk, a shot of caramel, and a bunch of whipped cream."

"Great choice," Jade says. "Is this a special day? You being adventurous and all?"

"Girl, at my age, every day is a special day."

Jade and the girl making the coffee, whose name badge says "Tyler," laugh. Tyler's a cute blonde with soft curls, blue eyes, and a smile that warms you as much as the coffee.

Jade rings up the sale, pulls the receipt from the cash register, and hands it to me. Unlike Tyler, something in Jade's eyes reminds me of a wilting flower. How odd. She seems to have everything going for her: youth, good looks, slender figure—from what I can see anyway. She wears baggy clothes, but doesn't everyone? A fashion, by the way, for which I'm thankful.

A cinnamon roll calls my name from the food showcase, but I deny myself the sugar binge, doggone it. Making my way to a table, I decide Jade's probably getting behind in her schoolwork and is grounded from her boyfriend on Saturday night. Life should be so easy.

I settle into my seat at the brown, wooden table by the window and take a drink of my mocha.

"What do you think?" Tyler asks.

"Pretty good."

"Uh-oh, that means something's, like, wrong with it."

"It's me. I have a sweet tooth, so I'd prefer a little more chocolate." I take another drink and open the lid. "Though I see you gave me extra whipped cream." I look up. "I'd give you my firstborn, but she just got married last week and abandoned me. So I guess that's out."

Tyler laughs. Jade clears off the table next to me.

Only a couple of other customers in the place: a young mother with a toddler and a businessman reading the morning paper. "You know, it baffles me that I rarely find old people in coffeehouses," I say to the girls. "Is it because they can't drink coffee anymore? When I'm old, will I have to give up coffee?"

"I hope not, because I'd be, like, so lost," Tyler says.

"They don't tell you that part. They throw around happy little clichés, such as, 'When I am old, I shall wear purple,' but nobody mentions the coffee part."

Looking up, I find the girls staring at me, obviously not quite sure what to think. I shrug. More customers enter the shop, and the girls scurry off to prepare drinks.

I sigh. Maybe the fact I am turning fifty tomorrow is affecting my moods. The big five-oh. Inside, I'm still sixteen; but the mirror tells me Grandma's here to stay. It would almost be a blessing if Gordon forgets the whole birthday thing. Heather's still on her honeymoon; Nick's at school; and Gordon already promised no party. But he won't let it slip by unnoticed. Gordon is very thoughtful, always has been. He's never missed an occasion to buy me a card, gift, whatever. My friends have been green with envy for years. No doubt if something happens to me, the single women will hover over him like vultures on a carcass.

The door jangles, shaking me from my musings. In steps my

friend from church, Louise Montgomery. I try not to groan. Louise is perfect. Too perfect.

I don't want to do perfect today.

I've never witnessed her with a bad hair day, though I'd love to see a good stiff wind come along and rough her up just once. Her size 10 body is always wrapped in the latest designer brand, and her stylish jewelry comes straight from Chico's. On top of everything else, she's got a heart of gold. I could hurt her, but then there's that whole "Love your neighbor as yourself" thing. I'm comforted in knowing that no one really knows the heart of another. Maybe inside her designer shoes are cracked heels, and behind that cute little DKNY dress beats a heart that hates her mother.

Okay, that's just cruel.

She sees me, waves, and heads straight for my table.

"Hi, Maggie. Out for some coffee, I see."

I smile and nod. "What are you up to today, Louise?"

"I thought I would grab a coffee before I head to the office." She glances at her watch. "Oh dear, I'd better hurry or I'll be late." She starts to turn away, then stops and swivels back to me. "I almost forgot. I've been trying to reach you, but you're never home. I hate answering machines, so I don't leave messages. Anyway, we're having the Habeggers, Heffrons, and Howies over for dinner tomorrow night. Would you and Gordon care to join us?"

I have a sneaking suspicion that she is hostessing her way through the church directory.

Gordon most likely has plans for my birthday, though he hasn't said so. Still, I better keep the night open. "I'm sorry, we're tied up. Maybe another time?" This will no doubt throw off everything, having to move us further down the alphabet.

"Sure." She wrinkles her perfect nose just a little before pasting a big smile back on her perfectly made-up face. "Talk to you later." She resembles a model on a runway as she glides toward the counter.

Good thing I didn't eat the cinnamon roll. I throw away my coffee cup, push through the door, and walk to my car. Jade must have finished her work shift because she is sitting in the white Focus next to my car, trying to get it started. The engine gives a forced gargle, then sputters and chokes to a dead stop. Sounds kinda like me in the morning. Jade looks over at me and shrugs. Her fingers tap the steering wheel impatiently. I walk to her car and rap on the window. She rolls it down.

"Do you want me to call your mom or dad to come get you?"

She shakes her head. "Sorry, no mom, and Dad is at work."

I want to ask her what she means by "no mom," but decide it's none of my business. "Want me to take you somewhere?" I offer.

She thinks a moment. "I don't want to be a bother."

"No problem. Where do you need to go?" Upon a closer inspection of her, I'd say she could use some lunch, but just because she could fit into my arm sleeve is no need to get bossy.

"Well, I don't have any classes today. I go to the community college in Rosetown," she explains.

I smile and nod.

"So, I can just go home and wait until Dad gets off work to tell him about my car."

"Okay, why don't you get in my car, and I'll take you there?"

"Thanks a lot," she says, reaching over to collect her things off the passenger seat. She gets out of her car and hops into mine. I can't remember the last time I hopped into anything.

I walk around to the driver's side. This was not on my agenda, but then I was only going to work in the attic. But like I said before, the stuff isn't going anywhere, and finding out more about Jade could be more interesting.

"What were your plans for today?" Jade asks, once we're settled into our seats.

Why does everyone want to make sure I have plans? Excuse me, but is "loser" stamped across my forehead or what? "Well, actually, I was going to work in the attic," I say. Without thinking, I reach up and feel my forehead. It's smooth. Okay, I feel better. "How about you?" I say brightly, as in, *Try and top that one, sister.*

"I needed to run into Rosetown to the department store to pick up a pair of jeans I've been saving for. They go on sale today." She frowns a little. "I know it's a lot to ask, um . . . Hey, I don't even know your name." Jade laughs self-consciously.

"It's Maggie, Maggie Hayden," I say.

"Well, Maggie—Do you mind if I call you by your first name?" Jade keeps going before I can answer. "If I give you some gas money, would you take me there? I'm afraid if I wait, the jeans will be gone."

I'm unnerved a little by her bold behavior. *Oh, sure, I have no life. Go ahead and reorder my day, kid. It's no big deal.* "Yes," I hear myself say, as in *whatever.* "And you don't need to pay me for gas. While we're there, I can pick up some makeup I've been meaning to get." I hadn't planned to get it today, mind you, but that's all right.

"Great. Oh, there's this new brand of eye shadow I've been dying to try. It is the coolest shade of green you've ever seen, and it sparkles with glitter."

She's all excited, and I'm thinking: *Somebody's been nippin' the espresso a little too hard here.* "Green glitter eye shadow?"

"Yeah." I pull up to the red traffic light and feel her gaze on me. "You know, you would look good in that with your dark eyes and hair."

"If I tried to wear sparkly green eye shadow, I could pass for Morticia of *The Addams Family.*" I chuckle at my own joke.

She stares at me blankly. "Who?"

"Never mind," I snap, our generation gap showing like teenage belly buttons and bra straps. I start to explain, then decide that some things are better left alone.

"Hey, they must be having a sale," Jade says, pointing to the lumber warehouse as we pass it. Amish buggies border the outside with horses tethered to a hitching post. Welcome to my world. It's like living on the set of *Little House on the Prairie*, which, by the way, is not a bad thing.

As we enter the store in Rosemont, the cosmetics counters are at the front, and the fragrances greet us when we enter. We approach one of the counters, and Jade picks up a tester bottle of perfume. She sprays the perfume on her wrist and takes a whiff.

"By the way," I ask her as she sniffs another scent, "didn't your mother ever tell you not to go off with strangers?"

"I told you, I don't have a mom."

Why do I get the feeling she's trying to tell me something here? I'm not sure what to say to that, so we wander over to look at the jeans before we check out the makeup. She finds the ones she wants, and I pick up a couple of "cool" T-shirts, as Jade puts it, and a pair of jeans she's talked me into buying.

Once we're satisfied with our clothes selections, Jade grabs my arm. "Maggie, you have to see this eye shadow I was telling you about. It will look great on you." She practically drags me down the aisle, while cosmetic clerks in white coats stand nearby, no doubt wondering if they should call security.

We stop in front of a counter. "Yes, I want to see your shimmering emerald eye shadow, please." Jade smiles at the worker, then turns to me. "If you like that one, they have a pink one that has sparkles in it too."

This girl really thinks she's helping me out, and I can't decide if it's because she likes me or if she thinks I look all washed out. I glance at a nearby mirror. Yikes! Not washed out. I'm going for the zombie look. I lift my chin a little and notice I have rings on my neck! What is up with that? They say you can tell how old a tree is by its rings. Same must be true of people. If every ring represents a decade, that would be just about right. I have five rings.

"I have some cream to help that," the other worker says, pointing to my neck. She has to be all of twelve. What could a twelve-year-old possibly know about rings around the neck?

"Thank you, I'm being waited on," I say as politely as I can while wishing my wrinkles on her.

Okay, attitude adjustment needed here. Something along the lines of divine intervention. I'm thinking forty days in the wilderness should do it.

"Here it is," Jade says, snapping open the cover of the shadow.

"Do you want to try it on?" another twelve-year-old behind the counter says. For crying out loud! It's an invasion of younglings. She and Jade both look at me. "In fact, I can do a makeover on you, if you want." The worker flashes her pearly whites.

When was the last time I had a makeover? Probably when *I* was twelve. I sigh.

"Come on, Maggie, it will be fun," Jade says as if we've been best friends for all of her young life.

Cosmetic Girl points to the stool in front of the counter and scrutinizes my face before I've even made up my mind if I want to do this. I'm feeling a little under the microscope, like the characters on *Honey, I Shrunk the Kids.* Jade looks on smiling and nods her encouragement.

A couple of Amish ladies walk by in their plain clothes, bare faces. They're laughing and talking together—content with their world. Why can't I be happy with mine?

I look in the mirror and see Grandma staring back at me. Oh, yeah. Now I remember.

Suddenly, visions of Gordon bending over legal files with the lovely Celine Loveland come to mind. *I wonder if she wears glitter eye shadow?*

I instantly climb onto the stool.

3

I'm fifty years old today, and still no sign of the Grim Reaper. Life is good.

With that thought in mind, I crawl out of bed, glance in the mirror—you'd think I'd learn my lesson—and I see green eye shadow smeared around my eyes. Great. A zombie with bruises. Not exactly the look I had hoped to achieve. I must have fallen asleep waiting for Gordon to come home last night.

After scrubbing my face, I reapply my makeup, glitter eye shadow and all. I make a resolve to celebrate this day and the rest of my life. I will get my body in shape, my attic cleaned out, and occupy my time with something more meaningful than shopping.

Proudly, I don one of my new, "cool" T-shirts for Gordon before he leaves for work. He pats my shoulder and asks me if I miss Heather so much that I am wearing her clothes now.

Perhaps Goodwill could sell these T-shirts.

To his credit, Gordon does give me a romantic birthday card before he leaves. Fifty years of life boils down to an empty house and a four-dollar card. At least it was from Hallmark.

After my shower, I decide—new life or not—I'm not spending my fiftieth birthday alone at work in the attic. I need a more rewarding project today. One look at our bathroom tells me the room could desperately use a facelift. I can so relate. The idea of transforming this room excites me. Maybe I'll stencil in pretty flowers, or just paint the walls a different color.

Energized by the idea of a real project, I quickly dress and attack the mess in our room, straightening and dusting before I head to the paint store. As I'm dusting Gordon's nightstand, the phone rings. It's Heather and Josh, singing "Happy Birthday"— a little off-key, I might add. Still, it brings tears to my eyes that they remembered my birthday, even on their honeymoon. Heather blows me kisses and says she can't stay on the phone because they are leaving to go snorkeling. *Ahh, that's the life.* I tell her good-bye and hang up, but before I can take my hand off the receiver, it rings again. This time, it's Lily.

"Hey, you want to meet for breakfast?" she asks.

Now, that's the kind of greeting I can appreciate. It's not like the bathroom project can't wait a few more hours. I wonder if Lily remembers it's my birthday. I decide to drop the teensiest of hints.

"Have you ever known me to pass up a meal, Lily, especially on, uh, a *beautiful day* like this?"

"Good point. Let's meet in ten minutes at Princess Pancakes," she says.

"You got it, girlfriend." I hang up the phone, slightly dismayed. Maybe she doesn't remember. I zip around our bedroom, dusting what is left and head out for breakfast.

The scents of coffee, fried sausage, and biscuits mingle through the air and greet me as I enter the restaurant. "Hey, Maggie." From the waiting area, Lily waves wildly, causing the flab beneath her left arm to dangle with abandon.

I love Lily.

As I get closer, I see a yellow package topped with a stiff yellow bow tucked beneath Lily's other arm. She didn't forget me.

"Hi," I say.

Lily smiles. "Bet you thought I forgot," she teases and points to the package.

"Of course not." I shake my head. "I knew you would never forget."

She squints her eyes and leans into me. Uh-oh, she notices. My back stiffens.

"Why, Maggie, you're wearing glitter eye shadow."

I shouldn't have let those teeny-boppers talk me into something so—so juvenile. "Do you think I'm too old for it?"

Lily smiles. "Not at all. I love the sparkles," she says with all the enthusiasm of a high schooler.

Okay, maybe it's actually a good thing. I'm a little proud even for being brave enough to wear it.

"What does Gordon think?"

"Haven't shown it to him yet."

"It makes you look sort of wild and mysterious." Lily wiggles her eyebrows.

Definitely an improvement over zombie with bruises.

The hostess shows us to our table. We settle into our seats.

"Happy birthday, Maggie." Lily shoves the package my way and acts all excited as though she's the one getting the present.

"Thanks." I tear into the gift. Inside the box is a plump decorative pillow in brown, gold, and russet shades. It's the one I have been wanting for my Tuscany guest room. The thought of taking a nap comes to mind, but I shove it away. "Oh, Lil, I love it!" I reach over and give her a hug. "Thank you so much."

The server comes and takes our orders.

"So what are your plans for the day?" Lily asks.

"Well, the bathroom needs a fresh coat of paint, and I'm thinking of going with a different shade this time. Change the look before Gordon gets home. He's out of town today on a deposition."

"Painting the bathroom on your birthday doesn't sound like much fun."

"It's better than going through all the kids' old stuff in the attic, which was my original plan. Besides, I imagine Gordon will take me to dinner when he gets home tonight. You know Gordon. He never tells me anything. But he also always takes me out on my birthday, so I know we'll do something."

"No question about that. In all the years I've known you, he's always been good about that."

I nod, feeling a surge of gratefulness for a husband like Gordon. "So, what are you up to today?"

"A couple of perms. I did have three, but one cancelled."

"Lil, is that okay? I mean, you've had a few cancellations lately. Does that hurt your income?"

Lily shakes her head. "Bob took good care of me." She smiles and holds her coffee cup up to the server, who promptly fills it. Opening a couple of yellow packets of sweetener, Lily dumps them into her cup.

The server lifts her carafe and pours the hot liquid into my cup. "Thank you," I say to her before adding cream and sweetener.

After taking a drink, Lily looks at me. "You know, I really don't know why I keep working. I guess it gives me something to do. Being my own boss helps," she says. "Doing a few cuts and perms now and then at my house is no big deal."

"That is nice for you." I take a drink.

"Have you heard from the kids?"

"Yeah. Heather and Josh are having a great time on their honeymoon. She wished me 'Happy Birthday' and promised to visit as soon as they get home."

"Oh, that sounds fun."

"You can join us when they come. I know Heather would love to see you too."

"Thanks. I might do that."

"Nick called last night. Says he has a card for me but forgot to mail it. He's probably waiting on me to send money for a stamp." I sure miss those kids.

Lily laughs. "He forgot to mail the birthday card? That's so Nick."

"Isn't it, though?" I smile in spite of the ache in my heart. "So, what are you doing tomorrow?" I ask, wanting to change the subject.

"To—tomorrow?"

Did I hear her voice catch? How curious.

"Hmm, oh, I don't know, exactly."

"Are you keeping something from me?" I ask her in a teasing way, but my Nancy Drew radar has kicked into motion.

She hesitates.

Okay, now I know Lily's up to something. She never has been good at lying. "Lil?"

"Uh, no—no."

Now I'm more than a little suspicious. "I know you're hiding something."

She cracks. Lily can never keep anything from me. "Oh, all right." She takes a deep breath. "Have I told you I've been meeting potential dates through an online dating service?"

I'm positively speechless. Lily has not dated once since her husband died. I've urged her to do so countless times. I want Lily to find love again. But this way? Over the Internet? "You're serious?"

"Yes."

"I don't believe it." Though Lily is a party waiting to happen, I don't quite see her as the adventurous type. Fun, crazy, hilarious? Yes. Bold, courageous, daring? No.

"It's true."

Something doesn't sound right to me, but then she's probably having second thoughts herself.

I *thump* back into my seat. "Well, I'm just amazed, Lil. Totally amazed."

"Do you think I shouldn't do it?" She looks as though it wouldn't take much to talk her out of it.

I'm not sure how to answer that. It's great she's starting to date. But meeting total strangers online? Something about the kind of people I imagine going to dating sites on the Internet scares me. Think Jack the Ripper here. "Are you sure those sites are safe?"

"As safe as anything else, I guess. I mean, aren't we taking a risk when we go out with anyone new?"

"Yeah, but at least you kind of get to know them before you go out."

"True, but I've gotten to know this man through our e-mails."

Silence stands between us.

"You think I'm wrong; I can tell."

"No, Lil, it's not that. I'm just, well, a little nervous about it." Uh-oh, Grandma's back.

"You, the adventurous one, always encouraging me to take a step on the wild side. You're nervous about it?"

"A little."

"Well, don't be. I'll be careful."

For crying out loud, she's a grown woman. I need to let it go. "So are you meeting someone tomorrow?"

"Yes. We're meeting at Prince Charming Restaurant at five thirty. I thought it wise to meet at a public place."

She's obviously thought it all out. "Well, what's his name? Tell me about him. Is he a Christian? Where's he from? Does he have any children?" *Oh goody, I not only look like Grandma, I sound like her too. This can't be good.* I hold up my hand. "Never mind. You don't owe me an explanation."

She doesn't give one.

I'm disappointed, but say nothing. Maybe I came on a little strong. I shouldn't have asked so many questions. Still, we've been best friends forever. I'm thinking that should count for something.

We continue in light conversation over breakfast, both of us leaving the subject of the Internet date alone. Knowing me as she does, she has to know she hasn't heard the last from me on the matter.

In fact, Gordon and I just may have to eat at Prince Charming tomorrow night.

• • •

"If your husband works late, avoids you when he gets home, and loses interest in romance, the signs are there. He may be moving on to greener pastures." The man's voice blaring from my bedroom TV stops my paintbrush midstroke. I stare at the screen as the host holds up the guest author's new book that's directed toward married couples.

"Watch for these signs to know if your spouse is losing interest," he says. "Then take steps to save your marriage."

Hmm . . . Gordon works late, then comes home and buries his nose in a magazine, and goes to sleep. If he has time off, he works on his car. There's no time left lately for romance or anything else for that matter.

By the time the author finishes his interview, I'm convinced my marriage is in trouble.

I zip through the bathroom painting in record time. The color is slightly off from the green accessories scattered about the room, but I ignore it and my aching muscles and step back to admire my handiwork.

After I put away the supplies and wash the paint from my face, arms, and legs, I hobble into our closet and rummage through my hanging clothes for something to wear tonight. I pull a new dress from the rack. It's black and gauzy. With silver jewelry, it will look perfect. When Gordon saw me in it, he told me it went great with my eyes and dark hair. It's very feminine and discreetly emphasizes the right places without fitting too tightly around my, um, problem areas. I need to look extra special tonight. I'll prove Mr. TV Man wrong.

In the bedroom, dirty socks peek out from under Gordon's side of the bed, alongside stacks of legal magazines. A couple of novels are scattered about. The *TV Guide*, a box of Kleenex, and an extra pair of glasses clutter his nightstand. Not the most romantic-looking room in the world, but I can fix that too.

I quickly pick up the mess and head over to the candle store. Tonight must be perfect. With the way I've been struggling over my appearance lately and the added problems of menopause, I've been less than thrilled with the whole intimacy thing. I want to fix that. I may be fifty, but there's still a whole lot of life left in me. *So take that, Mr. TV Man!*

• • •

After I get home and fix myself to perfection—well, as good as it gets, anyway—I look once more around the bedroom, plump the pillows on the bed, and spray perfume in the air. It's already eight o'clock, and I'm starting to worry about Gordon. It's odd that he hasn't called. He could be at the office, tied up in a meeting. I decide to call and find out. At least I'll know if he's back in town.

I walk into the kitchen and glance at the refrigerator before picking up the phone. Maybe I'll indulge in a couple of prebirthday-dinner slices of leftover pepperoni pizza. After all, I haven't officially started the all-out-war against my aging body. We're still at peace. At one with the universe, my body and I. So we blissfully enjoy the last scraps of pizza before I wash my hands and dial Gordon's work number. I settle onto the sofa.

"Yates, Comstock & Hayden," the evening receptionist says in a nasally singsong voice.

"Hi, Emma, this is Maggie Hayden."

"Oh, hi, Mrs. Hayden."

Why does she always have to say "Mrs." as if I'm so much older than she is, anyway? Okay, so I'm old enough to be her mother, but still.

"Is Gordon back yet, Emma?"

"Umm, let me check through the notes Heidi left."

Heidi is the dayshift receptionist. The senior partners are still old school and not willing to install voicemail just yet. They prefer the human touch, a practice for which most of their elderly estate clients are thankful. I hear some rustling of papers as I wipe a spot of pizza sauce from my wrist.

"Nope, they're still gone."

Dread crawls over me. "Th—they?" My voice cracks like an adolescent boy.

"Yeah, Celine went with him."

I clear my throat. "Oh yeah, that's right," I say, though I had no clue she was going. "Well, would you leave him a message that I called?"

"Will do, Mrs. Hayden. Talk to you later." With that, she clicks off.

I stare at the phone in my hands. He's with *her*. That's why he hasn't called. He hasn't thought of me once today, I'll bet. The thought of adding a two-pound bag of M&Ms to the pizza now churning in my stomach occurs to me, but I resist it. Rising from the sofa, I stuff the phone onto the cradle with a little more force than necessary. Crusher is sleeping on Gordon's recliner and lifts his head with a start. He can wet all over it for all I care.

Now panic starts to rise within me. "Mr. TV Man was right. He's with that woman, and he's forgotten my birthday!" I say to Crusher as if he can understand my pain. My mouth starts to quiver and tears sting my eyes, but I refuse to give in. Swallowing hard, I take a moment to get a grip on my emotions and pick up the phone once again.

"Hello?"

"Lil, this is Maggie. Can you meet me for coffee? Like, right now?"

"Sure. You okay?"

"I'm fine. I'll see you at The New Brew in fifteen minutes."

• • •

Listening to classical music on the radio calms me down a bit before I reach the coffeehouse. The thought of Gordon with that—that woman—hurts deeply, but I refuse to dwell on it. Gordon is always careful about not getting himself into sticky situations. I have no reason to believe he wasn't wise this time. I'm just overreacting—feeling menopausal—or so I keep telling myself.

The thing is, Emma didn't mention anyone else going along besides Celine. And Gordon rarely rides in a car alone with another woman. Always says it makes him feel uncomfortable, and he doesn't want to fuel the office gossips. I've appreciated that over the years. Hopefully, he still feels that way.

I take a deep breath and step into the coffee shop. Near the counter, Lily stands waiting in a pair of khakis and a powder-blue top that looks great with her bobbed blonde hair. She's wearing an enormous smile and whistles as I approach. Her perky attitude relaxes me a little more. "Hey, girlfriend, you sure look nice," she says.

I totally forgot about the new dress I'm wearing. Oh well, nothing to do about it now. "Long story."

Lily nudges me toward the table. "I've already ordered our drinks, so we can sit down."

"You didn't need to do that."

"My treat," Lily says, flashing another smile.

"What did you order?"

"A real mocha—not the skinny kind—with extra whipped cream."

Only Lily would think of giving me the fattening stuff on my birthday. "Have I mentioned you're my best friend?"

Lily looks heavenward. "Maybe once or twice."

We laugh.

Jade walks over to the table with our drinks. "Hi," she says as she hands some dollar bills to Lily.

"What's this?" Lily asks.

"You said it was Maggie's birthday. I wanted to treat her to the mocha." She turns to me. "I put in a shot of caramel—oh, and a little more chocolate. Tyler told me you like it better that way." She smiles.

Her generosity surprises me. "Thank you, Jade."

"No problem. You bailed me out with my car trouble, and I had a really great time shopping. Hope we can do it again sometime." She grins and walks away.

"Well, it appears to me that your empty nest is not so empty now," Lily observes.

Watching after Jade, I figure I'll bake her some goodies to fatten her up a little. I turn to Lily. "Maybe not."

"You've always been good with teenagers." Lily looks toward Jade. "You obviously still have the touch." She smiles.

I take a drink of coffee, wondering what to say or do next. Without warning, tears flood my cheeks, and Lily sees them before I can turn away.

"Maggie, what is it? And come to think of it, why aren't you out with Gordon having a romantic fiftieth birthday dinner?"

Thankful we're in a corner away from other customers, I pull my hands to my face.

"Gordon didn't come home tonight to take me out for my birthday," I wail behind my fingers. "He gave me a Hallmark this morning, and I haven't heard from him since." I reach for a tissue from my purse and wipe my face.

"Well, knowing Gordon the way I do, he must have a good reason."

"If he's not dead, he's in trouble."

Lily gasps.

"Okay, I don't mean that. I'm just mad." I blow my nose. Not the most ladylike sound I've ever made, but there you are.

"He hasn't called at all?"

I shake my head.

"Maybe he has no signal, or his phone is dead. He might not be able to take you out tonight, but I am sure he will make it up to you."

I shake my head again. "He probably hasn't thought of me once. He's with *her*." I say the last word with obvious distaste.

"Who?" Lily looks totally confused.

"Paris Hilton."

"He's with Paris Hilton? *The* Paris Hilton?" Her eyes are wide.

I frown. "Not the real one—Celine Loveland." My voice sounds thick with jealousy, very unusual for me—well, the me I used to know, anyway.

"What in the world are you talking about? Who is Celine Loveland?"

"Gordon's new paralegal who could pass for Paris Hilton's twin."

"Didn't I meet her *and her husband* at Heather's wedding?"

"Yeah. So what? That doesn't stop some women."

Lily's face softens. "Maggie, you're making far too much of this. Gordon isn't that way at all, and you know it. He's as devoted to you as any man I've ever seen. He loves you, Maggie. Most women would give their eyeteeth for a guy as good as Gordon."

"Yeah, well, I think *Paris* has her teeth locked onto him like a pit bull with a T-bone."

Ever the wise friend, Lily keeps silent, knowing I need to vent. I tell her about my phone call to the office.

"Why would he put himself in that situation, Lil? He's always been careful about that kind of stuff. And then he doesn't even bother to call me!"

"Maggie, you know there is nothing to this." She waits a moment and searches my face. "You're not acting like yourself. What's wrong?"

I wish I knew. *Nothing. Everything. Hormones. Lack of hormones,* I think. *I don't even know who I am anymore. Wait. How can Lily turn things around and make me the bad guy?* "This is not about me, Lil. This is about Gordon." I remind her sharply.

"Isn't this one of those times where you have to go on blind trust? You know, when you can't see the truth, so you choose to believe the best anyway?"

I hate it when she does that. Says the things I know are right, but I don't want to hear. I'm not going to agree with her. I'm not.

"Maggie?"

I'm not.

She's waiting for an answer like a pushy Sunday school teacher.

"Yes," I say through clenched teeth, but inside I'm still saying *no.*

"Maggie!" Gordon's voice calls from across the room. "I thought I might find you here!" He rushes to our table and whips out a bouquet of red roses from behind his back. My favorite, but for now I'm still pouting. "Happy birthday, honey." He reaches over as big as you please and gives me a kiss right on the mouth. Now I know something's up. He never kisses me that way in public. Wasn't that one of the things Mr. TV Man mentioned on the talk show? Tries to smooth things over?

"Woo-hoo," Jade calls from the next table where she's delivering a coffee.

Gordon smiles and settles in beside Lily and me. I will not be bought so easily. Humph, a dozen red roses. "I thought you forgot about my birthday dinner." I sniff for dramatic effect. But I do so love these roses.

Don't cave, Maggie. Don't cave.

"I could never forget, Maggie, you know that. Not with those little pink sticky reminders all over the house."

I gasp. "I did not leave reminders, Gordon Hayden."

He holds up his hands and laughs. "Kidding. I'm kidding."

I purse my lips and stare at him.

He continues. "I didn't throw a party because you said you didn't want me to make a big deal of you turning"—he whispers the number—"fifty. You remember telling me that, don't you?"

I nod.

"So I respected that. You still feel that way, right?"

"Right. No party."

"Oh, here's one more thing." He reaches into his pocket and pulls out an envelope.

I open it and find a generous gift certificate for a day spa in Rosetown. Pampering is good. I shove away the niggling thought that he must think I need a makeover. "Thank you, Gordon. This is wonderful." I want to throw my arms around him, but I'm still kind of mad at him.

"Do you know I have been trying to call you for the past four hours?"

I look up from the certificate with a start. "I'm listening."

"Would you look in your purse, please?"

"What for?"

"Your cell phone."

There is a sinking feeling in the pit of my stomach. Reaching in, I pull out the phone. The dead phone. The one-I-forgot-to-charge phone.

I'm not ready to give in just yet. "Did you try calling home?" I ask, eyebrows arched.

"Yes, I most certainly did."

"Well, why didn't I get it?" He's *so* busted.

"Were you home all day?"

My eyes lock with Lily's. "No, I went out for a little while." I try not to squirm. "But you weren't on the answering machine when I returned," I challenge.

"Did you by chance do some dusting today?"

There is that sick feeling again.

"Could it be that you turned off the answering machine again as you've done many times before when you dust it?"

I look away.

"Maggie?"

"Yeah, I dusted." Doggone it all anyway. I want to be good and mad at him, and somehow this turns out to be my fault. Although things are looking up, there are still some matters to settle with Gordon. I don't want to do it in front of Lily, though. I'll talk with him later.

We sit and visit a while longer, then drive home. Gordon pulls into the garage just after me.

"You look nice tonight," he says as we step into the house.

"Thanks."

"Just one thing." His face etched with concern. "Are you feeling okay?"

"I'm fine, why?"

"Your eyelids look sort of green." He points like I've got some infectious disease.

"It's eye shadow," I say dryly.

His eyes widen.

"I know. Morticia, right?"

Gordon gives me the same blank stare I got from Jade.

"You know, *The Addams Fam-i-ly.*" I sing the words like the TV jingle, snapping my fingers appropriately.

He laughs and pulls me into his arms. "You're beautiful the way you are, Maggie. You don't need that stuff."

I should have saved the money for mochas.

We're both a bit quiet as we go through our nighttime ritual. Gordon drops his handkerchief from the dresser, picks it up with his toes, practically skips over to the dirty clothes hamper, lifts his foot, and dumps in the soiled cloth. The man is a wonder.

I waver on whether to wear my pretty nightgown tonight. After all, he was with *that woman* all day. Still, he is *my* husband . . .

After dabbing on some perfume, I wrap myself in soft layers of chiffon, then slip beneath the covers. Gordon doesn't seem to notice. I wiggle a little closer, but he just reaches for a Kleenex and blows his nose—okay, *that's attractive*—not once mentioning the perfume. I sit up a little and pat his pillow. Putting on his bifocals, he picks up a law magazine.

With a sigh, I grab my Bible and put on my bifocals.

"Gordon?"

"Hmm," he says with highlighter in hand, already marking some references.

"Did anyone go with you today?" I ask nonchalantly, turning to my Old Testament reading in Genesis.

He finishes highlighting a passage and turns to me. "Yes, Ryan Butler and Celine went with me. Ryan is the associate working on the Walling case with me. You know, that personal injury matter involving the three-car pileup? And, of course, Celine went along as my paralegal. Why?" He turns his attention back to the magazine.

"Just wondered." How odd that Emma didn't mention Ryan. "I called your office to check on you, and Emma told me you and Celine weren't back yet. She didn't mention Ryan." Trying hard to cover my jealous-wife voice here and make it sound as though it doesn't really matter that much.

He doesn't say anything. I peek over at him. He still has his nose in the magazine.

"I know how careful you are about placing yourself in sticky situations with other women, so I wondered about that when Emma told me it was you and Celine." I turn a delicate page of my Bible as if only partially listening to what he might say.

Now he stops highlighting and looks at me. "Oh, that. Well, I am careful, honey, you know that. But Ryan has another case he's working on in that county. He had to go before us to make a court appearance. Celine and I traveled up later. When we were finished, she rode back to the office with him, and I came home."

Okay, I'm feeling a little better now—though it still rubs me the wrong way that she rode on *my* side of the car, in *my* seat for three hours, beside *my* husband.

"I'm sorry we had to do it that way. I didn't know how else to handle it. You okay with that?"

"Sure, it couldn't be helped." My voice is light with no hint now of the grizzly who had taken over my body only hours before.

I finish my Bible reading about Pharaoh's dream of skinny cows swallowing fat cows and Joseph's interpretation, and then I set it aside.

Finally, Gordon puts his magazine on top of a stack beside the bed, places his glasses on the stand, and turns out the light. I do the same. In the darkness, Gordon pulls me into his arms. I feel all dainty and feminine wrapped in chiffon and the strength of his embrace.

"You're the only one for me, baby." He whispers so close to my ear that it tickles. The smell of his cologne lingers, making me feel content, wanted, and loved.

"Besides, she's way too young for me," he says, his voice already thick with sleep.

I'm practically purring when his words hit me like a hot flash.

Translation: *She's young. You're old. I'll stick with you because you're like a comfortable old shirt that I don't want to part with.*

The old goat! I slip from his arms and pull myself up to give him a verbal thrashing. Before I can work up a healthy anger, he starts snoring. My mouth gapes as I stare in disbelief. I jostle the bed to wake him, just short of shaking his brains loose, but he's out . . . cold.

I snap my mouth closed, punch my pillow into place, and flop myself back down on the bed. In a frustrated huff, I shove earplugs into my ears.

I'll be doggoned if I'm gonna sit like a forgotten potted plant and wilt. I punch my pillow a couple more times and turn away from Gordon.

You best be moving over, Paris . . . Celine—whoever you are. I may be getting old, but this old gal's not dead yet!

4

Saturdays and I are not on speaking terms. After last night's birthday fiasco, I still didn't get to deliver my I-may-be-old-but-I'm-not-dead-yet speech to Gordon because—you guessed it—Gordon is working again. Still, the good news is I'm lounging around in my PJs, eating my favorite cereal, and I'm actually getting into the Saturday morning cartoons.

The bad news is that yesterday's pepperoni pizza has taken up residence on my hips, my birthday dinner and plans for romance went kaput, and to make matters worse, last night I had a horrible nightmare.

It was like this, I was sitting in the middle of an all-you-can-eat pizza fest where I gained twenty pounds in one sitting, while Celine what's-her-name perched her practically emaciated body—compared to me, anyway—in a dainty little chair and looked on smiling. Then, with no warning whatsoever, she opened her mouth and swallowed me in one huge gulp, just like the thin cows that ate the fat cows in Pharaoh's dream. End of nightmare.

Shouldn't there be some kind of warning about mixing the Scriptures with pepperoni pizza?

I can only hope I caused her heartburn.

There it is. That attitude problem again. Most days, spiritually speaking, I feel like I take two steps forward and three steps back—especially since menopause has kicked into gear. I believe the hormone army came in, kidnapped the nice person I used to be, and left an evil twin behind.

Anyway, that's my story, and I'm sticking to it.

Our air conditioning must not be working. It shows the temperature at seventy-two, but it's hotter than an Indiana heat wave in this house. I go to the bathroom, run cold water over a washcloth, and hold it next to my face and neck.

Okay, so maybe it's not the air conditioning, it's me. Just call me the Hot Flash Queen. The good news is this is the first time in my life I've qualified as a "hottie." I guess there is a silver lining in everything.

Once I get my internal thermometer under control, I stop by Heather's old room. My fingers run along her dresser, the bed-frame, pictures on her bulletin board. I glance at her favorite dolls clustered among the pillows of her bed.

Taking a deep breath, I lift my chin and snap my fingers. "I'll clean out the attic and the kids' bedrooms and have a garage sale, that's what I'll do," I say out loud, which is, by the way, kind of scary. Still, I keep going. "I'll call Heather and Nick and see what they want to keep, and we'll get rid of the rest."

I gather some boxes from the garage, go back to Heather's room, and set to work. Pulling things from her closet, I sort through old books, shoes, clothes, pictures, and school memorabilia, filling empty boxes as I go. Everything brings back memories, and I brush away tears or laugh out loud more than once. A couple of times, I even hold up items to show Crusher, but he just backs away and looks nervous. I would too. If anyone was peering in the windows, watching me hold up old baby dolls to show the dog, they'd call the men in the white coats. Once everything is packed, I scan the area. Heather's room feels bare and empty . . . kind of like my heart.

I shake off the threatening mood swing.

Crusher continues to look at me through cataracts. "I think we'll make this an exercise room, Crusher. Time we got into shape." His ear perks. He turns around and leaves the room. Sometimes I think that dog is nearly human.

Leaving the boxes in Heather's room, I head down the stairs to the kitchen to pour myself some coffee for a job well done. Just as I get comfortable on the sofa, the doorbell rings. It could be my neighbor, Elvira Pepple, the seventy-eight-year-old widow who comes over every week for sugar. She uses similar excuses to visit the rest of the neighbors on a weekly basis too. A cup of sugar here, a cup of flour there. Poor thing must be so lonely. Either that or she's hoarding food. I really don't mind, though. I've gotten so I buy an extra bag of sugar just for Elvira with every trip to the grocery store.

My shoes reverberate as I walk across the hardwood floor toward the front door. I tug it open.

"Mom!" Heather yells, and all at once arms are wrapped around bodies; hugs and kisses are flying everywhere. At the sight of my baby girl, tears prick my eyes, but I blink them back. I will get through this new stage of life. No sense in making Heather feel guilty while I work through it. Besides, I'm happy for her; and although Josh took her away from us, I love him like a son. Okay, the idea to stomp on his toe does occur to me, but I resist. That should count for something.

"Come in, come in," I gush, closing the door behind them. Heather's long, blonde hair has grown two inches this week, I'm sure of it. Her teeth flash white against her tanned skin, and her brown eyes sparkle with young love.

I take their jackets and hang them in the closet while Heather chatters on about how good it is to be home, as if it has been years since she's been here. I'm glad she feels that way, though.

"Sorry to make you get the door. I forgot my key," Heather says.

"No problem. So, you had a nice honeymoon?"

"The best," they both say, eyes sparkling, cheeks flushed.

We head for the living room and settle into our seats.

"Mom, our condo was perfect, and the Florida sun came out for us every day." Heather looks over at Josh, grabs his hand, and squeezes it.

"Yeah, we had a great time," he says.

"Well, I can certainly tell you've been in the sun. You both have beautiful tans," I say, all the while hoping Heather protected herself from the harmful rays, but wisely not mentioning it.

"I'm going to make us some iced tea. I'll be right back," I say, rising from the sofa. Rummaging around in the kitchen, I pull glasses from the cupboard, plunk ice cubes in them, and pour tea.

Just as I carry a tray into the living room, Heather shrieks. "Mom!"

The tray rattles in my hands, spilling a drop or two from the glasses. *Gulp. Guess she saw her room.* I bring the drinks to the coffee table. Josh looks worried and starts for the stairs.

"It's all right. I'll go talk to her," I say, waving him off. No need for him to get involved in a family showdown so soon in the marriage.

When I enter her room, she is standing with balled fists on her hips, staring at the starkness of the bare walls. She hears me and turns.

"What have you done?" She doesn't look happy.

"Your stuff is all there." I point to the boxes. "What's the matter?"

"I've barely been gone a week, and you redo my room? Thanks a lot, Mom."

"We both have to move on, Heather." I know that sounds like a bad break-up line, but I'm trying to convince myself here.

"What were you planning to do with my things?" Her voice holds accusation.

"I boxed them for you to go through. Whatever you don't want, I'll put in a garage sale."

"You didn't know I was coming here this weekend." Her chin lifts like she's caught me in a lie.

"True, but I decided to do this today and thought I would call you about it."

Her shoulders relax a little. She takes a deep breath and starts rummaging through the boxes. Soon, there are piles all around us as we reminisce over the dried corsages, science awards, and yearbooks of days gone by.

"You don't have to go through this stuff now, just maybe sometime while you're here."

"I still don't like it that you're moving me out already," she says, putting things down and heading toward the door.

"You moved yourself out last week, remember? Besides, this is still your home, Heather, you know that." I put my hands on her shoulders. "I couldn't bear to see your things all around; it just makes me miss you all the more."

She drops her guard and pulls me into a hug. "I'm sorry, Mom. Guess I tend to overreact—like someone else I know." She winks at me.

"It's not nice to talk about Lily like that."

"Yeah, whatever."

We go back downstairs and join Josh. Heather explains that I'm selling off her childhood. Josh looks from her to me and back to her. Smart guy that he is, he says nothing, just picks up his tea and drinks it. I'm thinking he's already learned a lot about marriage in a few short days. Yeah, he'll fit in nicely with our family.

"Oh, I almost forgot," Heather says, all excited again. She reaches into the huge bag she has by her feet and pulls out a wrapped present. She walks over to me. I stand up to meet her. "Sorry we weren't here for your birthday yesterday, Mom." She kisses my cheek and smiles.

For an instant she stands before me as a ten-year-old, complete with jeans and pigtails. I blink, and the ten-year-old is gone.

"Thank you, Heather," I say, tugging gently on the neatly wrapped package. My emotions are escalating and plunging with practically every breath.

"I know you are trying to keep this birthday low-key. Well, I hope you like your present."

"I'm sure I'll love it." Pulling off the final wrap, I turn the item around. There, in a beautifully carved wooden frame that says "Best Friends" across the top, is a collection of pictures showing Heather and me on our last big outing together before she got married. We rode the train to Chicago, spent the night in a fancy hotel, used the day to shop and see the sights, and then took the train home. It was one of the best weekends of my life.

Tears sting the back of my eyes. "Thank you, Heather." We hug again.

"Don't sell it in the garage sale," she warns.

I cross my heart with my index finger and make a solemn pledge with my hand.

Heather laughs. "So, you like it?"

Pulling a tissue from my pants' pocket, I shove it to the end of my nose and nod without looking up.

"Are you all right, Mom?"

I take a deep breath. "I'm fine." Still keeping my head down, I cry all the more and nod again. I try to gain control, I really do, but I'm such a mess.

Heather knows me well. "We'll visit often, Mom. I promise." She squeezes my shoulder.

"I'll be fine, honey." I take another deep breath and feel better. Thankfully, my little emotional storms leave as fast as they come. I dry my tears, look at them both, and smile. "The gift is perfect, Heather." I sit back down in my chair as if nothing has happened.

After taking a drink from my glass, I look up and see them both staring at me. "Is something wrong?"

"It's just that—well—" Heather seems to be searching for the appropriate words, but evidently she is unable to find them. Her face finally brightens. "I'm glad you like the gift, Mom."

"I love it." I get up and place the picture on a stand with countless other framed memories that tell our family's story. I turn to the kids. "How long do you get to stay?"

"Well, if it's all right with you and Dad, we thought we'd stay overnight, go to church with you in the morning, then leave after lunch tomorrow."

I clap my hands. "Wonderful! I need to call your dad and let him know you're here."

"Don't tell me he's working today?" Heather asks as she snuggles in beside Josh on the sofa.

Gordon and I used to do that. Now it's me and the little bald dog.

"Yeah. I guess they're busy these days." Before grabbing the phone, I pause to look at Heather. "Hey! I know just the place we can go for dinner."

"Oh?"

"Prince Charming Restaurant. Lil is meeting a man there."

"Mom, are you serious?"

"As a hen laying an egg."

Heather giggles. "Is this her first date since Uncle Bob?"

"Yep." Although Lily and Bob are not blood relatives, my kids have always called them aunt and uncle since they are like family to us.

Heather thinks a moment. "I can't believe it. I had given up on her finding romance again."

I lean in for the punch line. "She met him on the Internet."

Heather's eyes grow wide, her jaw drops. "No way!"

"Yes way!" I laugh.

Heather breaks into peals of laughter and looks over at a confused Josh. "You remember Aunt Lily?"

He nods.

"Can you believe it?"

"Yeah," he says, scratching the stubble on his jaw. "She seems kind of the adventurous type to me."

"Adventurous? No, no," Heather argues. "It took me forever to talk her into trying a peanut butter, honey, and banana sandwich. Does that sound like Indiana Jones to you? Trust me, she is not adventurous. Fun-loving? Yes. Indiana Jones? No."

Josh shrugs.

Heather leans in for the scoop. "So, tell me more, Mom." Her eyes are eager, her smile bright.

"That's all I know."

Her expression drops. "What do you mean that's all you know? Aunt Lily tells you everything."

"Not this time, I'm afraid. She's actually trying to be adventurous without me. Can you imagine?"

"Of all the nerve."

"That's exactly what I thought."

"So do you really want to go spy on her at dinner?" Heather feigns a look of outrage.

"Absolutely."

She claps her hands together. "Great! Let's do it!"

As my mother always says, the apple doesn't fall far from the tree.

My day has improved 100 percent since Heather and Josh walked into the house. I needed them to visit today. Maybe the fact they are here will cause Gordon to come home early from work. He's been working far too many weekends lately.

I pick up the phone and punch in the numbers. He's with a client. I tell Emma to let him know that Heather is home.

I turn to the kids. "Listen, this might be a good time for me to pick up some groceries for tomorrow's lunch."

"You want me to go with you?" Heather asks.

"Well, why don't I just go while you and Josh sort through some of your boxes?"

"Okay, if you're sure." She and Josh rise from the sofa and head for the stairway.

Once I'm in my car, I think about driving to Gordon's office. If his meeting is over, maybe I can coerce him into coming home with me, surprising the kids. With my mind made up, I head for Rosetown.

I spot Gordon's car when I near the old, stately brick building that looks every inch the law firm it is. I'm a little giddy with the prospect of telling Gordon about Heather. Hopefully, Emma hasn't told him already.

I start to pull into the parking lot when I see Gordon walking out with a woman. My foot eases up on the accelerator, and I squint to see if I know her. Something about her looks familiar. It doesn't look like Celine, but who is she?

My heart leaps into my throat as the woman places her hand possessively on Gordon's arm and looks up at him, saying something. I'm not liking this at all.

I pull into a parking spot on the street behind another car, so they can't see me. Reaching into my glove compartment, I yank out my sunglasses and put them on. My straw hat is in the back seat, so I reach for it, plunk it on my head, then slink down into my seat.

Gordon smiles at her, says something, and pats her on the arm. How quaint. They laugh together, and my adrenaline kicks in. Now I'm breathing heavily, and I'm almost sure if a hot flash occurred right about now, I could blow up the car. Just as I get ready to explode, the woman turns around. My heart slams into my chest and knocks the air from my lungs.

The woman is Debra Stiffler.

By the time the shock wears off, I consider confronting them, but Debra speeds off in her little sports car before I can get my door open. I imagine a high-speed chase, but I could so see me winding up in jail. With Heather home for the weekend, that just wouldn't be right.

• • •

After seeing Debra and Gordon together, I'm a little rough on the groceries as I throw them in the cart. What was she doing at his office, anyway? Where was her husband? Why is she staying so long in Charming? Was she seeing Gordon on business or paying him a social call? By the looks of things, he was getting some kind of personal invitation. And that just makes me steaming mad.

Here's the thing. Gordon is such a blockhead about the ways of women. No, I mean it. He's totally oblivious to feminine wiles, and it drives me crazy. He wouldn't know danger if it came with flashing neon signs. Or would he?

By the time I get home and put away the groceries, I've calmed myself. Nothing I can do about it right now anyway. Heather, Josh, and I head back down the hall to Heather's bedroom and spend the afternoon laughing and talking as we sort through the rest of Heather's childhood memorabilia. She keeps waffling back and forth on what to keep, what to let go. I wonder where she gets that?

Gordon arrives home in time for dinner. He exchanges hugs and greetings with the kids, and we all go to our rooms to get ready for the restaurant.

"So did you have a good day today?" I ask casually, hoping he'll bring up the Debra Stiffler thing.

"It was okay, I guess."

"Nothing out of the ordinary, huh?" I ask off-the-cuff like I'm just making conversation, though I'm still digging. He won't share specific details of a case with me, but the least he could do is 'fess up that Debra was there.

He shrugs. "Not really." He sits on the bed and pulls on some clean socks. "You know, I could have sworn I saw your car today."

Racing heart here. Do I confront him now? I don't want an argument before we go out with Heather and Josh. "Oh really, where?" I feign total innocence.

"By the office. Guess there's more than one red Beetle out there." He chuckles.

"Yeah, I guess so." Okay, I'd better just drop this whole thing. Gordon wouldn't like the idea of me spying on him. Not that it started out that way. I'm probably just being paranoid anyway. Hormones in overdrive, as usual. Debra probably needed to talk to him about something, that's all. Gordon loves me, wrinkles and all. Right? Sure he does.

The reflection in my mirror frowns at me. "Who asked you?" I grouse.

"Did you say something, honey?" Gordon asks.

"No." I step away from the mirror, while Gordon and I finish dressing for dinner.

My mind wanders over to thoughts of Lily. Internet dating seems mysterious and even a little dangerous. Part of me wants to scold her, and the other part of me wants to strike up a band for her adventurous spirit. Instead, I prepare to leave for the restaurant to do some serious sleuthing.

• • •

When we enter the restaurant, there is no sign of Lily or her friend. A shiver of panic races through me, but I refuse to give in to it. She's a grown woman, and I have to stop worrying about her. She'll be here soon.

Of course, the fact that she is not here presents me with a problem:

Where do we position ourselves? How can we watch her and Cyber Romeo if we don't know where they will sit?

The smell of fried steak and baked bread reaches me, and my stomach growls. I hope Lily hurries.

Two teenage girls come around the corner with an older man and woman. Both girls—barely out of junior high—are dressed in bell-bottomed jeans. The very same jeans I let Jade talk me into buying, and to my dismay, the very ones I'm wearing tonight.

Okay, the girls are fifteen. I'm fifty. What's wrong with this picture? They're dressing too old? I'm thinking no.

Said jeans are now going in the garage sale with the my-generation-gap-is-showing T-shirts.

"Hey, Maggie."

I turn to see Tyler from the coffee shop and a friend.

We exchange greetings, and I introduce her to my family.

"Cool jeans," she says, giving me the thumbs up. The other girl nods and smiles.

Okay, maybe I *can* wear these. I think I'll keep them.

We talk a few minutes, and they hurry on their way to the mall.

I glance around the restaurant and realize that there must be an upcoming IU-Purdue game scheduled. Patrons clad in red and white sweatshirts sit scattered throughout the room while black and gold apparel covers the other half of the crowd. You see, our town is divided. Part of the town roots for IU; the other part cheers for Purdue. It's all good, friendly rivalry.

"I don't see her, Mom, do you?" Heather asks.

"No, doggone it." Amusement twinkles in Gordon's eyes. "What?"

"Hard to know the best seat for spying, huh?"

He knows me well. I think a moment. There is a solution to every problem, I always say. We just have to find it. There is a bit of a line waiting, so I opt to go to the bathroom. "I'll be right back."

He nods, knowing full well my routine by now. We're so comfortable with each other, so aware of what the other is thinking. We have that "When one weeps, the other tastes salt" kind of thing going on. How could I ever think he would bring someone else into his life? He wouldn't, and that's all there is to it. I refuse to think about that anymore—well, at least for tonight. No promises about tomorrow. Baby steps. Tonight I'm here to enjoy our daughter, son-in-law, and Lily's *adventure.*

Once inside the bathroom, I touch up my makeup while my mind wanders. Lily and I normally sit in secluded corners so we can laugh, but since she hardly knows this guy, she'll probably pick a more public spot. Then again, she might not want to be seen by the people who know her. *Hmmm.* With a final brush of my hair, I decide to pick a spot near a corner. I'm thinking she'll opt for the out-of-the way place.

As it turns out, I didn't need to worry. Lily and her date arrived while I was in the bathroom, and they are already seated. They must have had reservations.

"We've been introduced, and he seems like an interesting fellow," Gordon says with a wink.

Of course that only piques my interest, especially when Heather smothers a giggle.

Okay, I've got to meet him. Now. I crane my neck to see where Gordon is trying to discreetly point out Lily. I take a step sideways to see the guy across from her, but there's a dumb plant in the way.

We're the next to be seated. I point out an empty table not far from Lily and her date. Gordon mumbles something to the hostess, and we're on our way. We pass Lily's table.

With my hand to my throat, I stop. "Why, Lily Newgent, my goodness, how nice to see you," I say with all the astonishment of someone who hasn't seen this particular friend in years.

Lily shoots a glare that says, "I'll take care of you later," and then smiles sweetly. "Hi, Maggie." She looks to her friend. "Maggie, this is Gerald Waterfield."

I bend over and lean toward the tall, dark, and lanky Internet date. "I will swallow you whole if you hurt my friend."

He blinks and scoots away from me.

Lily gives a nervous giggle.

I stand upright. "I'm just kidding," I say with a laugh. "Like I could swallow *you* whole?"

Lily stares daggers at me. Definitely daggers.

Some people just have no sense of humor.

Gerald looks around the room, no doubt, for a policeman. He runs his finger along the collar of his shirt and turns back to me. "Um, glad to make your acquaintance," he says like he doesn't really mean it. With notable reluctance, he gives me a weak handshake and pushes his sliding black glasses back up the bridge of his nose. For an instant, I imagine white tape across the nosepiece. I shake it off.

"Gerald is an accountant in Michigan," Lily says, making an obvious attempt to relieve some tension.

My eyebrows lift enough to give the air of one being impressed. He smiles and sits a little taller in his seat.

"I was just telling Lily if you average the per capita rate on the crowd here tonight, this restaurant is doing a fairly good business. Well, if we assume that most people will have steak from the menu, that is. Of course, if they take the chicken, it would be a little less—and then you have to factor in the women ordering only salads—but all in all, I'd say a decent business for one night." He tips his head as if to emphasize what he said, and his glasses slide back down his nose. He smiles while shoving them back into place.

I gape for a moment, then snap my mouth shut just short of drooling. This is a joke, right? Are we on *Candid Camera*? I look around for TV equipment. Nothing. I'm thinking she's safe with this guy.

I turn back to Gerald. "You know, that's something I hadn't considered—probably could have gone all night without considering it, as a matter of fact," I say with a chuckle until I lock eyes with Lily. "But you're probably right."

The man sits back in his chair, looking quite proud of his assessment.

I scan the area for Gordon. My safe haven. My woobie. I love Gordon. "I'd better go sit down so I can add to that per capita thing," I say before flitting off as fast as my legs can carry me, narrowly dodging a waitress with a full tray, who glares at me for an instant.

"Sorry," I say, as I slip into the booth.

"Well, what do you think, Sherlock?" Gordon asks.

"Interesting," I say with a positive flair, since I know I'm a little, well, picky when it comes to someone dating my best friend. Especially an Internet stranger who tallies restaurant totals. I pick up the menu to fan myself.

Heather plunks back against the booth. "I didn't think he looked quite like her type."

"Now, come on you two, you don't even know the guy. Give him a chance," Gordon says, tossing a wink to Josh, who is grinning from ear-to-ear.

"What?" I say, trying to sound positively aghast. "I didn't say anything bad." I stop fanning a moment, pull open my menu, and let the silence speak for itself. I venture a glance at Heather, and we both hide giggles behind the menus that now veil our faces.

"All I can say is heaven help the man who actually snags your best friend," Gordon says.

"What does that mean?" I ask, wondering how he would like me to poke him with my fork.

"Just that he has to go through you to get to her," he teases.

I wonder if Gordon realizes he will have to fight off me *and* Lily to get to Celine or Debra or anyone else! The words on the menu blur as I picture myself and Lily dressed in combat boots and fatigues. The picture isn't pretty.

5

"Where did you ever get a voice like that, Heather? I know for a fact your mother flunked out of fifth-grade choir." Lily laughs at her own joke—no one else dares join her—as she drops ice cubes into clear glasses for our after-church lunch.

"I *chose* not to be in the choir, thank you very little," I say with a definite edge to my voice. With that whole maternal thing going on, I turn to Heather. "You did sing beautifully in the service this morning, honey, but I am a little prejudiced." I wipe the beef gravy from my hands with a towel, walk over, and kiss Heather's baby-soft cheek.

"If you ask me, I think you're both prejudiced." Heather gives me a quick hug and tosses a wink to Lily.

I look at my best friend, and we both grin. "Okay, maybe a little, but we know talent when we hear it." We walk into the dining room to make sure all the food is out.

"Smells heavenly," Lily says as she hovers over the table filled with gravy-laden pot roast, mashed potatoes, scalloped corn, green bean casserole, dinner rolls, and salad.

In Indiana we know how to cook a Sunday dinner.

"You want to tell the guys lunch is ready?" Before Heather can comment, the front door opens. We exchange a glance, and I head for the door.

"Nick!" I scream with excitement, throwing my arms around my strapping six-foot-three-inch college boy, I mean, *man.* He hugs me back, then takes two steps into the room, and we all pounce on him like a litter of pups. When we've finished our friendly mauling, his brown eyes gaze up and a lazy grin lights his face. I smooth his ruffled hair.

"What brings you home?" I ask, so happy to see him. My little family, my life, is all together again.

"Laundry"—he lifts his nose appreciatively—"and lunch." He heaves in a duffel bag the size of Santa's.

I might have known.

Nick drags the bag across the hardwood floor with all the zest of a slug. Most likely so I'll feel sorry for him and send him back to school with clean clothes and groceries. The kid is a con artist.

Before lunch, Nick hands me a birthday card that teases me about my age, but softens the blow with a gift certificate to The New Brew.

"You know, I don't care what anybody else says about you, I think you're okay."

Nick shrugs, and I hug him, again.

In no time at all, we are seated around the dining room table where we say grace and immediately commence to chattering and passing bowls, clanking silverware, sounding very much like the Walton family.

It doesn't get any better than this. Family and friends gathered around a bountiful table. The conversation blurs while I offer a prayer of thanksgiving.

"It is nice, isn't it?" Gordon whispers in my ear.

I turn liquid eyes to him and nod. He squeezes my hand.

"So, how are we going to get all your laundry done before you go back to school tonight?" I ask Nick once I regain my composure.

"I don't have to go back until Tuesday, so I have the entire day tomorrow to get it done."

"Goodness, that long?"

He grins as he scoops another pile of potatoes onto his plate. "Just want you to feel needed, Mom," he says with his usual charm.

Gotta love that kid.

"How's the work coming on the Corvair, Dad?" Nick asks, referring to Gordon's hobby of fixing up old cars.

Gordon grins from ear to ear. "Oh, she's a beaut, Nick. You have to see her."

Why are cars referred to as females? I don't get that. I start to say something about that being a sexist comment, but let it go instead.

"What year is it again?"

"Nineteen sixty-four, red with a white top." Gordon lifts a proud smile as if he's just given birth to that hunk of metal.

"I want to see it after we eat. Is she about ready to drive?"

"Purrs like a kitten." Gordon brags, thumping back against his chair.

I'm thinking he must mean a kitten with croup.

"I still have a few things to fix on her yet, but she's getting there," Gordon adds.

Visions of the green Chevy Nova that Gordon used to drive when we were dating fill my mind, and my heart goes soft.

"Yep. That Corvair is one of a kind." Gordon's eyes are all dreamy.

Why doesn't he look like that when he talks about me?

"Isn't that the car the environmentalists say is unsafe? Something about being more prone to rollover accidents?" My son-in-law asks, oblivious to the fact that he has just thrown down the gauntlet.

At first, I want to flail my arms and say, "Danger, Will Robinson! Warning! Warning!" Then I remember that Josh stole our daughter from us, and I pretend I didn't hear a thing.

Frowning, Gordon sits up and prepares for round one of his debate with Josh. "Actually, Josh, that report . . ."

I perk up. The evil twin has resurfaced.

"Anybody want dessert?" Heather interrupts, giving her dad a pointed look.

Doggone it, she's ruining everything.

Everyone indicates they're up for the butterscotch pie. Once they're served, we start to eat again.

"So, Aunt Lily, what's this I hear about you dating some guy you met on the Internet?" Nick asks with a teasing glint in his eye.

Lily releases a sigh. "I guess all my potential prospects have to go through this entire family first."

We nod in unison. She finally gets it.

She scoops a piece of butterscotch pie onto her fork, brings it to her mouth, and waits. "Gerald is nothing to get excited about," she says before eating her pie.

"Now, there's a news flash." My hand flies to my mouth, the room grows silent, and my gaze collides with Lily's. She isn't smiling. "Did I say that out loud?"

Everyone nods.

"Sorry," I say.

Heather is the first to chuckle, then Lily relaxes and joins her. Pretty soon we're all laughing.

"Oh my goodness, all evening long he talked about the joys of figuring income taxes." Lily shrugs. "I suppose I should be thankful; he did give me a few pointers on things I can deduct in my business." She turns to me and fixes me with a stare. "He wasn't dangerous, though."

"How about a little strange?"

"Well, okay. I'll give you that one."

"At least you got that out of your system. Now I can relax without worrying about you and some Internet weirdo," I say. Then I catch the look on her face, and I know all is not well in Lilyland. "What?"

Everyone turns to Lily. Her face flushes, something that only happens when she's been confronted.

"Do you have a date with someone else, Aunt Lily?" Heather asks, disbelief on her face.

Nick chuckles before stuffing the fourth dinner roll into his mouth.

Lily's lips turn up ever so slightly at the corners. "Yes."

Gordon clears his throat and snatches the last dinner roll just as Josh reaches for it. Flashing a victory smile, Gordon takes a bite while Josh watches with a frown.

I turn back to Lily. "When? Where? Who?" I feel like I should scowl, cross my arms in front of me, and tap my toe.

"Now, Maggie—" Gordon begins.

I cut him off at the vocal cords with one glance.

"You worry too much, Maggie," Lily says with a nervous laugh.

I realize this is her way of skirting the issue, but she knows full well she hasn't heard the last from me. I snatch the last crumb of dinner roll from Gordon's hand and plop it in my mouth. He doesn't utter a word.

Heather and Lily help me with the dishes while the guys tinker in the garage over Gordon's "baby." Once we're finished, we go up to Heather's room.

"Wow, you really have cleared out this place," Lily exclaims when she walks in the room.

Heather makes a face at me. I wish Lily would keep her comments to herself.

"Mom's having a garage sale," Heather says.

"Yeah, that reminds me; I wanted to see if you want to bring your stuff over and join me." We talk about the date, and Lily promises to check her schedule.

"Are you sure you've gone through this stuff, Heather?"

"Yeah," she says with a sad voice.

"What's wrong?" I ask.

"It's just so hard to part with some of these things." She picks up one of her dolls and straightens its hair with her fingers. "I used to love this doll."

"Well, then keep her," I say. "You may have little girls who will want to play with her."

Heather stares at the doll a moment longer. "No, I don't need her. She has ink marks on her, her clothes are all soiled, and her hair is a mess. Our girls will want new dolls." She puts the doll in the box.

I shrug.

"Still . . ." She picks her up again.

This is not going to be easy. "Matrika Ethel," I say, pointing to another doll.

"What?" Lily looks at me like I've lost it.

I pull the Cabbage Patch doll from the box. "They came with their own names. This one was named Matrika Ethel."

"I think I'd rather be a flower," Lily says.

"You and Dad got her for me when they first came out. I loved that doll."

"You have her in the give-away pile," I point out.

Heather takes the doll from me and hugs it to her chest. "I've changed my mind."

"At this rate, you'll be taking all of this stuff home with you," I say.

She bites her pinkie nail. "I know, and we don't have the room." Pause. "Okay, I'll keep Matrika, but you keep that one." She hands the ink face doll to me.

I feel like we're negotiating a deal. "Done."

Though she and Josh went through the stack earlier, we go through it all again as Heather struggles with letting go of her past.

Like mother, like daughter.

We finally talk her down to keeping only two boxes. The rest will go in the garage sale, or maybe I'll try my hand at eBay.

By the time we head back to the living room, the "boys" have returned from the garage. We spend the rest of the afternoon playing board games, and all too soon our time together comes to an end. We say our good-byes to Lily and to Heather and Josh, who are leaving for their five-hour trip back to Illinois.

Before I can shut the front door, Gordon and Nick scurry back out to the garage to pick up where they left off on the Corvair, and I go upstairs to start tagging prices on Heather's things for the garage sale.

• • •

The next morning I pour liquid detergent into the washer and start it. After sorting through Nick's soiled white clothes, I stuff them into the machine and catch a whiff of his scent. My mind swirls with the suds, going back to the days of his youth.

Scolding myself for being so sentimental, I close the washer lid with a bang.

As I step into the kitchen, I meet our college man dressed in boxers and a T-shirt. He has a definite case of bed-head, and stubble covers his jaw. He yawns and scratches his belly.

"Hi, Mom. Any chance for pancakes?" He flashes his lopsided grin, and I melt down to my toes. I would move heaven and earth to get those pancakes for my boy. *Blueberries, chocolate chip? You name it, kiddo, it's yours.*

"I think I can manage that," I say with a smile, not wanting him to catch on to just how much I'm ready to spoil him.

"Yes!" He shoots a victory fist in the air like a football hero who's scored a touchdown—only with a little less gusto. Then he sits at the table—boxers, bed-head, and all.

"I haven't started yet, you know. You probably would have time to take your shower and get dressed before they're ready." I encourage.

Another grin and yawn. "Yeah, I know. But then I'd miss out on all that quality time with you." He winks, and we both know he's trying to borrow some slug time. He scratches behind his ear like an old hound dog on a lazy Sunday afternoon, and for the life of me, I can't make him go get dressed.

I shake my head and chuckle. He spots the newspaper at the end of the table and points to it so I'll scoot it toward him. I comply. So much for quality time together. He picks up *The Charming Chronicle*, and I set to work in the kitchen.

By the time he has worked his way to the classified ads, breakfast is ready. Placing the plate of pancakes on the table, I pour the blueberry syrup into a tiny pitcher.

Nick folds the newspaper and breathes deeply. "Wow, these look great, Mom."

I pour him a large glass of cold milk and place the butter dish in front of him. While the laundry whirs in the background, I pull out a chair and sit with him at the table. Nick closes his eyes and bows his head, and my heart is encouraged. He's still on track spiritually. I hope he's not just praying for my benefit.

He drowns his pancakes in syrup, spreads it until the cakes are squishy, picks up his fork, and starts to eat.

"So how are things at school, Nick?"

He holds out his palm to stop me from saying anything further. Closing his eyes, he chews slowly and deliberately, obviously not wanting me to interrupt this moment of bliss. Just like me with chocolate. Finally, he opens his eyes.

"You know I don't like to discuss school on an empty stomach,

Mom." Nick has never been one to mix business with pleasure. He turns his attention back to his plate.

I'm put off for now, but when those pancakes are gone, he'd better have the Tums on hand. He and Lily both should know by now that I have the determination of a bulldog.

All of a sudden, Nick points at my face. "Mom, are you okay? I think you have on a little too much makeup or something," Nick says, pointing to my face.

Without thinking, I feel my face with my hands. "It's just a flush."

"Huh?"

"It's nothing. Don't worry about it. It's a symptom of menopause. My face gets hot from the inside out."

His eyebrows rise, and he stares at me a little too long, like I'm scary or something. "Whatever." Nick says "whatever" when he doesn't want the details of something. I'm thinking compassion isn't one of his gifts.

Seems like forever since he has opened up to me like he used to do in his junior high days. Once he hit puberty, he worried about being dubbed a "Mama's boy" and pulled away accordingly. Some days I ache for my little boy Nick to come back.

"So, are there any girls in your life these days?"

"I've only been in school six weeks, Mom," he says dryly.

My eyes scan the ceiling. "So you should be on girlfriend number five or six by now," I say with a laugh, remembering his senior year in high school when he had three different girlfriends in three weeks' time.

A lopsided grin is all I get in response. He takes another bite, and I wait to see if he will answer.

"Okay, I'm seeing someone." He looks me full in the face. "But it's nothing serious, so don't start planning a wedding or anything."

"What's her name?"

"Promise you won't go to the police station and run a criminal check on her?"

"Ha, ha," I say, all the while wondering why he would mention that unless it's something for me to worry about.

"Melody Pearson."

"Melody? Has a nice ring to it."

He groans.

"So, what's she like?"

He shrugs. "I haven't given her a personality profile test yet, if that's what you mean. We've only gone to a couple of ball games and then out for pizza."

I breathe easier. The pizza-and-ball-game stage. He's right. There's plenty of time to reserve a place for the rehearsal dinner.

"Just remember to bring her home when it starts looking serious."

He nods and lifts his sticky plate. "Do you have any more?" He wiggles his eyebrows.

My heart goes soft, and I miss him already, even though he won't head back to school until tomorrow. I smile, take his plate, and pile the last three pancakes on top.

"Thanks, Mom. I don't know what I would do without you."

My heart catches. What he says off-the-cuff touches the deepest part of me, because I truly don't know what to do without Nick and Heather. I smile and turn away before my emotions bubble to the surface.

"I'm going to take a shower," I say, deciding I will definitely pick up some Siberian ginseng before the day is over.

6

Thankful for our visit together, I wave good-bye the next morning as Nick backs his beat-up Cavalier out of the driveway to return to school.

Gordon is at work, and I don't want to be alone all day. The attic holds no appeal, and the house is once again way too quiet. I call Lily, and we head to breakfast, then decide it might be fun to give ourselves a facial. We stop by the store, pick up some beauty supplies, and return to my house.

"I'm so glad you didn't have appointments today, Lil, so we could do this." I shrug off my jacket, put it on a hanger, then turn to her.

"Yeah, this will be fun." She hands me her sweater. "Do you have iced tea made?"

"Sure, help yourself."

"I'll get some for both of us while you put those away."

Soon we're sitting at the kitchen table. I put on my glasses. "Okay, it says here that it has to dry for thirty minutes. It will turn hard. They recommend soft music, no distractions, and also no talking or moving facial muscles or the mask will crack and it's less effective, evidently."

Lily shrugs. "Sounds easy enough. Let's do it."

I pour us both more tea. We wrap our hair in towels, sit at the table with makeup mirrors in hand, and smear on the mask.

"You know, I'm thinking I'd better get us some straws, or we won't be able to drink our tea with this stuff on."

"Oh, good idea," Lily says, placing the final touches on her chin. "Maggie, this is kind of fun. I feel like I'm at a spa." Lily twists the cap back on the tube.

I look at her and chuckle. "We are a sight, that's for sure."

Lily giggles. "Thankfully, there are no yearbook photographers nearby. Do you remember Wilbur Warner?"

"Oh my goodness, I forgot all about Wilbur!"

"He was always sneaking around, taking pictures when you least expected it."

"Right! We tried never to come out of gym class without makeup, because we just knew Wilbur was lurking somewhere." I think for a minute. "Wonder whatever happened to Wilbur."

"Oh, you didn't know? He's the photographer for some gossip magazine for the stars. Lives in Los Angeles."

"Wow. Wilbur's part of the *paparazzi*." I shake my head. "Well, if anyone can snap great pictures of stars when they least expect it, it's Wilbur."

We both laugh. My hand touches my face. "You know, this is starting to harden. Maybe we should go in the living room and just rest. Better not talk or look at each other so we don't crack."

"Good idea," Lily says.

I pop an instrumental CD in the player and sit in Gordon's recliner. Lily gets comfortable on the sofa. We turn away from each other. I lean my head back and close my eyes. This feels wonderful after the emotional upheavals I've been going through. Lily's right, I do overreact. Gordon would never be unfaithful to me.

In no time, I actually doze off when the doorbell rings and

startles me. Momentarily disoriented, I jump up and run to the door to answer it.

My hand yanks the knob, and before I can think, I'm face-to-face with Debra Stiffler. It's only upon seeing the look of horror on her face that I remember about the mask on my face.

Okay, this is awkward. My fingers reach up to my cheeks, and I gulp. Out loud.

"I must have picked this up with my things the other day when I was with Gordon, and I didn't want to go all the way to Rosetown, so I thought I would return it here."

I blink. My eyelids are the only things on my face I can move. Debra hardly pauses for a breath.

"I'm sorry, I should have called first, but I was in the area and thought I would stop. If—"

I hold up my hand before her lungs collapse from lack of air. "It's okay, Debra," I mumble, a real feat since my mouth won't open wide enough to slip in a stick of gum.

She hands me Gordon's calendar when it hits me. This woman has Gordon's calendar. *Hello? What is she doing with Gordon's calendar?* Okay, I want to frown big-time here, but my eyebrows just won't move. My face is like Indiana soil after a harsh winter. Bedford limestone comes to mind.

I want to ask her what she's doing in Charming, where her husband is, and what she was doing with mine. But since I can't move my lips, I'm a little, well, limited.

She scurries off before I can say another word. If I could open my mouth, she'd be in for it.

I'm thinking God saw this happening and put the facial mask idea in my head. You know, character building and all that.

With calendar in hand, I stomp back into the living room to tell Lily what happened. One look at her and all anger flees. There are no words for what I'm staring at right this minute. Obviously, the same must be true of me because we both start to laugh. I mean, I have this belly laugh working its way up into my throat, trying like crazy to squeeze out through my pitiful excuse for a mouth. Then she snorts, and I know right then and there we're goners.

Pain follows. Big pain. And cracking. My face is cracking. Think San Andreas Fault here.

I try to stop myself, but it's not happening. The more we try to stop laughing, the more we can't stop ourselves. Tears escape and run over the hardened mud on my face.

I point to Lily. "You should see yourself." I practically fall over Gordon's chair.

More laughter mixed with groans. "We have to get this off," she says.

"Oh my goodness, Lil, you could be a ventriloquist! Your lips did not move once."

"You want to be the dummy?" Lily laughs. Our masks shed with every word, dropping bits of plaster upon the floor.

"Okay, Shari Lewis, I'll be Lambchop. Let's go wash our faces." I pull Lily up, and we head over to the sink where we set to work.

"I feel like that woman on the *Twilight Zone* who had plastic surgery, and when they peeled off the mask, she had a totally different face. Hey, maybe I'll be Jaclyn Smith," I mutter beneath my washcloth.

"Yeah, right, and I'm Farrah Fawcett."

After applying the warm water and scrubbing softly with the cloth, we finally rinse away the last of the facial. Still holding our washcloths over our faces, I mumble, "Hey, Farrah, I'll take mine down if you will."

"Deal."

We drop the cloths at the same time and laugh.

"Still Lily Newgent?" she asks.

I nod. "How about me?"

"Maggie Hayden."

"Oh well, they promised good skin, not miracles." My face feels absolutely fresh, soft, and tingly. I look closer at Lily.

"Wow, Lil, your skin looks great." Her face is all aglow in piglet pink. I'm not about to tell her that, though.

She picks up her mirror and runs her fingers across her cheeks. "Hey, this stuff does feel pretty good."

I look at my face in the mirror and agree. My skin looks baby-pig pink too. Pink is nice. Not Jaclyn Smith nice, but it works for me.

Lily gets a call on her cell phone from a customer who wants a haircut now. She is out the door before I can blink. It's only after she leaves that I remember I didn't get to tell her about Gordon's calendar.

• • •

By afternoon I've almost convinced myself that Debra picked up Gordon's calendar by mistake when she was at his office on purely business the other day. If they were sneaking around to see each other, she wouldn't have bothered to return the calendar to our home. She would have made the trip to Rosetown to give it to him personally. My paranoia settles down.

I decide to check into some kind of exercise program to help me get back in shape and lower my stress level. In the afternoon I drive over to Curves, the fitness center for women that I've been meaning to try for some time now.

Pulling into the parking lot, I shut off the engine. It feels good to take charge of my body like this. I'll get a handle on this age thing if it kills me.

Peppy music greets me upon entrance. Women of all ages are moving to the beat on "stations" in a circular setting. Some stations have exercise equipment; some are merely wooden squares for aerobic workouts to keep the heart rate up in between machines. The women working out are kicking up their heels, stretching, bending, lifting, and grunting to the techno music. A youngling with virgin teeth—as in white teeth that have never known coffee—makes her way toward me.

"May I help you?" she asks. Her eyes are bright and alert, her body brimming with energy.

I explain my interest in Curves and say I want to know more about the program. She proceeds to enthusiastically demonstrate the process, and before I know it I'm on the circuit trying out a round of the routine. I'm not exactly dressed for the occasion, but I attempt to work out.

If I wasn't in such pain, I'd be laughing right now at the mix of ladies in this place. We've got your basic exercise gurus, a sprinkling of moms who are trying to get back into shape, a few midlifers whose zip appears zapped, and then the seniors who are just plain happy to be alive and moving, if only barely.

As luck would have it today, I'm working out beside an exercise guru. I barely cause a stir as I run in place. Greta Guru, on the other hand, runs as though her life depends on it without so much as breaking into a sweat. Her perky ponytail swishes back and forth, and there's not a tiny ounce of fat to be found anywhere on her slim body. If I could only get a glimpse of some flab jiggling out of control somewhere on her body, my joy would know no bounds.

My gaze wanders down to my kindred spirit, Molly Midlife—okay, post-midlife, I admit it—and I see that I'm doing as well as can be expected. We're tired, Molly and I. Maybe if we could visualize a chocolate truffle just beyond reach, we'd kick up our heels a notch.

I glance at Sally Senior. Her cheeks drop further with every bounce she takes, her steps are slowing, and the frown on her face says she could go postal on us—if she had the strength.

This place is like wandering through a photo album. I see the ghosts of Maggie past, present, and Maggie of the future. *God bless us, every one.*

By the time I leave Curves, the muscles in the backs of my legs are giving me what-for, but I'm proud of myself for taking action. The thought of celebrating with a mocha occurs to me, but I opt for a bottled water at home.

A voice calls out to me as I walk toward my car.

"Hi, Maggie."

Debra Stiffler walks up beside me. Is this woman stalking me?

She chuckles. "You a look a little different than you did this morning," she says with a smile.

I can tell she means nothing bad by her comment, but who wouldn't feel a little self-conscious in front of Miss Former Cheerleader after that whole mask thing? "Better, I hope," I say with a laugh.

She smiles.

"So, Debra, what brings you to Charming? Visiting your folks?" I try to ask the questions as though I'm not being nosy.

"Actually, I've moved back. Greg and I recently divorced, so there was nothing holding me in Colorado. I felt my place was here to help Mom and Dad in their old age."

"Oh, I'm sorry," I say, and I truly am—but sorry for her or for me, I'm not so sure. Truth be told, I don't want to worry about Debra strutting all around Charming with her cute little figure and wrinkle-free skin, visiting my husband at his office. I know it's horrible to have those thoughts, but there you go.

She shrugs. "Life happens. Hey, I didn't know you come to Curves." I don't miss the fact that she glances at my thick midsection.

Refusing to be intimidated, I lift my chin. Okay, both of them. "I'm just checking it out."

She smiles.

"Well, I'd better get to work. Got to keep that fat from forming, you know. See you later." She practically bounces toward the door.

I'd like to throw some of my cellulite her way. I should be ashamed at the places my thoughts have taken me lately. One more glance at Debra.

I should be, but I'm not—all right, maybe a little.

She probably went to Gordon for legal advice, maybe relating to her divorce. That must be how she ended up with his calendar. I climb into my car.

Passing the Christian bookstore, I want to stop but wonder if I should go out in public after that workout. With my present attitude, I'm thinking it would be a good thing to stop, no matter what I look like. There are only a few cars in the lot. I'll just dash in and dash out.

Once inside, I browse through the latest novels and pick up a lighthearted romance and a nonfiction title on dealing with menopause. Before checking out, I spot a row of journals. That's something I used to do quite some time ago. Since it's hard to collect my thoughts these days, this might be a good time to start one again. It could help me think more clearly, even pray with more effectiveness.

After paying for my purchases, I head back to the car.

I'm taking charge of my life, trying to improve myself, and it feels pretty good. Glowing skin, toned body, stimulated mind. The attitude thing is going to take a major overhaul, but I'll get there. I'm thinking I could do a Total cereal commercial. You know, that "Today is the first day of the rest of your life" thing. Time may be working against me, but I can at least grow old gracefully. When I get through with the new me, Gordon won't give Paris-Celine or Debra Divorcée a second thought.

Right? Please, God, let me be right.

• • •

I pull the car into the driveway and notice Elvira is rolling her garbage cart out to the street. God bless her. Elvira is a sweetheart, but she's also the epitome of what I don't want to be when I grow old. She's wearing a simple brown cotton dress that hangs on her like an oversized tent. White bobby socks stop at her ankles, and her sneakers squeak when she walks. Her hair is powder blue today. She colors it herself every other Wednesday morning. By tomorrow she will boast a bright blue do. Every time I see her after a dye job, I get a craving for cotton candy. Her colorful lipstick—one never knows what she might choose—rarely stays within the lines.

But she has a heart of gold.

It's not as though Elvira doesn't have the money to dress better. She does. She and her husband inherited money after the death of his rich aunt more than twenty years ago. That's about how long they've been in the neighborhood. No one can say for sure what Elvira Pepple does with her money. I figure she stuffs it under a mattress.

Wanting to be neighborly, I park outside the garage. "Hi, Elvira." I walk over to assist her with the garbage container.

She brushes her hands together, then plants her fists on her hips. "Well, aren't you just the sweetest thing?" she says, watching me take over and move her container to the edge of the street.

I turn to her and smile. "How are you?" Her lipstick has an artistic flair today. The color is bold red, and her lips are big. Really big. Think bad experience with collagen here.

"I'm fit as a fiddle," she says in a loud voice. Elvira is hard of hearing but won't admit it. She's become a master at reading lips, but when she talks, it's about three notches above normal.

I cringe but try not to show it.

"How could I not feel great with wonderful folks like you living next door?"

My heart softens in spite of myself. I can't help but love this woman, but I don't understand why she doesn't take better care of her appearance. I have a feeling she is really quite attractive underneath the smeared collagen lips and unusual wardrobe.

"So what are you doing on this lovely day?" Elvira asks as we make our way back up the driveway.

I tell her about my trip to Curves and the Christian bookstore.

"Well, it sounds like you've had a fine day." She looks up at the sky. "Not one cloud today. Can't ask for better."

I nod.

"Haven't seen Crusher in a while. He doing okay?"

"Crusher is fine." Well, except for that whole bladder-control thing. She always worries about Crusher. They've bonded because she thinks Crusher is her age in dog years. The way I figure it, Crusher's doing a little better. At least he still has three teeth of his own. Elvira's pearly whites, on the other hand, soak in a cup of Efferdent each night. She told me so.

"Gordon doing okay?"

"Gordon is fine."

"I saw those kids were home for the weekend. Got to talk to Nick for a little bit. Heather came over and gave me a hug. She's just like her mama." Elvira winks.

"You know they love you. Practically consider you their grandma," I say, meaning it.

She shakes her head. "I love those kids like they are my own grandchildren. And since me and Harold didn't have any kids, I figure I can claim them."

"You sure can," I say with a smile. "Well, I'd better get inside. Nice talking with you."

"You, too, dearie. Thanks for helping me with the garbage bin."

With a wave, I head into the house, packages in hand. Once inside, I drop everything on the counter and go over to the Crock-Pot to stir the chicken and noodles I had started earlier. Though Gordon is still on his low-carb diet, occasionally he will indulge. A gust of steam lifts the delicious aroma around the room.

With the spoon I lift a few noodles and sauce from the pot and turn away with it. After blowing gently to cool it off, I taste it. Melt-in-your-mouth noodles with a creamy sauce, just the way Gordon likes it. I can hardly wait until he comes home.

I head up to Heather's room. My arms quiver like gelatin as I carry the boxes full of garage-sale items out to the garage. Maybe I should start lifting weights.

Yeah, right, like that's gonna happen.

Setting the boxes down, I brush the dust from my hands, and look at all the stuff we've accumulated over the years. Things I pass nearly every day, but never really *see.* I wonder if that's what's happened in our marriage. Gordon sees me every day, but does he ever really *see* me anymore? Feeling the heat rise up in my neck and cheeks, I head back into the house.

Tonight, I'll make him see me!

7

As I start to set the table, the phone rings.

"Now, there's the voice that can still make my heart flutter," Gordon says.

I want to crawl through the phone wires and hug him, but I have the sneaking suspicion he's buttering me up.

"What have you been up to today?"

I tell him about Curves and my decision to try it for a month. "Oh, yeah, and Debra Stiffler stopped by the house this morning."

"Oh?"

"She returned your calendar."

"So that's where it was," he says. "I've been looking everywhere for that. She must have picked it up the other day when she was here. Just put it on my dresser. It's a relief to find it."

He doesn't bother to hide the fact she was there, so I have to assume this is all business-related stuff. Now I'm feeling better . . . I think.

"By the way, there are a couple of baseball bats in the garage, and Nick said he didn't want them. Is it all right if I put them in the garage sale?" I ask.

"Sure."

"How about the extra mower that we never use, can I put that in?"

"Well, I guess . . ."

"And the tool set your Uncle Harry got you that's stuffed in a remote corner, covered with cobwebs because you use a bigger one?"

"This sounds serious. You're cleaning out my stuff. Should I come home before you give the house away?"

"I won't put the house in the garage sale."

"Whew."

"I can get more for it on eBay."

Gordan groans. "Listen, Maggie, the reason I'm calling is I have to work late tonight."

So much for making him see me, piglet-pink skin and all.

"Oh, Gordon, not again." Crusher and the evening news. Another swinging night for Maggie at the Haydens' house.

"I'm sorry, babe. I'll make it up to you; I promise."

I roll my eyes. I've heard that one before. All he does is work anymore. Since when did he become such a workaholic? Oh yeah, right, since Celine started working for him. Or maybe since Debra became a client?

Silence.

"You okay?"

Hello? I'm spending the evening with a dog that has three teeth and a bladder-control issue. Would you be okay with that?

"I'm fine." No point in whining about it. My nagging would only shove him further away. "What will you do for dinner?"

"Well, several of us are working on the Keller estate. Celine offered to pick up some pizza."

Okay, now that just makes me mad. "Fine," I say with all the stiffness of a starched shirt.

"You sure you're okay with this?"

Like I have a choice. "Well, Gordon, if you tell me you *have* to work late on a case, you obviously have to or you wouldn't, right?" I've got him now.

"That's true, I wouldn't."

Yeah, right, I want to say, but I clamp my mouth shut.

"I hope you didn't start dinner yet."

I glance toward the Crock-Pot. "The chicken and noodles can be warmed in the microwave tomorrow."

"Oh, I'm sorry, honey."

"No problem," I say, trying to swallow past the sudden knot in my throat.

"You're the greatest, Maggie. I'll probably be home pretty late. Don't wait up for me. Love you." Click.

"Don't worry, I won't," I say to the dial tone.

• • •

Before I can think what to do next, the doorbell rings. I walk to the door and open it. There stands Elvira. But instead of holding a measuring cup, this time she's holding a photograph album.

"Maggie, do you have a minute?" She looks hopeful. How can I refuse? It's not like I have anything better to do, anyway.

"Sure, come on in."

She steps inside. "Thank you." She smoothes down her windblown hair. "After seeing you outside, I just had to bring this over and share it with you. You sure I'm not interrupting anything?"

"Nothing at all," I say in all honesty. "Would you like some chicken and noodles? I made some for dinner, and Gordon isn't coming home until later."

"Oh no, thank you, dearie. I'm not all that hungry. I'll eat a light dinner in a little while at home."

"Come to think of it, I'm not all that hungry, either."

Elvira smiles brightly and hobbles over to the sofa. "I brought my photo album." Her loud voice booms through the house. Crusher stares at her, yips a time or two, then covers his eyes with his paws. Elvira lifts her album in the air like a prize trophy. "Today would have been Harold's and my fifty-fifth anniversary." Her teeth clack for emphasis. "Thought you might like to see us in our younger days. We looked a little different then." She cackles.

"You make yourself at home, Elvira, and I'll get us some tea," I say, gearing up for our usual routine.

She turns the pages in her album while I head for the kitchen. I put the water on to boil, turn the Crock-Pot off, and put the noodles in the refrigerator. As soon as the tea is ready, I pour it in the carafe, put some cups on a tray, and carry all the fixings into the living room.

Elvira is dozing. Bless her heart. Happens almost every time she comes over when I go get the tea. Must be an age thing. Activity leaves the room, and boom, she's out cold. Not wanting to startle her, I make a quiet little commotion as I settle onto the sofa.

Her eyelids flutter open, and I act as though I haven't noticed her short visit with the Sandman.

"Here we are," I say, pouring the hot brew into our cups. I stir in the usual sweetener for me and sugar for Elvira and then hand her a cup.

"Thank you, dearie," she says sweetly before taking a sip and placing her cup back on the coffee table. She opens her treasured album. "Now, this picture here is our weddin' day." Gnarled fingers point to a young couple standing inside a plain church with a gathering of people. I am astonished at the simple beauty in the woman. There is a faint resemblance of the woman on the page and the woman beside me, but the younger version appears far more refined and fashionable than the lady in the tent dress beside me.

I feel almost guilty that my thoughts have traveled to such a place, but I can't get over the differences. It's more than age; it's something I can't quite put my finger on.

While Elvira strolls through her memories of each picture, I take a peek at her face. She still is very much full of life. Her eyes twinkle. There's a certain glow about her. But there's the lipstick, false teeth, and dress thing I can't get past. Not to mention the hearing problem. Age has taken its toll. No doubt when I'm her age, I won't care about my appearance so much anymore. After all, there's only so much a body can do. Elvira probably just gave up the fight and opted to roll with it.

As we peruse her pictures, Elvira recounts the days of her past. Now I know why they say to make memories every day. If I fail to make worthwhile memories now, I'll have nothing meaningful to reflect upon when I'm old.

Okay, that's depressing. Besides, our family has made some great memories together. Elvira's words fade as I reflect on past days with the kids, picnics in the park, and Sunday afternoon rides.

We spend a little more time with the album, and by the end of our visit, it occurs to me that Elvira's had a wonderful life. Plus, she doesn't seem unhappy with where she is now. I'm the one who struggles with what Elvira looks like now. She's obviously fine with it. I can handle being old and all—I think—I'm just not ready to go there yet. And well, no offense to Elvira, but I don't want to be like her when I'm old. I want to be spry, thin, fashionable. Is that so wrong?

After we finish talking, she announces she's going home.

"Well, thank you for sharing part of your evening with me, Maggie." She looks up at me and smiles. "You're a special young lady, and if Harold and I had had a daughter, I would have wanted her to be just like you." Without hesitation, she reaches up and gives me a peck on the cheek.

I melt. This precious lady friend has given me a wonderful gift. She shares her memories with me, and all I can think about is how I don't want to be like her when I'm old. I stare into her face and see the smile in her eyes. I could do a lot worse than ending up like Elvira Pepple.

I have a feeling this is a memory I'll visit again one day.

• • •

After Elvira leaves, I eat a few noodles and decide to go to the coffeehouse. It's only seven o'clock, and I'm restless.

The place has fewer customers than I thought they might have tonight, which suits me. With journal in hand, I order my skinny mocha and find a far corner table near a window. Before I sit down, I throw away an empty cup and used napkin from the table next to me.

"You're better at keeping the tables cleaned off than we are," Tyler calls out pleasantly.

Turning to her, I smile. "It's the Mom in me."

While waiting for my drink, I settle in at my table and glance out the window. Jade is outside talking with some boy. She looks upset.

"Here's your mocha," Tyler says, drawing my attention to her.

We talk a moment about how she's doing at school. The bell jangles over the door, and Jade steps inside. Her eyes are red and swollen. Tyler and I exchange a glance; then Tyler follows Jade to the back room.

I write a little bit in my journal until Jade straightens some chairs nearby, causing me to look up. Her eyes are still red.

"Jade, are you all right?" I ask when she is within earshot.

She nods, but her chin quivers. Poor kid probably broke up with her boyfriend or something.

"Can I do anything for you?"

She shakes her head.

Not wanting to pry, I turn my attention back to the journal, but my thoughts are still on Jade. There's nothing worse than a broken heart. Within minutes, the bell on the door jangles again, and I look up. Jade is leaving.

More customers come in before I have a chance to talk to Tyler and see if Jade is okay.

I don't stay long at the coffeehouse tonight. I finish a little journaling and leave. When I arrive home, the house is still empty. I'm feeling charged up—whether from caffeine or frustration at coming home, yet again, to an empty house, I don't know.

Picking up the package of beauty supplies I bought this morning with Lily, I pull the stuff from the bag and look through them. Cleanser, toner, age-fighting moisturizer, nighttime anti-wrinkle cream. I even purchased an exfoliating cream and resurfacing tool to "stimulate my skin, make it healthier, and give it a glow." Or so the salesgirl told me. A lot of good it does me if Gordon's never home to see me shine.

I pull the last item from my bag. Okay, this one was definitely an impulse buy. It's a workout DVD. And I got this, why? Oh yeah, I thought it might be fun to exercise to music from the '70s. That is, if I ever exercise.

With a sigh, I take the DVD into the living room and stick it beside three other exercise DVDs, also impulse buys. Well, it's either try one or drag out a bag of chips to munch on and just watch the exercise guru knock herself out.

I grab a bottled water from the fridge. The more I think about Gordon working late and eating pizza with Celine, the madder I get. Enough adrenaline runs through me to enter the Iron Man competition. Though I already exercised at Curves, I've got too much energy pumping through me to sit.

Pulling out my new exercise DVD, I rip off the cellophane wrapper. "Working late, my foot." I drop the unopened DVD on the sofa and stomp toward the bedroom, where I put on my sweats.

By the time I'm in my exercise attire, my adrenaline surge has calmed a little, but not much. I step into the living room, turn on the DVD, and begin my routine. *One, two, three, kick, four, five, six, punch.* "This is for you, Gordon Paul Hayden." I punch with all my fury and feel my shoulder muscles protest. "Seven, eight, nine," bend. "If you can't eat dinner with me, that's just fine." My breath is ragged and short. My emotions are all stirred up again. I'm starting to sweat, and I'm only two minutes into the DVD. This can't be good.

When I've finished the exercise workout thirty minutes later, I consider calling 9-1-1, but that would mean I'd have to get up and walk to the phone, so I nix the idea.

Oh, well, at least I'm not mad anymore. I'm sure Gordon has his reason for working late. I just hope the reason is not a certain twenty-nine-year-old bombshell.

I prepare for bed and slather on all the beauty remedies. With any luck, I'll resemble Catherine Zeta-Jones when I wake up tomorrow morning.

8

Help! I'm a freak!

The beauty products betrayed me. I lean into the mirror. Little red bumps are splattered all over my face. Can a fifty-year-old get measles?

"Well, aren't you the early bird?" Gordon says in his still-sleepy voice.

I step into the shadows, away from the mirror and the morning light that's filtering through our windows, so he can't see me.

"What time did you get in last night?" I act only slightly interested.

"You don't want to know." He groans and pulls the pillow back over his head.

I consider sitting on it.

The alarm goes off, and Gordon removes the pillow from his head before I can do my dastardly deed.

"I guess it's that time again." He yawns, scratches his head a time or two, and pulls off the covers. A feather from his pillow flutters to the ground, and he strategically picks it up with his toes. This time he lifts it up to his hand, carries it to the trash, and deposits it. On his way to the bathroom, he drops a kiss on my head.

Feeling frantic, I look around while he's gone to see what I can do to hide this mess on my face. He can't see me like this before he goes to the office and spends the day with Miss Beauty Queen. I reach for my makeup bag.

"Honey, could you start the coffee?" Gordon calls out from the bathroom. I hear the squeak of the shower knobs, followed by water spraying against the stall. Obviously, he's not waiting on my answer.

Holding the makeup bag in my hand, I look longingly at it, then put it down. I'll just get the coffee going, then apply the foundation to my face. Pulling on my housecoat and slippers, I edge down the hallway and stumble into the kitchen.

Puttering around the room, I get the coffee started. The rich aroma causes my senses to awaken. Soon the machine is working its magic, and I can almost taste the dark brew.

My face starts to burn, and I realize I've been scratching it. Walking over to the sink, I wash my hands. My face feels tight now, and I work my muscles to loosen things up a bit, but not too much. I don't want my cheeks to drop to my shoulders.

Gordon walks into the kitchen behind me. He smells fresh, clean, and drenched in Tommy cologne. For a moment, I close my eyes and drink in his scent. The fire in my face doesn't let me linger too long, though. I have to get out of here, and fast, so Gordon won't see me like this.

Before I can move, his arms wrap around my waist, and I feel the brush of his lips on my neck. "Good morning, Maggie." His whispered words, along with the tickle of his goatee, send shivers through me. He starts to turn me around.

"I need to get something," I say, dashing off to the bedroom like Wonder Woman on a mission. I flip on the light switch. Time is of the essence, so I unzip my makeup bag, grab the foundation, shake it a few times, and open it. With the bottle in hand, I step up to my mirror. I look like Bob the Tomato.

"Maggie, you okay?" Gordon's voice reaches me before he does. Just then he pokes his head in the door and gets a good look at me. "Maggie! What happened?"

I play dumb. "What?"

He steps inside and stares right into my face. "Wow, that is one major hot flash."

"You're kidding, right?"

"It's not a hot flash?" he asks.

I stop my tongue from saying, *"Hey, you with the brain, use it!"* Instead, I shake my head.

"Then we have to get you to the hospital."

Hospital? I hate hospitals. "I'll be fine. I'm thinking this is a reaction to my new wrinkle cream."

"Maggie, listen to me. Your face is red and . . . and"—I notice he treads easy here—"swollen."

"Well, I'll be. You noticed that too?"

He glares at me and tugs on my arm. "Let's go."

"I can't wear my nightgown. I'd get arrested." Besides, they'd confiscate it, and it's the only one I have left that still fits me.

"Okay, but make it quick. I don't want to mess around with that." He points at me and cringes like I have leprosy.

While I get dressed, Gordon calls his office to let them know he'll be in later.

As we travel to Rosetown Community Hospital, my cheeks continue to itch and burn. When I was a kid, Mom would pull my hair into a tight ponytail, causing my eyes to narrow into slits. I couldn't move my lips to save me. That's how my face is starting to feel . . . way too tight.

And to think I worried about a few wrinkles—which, by the way, are gone now.

The smell of antiseptic and coffee greets us as we enter through the emergency room double doors. People stare as we go by. A little girl with golden curls says something to her mother and then points, causing others to look my way. I want to shout "Boo!" as I go by, but I keep silent.

We fill out the necessary paperwork, answer endless questions, and I take my seat among the throng of patients. Fortunately, they don't make us wait long, and we soon find ourselves in the inner chambers.

"So, what can we do for you today?" a cheerful nurse with a smooth, clean complexion asks me.

Hello? Check out the face. Does this look normal to you? I rein in my thoughts and tell her my symptoms. She writes something down on her chart and checks my vitals.

"The doctor will be with you shortly." She smiles kindly and pats my hand before walking away. Nurses don't pat you unless you're old. And I'm almost sure she talked a little louder to me than she did to the lady in the next bed.

My face itches and burns, and I'm getting cranky. This is the thanks I get for trying to make myself beautiful.

"Will you be okay if I go down the hall for a cup of coffee?" Gordon asks.

"I look like a tomato, Gordon. What else could happen?"

He winces. "Sorry. I'll be right back."

He leaves the room, and I feel awful that I snapped at him. With a sigh, I look around my sterile cubicle. Oh well, it's not as though I had anything planned today. Why not spend my morning in the ER? I can think of worse things. Let's see, there's solitary confinement, going through junk in the attic, listening to Lily's last date drone on and on about the per capita something or other . . .

"I've told you about meeting up with strangers." The older woman's voice in the next cubicle is sharp and curt.

A soft whimper comes from a younger voice. "I thought I knew him. We had been talking on the phone."

"It's dangerous. You should never be alone with strangers."

Fear strikes and spreads through me like cobra venom.

"But I never expected him to—to beat me up."

I gasp and cover my mouth with my hand.

"People are crazy. You can't trust a stranger," the woman barks.

The young woman sobs.

My throat threatens to close, and I can hardly breathe. That could be Lily. I can't let her do this Internet dating thing. I can't. I won't.

Gordon returns with his coffee, and soon the doctor enters. He digs for information and finally decides the problem is not the beauty cream, since the dots can now be seen faintly all over my arms and legs too. It seems I've had a reaction to the Siberian ginseng. Thanks a lot, Lily. He gives me a shot of cortisone and a prescription, and we're on our way. But I can't get that young woman out of my mind.

I barely notice the hum of our car motor or the clicking turn signal. I don't care that my face itches and burns. Lily is in danger, and I've got to stop her.

Before it's too late.

• • •

I should just pray about Lily and let the Lord handle it, but there's that whole problem with concentration. Honestly, I don't know why I'm even trying to help her after what she did to my face.

Lily is stubborn, so I have to be careful how I approach this. Knowing that I worry, Lily won't give me any more information than necessary. I'm sure of that. I have to come up with a way to wiggle it out of her.

After the shot and two pills, my face feels better already. The itching has somewhat subsided, and the burning has calmed. I pick up the phone and call Lily.

"Do you have a customer?" I ask after she answers the phone.

"No, I'm free as a bird 'til my cut-and-perm in another hour. I hear the squeak of her leather chair as she settles in for a good chat. "She was supposed to be here earlier, but had some nausea. I told her to drink chamomile tea and grated ginger root. She's good as new now. What have you been up to today?"

Too bad I have to point out the ginseng thing, but, well, she asked.

"Leave it to you to have the wrong body chemistry."

"Oh sure, it's all my fault, Lil," I say dryly. "At least I can still use my beauty creams."

"You know, Maggie, you worry too much about aging. You need to lighten up and just go with the flow."

"Yeah, I guess." If she owned my mirror, she would understand. "So, what's up with you and Gerald whoever?"

"Waterfield."

"Yeah, that's him."

"Well, I wrote him an e-mail and told him I had a nice time last week, but I didn't really see a future for us. He understood, and that was that."

"So you never did tell me about this other guy you're going out with," I say with a slight tease to my voice. I have to keep this light, or she'll clam up on me.

"Maggie Hayden, are you snooping?"

"Yeah, why? You got a problem with that?"

"Only because I don't want you stalking me and my dates."

"I don't stalk. Place myself strategically, maybe, but I don't stalk."

"You stalk."

"Do not."

Lily sighs. "You don't need to worry. I'm being careful."

I want to spill my guts and tell her about the woman at the hospital, but that will only make her more determined to keep things from me.

"I promise, no stalking. But I have to say if you don't tell me about this guy, I'm going to talk about you-know-what."

"Oh, Maggie, don't say it!"

Lily hates the texture of peaches. How weird is that? The mere thought of them to her is like nails on a blackboard.

"Peaaa-chesss," I say in a spooky voice.

"Okay, that's just ugly."

"Come on, Lil, I'm your best friend. I want to know what's going on in your life."

"You promise you won't stalk?"

"I won't stalk." *Snoop, yes. Stalk, no.*

"And you'll stop saying the P word?"

"My lips are sealed."

"Okay. Remember, you promised."

I grab a pen and paper to take notes, just in case I need them later.

"Walter Thumbly."

"What?"

"Walter Thumbly."

I try not to laugh.

"Now, stop that."

"What?"

"I know you want to laugh."

We're kindred spirits, Lily and I. "Why would you, uh, think that?" I lift the mouthpiece of the phone away from my lips so she can't hear me giggle.

"Because his name is funny." Lily giggles too. "But that doesn't mean he's not a nice guy," she says defensively.

I have to admit I'm not exactly worried that Walter Thumbly is a serial killer. He'd be laughed right out of prison. "I'm sure you're right. He's probably a very nice guy." Short, but nice. Think thumb with a face here. I purse my lips together. Firmly.

"He seems nice enough on e-mail."

"Divorced?"

"Nope, never married."

"Uh-oh."

"What?"

"Oh, nothing."

"Come on, Maggie, you and I both know that 'uh-oh' means something. Spill it."

"Well, 'never married' does kind of make you wonder why."

"Why does society think people are weird if they're over fifty and have never married?"

"Well, several things come to mind."

"Let it go, Maggie."

"Okay."

"See, that's why I don't want to tell you about these things."

"Why?"

"Because you find fault with everyone."

Okay, maybe Lily's right. "I'm sorry."

She sighs. "I know you care about me, but don't worry so much, all right?"

"All right," I say with what I hope sounds like an appropriate amount of remorse. "So are you going out with"—I hesitate, but only for a moment—"Walter?"

She pauses. "Yes."

"In a public place?"

"Yes."

"When?"

"Soon."

"How soon?"

"Very."

"Come on, Lil, you know you can't keep secrets. I'll say the P word," I threaten.

"You can't. You promised." She takes a deep breath and lets it out slowly. "We're going to dinner and a movie on Friday night."

Friday night. I mentally check my calendar. I'm coming up with a free night. Saturday is the garage sale, but Friday is wide open.

"Great." *I can make it.*

"Great? Are you sick?"

"No—well, other than the whole swollen-face-with-bumps thing," I say with a laugh. "I'm just glad you're keeping these dates public." The tone of my voice implies the whole matter doesn't bother me in the least.

"I told you; I'm being careful."

After finding out when and where they are meeting for dinner and what movie they are going to see, we end our conversation. Then I begin making my plans for Friday night. I could probably let this Walter Thumbly deal go, but a girl can't be too careful—especially with her best friend.

The phone rings.

"Hello?"

"How's my girl?"

My insides turn squishy at the sound of Gordon's voice. "I'm doing much better."

"I hated leaving you this morning. You looked so—"

"Pathetic?" I groan.

"I was thinking more along the lines of vulnerable."

"Okay, that too."

"I'm just glad you're getting better. I know you're happy you get to keep your new wrinkle cream—which, by the way, you don't need, Maggie. You look as young as you did the day I married you."

I make a mental note to put his slippers and newspaper by the door to greet him when he gets home. "You say all the right things, Gordon."

"I mean it, Maggie. I know you've been obsessing about your appearance lately—"

Wait. Did he say "obsessing"? I don't obsess. I think through thoroughly. Right? Right??? I realize Gordon is still talking, so I try to concentrate.

"—and I want you to know I think you're beautiful."

Backup. Rewind. Time out here. Let's replay that, please. *Beautiful,* did Gordon mention that I am beautiful?

"Are you still there?"

"I'm here. Thank you, Gordon."

"I mean it, Maggie. I love you."

Wait a minute, something's up. Gordon doesn't get this mushy on the telephone. "Who are you, and what have you done with my husband?"

He chuckles. "What's the matter? Can't a guy be nice to his wife?"

My face is feeling warm again, but this time it's not the bumps or a hot flash, just a rush of pure affection for this man I married. "I love you too."

"I called to see how you're doing and to tell you I'll be home early tonight. If you're feeling better, maybe we could go out. I know we have choir practice, but since we never get any time together, I was hoping you wouldn't mind if we skipped just this once."

I bolt up in my chair. "Really?"

"Really." I hear the smile in his voice. "You've been such a good sport lately, Maggie, with all the extra hours I've had to put in at work."

My efforts were not in vain. Take that, Debra Stiffler.

"So is it a date?"

"It's a date." We hang up, and I feel giddy. Maybe I'll go shopping for a new outfit. No, I'll check my closet first. While pondering what to wear, I glance at the garbage can in the kitchen and see it needs to be emptied. I lift the bag out and take it outside to the bin. Elvira waves from her backyard. It's Wednesday. Her hair is bright blue.

That gives me an idea. I'll color my hair for a different look tonight. It might spice things up a bit, not to mention the fact it will get rid of my sprouting gray. After waving to Elvira, I slip back into the house. I want to ask Lily to dye my hair, but she has a perm scheduled this afternoon. She wouldn't have time to fit me in.

Next thing I know, I'm at the store picking out hair dye. I have no idea which brands are better. This is a new experience for me. A red highlight might be fun. I spot a brand marked "Scarlet." Feeling a bit daring, I pick up the box, buy it, and I'm on my way.

This will be a special night for Gordon and me. We've had so little time to ourselves lately. When we do have the time, we're both so tired.

I put candles all around the bedroom, plump the pillows, and make sure everything looks and smells nice.

After following the directions on the box, I wrap my hair in plastic and wait on it to "set." I browse through our food pantry and realize it's a good thing we're going out tonight. We're down to the bare minimum. I'll have to go grocery shopping tomorrow.

There's something refreshing about changing one's hair color. Maybe I'm just tired of the same old thing. I need this pick-me-up today. They say it gives hair a lift if you bend over and blow dry it underneath, at the roots. So after rinsing out the dye, I flip my hair over to dry it just that way, then straighten up and fluff it back into place. The dreaded mirror is waiting for me to turn around. I can feel it. I take a deep breath and try to work up my nerve. Finally, unable to contain my excitement any longer, I turn around to face the fabulous new me . . . and I gasp.

9

Just call me Little Orphan Annie. Minus the curls. Okay, and the "little" part. I don't know whether to laugh, cry, or break into my own rendition of "Tomorrow."

Let's face it. With my red bumps and bright hair color, I look like a walking torch. I can't go out like this. Gordon deserves better. Whether from the trauma of the day or the medicine from the hospital, I collapse on the bed and quickly fall into a deep sleep. My eyelids don't open until Gordon calls out to me.

"Maggie?"

"Hi," I say, still groggy from sleep.

"What happened? I mean, your—well . . ." he points to my head. My hand reaches for my hair, and everything comes back to me in an instant. I bolt upright, and then try to cover my hair with my hands.

"Don't look," I say, as if he hasn't seen enough already. I run to the mirror.

Gordon is silent. That's not a good sign. He follows what his mother taught him as a child. If he can't think of anything good to say, he says nothing at all.

One glance at my reflection tells me nothing has changed since I fell asleep.

After the moment of shock wears off, Gordon recovers and says cheerfully, "Do you know where you want to eat tonight?"

"Yes. Here," I say with a pout.

His muffled footsteps stop just behind me. "You know what, Maggie? Your hair color is rather mysterious and sexy," he says with his familiar nuzzle into my neck.

"I'm a walking fireball."

"In more ways than one," he growls teasingly.

"Gordon, this is serious." I turn to face him.

"World hunger is serious. The threat of nuclear war? Serious. This"—he says, lifting a strand of red hair between his fingers—"is not serious." He kisses the strand.

"I'm sorry, Gordon. I wanted everything to be so perfect tonight. But look at me, I'm a mess. Bumps on my face, hair the color of—"

He puts his fingers on my mouth to silence me and smiles as he leans in to kiss me. His lips are soft and warm. "Maggie, I don't care if you're a brunette or a redhead, I think you look beautiful," he says in a way that draws the air from my lungs. He holds me for a full minute, and I almost forget my worries and my blunders.

Almost.

"Let's go eat." Gordon interrupts my reverie.

"Can we eat here? I don't want to go out in public."

"Come on, babe, you have to go out sometime."

"Gordon, let me hide, at least for tonight."

He sighs. "All right, if that's what you want."

I nod and lift a weak smile,

"Do you want any help with dinner?"

I shake my head.

"Okay, let me know when dinner is ready." Gordon heads for the garage to work on his Corvair.

Great. I should have opted to go out. That car gets more attention than I do. Between legal cases, lurking women, and rusted out machines, he has nothing left for me. Maybe I should hire him to help me sue the hair-dye company for doing this to my hair. At least that way I'd get to see him almost as much as Celine does.

In no time we are sitting down to a candlelight dinner of leftover chicken and noodles and wilted salad. I try not to think about the fact that I've ruined what could have been a wonderful evening together. We are just about finished eating when Gordon starts to chuckle. I glance up.

"What is it?"

"Just thinking about you and your day. The allergic reaction. The hair. I'm sorry, Maggie, but only you could pull that off." He chuckles some more, then breaks out into a full-fledged guffaw.

I'm thinking I ought to be offended, but for the life of me, I'm not. His laughter is contagious, so I give up and join in. Next thing I know, we're cuddled up on the sofa, sharing a bowl of popcorn, and watching the classic *An Affair to Remember.*

When the movie is over, I light our bedroom candles while Gordon is in the bathroom. He soon joins me. With a smile that starts in his eyes and spreads to his lips—have I ever mentioned that Gordon has great lips?—he pulls me into one arm, while closing the bedroom door with the other . . .

• • •

Two days later my skin has finally cleared up, and I've washed my hair enough to fade it to a softer shade of red.

Tonight is Lily's big date with Walter Thumb Man (I know, Thumbly), so I've tried not to restore my hair completely to its original brown in order to travel incognito when I "strategically place" myself—all right, *snoop*—tonight. Gordon is working late as usual, but I don't mind so much this time. There is work to do. It's Superfriend to the rescue!

Since Lily is taking Walter to Prince Charming Restaurant at six o'clock, I plan to get there about six fifteen. Hopefully, Lily won't be facing the entrance, and I can sneak in.

First, I curl my hair into ringlets with a curling iron Heather left behind. Then, I pull the curls into a clip at the back of my head. I brush on red nail polish and apply red lipstick, being careful to stay within the lines. I shrug on navy pants and a matching navy-and-white-striped top. To add the finishing touch, I slide on a pair of sunglasses. Okay, this maybe looks a little ridiculous, but my best friend's life is at stake here. You do what you gotta do.

I park toward the back of the lot so Lily won't spot my car. Thankfully, Prince Charming has a lot of planters decorating the room, so I strive to hide behind them while I look for Lily.

Bingo. Left corner, near the front. I can easily slip by without her seeing me. I tell the hostess where I'd prefer to sit, and she takes me to the perfect place for snooping. If Lily turns toward me, I'll just lower my head, so all she sees is red curls. She'll never know it's me.

I peek over the top of my menu. Walter Thumbly is better looking than I had imagined. He appears to be about five feet ten or eleven inches. Dressed in a sweater and pants that announce they've just returned from the dry cleaners. Short, blond hair perfectly in place. My eyes narrow as I look more closely. Absolutely perfectly in place. I think for a moment. I read somewhere that coldhearted murderers can be very neat in appearance. Very calculating and orderly. I swallow hard and continue watching.

Lily says something, and her date smiles pleasantly. Lily smiles back. What is she doing smiling? She hardly knows this man, for crying out loud.

"Maggie Hayden? Why, Maggie Hayden, is that you?" A voice calls.

I drop my menu and look up to see Louise and Don Montgomery

standing there. Can't they see that I'm busy? With a sinking feeling in the middle of my stomach, I slowly pull off my sunglasses.

"What are you doing here?" she asks.

"Eating?"

"Why, you've changed your hair color," she says a little too loudly for comfort.

I slink down in my chair and glance over at Lily, but she's still engrossed in conversation with Thumb Man.

"I like it," she adds.

"Where's Gordon tonight?" her husband joins in.

Lily could be sitting in this very room with a murderer. Please go away. "He's working late tonight." I don't miss the rise in their eyebrows.

"Did you have an eye appointment today?"

"What?"

Louise points to my sunglasses. "Oh, that," I say, waving them with my hand. "I—I've kind of—" I am searching for something to say without telling a fib when the server arrives with my Diet Pepsi. She takes a minute to place it in front of me and hands me a straw. "Well, so good to see the two of you," I say, dismissing the question entirely.

Louise looks at me funny, blinks, then smiles. They turn to go; then she stops and faces me once again. "We're having the Herndons, Hills, and Huxleys over next Friday. Could you and Gordon join us then?"

Bless her heart; she can't seem to make it through the letter *H* of the church directory. I start to answer Louise, then notice that Lily is looking my way, and panic hits me. I purposely drop my napkin on the floor and reach down to pick it up. Louise waits for an answer. *Don't you have a roast to put in the oven, Louise? Go away.* Feet shuffle past my table, and I glance up to see a server with a tray of food in hand struggling to move past her. I turn, and the couple at the next table is staring at me.

"Oh, hello," I say, as politely as possible while all the blood rushes to my head. Still ducking down beside my table, I look over at Lily. She is no longer facing my way. I bolt upright, banging my head on the edge of the table and nearly knocking my drink over.

"Are you all right?" I've completely forgotten about Louise and Don. Louise is staring at me with concern.

"Oh, sorry. Can I call you on that?" I ask, rubbing the knot on my head. "I'll have to check with Gordon."

"Sure, that would be fine. Ta-ta," Louise says, backing up with a dainty wave and a slight tinkle of her charm bracelet.

I hold my breath, praying she and Don won't pass Lily's table and tell her I'm here. Another patron gets in their way, heading them off at the pass, and the Montgomerys go another direction. Phew! That was a close call.

When the server returns, I order my usual chicken salad and low-fat ranch dressing. She tugs at the menu in my hand, but I refuse to let go. Our eyes lock.

"Could I keep this for a little while?" I ask, hanging on to it for dear life.

The server frowns, then finally releases her death grip.

"There is someone here I am trying to avoid," I say sheepishly, holding up the menu like a veil so she gets the idea.

"Oh," she says, as if the lights just came on. She leans into the table. "I've dated some real losers, too, so I can relate. You hang on to it as long as you need to." She smiles as though we share a secret and walks away.

I put my sunglasses back on and peek over the top of my menu. Lily and Walter are laughing some more. Did he just brush his hand against her hand? My back stiffens. I'm almost sure I saw him do that. Why, I have half a mind to—

"Mrs. Hayden, is that you?" *For crying out loud, is all of Charming here tonight?*

I look up and see Celine Loveland standing there in all her Paris Hilton glory. Okay, just shoot me now.

"Yes," I squeak. "How are you, Celine?"

"I'm fine. I wasn't sure if that was you. Your hair is a little, uh, different than I remember."

"Well, yes—yes, it is." I see a handsome man standing beside her, and I feel better instantly.

"I like it," she says before flashing her blinding smile. I should have left on my sunglasses.

"Thank you." I look toward the young man.

"Oh, I'm sorry, this is my brother, Craig," she says, and my spirits sink. Somehow I'd feel better if this good-looking young man was her husband. Although Celine and her husband attended Heather's wedding, I don't remember him all that well. I wonder where he is tonight.

We exchange greetings, and I look back to Celine. "I thought you were working late tonight." Though I'm relieved to see she isn't.

"No, we finished early. Gordon"—*Okay, so he's Gordon and I'm Mrs. Hayden?*—"left a while ago too. You probably just missed him."

I nod. "By the way, please feel free to call me Margaret." It's not that I mind her calling me Maggie; but, well, when I'm around her, I want to be a princess.

She smiles. "Margaret."

"You know, I'm surprised Gordon hasn't called my cell phone," I say more to myself than to Celine. Digging it from my purse, I look at it and cringe. "The battery is dead." A nervous laugh comes from my throat.

She raises her eyebrows, then smiles. "Well, it's certainly nice to see you."

"Nice to see you both," I say before they walk away. She takes the gaze of most of the men in the room with her.

Great. Gordon is home. He's probably tried to call me, and my cell phone—as usual—is dead. Lily is most likely sitting with an ax murderer, and half the town has turned up in Prince Charming

Restaurant tonight. And I thought people would not recognize me. This is a small community. I've lived here forever. My hair is red. I'm not bald. It's a miracle Lily hasn't spotted me yet.

"Well, Maggie, I just keep bumping into you." Debra Stiffler has just flounced her perky cheerleader self right up to my table. *Give me a G, give me an O—what's it spell? GO! As in, GO away!*

"Hi, Debra."

"Is Gordon working late *again*?" she asks. *How does she know my husband's working hours?* "He must really like his job." *Okay, do her words contain a hint of sarcasm, or is it just me?*

"Gordon is a hard worker, and, well, he likes to indulge me in the finer things in life." I chuckle. *Did I just say that?*

Debra gives my casual top a pointed glance, then looks back at me.

Okay, that was harsh.

I suddenly picture Debra and me in a mud fight, and I'm winning. *Bad, Maggie!*

"Well, I just wanted to say hello." She gives the obligatory wave and sashays toward the door.

"Hey, this is a name-brand top," I want to shout after her. She doesn't have to know I bought it on eBay. I see people staring at me. I realize I actually *did* shout it. Evidently pretty loudly. Then I remember Lily. I throw a frantic glance toward her table, and our eyes lock.

Busted.

I drop my fork this time and stay down longer than necessary to make sure she's not watching me. The couple in the next table stares at me again. I just smile. As I start to reach for my fork, I see a woman's shoe, tapping rather impatiently, beside it. The shoe is Lily's. I'm tempted to prick her toe. Instead, I muster what's left of my dignity, pick up my fork as if nothing at all has happened, sit up in my chair, and look at her.

I pull off my sunglasses. "Well, Lil, how are you?"

Her arms are folded across her chest, and she's still tapping her foot.

"I'm having chicken salad. Do you want to join me?" Uh-oh, hot flash moment here.

"Margaret Lynn Hayden. What are you doing here?" Her face is pinched, making her look every inch the schoolmarm.

I dab at the back of my neck with a napkin. "Why do people keep asking me that? I want to eat. Is that a crime?"

Lily's eyes narrow. "You're stalking."

"Am not."

"Are too."

"Am not." I root through my purse for a used church bulletin, pull it out, and start fanning like the dickens.

"Lily, is everything okay?" Walter walks up beside her.

The server walks by carrying a pitcher of ice water. "Could I have that?" I ask.

"The pitcher?" she asks.

"Yes."

"Well, I was taking it to another table."

"Could you please get them another one and leave this with me?" There's a slight growl in my voice here. The look on her face tells me she gets it. She puts the pitcher on the table and walks away. No questions asked.

I pick it up. Resisting the urge to pour it over my head or throw it on Walter, I merely hold it between my hands and smile up at the two of them.

They both stare at me a moment before Lily finds her voice. "Walter, this is my friend"—I notice she kind of grinds the last word out through clenched teeth while she glares at me— "Maggie Hayden."

I smile sweetly as Walter shakes my hand. It's all wet and cold from the pitcher. Serves him right. He smiles and tries to discreetly wipe his palm on his pants. He has a fairly firm handshake, I'll give him that, but his hands are soft. Sissy soft.

I don't like him.

An awkward silence ensues. "As I was saying, Maggie, what are you doing here tonight? Didn't you and Gordon have plans?"

I flash a sweet smile and bat my eyelashes a time or two. "I'm sorry to say Gordon had to work tonight." Hot flash at an all-time high here. I'm getting frantic. "Oh, look, there's—" I point behind them and quickly scoop an ice cube from the pitcher while they're turned away. They turn back to me and I smile. "I thought it was—oh, never mind." I hold the ice cube on the back of my neck. Bliss. Sheer bliss.

"That is too bad Gordon had to work," she says, and I'm sure she means it. "Well, we don't want to miss our movie. Enjoy your dinner." She smiles sweetly until Walter turns his head; then she throws me a you-had-better-stay-away-from-us look. Good grief. I don't know why she's so touchy all of a sudden.

Before the server returns with my salad, I've greeted more people than I normally do at the annual town fish fry, and my appetite is gone. Not to mention that I'm sure Gordon is furious with me, Lily is in the movie theater with an axe murderer, and I'm generating enough heat to see Charming through the winter.

"Do you have a telephone I can use?" I ask the server.

She points me in the right direction, and I call home. By the time my ice cube has dissolved to the size of a pea, my hot flash subsides.

"Hello?"

Before Gordon can say another word, I grovel an apology and promise him all but my Visa card. And before we hang up, he agrees to meet me at the theater for the seven forty-five showing of the blockbuster romantic comedy now playing.

I love Gordon.

• • •

The movie is fine, but I haven't spotted Lily in the theater at all, and I'm starting to worry. I shouldn't, but, come on, she's so vulnerable.

She hasn't dated for years. She has no idea what kinds of men are out there, especially the kind who get on Internet dating services and take advantage of women. They're probably hoping that since she's widowed she has a lot of money. I have to warn her.

"Maggie, you ready?"

"Hmm?"

"Are you ready? The movie is over, in case you haven't noticed."

"Oh." I smile. "Sure, let's go."

Gordon helps me out of my seat, and we make our way down the aisle after most people have left. "Well, are you going to tell me?"

"Tell you what?"

"Why we're really here." I hate it that he and Lily know me so well.

"That movie got great reviews."

"That's true. But it's not about the movie, is it?"

It's times like this when I wish I could at least get away with a teensy little fib.

"Maggie?"

Why does he pressure me like this? I don't like it.

"Margaret Lynn Hayden?"

Uh-oh, he's using my full name. Now I have to tell him.

"Is Lily here?" he asks as we push through the doors of the theater and step outside onto the cemented entrance.

"Lily?"

"You know, as in Newgent, best friend since grade school? Any of this ringing a bell?"

"Oh, *that* Lily."

Gordon stops, folds his arms across his chest, and looks at me. Why do he and Lily do that? It's like they've had the same training, and that's step two in the inquisition process.

"I haven't seen her here. Have you?" That's not a lie. I haven't seen her at the theater at all. Do I have to tell him about the restaurant episode? I think not.

For just a moment, he falters. "Well, no, I haven't seen her." He rubs his jaw. He knows something's up, but I'm not about to help him put two and two together.

"Well, fancy meeting you two here," Lily's voice calls behind us.

I gulp, then glance at Gordon who is now peering over the rim of his glasses at me. "I'll talk to you later," he whispers before we turn around.

There stands a smiling Lily and a surprised Walter. Lily makes the introductions, and before long we all end up at The New Brew, sipping lattes and mochas, and enjoying friendly conversation.

"So what movie did you go see?" Lily whispers with a mischievous grin. The guys are engrossed in their own conversation about the price of cars today.

"Same one as you," I say, then clamp my hand over my mouth.

She grins triumphantly and shakes her head. "I changed it at the last minute. I knew you would come!"

"Doggone it, Lil, you made me sit through two hours of that dumb movie while I worried about you," I snap with as much punch as you can communicate in a whisper.

"That's what you get for stalking," she says, trying to glare at me but unable to conceal a grin. Pretty soon we both start laughing.

Before the night is over, we confirm that Walter still lives at home with his mother, has never married, has never had a traffic ticket in his life, and that as a young man he was pushed through the ranks all the way to Eagle Scouts. He has bad allergies, but hey, nobody's perfect.

I like Walter.

10

I'm a half hour into my garage sale when Lily's car arrives.

"Good morning," she says, walking up my driveway with a box of things she plans to sell. I'm thinking maybe I should apologize to her about last night, so with no one else here at the moment, I figure now is a good time.

"Do you forgive me, Lily?" I blurt, before she has time to say, "Good morning."

"Of course I forgive you, you goof." She walks through the table-filled garage to set her purse down inside the house, then comes back to me. "But one of these days your stalking is going to get you in trouble."

"And one of these days your Internet dating is going to get you in trouble." She glares because she knows we're even. A thought occurs to me. "Maybe I should go into business. Become a private investigator. Do you think there's money in it?"

"Oh, so you admit you're a stalker?"

Lily's fast; I'll give her that. "Do we have to go there again?"

She laughs. "Did you sell anything yet?"

"Lil, it's only seven thirty a.m.," I say with a yawn. "But actually, yes. A couple of knickknacks, some kitchenware, that type of thing. One man is bringing his brother back to look at the lawnmower."

She nods, pulling things out of her box and arranging them on the tables.

"So what'd you think? Do you like him?" I ask.

"You never give up, do you?"

"No. And you love me for it."

"Well, sometimes I love you for it. Sometimes you're a *royal* pain in the neck, Princess Margaret." She pauses. "You know, he's all right, but I don't hear wedding bells or anything."

"I like him."

"Why, because I don't hear wedding bells?"

"No."

"Okay, what's the deal?"

"What's up with that? You're suspicious if I don't like the guy, and suspicious if I do," I say, acting all offended.

"You've never liked anyone I've dated except for Bob." She slips into her chair beside me.

"Well, there you are."

"What does that mean?"

"There's no one like Bob." The minute I say the words, I wish I hadn't. We both get quiet.

"I'm sorry, Lil."

"No, it's okay. You're right; there is no one like Bob. But the thing is, Maggie, I'm not trying to find another Bob. I'm trying to find someone who will fit in my life now, today. Do you see?"

"I think so," I say, but I'm not sure. Deep-down inside, I don't want anyone else but Bob for Lily. They were so perfect for each other.

"We have to let him go, Maggie."

"I know." Our conversation has turned heavy, and it makes me uncomfortable.

"He would want me to date, you know," she says almost in a whisper.

"I know. You're right."

A car door slams, startling us out of our reverie, and a woman walks up the driveway. She spots Heather's ink-face doll, picks her up, and comes over to the table to pay for her. "I'll give you fifty cents for this."

"No, I don't think so."

"The woman gives a frustrated sigh. "All right, seventy-five then."

That was one of Heather's favorite dolls, ink spots or not. "No, I don't think so."

"Well, that's the price you have on it here."

"I know." I reach for the doll, but the woman has a firm grasp on it. I grab the doll's feet, and the woman strengthens her grip. We enter a tug-of-war, glaring at each other, and I'm almost sure I see her lip snarl here. With one quick tug, I wrench the baby doll away from her. "I'm sorry," I say sweetly. "I've changed my mind about selling this one. It was one of my daughter's favorites."

The woman turns and stomps off, muttering something about crazy people.

"Whoa, don't mess with Maggie Hayden." Lily straightens some sweaters nearby. "What was that all about, anyway?"

"I decided not to get rid of the doll, that's all." My words are curt. "I'll just keep it for Heather to have at our house."

Before Lily can comment, other people show up. "How much do you want for these Transformers?" One man asks, holding up Nick's old toys. I remember when our little boy used to play with those day-in and day-out.

"Oh, I'm sorry, those weren't supposed to be on the table. They're spoken for." Now I can feel Lily's gaze practically boring a hole through my back, but I ignore her as I gather the Transformers into my arms and carry them over to hide them under the table where we're collecting the money.

"So back to what we were talking about," I say, continuing to ignore her questioning gaze. "You understand I don't have a problem with you dating. It's just the stranger part that worries me."

"Maggie, we both know there is no one in town I can date."

"What about Roy down at the barber shop?" We keep our voices down because people are mulling around in the garage.

"Roy cuts hair; I cut hair. We'd be forever snipping at each other."

We both giggle.

"Besides, there's something exciting about looking beyond Charming for someone. And I told you I'm being careful."

"It's just so unlike you to be this adventurous."

"I know. To tell you the truth, it's a little freeing to do this. You know I'm not the adventurous type, so I'm proud of myself for doing something different, stepping out of my comfort zone, so to speak."

When was the last time I stepped out of my comfort zone? These days I'm as adventurous as a rock—well, beyond Curves, wrinkle cream, and the new hair color. But those hardly qualify as adventure. "Maybe that's what I need to do."

"What?"

"I don't know, something adventurous. A belly-button piercing, a tattoo, a climb up Mt. Everest, maybe. The possibilities are endless."

The guy comes back and buys the lawnmower. I take his money, turn to Lily, and smile triumphantly.

"Well, I'm glad to see you sold something. I was beginning to think you were going to keep it all."

"Why? Just because I changed my mind on a few things?"

She lifts her motherly look my way. "Maggie, you've got to let things go."

"I am letting go."

A woman buys a lamp, a Scrabble game, and a card table. Lily takes over the money box as I help the woman carry her purchases to her car. "See, I'm letting go," I call over my shoulder to Lily, who just shakes her head.

"So, are you trying to make a point with the whole belly-button piercing-tattoos-climbing-Mt. Everest comment?" Lily asks when I return.

"Whatever do you mean?" I feign innocence.

"Like perhaps that some adventures are okay and some are better left alone?"

"My lips are sealed."

"Just as I thought. Remember, I'm being careful. I'll always meet these guys in public. I won't be alone with them until I know them very well."

"Okay, but it's just hard to know whether you can trust them."

"So you're going to be good and not stalk my dates in the future?"

"I'll try." I just can't promise any more than that.

"Well, I suppose that's the most I can hope for," Lily says with a sigh.

"Am I a thorn in your flesh, Lil?" I ask, thinking of Paul's "thorn in the flesh" in my Scripture reading this morning.

"Not a thorn exactly, but maybe a little prickly now and then." She laughs.

"Okay, but if your next date has horns coming out of his head, you'll call me, right?"

"You're pathetic."

"I know."

"How much do you want for this, ma'am?" The woman lifts a box of dishes that Nick and Heather bought for me one Mother's Day. They're cheap dishes; don't know why I didn't get rid of them before. Still, I can feel the lump in my throat. I quickly quote her much too high a price, but she takes it.

"These will go very nicely with my kitchen," she says, all excited.

I smile, though I can hardly breathe. She walks away with my junk, which suddenly looks for all the world like a treasure.

"I'll be right back, Lily," I say, going into the house. I grab some money from a kitchen drawer and sneak out the front door to catch the lady. "Ma'am?"

She turns to me.

"I know this sounds crazy, but I'll pay you twice what you gave me for those if you give them back."

She looks at me like I have a screw loose. "You kiddin' me?"

"Nope." I feel hope spring up inside me.

She shrugs. "Okay, I don't need them that bad."

I smile, give her the money, and she hands me the box. I turn to sneak it back in the house and see Lily standing at the edge of the garage door, arms folded across her chest, doing the whole foot-tapping thing and shaking her head. I lift my chin and walk inside, just as the phone rings. I set the dishes down to chat with Eric Galloway, a friend of ours who owns Galloway's Auto Sales. We spend a minute or two catching up on our families.

"Listen, Maggie, I don't know if Gordon would be interested, but I just got a 1971 Chevrolet Nova on a trade-in. It needs some repair, and by the looks of it, it will need a new paint job. But I remembered how Gordon loved his Nova in high school, and thought he might want to know about it. Especially since he enjoys fixing up cars."

Eric seems to have a sixth sense about Gordon. Just when Gordon is about to finish with one car, Eric is ready to sell him another one.

"He did love that car, didn't he?"

"He sure did."

"Gordon is almost finished with the Corvair. I suspect he'll be ready for another car soon. But he's been working so much lately he hardly has any time to tinker with cars. Let me run it by him, and I'll have him call you."

"That would be great. You know, I can still see the two of you driving off in that car when we won our big homecoming game. You remember that night?"

"I'll never forget it," I say dreamily, almost embarrassing myself.

"Seems like yesterday. 'Course, looking at the rust on this thing, I can see that it's been a lot longer than I care to admit."

"Ain't it the truth," I say with a laugh.

"Well, I'll wait to hear from you or Gordon then." We say our good-byes. I put the phone down and stare into space a moment.

"Well, what do you think?" Gordon asks as we slide into his new Nova.

I close my eyes and take a deep breath. "Mmm, it smells like a new doll," I say, opening my eyes and smiling.

Gordon wrinkles his nose. "A doll?"

"Never mind. You wouldn't relate to that, I guess. It smells new, anyway."

He flashes a wide grin. "Isn't it groovy, Maggie? Check out the stereo speakers." He pushes in the eight track, and Chicago breaks into "Does Anybody Really Know What Time It Is?"

I'm impressed, and he knows it. We leave the school parking lot, music blaring as we wave good-bye to friends along the way.

We stop at McDonald's, place our order, and eat it in the car where we can be alone. After we finish, Gordon takes my hand.

"I know this isn't the best time or place, Maggie, but, well, you know how I feel about you, and I think I know how you feel about me. Do you want to go steady?" He takes off his class ring and holds it out to me, fear in his eyes.

My heart blips. I smile and nod. He hands it to me since it's too big to put on my finger. I dig a rubber band out of my purse, wrap it around the top, and slip his ring on my finger. "First chance I get I'll buy some angora yarn to wrap around it so it will fit without the rubber band. I can hardly wait to show Lily."

Gordon smiles. "Bob won't believe I finally got up the nerve. Took him a while to ask her, too, you know," he says defensively.

I smile.

Gordon reaches over and gives me a kiss and a hug, and thus we seal our future together.

I shake myself from the daydream. "A future that has lasted for more than thirty years." At this, Crusher looks up.

"What? You find that so hard to believe?"

Crusher studies me a moment, then buries his nose beneath his paw.

Those were the days. Gordon and I were quite the couple. Everyone predicted we would marry one day. Our yearbooks testify to that. Still, I was always afraid to hope. I figured since he would be at college a whole year before me, he was sure to meet someone else, and I would be history. As it turned out, he met plenty of girls, but he chose me.

Gordon was so proud of his Nova. In fact, it served us well for a couple of years after we were married. When it came time, he hated to sell it, though it seemed the wisest thing to do. He probably would like to have one again. Of course, he would have to sell the Corvair, but that doesn't seem to be a problem since quite a few garage salers asked me about it this morning.

Then I'm struck with inspiration. It just might work.

I pick up the phone and punch in the number.

"Hi, Eric. It's Maggie again. Can we hold off on you telling Gordon about that car? I'd like to talk to you about it myself first. Could I come down there sometime next week?"

"Sure. Drop in anytime. I'm usually here."

We say good-bye, and I'm excited. Really excited. I want to buy the Nova myself and present it to Gordon for our thirtieth anniversary, hoping it will take him back to those romantic high-school days too.

On the other hand, it might just make him feel old. No, he will like it, right? I mean, this will be fun. Okay, now I'm not so sure.

I head back to the garage to run the plan by Lily.

"I think you should definitely do it," Lily confirms.

Okay, I'm feeling better now. "You're absolutely right. I will." With that settled, I turn my attention back to the customers milling around my drive.

Lily sells a couple of sweaters, a teapot, and some books. The garage is empty once again when she turns back to me. "Uh-oh, you've got that glazed look in your eyes. What are you thinking about now?"

"I just keep wondering where my life is going from here, Lil. I mean, Gordon has his work and his cars. Heather has Josh. Nick has school. You have scary Internet dates . . ." At this, Lily arches her left eyebrow. I smile. "I have an empty house, an old dog, and faded memories." I shrug. "That's about it."

"You really are going through a midlife crisis or something, I think. Maggie, we've got so much life still in us. It's not over just because you've turned fifty. We're only getting started! Look at me," she says with energy, "I'm having the time of my life. I don't care about impressing anyone. If I find a man I like in this group, great. If not, that's okay too. I don't need a man to be happy. But I'm having fun, enjoying the journey, you know?"

"Yeah."

"You're still worrying about Gordon and his paralegal, aren't you?"

"Among other things."

"Such as?"

"Oh, I don't know. I saw Debra Stiffler come out of his law office with him last week, and they looked pretty cozy as they stood in the parking lot talking. Plus, he didn't mention it to me when he got home."

"Is that a crime?"

"No, but why didn't he mention it?"

"You know men are clueless. And if he did think of it, well, he might have been afraid to tell you for fear of how you would react. You're not exactly yourself these days, Maggie."

"I'll give you that. But, well, here's the other thing. When I see her around men, she acts, I don't know, lonely and vulnerable. I don't want her pulling that routine around Gordon. It's like she's wanting his attention."

"Maggie, I think you're reading too much into it."

"Maybe. I just don't want Gordon to lose interest in me."

"You can't be serious."

"I am."

"Gordon loves you, Maggie. You have nothing to worry about."

"But he has all the signs. I told you about that talk show. He works late; he stays in the garage when he's home. Maybe it's because he doesn't want to be with me." I shake my head. "I feel stupid just talking like this. I sound like such a whiner."

"Actually, you do, and that's not like you. We'll chalk it up to the big M."

I nod. "I want to get him the Nova, but then if I do, he'll spend even more hours in the garage once he gets home from the office."

"Yeah, but you know it's something he loves to do. Probably his way of handling stress."

"What about me?"

"You can go to the coffee shop with me." She puts her arm around me and gives me a squeeze. "Now, stop worrying."

A few hours later, we decide to close up shop. I peer at my profits. "Well, we made a little money today. Looks like you made out a lot better than I did," I say to Lily as I look over at her pile compared to the piddly offering in my money box.

"That's because I sold my things when people wanted them."

I ignore her.

She gives me another hug. "I'm going home."

"Thanks for your help, Lil. I owe you a truffle."

She turns to me. "You owe me a box of truffles."

She negotiates just like Heather.

After the semisuccessful garage sale, I treat myself to a trip to The New Brew and spend the afternoon discussing life, love, and other important issues with Tyler and Jade. I'm really beginning to love those girls, and they seem to look forward to seeing me too. Kind of helps fill the void of my kids being gone.

Worn out from work and the sale, Gordon and I spend a comfortable evening curled up on the couch in front of a movie before we call it a night and head for bed.

11

After church on Sunday, Gordon helped me clear "his side" of the garage so he could move the Corvair back into it. We spent the afternoon puttering around the garage together—me sorting through the leftover stuff and trying to get rid of some of it, him underneath the Corvair, banging and tinkering.

When we're together like that, I think nothing could come between us. I can tell which tool he wants by which grunt he utters. He instinctively knows when to rush to my rescue when I grab a box that almost topples me over. He is the yin to my yang. The rhythm to my melody. It takes years of learning and loving each other to perfect a dance like ours. No Debra, Celine, or Paris could replace that. Right?

How easy it is to believe that when we're together on the weekends, but now on Monday morning as Gordon heads off for work, fears build like a mounting storm.

The attic is on my agenda today. I can add the stuff from the attic to the boxes that need to go to Goodwill.

My head hurts this morning. "Dr." Lily mentioned that for headaches I should get Vitex or Wild Yam—I'm pretty sure that's what it was, because as soon as she said it, I thought of candied yams with marshmallows. All that herbal stuff is confusing to me, and the ginseng wasn't exactly helpful, so I opt to go with a good old pain reliever.

After taking the meds, I grab my coffee and turn toward the attic when a crumpled paper on the kitchen floor catches my attention. I reach for it and start to toss it in the trash. Then wondering if it could be something important that spilled from Gordon's pocket, I smooth it open. My heart turns to ice as I read the words: "I've never met anyone like you before. What we share is special, even through the obstacles. You seem to understand that. Thank you for everything. Celine."

An acid taste climbs my throat. My head throbs behind my eyes. I stagger over to the sofa and sag onto it. There has to be a logical explanation. None of this makes sense. *Oh, God, please don't let it be*—I can't even say it. I look at it again, reading each word slowly, squinting to see the unwritten message that lurks on the cold paper. The paper that could change my entire future.

I start to get up, but the room spins. With trembling fingers, I pick up the phone.

"Lil, can you come over?" My voice quivers, sounding frightened and old. *Please say yes, please say yes.*

"You okay, Maggie?" she asks with a measure of alarm.

"No. I need to talk to you."

"You got it. I'll be there in fifteen minutes."

"Thanks, Lil," I say, struggling to choke back the tears.

"Maggie?"

"Yeah."

"You gonna be okay 'til I get there?"

She knows I'm going to cry. Why can't I be strong? This is probably nothing. There must be an explanation. It can't be happening with Gordon and me. He loves me. He said so just this morning. "I'll be okay." My voice is barely audible.

"Be right there." Lily clicks off the phone.

She gets to my house in record time. I've not even moved off the sofa. My mind is blank. My heart feels as though it's stopped beating. The world seems to stand still. The room feels dark and cold. Bitterly cold. Hollow. Lonely.

The doorbell rings. I rise from the sofa and steady myself, still feeling a bit woozy. When I open the door, Lily rushes in. "Oh, you poor thing!" She puts her arms around me. "What's wrong?"

I crumple and let the tears fall while Lily holds me against her, patting my back, saying nothing. When I finally regain my composure, we walk into the living room and sit on the sofa.

I tell her everything about my morning, Gordon's loving words before he left; then I show her the incriminating paper. Lily sits wide-eyed and mute the entire time, nodding now and then, but giving away little beyond that. When I've run out of words, she looks at me, still holding the hard evidence in her hand.

"I know it looks bad, Maggie, but I just have trouble believing this of Gordon. I see how he looks at you with love in his eyes. He's not a man looking for someone else. He just doesn't have that *look*. Gordon loves you as much today as he did thirty years ago."

I cry again. "I don't think so. Why would Celine say, 'What we share is special, even through the obstacles,' Lil? I don't get it. What do they share? Call me paranoid, but all this implies an intimacy beyond a business relationship."

"I don't know." Lily looks into space. "I just don't know." She turns back to me. "But I do know Gordon. And you do too. He loves the Lord, Maggie. Do you think he would throw away his relationship with the Lord for a young girl?"

"It happens."

"That's true, it does happen, but I don't see it happening with Gordon. Besides, I thought you were worried about him and Debra. Surely you don't think Gordon is fooling around with two women?"

"I don't know what to think anymore. If only I hadn't let myself go, maybe—"

"What? Maggie, you look fine. Why are you so hard on yourself? We can't compete with twenty-year-olds. We are who we are. Sure, we need to take care of ourselves the best we can—and you're doing that. You need to stop putting that kind of pressure on yourself. Gordon isn't twenty, either, you know."

"It's different for men, and you know it."

Lily shrugs. "I still say there's an explanation."

"What should I do about this? Should I confront him on it or what? If I find out he's lying to me, I'm not sure I could bear it."

"Well, if you confront him, it might hurt him that you would think he was unfaithful, Maggie."

"But I have to know."

"Maggie, you *do* know. You know deep in your heart that Gordon loves you."

"He works late almost every night. He's never here, and when he is, he works on his car or falls asleep in his recliner."

"But he tries to make it up to you."

I want to believe Lily with all my heart, but I just don't know.

"Let's pray about it together, Maggie. The Lord knows the truth, and He can help keep you calm so you can listen as He guides you through this."

I nod. Lily reaches over, grabs my hand, then leads me through a beautiful prayer that makes me more determined to keep my emotions in check and wait on the Lord.

My headache is starting to subside a little. "Thanks, Lil," I say, drying my face with a tissue. "I don't know what I'd do without you."

She squeezes my hand. "You're my best friend, Maggie. Gordon is a close second." She smiles. "I know there's an explanation. I don't believe for a minute that Gordon would do anything to harm you, your marriage, or his relationship with the Lord."

I take a deep breath and nod, praying all the while she is right.

"So what were your plans for the day?" Lily asks.

"I was going to sort through our stuff and weed out what we don't use or wear anymore. Get back to work in the attic."

"What's with the cleaning frenzy? I'd almost think you were pregnant. You know, with the whole nesting deal going on." She laughs.

"Bite your tongue! I miss the kids, but I'm not ready to do the Sarah thing," I say, referring to Abraham's wife in the Bible who was an AARP member before she got pregnant with their son.

"Well, you're certainly ambitious."

"Yeah, if only I could get things done before getting sidetracked."

"That's true." Lily laughs.

Lily looks toward our bookcase. "I didn't know you kept your yearbooks in here," she says, reaching for a yearbook and pulling it from the shelf. She sits down beside me and flips through the pages. "Oh, my goodness, we looked awful back then."

"Hey, speak for yourself," I say, looking through the pages with her and laughing.

"Oh, my goodness, look at Katie Phillip's elephant bells! The way we dressed back then! Remember those, the really big-belled pants?"

"'Course I remember. You bought me a pair one year for Christmas!" I'm cracking up just thinking about it. "They were plaid."

Lily groans. "They were awful. I can't believe we liked them!"

"Look at Gordon's pants in this band picture. I'd have enough material to make Elvira two good housedresses."

Lily laughs. "And look how long his hair and sideburns are! What a hippie."

One look at the picture and my heart squeezes in a Pavlovian response at the sight of the man who has turned my insides to mush for more than thirty years.

We laugh.

"Remember how mad our moms used to get over the miniskirts?" I ask.

"Boy, do I ever. That's why I wore maxidresses all the time."

"Hey! I have an idea," I say.

"Uh-oh, that always scares me."

I'm not so easily put off. "Can you stick around for a little while? I'll drag out my 45s. We can relive the good old days, and I'll even fix you lunch."

"You still have a record player that can play those things?"

"Are you kidding? Gordon would never part with it." I laugh. It suddenly occurs to me that by fixing up old cars and keeping record players, maybe Gordon is trying to hang on to his youth too.

"Okay, twinkle toes, you're on," Lily says with a laugh. "I'm going to run to your bathroom real quick." Lily takes off down the hall.

I glance once more at Gordon staring up from the page. Leaning my head on the back of the sofa, I close my eyes. A young Gordon approaches me with his winning smile and asks me out for our first date. I feel the brush of his lips on mine with our first kiss. I hear his Toyota with the rusty muffler making its way toward our house. In the next scene, I step outside to see his new Chevy Nova with that state-of-the-art, eight-track stereo system. He whisks me down the road with the sound of Chicago's "Make Me Smile," wafting out our open windows.

I open my eyes and hurry to the place in the garage where Gordon has stored our records. Thumbing through the stack, I pick out ones I'm sure Lily will remember. The very idea makes me hyper. Maybe I should pull out the song, "They're Coming to Take Me Away, Ha-Ha." It seems rather appropriate. Well, I suppose it's okay to do this once in a while, as long as I don't get stuck in a time warp and pile my hair up in a beehive.

"Is this totally insane or what?" I say, bringing in the record player and stacks of records.

We sit on the sofa and sort through our 45s like a couple of high schoolers at a slumber party.

"Oh my goodness, Maggie, do you remember this song by Bread?"

"How could I forget?" We break out in song. "Baby, I'm-a Want You—" We both draw a blank on the rest of the words and erupt into laughter.

Lily nods. "Oh! Look at this, 'Puppy Love' by Donny Osmond!"

I squeal and take it from her. "You used to have the biggest crush on him."

"Did not. He was too young for me."

"You did too. You just didn't want to admit it."

"Okay, so I did. You were just as crazy about Kurt Russell. You know, *Super Dad* and all that?"

"Wasn't he so *groovy*?" I say, putting a heavy emphasis on our hip word of the '70s.

We laugh.

"Remember the time we had a fight because I smeared a piece of banana on your Kurt Russell poster? You were so mad we almost came to blows."

"I almost never forgave you for that one." A fresh wave of bitterness assaults me. "The banana bleached his lips orange."

Lily busts up again.

I get us some iced tea and set the glasses on a stand. Before I know it, we're dancing around the living room to tunes by Chicago, Three Dog Night, the Osmonds, and the Jackson 5. Finally, we belt out "Top of the World" by the Carpenters and then collapse onto the sofa in a sweaty heap.

"I can't remember when I've had such fun, Maggie," Lily says, wiping the perspiration from her forehead.

"Me too. This is the most I've exercised since, well, Nick was born."

Lily laughs. "That's so not true. You've even gone to Curves."

We pause to drink our iced tea. Lily glances at the clock. "Oh, it's eleven thirty. I have to get going."

"But we haven't had lunch yet."

"I'll take a rain check," she says, dumping the ice cubes from her glass into the sink and rinsing out her glass. "I need to get home and get the house picked up before my afternoon appointment." She turns to me. "I've had the best time, Maggie."

"Me too, Lil. And thanks for the prayers for Gordon and me."

"Don't you worry. It will be all right; you'll see." She grabs her sweater from the hall closet. "I'll call you later."

With that she is gone.

The tunes continue to play in my head while I put everything away.

That was a fun way to exercise. I feel good. Really good. And Lily has completely dissolved my fears over Gordon and Celine.

Well, almost.

12

Colored pennants flap in the afternoon breeze, and sleek, shiny cars line the parking lot at Galloway's Autos. The new models sit proudly across the front of the lot, while the used ones fill the back. Eric Galloway is a good businessman, and his success proves it. People trust him. They know he has their best interests at heart and will do the right thing by them. That's a rare thing in car sales, which is why he is so successful. A little integrity still goes a long way.

I step inside the office building with the small waiting area. The smell of coffee and upholstery mingles through the air.

"Hi, Rhonda, how are you?" I say to the receptionist at the front desk.

"Doing great, Mrs. Hayden. Have you heard from the newlyweds?" Rhonda is a former high-school classmate of Heather's, and I always liked her peppy spirit. With a mass of dark curls on her head, she reminds me of a French poodle. I feel a compulsion to stick a tiny red bow in the front. Her face is round, and her eyes twinkle. Those friendly eyes, no doubt, will cost her wrinkles by the time she's my age. Her slightly pudgy frame suits her. I can almost imagine her sitting on the floor with half a dozen kids playing happily beside her.

"Yes, they were at our house last weekend."

She smiles. "The wedding was beautiful. I'm so happy for Heather. Josh seems like a nice guy."

"He is," I say with a smile. *'Course, there's that whole he-stole-my-daughter thing, but I'm trying to let it go.*

"You here to see Eric?"

I nod.

"I'll let him know you're here." She picks up the phone and speaks into the intercom. Her voice immediately changes from perky to nasal.

Making my way to the seating area, I sift through a table full of car, entertainment, and health magazines. An article on menopause catches my attention—I seem to be drawn to those. Picking up the magazine, I walk over to my chair and rummage through my purse for my glasses, then settle in for a good read.

The article goes over the usual symptoms: hot flashes—been there, done that. Weight gain, ditto. Irritability, who, me? And then, of course, there's always the dreaded facial hair. I don't even want to think about that one.

"Hey, Maggie, good to see you." Eric gives my hand a hearty shake. You know, age is cruel to more than just me. Here is this former high-school football star, and now the last few wisps of hair on the top of his head seem to be hanging on for dear life, and his midsection has expanded like a helium balloon since I last saw him.

He's probably thinking the same thing about me.

"You've got some nice cars out there, Eric. Business must be good; it looks like you've sold a few since we last drove by," I say, as we make our way down a long, narrow aisle to his office.

"Yeah, we're gearing up for the next shipment."

We step into his office, and I'm thinking he spends little time in here. Papers clutter his desk. Stale coffee mugs line the credenza behind his chair. Crumpled paper fills his trash can.

He sees me scanning the room. "Sorry for the mess." He scratches his nearly bald head. "I've been so busy lately, I don't know whether I'm coming or going."

"I can relate to that." Why did I say that? That's how my life used to be. Now I share endless days with Crusher. We stare at spots on the floor for hours at a time. Okay, maybe it's not quite that bad.

Eric points to a chair for me to sit in and plops down in the seat behind his desk. Placing his elbows on top, he steeples his fingers together and suddenly looks salesman-serious. "So, Maggie, what can I do for you?"

At this point my mouth gets dry as dirt. Am I doing the right thing? Will Gordon be okay with this? What if he doesn't like the car? What if it has problems beyond what he can fix? What if—

"Maggie?"

"Sorry, Eric." I chew on my lower lip, still wondering if this is the right thing. "You mentioned that Nova, and, well, you're Gordon's friend."

He nods.

"You know what he likes in a car and whether he can handle the problems on it, right?"

He looks puzzled. "I think so." His words sound noncommittal, but his body language tells me he's pretty confident. He sits back in his chair. "What's on your mind?"

"Well," I reach into my purse and pull out an envelope with cash in it. Eric's eyes grow wide. "I have a little money saved to give you as a down payment. Hopefully, that will hold it for a while." His elbows are back on the desk, fingers steepled. "Go on."

"Gordon and I will be celebrating our thirtieth anniversary in a little while and, well, I would like to surprise him with this car. Of course, I'd like to look at it first."

"Of course."

We discuss the price, what my payments would be, and then he takes me out to the lot to see it. I know very little about cars, but I trust Eric. So if he says there's potential in the car, I believe him.

I look at the body and interior.

"I told you it would need a paint job, but it's pretty cool that it's the same color as Gordon's old car."

I nod. "He will be thrilled."

Eric smiles and shoves his hand in his pocket. "I'm glad you're doing this for him, Maggie," he says like the true friend that he is.

After scrutinizing the car, cosmetically speaking, I look up at Eric. "Would it be possible to keep it here until our anniversary?"

"No problem, Maggie. I'll just put a sold sign on it and move it to the back out of sight."

"Great." We walk back to his office where I give him my deposit, and we finalize all the details.

I leave feeling energized by my secret for Gordon. Then out of nowhere, Celine Loveland and Debra Stiffler come to mind, and I hear a voice inside me sneer, "*If you make it to your anniversary.*"

I push back my fears and head for my car. "Gordon will love the Nova," I say to myself with confidence.

With a little less confidence, I pray he will still love me.

• • •

Despite my struggling self-esteem, I enjoy the drive home. A bright autumn sun sprays across the open fields and pastures where cattle and horses graze. I roll down my window and take a deep breath of the country air. I quickly roll my window back up. Sometimes that country air thing is way overrated.

An Amish buggy holding a man and woman passes. The woman

looks over at me and smiles. We exchange a wave. She's plain-faced, dressed in black.

Takes a lot of the pressure off to dress like those people. You live with the face God gave you, and there's no problem deciding what to wear in the morning.

Wonder if I could join the Amish order? No, wait. I don't do outhouses.

Pulling into the garage, I see that Gordon is already home, tinkering with the Corvair. My heart leaps.

I get out of the car and walk over to him. "Hi." I decide not to mention the note. Lily helped me put it into perspective. Hopefully, she's right.

He peeks out from under the hood. "Hi, yourself." He gives me a kiss.

"You're home early."

"Uh-huh," he says, tightening some kind of knob.

His hands are dirty, and he has a smudge of oil on his face. He looks like the teenager I remember. Maybe he feels like one too. Maybe that's why he loves this so much. I feel a private thrill of excitement about the Nova.

Have I mentioned that I'm bad at keeping surprises to myself? Lily can't keep a secret, but I'm just as bad with presents. I want to blurt out, "Oh, Gordon, I just went over to Eric's today and bought you a 1971 Chevrolet Nova that has a good body, needs a paint job, and a little minor repair on the engine (sounds like me). Guess what? That baby is yours. We can go cruising through the streets of Charming like we did thirty years ago!" Instead, I grit my teeth to keep my tongue in place.

"So, how are things coming along in here?" I ask nonchalantly, acting like all those internal wires mean something to me.

Gordon adjusts some kind of plug and turns a nozzle. "I think she's coming right along, Maggie." He wipes his hands off and throws a grin my way. *Be still my heart.* "She's almost ready to find a home." He drops the hood down with a bang.

"I don't know why you spend all that time fixing up cars and don't keep them long enough to enjoy them."

Gordon follows me into the house. "Because it's the fixing part I enjoy. By the time I finish them, I'm itching to start a new project." He laughs.

I scratch my head.

"Don't try to figure it out. It's a man-thing," he says and wiggles his eyebrows at me, all studlike. I can't help but chuckle, then lean into his arms, grease and all.

After dinner we relax awhile in the living room, talking about the kids; then we settle in to read the newspaper, and I'm thankful Gordon isn't in the garage.

The grandfather clock in the hallway ticks off the time. I used to love that clock with its beautiful wood grain. Its rhythmic ticking added a warm, cozy charm to our home. Now that the kids are no longer here, the sound reverberates off the walls, emphasizing the hollow, empty shell in which I now live.

Enough of that! Soon I'll be thinking about that stupid note again. No, I refuse. Lily said to leave it alone for now, and that's what I am going to do. I take a deep breath and open the paper to the classified ads. Browsing through the employment opportunities, I stumble upon an ad for a real estate class to be offered in town. Now, there's something to consider. I love looking through homes, know this town like the back of my hand, and I enjoy helping people. It seems like the perfect fit.

"You know, Gordon, I would like to get a job."

"Hmm," he says, only half listening. "That's nice, honey."

"Did you hear me?"

Gordon closes his paper and turns to me. "I'm sorry, honey. Just finished reading an article about the gas hike. Always something." He shakes his head, then lifts a smile. "Now, what did you say?"

"I want to get a job."

His eyebrows raise. "Really?"

"Do you mind?"

"Of course not, honey, if that makes you happy. But if it's the money—"

"No, it's not the money"—*Well, okay, maybe a little, but I can't tell him about the car, not yet anyway*—"I just need something to do with myself while you're gone all day."

He studies my face. "You're really missing the kids, aren't you?"

"Hello? News flash! Of course I miss the kids! If you were home more, you would know that." Uh-oh, I'm beginning to snap like a turtle.

Our eyes lock.

"Sorry. Hormonal spell over." My face is burning, but not from a hot flash this time.

"I'm sorry, Maggie. I didn't know things were bothering you so much."

I don't want him to feel sorry for me. I can do this. "I do miss them, and I need something to do with my time." My voice sounds almost professional here.

He gives me an understanding smile. Before I can elevate him to sainthood, I remember—nope, I'm not going to say it.

"Honey, if that's what you want, then I support you. Do you have anything in particular in mind?"

I bite my lower lip a second and reach for the paper. "It says something here about a real estate class being offered at the high school—"

"You're kidding, right?"

His comment startles me. "What? You think I can't handle the class?"

"It's not the class I'm worried about. Have you ever noticed how you get lost two blocks from home?" There's a teasing sparkle to his eyes, but I'm just a little too put out at the moment to appreciate it.

"Excuse me? If memory serves me well—and it does—the city did some major changes to the road two blocks from here. I got a little disoriented," I say in a huff.

He chuckles. "Well, suit yourself." He picks up his paper once again. "I'd just hate to see you get lost, that's all."

I bite my lower lip again. He knows how I hate getting lost. One afternoon I ventured into the next county and got lost in some farming community. I wandered for hours on country roads with only Jersey cows as landmarks. I can only imagine what they were thinking while they grazed and watched me circle their pastures like a race car driver on a track. "Look, Elsie, there she goes again. The poor dear. Farmer Joe ought to throw her a map." Gordon *would* have to bring that whole thing up.

I sag into my chair and ponder other employment ideas.

"Now, don't get discouraged," Gordon says. "If that's what you want to do, go for it. I have no doubt you can do anything you set your mind to."

Now, that's the Gordon I love and cherish. His encouragement can lift me higher than a sale at Isabella's Boutique. Well, it's a close second, anyway.

"Thanks, Gordon. But you're right. I probably wouldn't be happy if I had to spend most of my time asking for directions. I'll check into some other options."

He winks and smiles. "Say, I need to look over a file tonight, and I left it at the office. You want to ride with me to Rosetown? We could go to Starbucks afterwards."

I think a moment, wondering if I should take time to fix up a little in case we run into Celine or Debra.

"What's the matter? You trying to figure out where Lily might be meeting Walter?" He winks again.

I ignore him. "Starbucks sounds great." I decide to touch up my makeup in the car. He brings up a valid point about Lily and Walter.

I wonder if he's still in town or if he's back home with Mom. How did I let Lily slip by without telling me if he's still here? Oh, well. Tomorrow is another day.

We get in the car and drive over to Gordon's office where he gathers what he needs to bring home. Afterwards, he takes me to the nearest Starbucks, and when we walk inside, I spot Jade sitting alone in a dark corner. While Gordon orders our drinks, I walk over to talk to her.

"Hi," I say, walking up to her table. "Aren't you in the wrong coffeehouse?"

She looks surprised to see me but musters a smile. "Hi, Maggie. What are you doing here?"

I explain about going to Gordon's office. "How about you? Big test on Monday?" I ask, noting the psychology book and open notebook on her table.

She nods. "You okay? Your eyes look kind of puffy."

"Yeah." Great. My emotional storms are catching up with me. I must look like Rory Raccoon.

There are three empty coffee cups on her table.

"It's the regular kind, nothing special," she explains. "I need the caffeine so I can study. Otherwise, I fall asleep."

I have to wonder if it's good for her to have that much caffeine. She has dark circles under her eyes, and her face is the color of old milk. That can't be good.

"Listen, Jade," I tread easy here because she's rather private about her life, "are you okay?"

She forces a smile that never reaches her eyes. "I'm doing fine. Just a little tired from studying, that's all. If you're referring to what happened at The New Brew, I was just upset with my mom. No biggie, really." She shrugs it off.

I'm confused.

"Oh yeah, I told you I didn't have a mom. That's not entirely true. My parents are divorced, I live with my dad, and my mom and I—well, we don't get along."

I get the feeling Jade is dealing with something deep here, but I have no idea how to help her. I shoot a quick prayer dart for some help.

"You know, Jade, when I was in college, I used to journal." She looks at me like I'm crazy. "I know it sounds dumb when you already have so much reading and writing to do, but somehow journaling helps organize your thoughts, gets everything on paper, you know, and just—oh, I don't know, it makes you feel better. It did me, anyway."

This time she looks at me almost as if she's considering the idea. "Well, I don't have a journal."

I make a mental note to buy her one and not push the matter any further for now.

"Just a thought. Anyway, I wanted to stop over and say 'hi'." I smile and start to walk away.

"Maggie?"

I turn back around.

"Thanks."

My insides go soft. "You're welcome." I walk over to the table to join Gordon.

Now I know why she wears those baggy clothes. She's covering a broken heart.

13

"Hi, Mom." Cough, sniffle. I'm thankful for phone wires that hold the cold germs at bay.

"Heather, is that you?" She sounds like Tennessee Ernie Ford.

"Yeah, it's me." She blows her nose here. Lovely.

I want to forget the laundry on my to-do list and travel to Illinois to take my kid some chicken noodle soup.

"Has Dad left for work yet?"

"Yeah, he just left. Did you need to talk to him?"

"No, just didn't want to interrupt your morning coffee."

"So when did you get sick?" I ask, holding the cordless phone between my shoulder and my ear as I finish sorting the laundry.

She tells me about her cold and how she's been home since last Friday with it. "Anyway, all that to say, I miss my mommy."

We share a laugh, and my nurturing side kicks in, all toasty warm. "You have Josh get you some chicken noodle soup and load you up on Vitamin C." I'm beginning to sound like Dr. Lily.

"Just hearing you take charge makes me feel better already," she says.

I'm about to melt down to my toes. "Did you get a sub for your class yesterday and today?" I ask, referring to her job as a second-grade teacher.

"Yeah, they called in a substitute." She blows her nose again.

"So how is married life, besides the cold, I mean?"

"It's great, Mom. Josh is wonderful. We're so in love."

"That's always nice to hear after spending all that money on the wedding." I finish sorting the clothes and manage to put the first load of whites in the washer and start it up.

She laughs.

I tell her about the things I kept for her from the garage sale, and she perks up.

"I'm really getting to know Josh's parents, and I like them a lot. Mom is very gifted with decorating—"

I've just settled onto the sofa with the phone to my ear when my heart skids to a halt. Time out here. *Excuse me, but did you just call her Mom? Was she the one who walked the floors with you at night when you had the flu? Did she change your dirty diapers? Did she see you through your heartbreaks and measles? High school? College? Hello? I don't think so.*

Take a deep breath, Maggie.

Of course she called her Mom. That's her mother-in-law; it's natural for Heather to call her Mom. I just hadn't thought about her doing that until this very minute. I feel as though a porcupine is crawling all over my heart.

"Mom, you still there?"

"Uh, yes," I say, trying desperately to ignore the jealousy that creeps through me like a slow-moving fog.

She drones on about Marilyn Stewart's talents and how she is teaching her so many new things about decorating. Like I failed miserably? Is that what she means? I look around the house. Okay, maybe I'm not Martha Stewart here, but neither am I Ma Kettle.

We talk a while longer, but for the life of me, I can't seem to move past the "Mom" thing, though I do try my best not to let Heather sense it. A hormonal moment. That's all this is. This, too, shall pass.

After our conversation, I feel better in some ways just having heard Heather's voice, but still feel the need for a distraction. If I get my laundry finished, I might go to Curves this afternoon, but for now I opt to run through my new exercise DVD.

I put on my exercise clothes, and in no time I'm sweatin' to the oldies and having the time of my life—well, okay, my muscles are screaming almost as loud as the music, but this is good. "No pain, no gain," and all that. I'm *so* not into this. I'm beginning to understand that whole slug thing with Nick. He gets it from me.

Crusher is resting peacefully on Gordon's recliner. Life can be so unfair. Why can't I melt into a chair all day and only weigh four pounds? My evil twin kicks in, and I'm wishing for a dog whistle. That would fix him. I can be so mean when I'm exercising. Of course, knowing Crusher's lack of bladder control, the joke would probably be on me.

By the time the DVD is over, I'm breathing like an obscene phone caller, and my body is threatening to go on strike. When life comes back to my legs, I drag myself with all the grace of Igor over to the refrigerator and grab a bottled water.

The water chills my throat and refreshes my spirit. Replacing the cap on the water bottle, I head for the shower. Once I'm clean and dressed, I'm feeling much better for taking charge of this menopause thing. I am woman, hear me roar, and all that. I can almost hear strains of the "Hallelujah Chorus."

• • •

"Hey, babe, how's your day going?" Gordon's voice still makes my heart race.

"It's going well. Heather has a cold and misses us, but she's okay. How's your day?" I carry the phone headset to the sofa, sit down, and get comfortable.

"Getting lots done. That Celine is a wonder."

Great. She's not only beautiful, but smart too.

"We're ahead of the game, so I'm happy about that. As you know, my schedule is usually lagging behind."

I brighten. "So I guess that means you'll be coming home earlier tonight?"

"Oh, well, no. I'm sorry, honey. Still a lot to do, but we're on track and doing better every day. The Keller case is coming along, and good days are ahead."

He sounds spirited like he did back in the days of his Nova. Alive. Vibrant. Maybe he is going through some kind of change too. Why is it men going through a change seem energized while women just long for a nap?

No doubt seeing a young, beautiful woman is making Gordon relive the days of his youth. Great. He spends his morning with Celine. I spend my morning sweating with the oldies and Crusher.

"You still there?"

"I'm here," I say as cheerfully as possible. If he starts blow-drying his chest hair, I'll have to take some action. Wait. Who am I to point fingers? Haven't I been buying wrinkle creams, dieting—well, I've had a carrot or two here and there—hanging on to what's left of my youth like an aging film star clutching her movie reels?

"Any chance we could do lunch today, Gordon?"

"I'm sorry, honey. I have to go out for a meeting with a client in a half hour, then I'm coming back to the office to get right back to it."

"So what time do you think you'll be home tonight?"

He pauses. "I'm not sure. Don't worry about dinner. I'll order something out."

I try not to sound irritated, though I am.

"This will be over soon, I promise," he says.

Yeah, right. "That's okay. I know you'll come home when you can. If you don't, I'll have to hurt you."

Gordon hesitates, then lets out a weak laugh. I don't make a single sound. He clears his throat. "Hey, the reason I called was to let you know there are a couple of legal secretarial openings in town. I didn't know if you would be interested."

I perk just a little.

"Now, so you know, I don't care if you work or not. This is totally up to you. But you had mentioned that you were considering a job, and when I heard about these, I thought I would let you know."

If he had anything going on with his paralegal, would he want me working in the legal community? It seems unlikely, but still one can't be too careful. "Could you give me the phone numbers and the names of who I should contact?"

"Sure. Just a second." A rustling of papers here—no doubt he's going through one of his many stacks. "Here it is." He gives me the information. "Those are both nice law firms. I think you would be happy there, if you decide law is the place you want to work. Remember, it's totally up to you."

"Thanks, Gordon."

"You're welcome, babe. I love you, you know that?"

"Yeah." My face warms. "I love you too."

"See you tonight." He hangs up, and I stare at the phone.

Legal secretary. This means I'll have to pass on my visit to Curves today. Good thing I exercised this morning.

I take a deep breath and call the law offices. By the time I'm finished, I have a two o'clock and three o'clock appointment with the law firms.

I fold the laundry and decide to finish the rest later. It's close to lunchtime, so I head for the kitchen to grab a sandwich. One glance in the refrigerator tells me my nerves couldn't handle food right now.

I go to the closet to pick out a suit for my appointments. This should be an interesting afternoon.

• • •

Though there's plenty of time before my first appointment, I leave early anyway. Nerves always make me do that. Well, and that whole getting lost thing.

Once I arrive in Rosetown, I spot Gordon's car in the parking lot of a popular restaurant. How odd to find him here. He said he had to be out earlier, but he also said he couldn't do lunch. Too much work, as I recall. Maybe his plans changed, but, hey, I asked him first. You'd think he would have let me know. With a little time yet before my interview, I pull into the parking lot. I'm feeling very sophisticated in my black business suit, so I step out of the car and head into the restaurant, hoping to surprise Gordon.

I slip inside, all excited with the idea of seeing Gordon. He's sitting by himself at a table across the crowded room. My heart leaps as I inch my way toward him. Just then a woman steps up to his table, and I stop in my tracks. She says something and laughs, turning enough for me to see her. Her familiar face causes my heart to pause. I'm the one who gets the surprise, because apparently Gordon is having lunch with Debra Stiffler!

I'm too mad to cry. With my eyes fixed on them, I stomp forward with a vengeance—which is hard to do in heels—but doggone it, I am determined to give Gordon Paul Hayden a piece of my mind.

"Well, Maggie Hayden, fancy meetin' you here," a sweet voice calls out a little too loud for comfort.

I turn to see Elvira standing there in a flowered housedress, a frail, gray-haired lady standing beside her.

"Oh, hello, Elvira, how are you?" I try to concentrate, all the while looking beyond her at Debra Stiffler and my husband.

"I'm doing just great, kiddo," she says, thumping her hand against my arm and blocking my view. "This here is my friend, Freida. She lives here in Rosetown," Elvira says.

"Hello." Gordon and Debra are standing now. I turn back to Elvira. "I'm on my way to an appointment," I say, hoping to hurry this visit along.

"You gonna get a waitressing job?" Elvira wants to know.

"What? Oh no, I just stopped to"—*snoop on my husband comes to mind, but I ignore it*—"have a quick lunch." Which is totally true. I wanted to have lunch. With my husband. I look up just as Gordon and Debra are about to reach the door on the other side of the room.

"No, wait!" I call out. I look to Elvira. "I'm sorry, Elvira, I have to go." I look at Freida. "Nice to meet you."

I rush off toward Gordon, and the thin heel of my shoe gets caught in a rectangular floor register. In a panic, I try to yank free, and when I do, the small register comes up out of the floor, still attached to my shoe. The weight of the struggle tips me off balance just as a server is passing. I topple against him, knocking his tray to the ground and causing green peas to scatter all over the floor.

By the time I regain my dignity and assess the matter, I find that Gordon and Debra are gone, apparently having missed the whole "pea" episode. I make my apologies to the waiter and help Elvira and Freida avoid the peas, then quickly make my way out the door. Now that the fiasco is over, I get inside my car and sit for a minute to calm down. I brush off the front of my suit, which miraculously escaped injury.

Why didn't Gordon tell me he was meeting Debra Stiffler? Because he knew I would overreact? All right, so maybe trying to make a mad dash for him and Debra and getting my foot stuck in a register, scattering hundreds of peas to the floor is overreacting. A little. Okay, a lot. Gordon was just having a business lunch, right? Debra is obviously in need of legal help.

Come to think of it, if this keeps up, *I* might have to look for a good criminal attorney myself.

A glance at my watch tells me there's no time to think about it now. A job interview awaits me. I will be calm and professional. I can hurt my husband later.

I'm just kidding. I think.

Inside the warmth of the law office reception area I shed my suit jacket. Three other women glance through magazine pages and look up when I enter. We exchange smiles, and they return to their magazines. They look younger than Heather.

After reporting to the receptionist, I take my place with the others. By the time I settle in my seat, I'm feeling better about Gordon and Debra. I'm sure he has his reasons for not telling me about their lunch. I trust him. I do.

Looking around, I'm instantly aware of my age. I feel like a school marm waiting with anxious students for the announcement of the spelling bee finalists.

Their thin bodies are dressed in short skirts, tight tops, and fashionable shoes. I, on the other hand, am dressed in a classic black, knee-length suit, with sensible shoes, and matching purse. Throw in a pair of dainty gloves, and I'd look like June Cleaver going to market.

I pick up a magazine and glance through it. Okay, the first article is by the same author that was on TV the other day talking about troubled marriages. Is this a sign?

All the other ladies are probably reading about how to find a man. I'm trying to figure out how to keep one.

I read through the article and suddenly wonder how a beautiful woman like Debra Stiffler could lose her husband. After all, if someone as gorgeous as Debra can lose her husband, I haven't a prayer of keeping mine. My spirits deflate.

Still, the fact that Gordon and I have been married almost thirty years should count for something. For a moment, I wonder what would happen if they hired me to write these articles about relationships. A voice of authority, really. I could tell these young girls that there's more to a relationship than wearing "hot" clothes and keeping your man "satisfied in bed" like these articles say. It's seeing your husband at his worst and loving him anyway. It's supporting him through thick and thin. It's trusting him when all the evidence is stacked against him.

No, wait. Better leave that one out. I don't have that one down yet.

"Mrs. Hayden?" A young, thin woman stands before me, dressed in preppy clothes and a smile. "If you'll follow me, please?"

I *so* do not belong here.

My afternoon consists of taking typing tests, answering endless questions, scribbling notes, and viewing the offices. The interview comes off without a hitch, all except for when that pea slid out from under my suit, rolled across the floor, and came to a stop at the tip of the attorney's shoe. *Thanks a lot, Gordon.*

At least now I'm finally free to go home.

I've learned something about myself today. Legal secretary is not my career choice.

I trudge my way home and think I'll call Lily for dinner. Once there, I take care of Crusher, then sit down and pick up the phone.

"Hey, Lily, are you free?"

"Yes, my last appointment left forty-five minutes ago. What's up?"

"A couple of questions for you. First off, what can I take for face flushes?" I can't believe I'm encouraging her to practice without a license. "My face is sizzling like a heated frying pan."

"Black Cohosh is good for that."

"Great."

"Secondly, do you want to grab a sandwich with me at Wendy's tonight?"

Hesitation here.

"Is that a problem?" She's usually free in the evenings.

"Uh, well," she stammers and waits some more.

"Okay, Lily, what's going on?"

"You promise not to say the P word?"

I can almost see her shiver here. This must be serious. "That can only mean one thing."

"Listen here, Maggie, I want you to stay home. Do you hear me?"

Just as I thought. "P-pe-pea-p—"

"Now, cut that out!"

"Oh, all right," I say, deciding she's no fun at all. "So who is it this time?"

"Walter is back in town. We're going for dinner tonight."

Another date? She's going on another date with Walter? This could be serious.

"Promise not to stalk?"

"Celery stalks, Lily. I merely snoop."

"No snooping," she quips.

"You'll thank me one day."

"For what?"

"For saving your life." Pause. "I heard that."

"Heard what?"

"You rolled your eyes."

Lily starts to giggle. "I wish you'd stop that."

"Stop what?"

"Stop making me laugh when I want to be mad at you."

I smile. "That's what friends are for," I say, enjoying our banter.

"Gotta go. Someone is here," she says. "No stalking."

"Killjoy."

"No snooping."

"Scrooge. Do I win?"

Click.

14

I've barely had time to eat a sandwich when Lily calls me back. "Thought you had a big date tonight?"

"Walter wasn't feeling well, so he went on home."

"Oh, I'm sorry, hope it's nothing serious."

"I don't think so. Just a flu bug. By the way, how's Heather feeling? Did you tell her to take some ginger root and cinnamon?"

I curl my feet beneath me on the sofa and smile. "Yes, Dr. Lily, Heather is better. And yes, she knows about the herbs."

"Did you get a sandwich yet?"

"Just finished one."

"Is Gordon working tonight?"

"Do chickens have lips?"

"No, I don't think so."

"Oh, okay, does McDonald's have Big Macs?"

"Does that mean that Gordon is working?"

"You got it."

"I taped Oprah and wondered if you wanted me to bring it over so we could watch it."

"Oh, that would be super! I missed it today because of those interviews."

"I want to hear about those. I'll grab a quick bite to eat and be over in a jif, okay?"

"Save room for popcorn."

The iced tea and popcorn are ready by the time Lily arrives. We settle onto the sofa, the bowl of popcorn between us, Oprah telling us that the theme of her show is anorexia. Pictures of skeletal-looking women flash upon the TV screen, women who give their testimony of overcoming their struggle with the devastating eating disorder.

"It's a mind-set," one says. "No matter what anyone said, no matter what the mirror told me, I still thought I was fat. I could think of nothing else but getting thin."

"I watched her waste away, day after day, and felt totally helpless," a mother says, her arm around her daughter.

The show breaks for a commercial.

"It's hard to imagine women abusing their bodies that way, isn't it?" I say.

"Our minds can convince us of many things," Lily says, before cramming popcorn into her mouth.

Such a simple statement but very profound.

Lily looks at me. "What?"

I smile. "I was just thinking how wise you are."

She sits up taller. "There'll be no living with me if you keep talking like that."

The program returns, and for the next hour we listen to the ladies talk about their food issues and self-esteem problems. When it's over, I click off the TV with the remote.

"It is so sad what some women go through. There is one thing I know for sure."

"What's that?" Lily asks before taking the last drink of her tea.

"I don't have that problem. Want a truffle?"

We head for the kitchen, with Crusher not far behind . . .

• • •

Early Thursday morning Gordon's in the shower, when I throw off the covers. It's time to get up to make myself presentable. No more sending my man off to the office while I slug around in a housecoat and slippers.

Racing against time, I fluff my hair and put on my clothes for the day—since I showered last night. I grab my makeup bag and start to apply my foundation when I notice my magnifying mirror lying on the dresser, collecting dust. You know, the one that's magnified six times? The one that shows the real you, the you that you pray with all your heart that no one can see but God? That's the one. I haven't used it in forever. There's something about ignorance being bliss, you know?

Well, today I feel brave, so I lift the magnifying mirror to my face and gasp. Manly hormones have arrived in droves. I have a mustache that would be the envy of eighth-grade boys everywhere, and spikes the size of porcupine needles are poking out of my chin.

Now, I figure it's my wifely duty to keep the less-than-feminine things in life from my husband. He doesn't need to know *how* I keep myself beautiful, only that I *am* beautiful, right? So, I have to take care of this latest problem . . . and fast.

The shower door squeaks as Gordon steps out of the shower. Without a moment to lose, I grab my nifty new bottle of hair removal cream and pray that it works quickly. While Gordon prepares for his day, I slather cream on my upper lip and chin. It has to stay on there for ten minutes.

When he finally walks into the bedroom, I keep my face turned and start to go out the door so he won't see me. Just as I'm stepping into the hallway, he ever-so-sweetly calls out right behind me, "You're so beautiful, Maggie."

I skid to a halt.

Now, Gordon is a romantic most of the time, and I appreciate it. I really do. But sometimes it's just aggravating when he tells me I'm beautiful without really looking at me. I mean, how heartfelt can that be?

So, while I do not want him to see me in this state, the temptation to teach him a lesson is far too great. On the other hand, I don't want him to remember me this way when he spends the day with Celine. I teeter with indecision. Doggone it, if Gordon is going to tell me I'm beautiful, he had better get a good look before he says it.

So, lathered in facial cream like a man in a barber chair, I turn to him in all my glory. Sometimes a picture is worth a thousand words, you know?

Gordon goes all wide-eyed and, well, speechless.

"Beautiful?" I ask, sputtering flecks of facial cream upon his undershirt.

He gets my point.

After he finds his tongue, he goes into this whole "beauty is more than skin deep" thing and mumbles some spiritual application.

I'm not buying it.

Let's face it, I'm not twenty anymore, and *beautiful* just does not apply. I'm thinking *ripe* might be the better word here, but I leave it alone to let him ponder what just happened. We spend the rest of our morning in silence.

I think I've frightened him.

By the time Gordon leaves for the office, I'm feeling kind of bad about the whole thing; and I'm seeing Dr. Phil books in our future.

I finally shrug it off and decide to check for some nutrition supplements on the Internet. After ordering a few bottles of supplements that promise to give me strong, healthy bones while lessening my menopausal symptoms, I switch over to e-mail.

Nick usually tries to write every now and then. I think he considers phones obsolete, or maybe that's his way of trying to force us into buying him a cell phone. One can never be sure with Nick. As I've said before, the kid is a con artist.

Sure enough, there's a post from our son. My heart leaps. I love to hear from our kids.

> Hi, Mom! School is going great. *Send Nick some money.* My classes couldn't be better, and there are girls a plenty. *Send Nick some money.* They say we average about four girls for every guy out here. *Send Nick some money.* It's a college man's dream. *Send Nick some money.* Well, just wanted you to know I love you and Dad, and I'm thinking about you. *Send Nick some money.* Don't worry about me; I'm eating as much as I need—besides, losing weight is good. *Send Nick some money.* And I'm sharing a workbook from lit class, so don't give it another thought. *Send Nick some money.* One more thing, you'll be happy to know I've made up my mind that I don't have to go to all the school games. *Send Nick some money.* After all, college isn't about a social life, right? Love, Nick.

I never quite understood that whole subliminal message thing in the '70s where records supposedly had a hidden message in them if you played them backwards. Still, call me psychic, but something about this message makes me think he's trying to tell me something here.

Just how should a mother respond to that? I think about it a minute, then roll up my sleeves and get to work.

> Nick, so good to hear from you! *No money, get a job.* Glad to hear the classes are going well and the girl-to-guy ratio has turned out so well for you. *No money, get a job.* It's every mother's dream for her college boy. *No money, get a job.* We love you and are thinking about you too. *No money, get a job.* Keeping an eye on your weight is good for your heart. *No money, get a job.* About the workbook for lit class, I'm glad you're learning to share. It makes me feel justified in hav-

ing sent you to preschool. *No money, get a job.* You're so right; college isn't about a social life. *No money, get a job.* You've learned a valuable lesson, son. And to think your college days have only begun? Well, that just makes us proud. Love, Mom.

I chuckle as I push send. Nick and I have this sort of crazy humor between us. I miss that about him. So while he is a bit of a con artist, I enjoy his antics every now and then. Maybe I'll send the little con some money.

Turning off the computer, I decide against staying in the house today. Besides, the coffee shop is calling my name.

I grab my journal and purse, and the journal I purchased for Jade, then head for the garage. I step outside to check the mail, but the box is empty. Dazzling sunlight splays across our front yard, and our maple tree has shed a fair amount of its covering, spotting our lawn with russet and gold leaves.

Autumn is my favorite time of year. Funny how the leaves look the most beautiful just before they crack and fade into oblivion. I wish I could do that. Most likely, I'll just crack and fade. Forget the beauty part. Won't happen. What's up with that? Maybe I'll explore these feelings in my journal.

As I drive to The New Brew, my thoughts flit to Gordon. I hope he's managed to put the image of me and my facial cream out of his mind. I should have resisted the temptation to turn around, but what's done is done.

Upon entering The New Brew, Jade and I exchange a smile.

"Skinny mocha, whipped cream?" she asks.

I nod.

"How are you today?" she asks while measuring the coffee.

"Pretty good." After watching that anorexia thing, now I notice how her clothes seem to be hanging on her more than usual. Superman eyes would come in handy right about now—that whole x-ray vision thing. Baggy is in, so who can tell on kids these days?

Hey, I love baggy. I mean, it can hide my pizza and truffles without a problem, and no one is the wiser. Well, at least until they bump into me and learn that, why yes, she is that big.

Jade shuffles around the counter as she prepares my drink. Her feet drag when she walks, and she goes through the motions like she could do it in her sleep. I'm waiting on her to finish before giving her the journal.

Meanwhile, I see a dirty table, and my compulsion to clean moves me to remove the debris and wipe the spilled coffee drops with a napkin.

"You don't have to do that, you know," Jade says with a smile.

"It's no problem," I say happily. And it isn't. It's just my way of giving back to this place, and it makes me feel needed somehow.

Finally, she sprays the whipped cream, snaps on the lid, and then turns a weak smile my way. Dark shadows still color her sunken eyes, and her skin has lost its glow—if it ever had one.

"Thanks. Uh, by the way, I got you something." I hand her the journal.

Surprise lights her eyes; then she looks back to me. She looks kind of choked up. "Thank you, Maggie." That's all she says.

It's enough.

I pick up my coffee and settle into a chair at a table. Once I'm situated, I pull open my journal. Staring into the blank pages, I think about Jade, about my life since Heather's wedding. All the changes. Gordon. Celine. Debra. Lily's Internet adventure. I've been so caught up in these things that I haven't noticed what's changed the most in my life.

My relationship with the Lord.

I've been busy? Yeah, right. Time to face facts. I haven't wanted to pray or read my Bible. True, I can blame some of it on the menopause thing with the lack of concentration and all, but I can't help feeling it's more than that. I still love the Lord; we're just not as close as we used to be. And they always say if that happens, you know who moved. Obviously, it wasn't Him.

Great. There's a revelation I didn't really want. Don't I have enough to deal with here? Do we have to throw in a rusty spiritual life too? Rusty. Like everything else in my life these days.

I pick up my pen and spill my heart onto the pages.

Lord, why does life have to get so complicated? I mean, whatever happened to my days that were filled with carting kids to and from school, occasional dinners out with Gordon; where all I had to do was take a shower, run a brush through my hair, and I was good to go? Now hours in front of the mirror won't help. I remember when my skin used to be flexible. Now my skin gives a whole new meaning to that "hang loose" thing.

I realize I'm wallowing in self-pity here, but if I can't share how I really feel with the Lord, who else is there?

"So, how is it?"

I look up to see Jade standing there, the sunlight glinting on the silver stud in her nose.

"Your drink. Is it okay?" she asks, pointing to my cup.

"Oh, it's great." I smile.

Jade just stands there, looking at the toe of her shoe as she draws circles on the floor. She acts like she wants to talk, so I wait to see if she'll say anything. Lifting a strand of hair, she twirls it between her fingers then looks back up at me. "Do you have a minute?" she asks.

"Sure. Sit down." I pull out a chair for her.

"You do know we're usually pretty busy? You just happen to come at our down times," she says.

"That's why I come during the afternoon. Without all the noise."

She looks at my journal. "Oh, I shouldn't bother you." Jade starts to get up.

"No, no, please. Talk to me."

She still looks like she wants to bolt, but she sits back into her seat, and I breathe easier.

She waits a moment and says finally, "Well, it's like this. I have this friend, who, well, her mom left their family for her husband's best friend." Her fingernail, chewed to the quick, rubs across a spot on the table. She looks up for a second. "Well, anyway, this friend," she says, resuming her rubbing at the imaginary stain, "she's doing okay, but her dad is really hurting." Her hand stops, and she looks me full in the face. "I think he needs help." There is a plea in her voice here.

"What kind of help?" I ask.

"I don't know, like friendship kind of help."

"Doesn't he have any friends?"

Jade draws on the table with her fingers. "Not really. I think Mom and—" Her head shoots up, and fearful eyes look at me. My expression doesn't change. "I mean, *his wife* and his daughter were his life. So when she walked out, I don't know, it did something to him."

"That's too bad." I study her. She squirms beneath my gaze.

"I don't know why I'm telling you, really. It's just that you're easy to talk to, and you're an adult and all."

I know I haven't spent a lot of time with you lately, Lord, but I sure could use some help here. Doesn't have to be a lightning bolt or anything, but a couple of words of wisdom would be nice.

"That's a tough one," I say, stalling for time just in case the Lord needs it. "Does her dad go to church anywhere?"

The question startles her. "Huh? Oh, church? Um—" She pretends to think about it a moment. "You know, he used to, but not anymore."

"I was just thinking he could talk to the pastor and also develop some friendships that might help him through it. But if he's not going anywhere, maybe you could suggest to him—to your friend, to talk to her dad about that. He could get involved in other things, too, of course, a softball team, men's Bible study, anything that would get him out with other people and maybe help him make some new friends."

Jade thinks about that a moment, then smiles. "I think that's a good idea. I'll tell him—my friend, about that. Thanks." She starts to get up.

"What about your friend?"

"Huh?"

"Your friend? How is she doing with all this?"

"Oh"—she waves her hand—"she's doing okay." She stands and turns to walk away.

"Because I know something like a mom walking out could be pretty traumatizing to a kid still living at home."

She swivels back around. "Well, she's not exactly a kid. She's practically an adult. Actually, she is an adult. She's eighteen. She can vote, fight in a war, all that." Her chin is slightly lifted.

"Still, it has to hurt."

I don't miss the fact that she swallows hard, and her eyes get watery.

"You know, if you ever want my husband to talk to your friend's dad, I mean, if you could work it out somehow, I know Gordon would be happy to do what he could to help him."

"Really?" She brightens.

I smile. "Really."

"I'll let her know. Thanks, Maggie."

"You're welcome."

"And thanks again for the journal." She walks away and helps a customer who strolled into the shop.

Our conversation makes me feel better. Although we haven't actually solved anything, I feel good that she's sharing with me. It's obvious she was talking about her family. She's been hurting over the divorce. She's mad at her mom and missing her at the same time. Kind of like I feel when Gordon and the kids are gone. She'll get through this. Maybe one day she'll even confess that the friend is really her.

I'm thinking the gift of the journal opened doors somehow. Such a little gesture, yet God used it to make a difference.

I look upward.

"Thanks."

15

"I've been thinking it's about time to sell the Corvair and start looking for another project," Gordon says over morning coffee.

"I figured it was getting that time again." I tingle with the anticipation of presenting him with the Nova. Happily, I take another sip from my cup.

"In fact"—he kind of hesitates here—"I've got my eye on a 1969 Mustang over in Rosetown."

A lead weight drops in my stomach.

"What, do you want me to wait awhile?"

"Hmm?" I feign innocence.

"You look kind of upset."

"Oh, that." I make a face. "Too much sweetener in my coffee." I put my mug on the stand beside me.

He nods. "So, you're okay with that?"

"With what?" I fluff a pillow on the sofa and look back at him.

"With me maybe buying the Mustang?" The sparkle in his blue eyes melts me down to my toes just the way it did when we were in high school.

"Do you think you should wait until you sell the Corvair?" I tear my gaze away from those perfect eyes and fidget with the cover on the arm of the sofa, acting only partially interested in the conversation. He must not get suspicious over my concern.

"Yeah, I guess you're right." There's a hint of disappointment in his voice. My heart constricts.

"I'm sure you'll have no problem selling the Corvair. You've got it running great, and it looks really nice since you've painted it."

He brightens. "Yeah, I should be able to get it sold fairly soon." He pulls out his pocket PC and pokes at it with his stylus. "I think I'll just make myself a note to get the word out to a few dealers that I'm selling it." After he scribbles something, he looks up and smiles. "Honey, you should see that Mustang. She's red and a real beaut."

There he goes again with that car gender thing. "If she's a beaut, what will you do to fix *her* up?"

"She doesn't need much. A few rust spots to go over, slow-moving parts, that kind of thing. I'll put her body back in order, give her ticker a check, then a scrub and a polish should do the trick. She'll be good as new." He winks.

"Could you do the same for me?"

"Huh?"

"Never mind. I'm thinking if you don't have much to do to fix her up, the car will probably cost more, right?"

"Well, you see, that's the thing. It does cost more. That's why I hadn't mentioned it to you yet. We can see what I get for the Corvair and go from there."

My mind scrambles to think of what I can do to hold Gordon off from buying that Mustang until I can give him the Nova. With our anniversary not that far off, I'm not sure what to do.

"Well, I'd better get to work, or I won't be able to afford that Mustang," he says with another wink.

We both stand and head for the kitchen. Gordon grabs his laptop, then bends over to kiss me. It's short and quick. "Oh, let me try that again." He puts his laptop back on the floor, places both arms around me, and pulls me to him. He kisses me firmly on the lips, and by the time he pulls away, I'm seeing stars. 'Course, it could be the caffeine, but I'm thinking it's Gordon.

"I love you, Margaret Lynn Hayden." His baritone voice is soft and husky. He holds me close. "I hate working these hours. I miss you."

My heart pounds so hard against my chest, I think it will jump right out of my skin. *Hooray! He misses me!* "I miss you too, Gordon."

With his arms on my shoulders, he leans away a bit to look me in the face. "It will calm down soon, I promise."

All of a sudden I feel shy, the same as I did when he looked at me that way in high school. I nod.

One more hug, then he's out the door, leaving me standing alone in the kitchen with my heart reeling.

• • •

I want to check out a few more herbal remedies online that Lily told me about, but when I try to get on the Internet, it doesn't work. I also need to check some items I'm trying to sell on eBay. The auction is over today for a couple of them.

Since the eBay thing is all I have to look forward to right now, I call Gordon to see if I can use his computer. He's out of the office most of the morning, and Emma tells me I can come in and use his computer.

The mahogany leather squeaks beneath me as I make semicircles in Gordon's chair while waiting on the computer to boot up. I'm feeling quite important sitting here. Huge wooden desk—covered with stacks, I might add—and this big chair. Remembering my tiny computer desk I have at home, I have to question whether life is fair.

After checking out my eBay sales and ordering one bottle of

black cohosh, I turn off Gordon's computer and prepare to leave. I reach for my purse and knock a pen from Gordon's desk. While I climb under the desk to retrieve it, footsteps sound in the hallway, and I hear a woman's voice.

"Hey, Gordon, how about you and I go out to dinner together, just the two of us?" her voice coos.

My pulse pounds in my head. Huddled beneath Gordon's desk, I gulp hard.

"I don't know, Brenda, how do you think Rick will feel about that?" The teasing note in Gordon's voice makes me drop the pen from my hands. It goes rolling out from under the desk. I gasp and pull my hand to my mouth.

Suddenly, the momentary silence is deafening. Footsteps draw near. Very near. The tips of Gordon's shoes are showing.

I could go for an earthquake right about now. You know, where the ground opens up and swallows me whole. But since I'm in Indiana, I don't see that happening.

"Maggie? What are you doing under there?"

Another gulp. It's bad enough that he's caught me hiding beneath his desk, but now I have to figure out how to unwind myself from this pretzled position without calling in the Jaws of Life.

I look up. "Hi, honey." I wave. My hand is the only thing I can move at this point. More footsteps. I turn to see sparkly painted toenails in colorful sandals stop beside Gordon's feet. *I could sure use that earthquake, God. How about a tornado? Fire drill? Hello, any of this getting through?*

I look back to Gordon, and his face just scares me. I'm thinking he's running through his marriage vows to see if this one is covered.

"What are you doing under there?" he asks again, extending his hand to help me out.

It takes concerted effort by everyone—including Sparkle Toes—to uncoil me from beneath the desk.

"Well?" he repeats.

"Checking your carpet for fleas," I say before I have time to think.

Gordon frowns. The lady beside him chuckles, causing us both to look at her.

Gordon makes the introductions, and I explain what happened. Everyone gets a good chuckle, and Gordon walks me out to my car. He looks at me as if he can't quite figure me out as he leans down to kiss me good-bye. I wave, pull my car out of the parking lot, and head down the road before I remember—

Miss Brenda Sparkle Toes made a pass at my husband.

• • •

I spend the afternoon running errands, picking up groceries, stopping by the church to pick up a choir song I need to practice, and dropping a package for Nick in the mail. When I get home, Gordon is still gone, so I figure it's a good time to call Eric. Though after the episode with Sparkle Toes today, I wonder why I'm bothering with this whole car thing.

"Galloway's Autos."

"Hi, Eric. This is Maggie. Just wanted to check in and see how the car was doing."

"Oh, she's doing all right. Still tucked away in the corner of the lot. I've had some interest in her, though."

My heart quickens. "My deposit holds her, doesn't it?" Now they've got me referring to a car as a female. Good grief.

"Yes, Maggie. As long as you get the payments to me, which I know you will, the car is yours."

"Thanks so much, Eric."

"You're welcome. Just make sure you have Gordon come by with her once in a while after you give her to him."

I don't like the sound of that last statement at all. "Once I give her to him?" Why can't we call that hunk of metal an "it"? "Okay, will do, Eric."

We no sooner hang up than the phone rings. "Hello?"

"Hi, Mom!"

"Hi, Nick! I've been enjoying your e-mails."

"Great. That's why I called."

Uh-oh, now we enter the begging-for-money phase. "Yeah?"

"I got a job."

I drop the phone and grapple with it until I get it fixed firmly in my hand again.

"Mom, are you all right?"

"Yeah, sorry about that."

"I knew you'd be excited, but I didn't expect you to get that excited."

"Well, it does come as quite a shock. Where are you working?"

"I'll be working at the Tan-and-Fan."

"I'm afraid to ask."

"It's a tanning-booth shop, but I make a decent wage, and they're flexible with my school schedule. The best part is I get to tan for free."

"Imagine, melanoma at no extra charge."

"Aw, it's not that bad, Mom."

"I don't know, Nick. There's just something about lying in a hot bed, frying like a piece of meat. It just doesn't set well with me."

"I use the proper lotions."

"Wonderful. Marinated meat."

"I thought you would be happy."

There is disappointment in his voice, and I feel badly. I mean, he's trying, after all, and I need to quit my constant worrying about Nick, about Gordon, Heather, Lily, my wrinkles, extra weight, everything. Sheesh, just listing them off wears me out. No wonder I'm tired all the time.

"I'm sorry, Nick. If that's what you want to do, that's great. Just be careful, okay?" Hey, I can't change overnight.

"Thanks, Mom."

Nick goes on to talk about how his classes are going. He's still dating Melody, though it's not serious, or so he tells me. He sends his love to his dad and says he'll be home soon.

As easily as my boy tans, he'll look pretty much like a Hawaiian native by the time he gets here.

I glance at my pale skin. I've never darkened the door of a tanning spa, and I'm wondering what a couple of sessions would do for me.

Bahama Mama comes to mind. Is this where stretching comes in? Maybe I'll call the tanning place in town, just find out a little more about it . . .

• • •

When Gordon gets home, we talk about Brenda, aka, Sparkle Toes. He insists she was kidding, but I don't buy it. Still, I let it drop for now. I'm fixing dinner when the doorbell rings.

"Gordon, would you mind getting that for me?"

"Sure."

It's so nice to have him home early tonight. No doubt he made the extra effort because I "caught" him when Brenda was coming on to him, but at least he's home.

I stir the vegetables and chicken in the wok. Steam rises, and the delicious aroma blended with a generous amount of soy sauce escapes. Gordon comes up behind me and puts his arms around me.

"Who was at the door?"

He nibbles my ear. "Hmm?"

I put the lid on the wok and wiggle around to look into his eyes. *Please say you'll love me forever, that you'll never leave me.*

"You know, there's something very appealing about you in an apron," he teases.

I slug him. "You'd better be careful. I know a good attorney who won't hesitate to fill out harassment papers."

"How good is he?"

"The best."

He quirks an eyebrow. "Really? Guess I'd better behave then." He kisses me full on the lips.

"You didn't answer my question," I say, dreamily.

"What question?"

It feels pretty good to know I've made him forget my question. "Who was at the door?"

"Oh, the boy from down the street, Trevor somebody."

I pull away and look at him. "What did he want?"

"He was selling candy for the band boosters."

"Oh no." Now, Gordon is a man of compassion. He's always for the underdog. If someone is in trouble, Gordon is right there. Kind of like Superman—except Gordon wouldn't be caught dead in a pair of tights and a cape. Anyway, this whole compassion thing has gotten him into trouble more than once.

"How much?"

He pretends innocence. "How much what?"

"Spill it, Gordy. How much candy did you buy this time?"

"I can take it to the office."

I walk over to a cabinet and open it. Inside are eight unopened boxes of chocolate—evidence of Gordon's soft heart. He peers inside and grimaces.

I stand in front of him like the Gestapo. "How much did you spend this time? Do we need to get a loan?"

"Of course not. Ever heard of credit cards?"

I groan.

"I'm kidding. I spent about, oh, I don't know, thirty dollars." He says the amount in a mere whisper.

I shove my fists on my hips. "Gordon Paul Hayden. Thirty

dollars for candy? How can you possibly afford that Mustang doing things like that?"

I'm still trying to decide whether to change my mind or not on the Nova so Gordon can get the Mustang he wants. I just don't know what to do.

He shrugs. "Poor kid's trying to earn a trip to Florida for the school band. How could I not help out?"

"You're hopeless, you know that?"

He lifts a sheepish grin. "Yeah, I know."

He droops those baby blues in a hound-dog sort of way, and I struggle to stay firm. "Are you still giving to the homeless shelter?"

"Yeah."

"Feeding children in Africa?"

"Yeah."

"Buying groceries for our church food bank?"

He nods.

"Donating to Habitat for Humanity?"

"Uh-huh."

"Girl Scout cookies?"

"Check."

"Investing in the neighborhood lemonade stand?"

"Yep."

My heart softens. I close the cabinet door and shake my head. "You're a good man, Gordon Hayden." I wriggle into his arms once again.

"Really?"

"Really."

"I thought I was in for it."

"Nope. How could I not love someone with such a big heart?"

Gordon kisses the top of my head. "And we get a ton of chocolate to boot."

"Don't remind me of that part." I turn back to the wok and

move the stir fry around once again. "If you'll get the plates on the table, this is almost ready."

"Great." He walks over and pulls the stoneware from the cabinet, then sets the table for us.

I empty the steaming contents from the wok into a pretty glass bowl, get our drinks, pull the salad bowl from the refrigerator, and we're good to go. Gordon says our prayer, and we start to eat.

I watch him and wish I could just put away all these fears about him and other women. In all honesty, I have no reason not to trust him. And the truth is I have no reason not to trust the women, either, other than the fact that they are beautiful. But to judge them solely for their beauty? That's just not fair.

Then again, who said life was fair?

Uh-oh, the evil twin has emerged once again. *Down, girl. Down, I say!*

"You're awfully quiet. Everything okay?" Gordon asks before taking a bite of chicken and snow peas.

"Yeah, everything's fine." A sharp ring of the phone blasts through our conversation. Saved by the bell. "Excuse me," I say, walking over to the phone.

"Hello, Margaret? This is Celine. I'm sorry to bother Gordon at home, but may I speak to him, please?"

I feel my back bristle a tad, okay, a lot—you can pretty much picture a cat at Halloween here—but I somehow manage to maintain my princess composure over the phone. After all, she did call me Margaret. "Just a moment, please," I say in my nicest princess voice. I turn to my husband. *My* husband, mind you. I cover the mouthpiece of the phone. "Gordon, it's your paralegal." I try to show no emotion whatsoever. I refuse to play the part of the sniveling wife.

Princess. I am a princess. As in one false move, and I'll have your head!

Gordon wipes his mouth with the cloth napkin and walks over

to the phone. He smiles at me, but I can tell by the look on his face, he has no clue whatsoever that Celine bothers me in the least. I hand him the phone and try to tiptoe back to the table so I can hear what he says. Doggone hardwood floors. My shoes clack and echo so loudly that I consider sitting on the floor and scooting my way back. He might notice, though, so I decide against it.

Gordon finally returns to the table. I flip my napkin on my lap, spear a bite of chicken with my fork, and raise it to my lips.

"So what was that about?" I ask, as though I'm asking out of courtesy.

"Work stuff." He wrinkles his nose like it's not worth talking about.

Try me, big boy. I can handle it. But the only sound he makes is the scraping of his fork against his plate.

If I'm going to learn anything from this man, I'm going to have to think of better tactics.

16

After dinner, I walk into the garage where Gordon is hunched over the Corvair engine. "You know, I'm kind of worried about Lily."

"Why?" he asks without looking up.

"Well, I called her earlier, and she hasn't called me back. That's just not like her. Especially with it being so late and all."

Gordon shrugs, grabbing a wrench from his back pocket and working it underneath the hood. "I'm sure it's nothing to worry about, Maggie. It is Friday night, after all. You act like she's the kid sister you never had." He glances over at me and winks.

My shoulders sag. "I guess, but it's only because I care about her." I turn toward the house and stop in my tracks. I yell out, "I'll bet she's with that Walter guy again!"

"What?" Gordon jerks up too soon and bumps his head on the hood. He makes a mad face and rubs his noggin.

I wince. "Sorry, honey." I allow him a moment of silence. "As I was saying, I'll bet Lily's with Walter; that's why she didn't tell me. She didn't want me to stalk—I mean—know."

His mood is growing dark here, as though it's my fault he bumped his head. "He was an Eagle Scout, Maggie."

"They're the ones we never suspect."

He groans. "You didn't act this bad when Heather dated."

"Heather didn't date an Internet freak."

"Just because he's on the Internet doesn't make him a freak, Maggie."

"Cyber junkie?"

"No."

"Weirdo?"

"Same thing as freak."

"Geek?"

He shakes his head. "Why do I try?"

"Why is it you men always stick together?"

"It's an unwritten law." Gordon goes back to work on the engine.

"Fine, but if Lily ends up at the bottom of some river, don't blame me." It gives me the creeps just saying that.

I head for the house and try to think what to do. Gordon won't let me go out now that he knows what's on my mind. I call Lily again. No answer. Maybe it has nothing to do with Walter. Maybe she's at home, hurt or something. I really start to panic and go back into the garage.

"Gordon, I'm really getting worried."

"Maggie," he says in his courtroom voice.

"Well, I mean it. What if it has nothing to do with Walter? What if she's hurt and all alone at home?"

Gordon heaves a big sigh, pulls the dirty rag from his back pocket, and stands and looks at me. "Maggie Hayden, you make me crazy some days. Do you know that?" he says, wiping oil from his hands. He puts tools back in his toolbox.

"What are you doing?"

"Well, you want to check on her, don't you?"

My heart quickens. "Yes."

"Get your coat on. We'll drive over."

"You're the best!" I say, running for the closet to get our jackets.

My nerves are jumpy as we drive to Lily's house. We pass The New Brew on our way, and I think that a coffee might taste good on the way back. Just as I'm dreaming of coffee, I spot Lily's car in the parking lot.

"There!"

Gordon hits his brakes. "What is it?"

"Lily's car is in The New Brew parking lot. Pull in there," I say, arm waving, my voice high and loud.

Gordon sighs and does what I ask. He pulls into a parking space, shuts off the engine, and turns to me. "Now what? You want to get some coffee?"

My adrenaline is charged at full speed. I chew on my lower lip a minute. "No, no, we can't do that. If she's with Walter, she'll accuse me of spying again."

"Well, isn't that what this is?"

I shake my head nervously.

"Did you down a pot of espresso before we came here?"

"No." I try to make a face here, but I feel like a nervous Chihuahua dancing around on a hardwood floor. Now I know how Crusher feels.

Gordon looks impatient. "Come on, Maggie, just go make sure that's her car. If it is, you know she's not alone and hurt in her house, and we can go home and relax like normal people."

"I want to take a quick peek in the coffeehouse and see if she's there."

"You can't just check her car because you want to see if she's with Walter, right?"

"I'm not a stalker, just a concerned friend."

"Of all the women there are in the world, and I had to marry Jessica Fletcher."

"Ha, ha," I say with sarcasm. "I'll only be a minute."

I sneak out of the car and walk toward the shop. Upon reaching the entrance, I cup my hands on the door window and peek in to see if Lily is in there. Bingo. She's there with Walter! Before I can think what to do next, they get up and walk toward the door. With no time to think and not wanting her to see me, I dive into the tall bush on the right of the door.

I think I've landed wrong because my left arm hurts like the dickens. Not only that, but I'm thinking this must be a coffee bush—is there such a thing? The smell of coffee is so strong, it makes my eyes water. I hear the door open and struggle to get situated, making sure they don't hear me, but when I move, a sharp pain runs through my lower arm. I groan, then clamp my good hand over my mouth.

"Wait," Lily says. Walter stops beside her.

My heart is thumping like I've just discovered the fountain of youth. Could they just move on, please?

"What is it?" Walter asks.

"Did you hear that?"

"Hear what?"

"I don't know, like someone moaning or something."

I hold my wounded arm at my side and wish with all my heart they'd hurry up and leave.

"I didn't hear it."

"I swear I'm so used to Maggie Hayden following me that I think I can hear her even when she's not around." Lily chuckles.

I fume. The nerve of her talking to Walter about me. Walter, a man whom she hardly knows. And me, her best friend for all these years.

It's then that I look down and see my shoe has slipped off, and my sock is caught on the stem of one of the branches. I try to maneuver my way free, but I'm snagged good. I continue to shake my foot, trying to wrangle away without Lily hearing me again. Little flecks of something splatter onto me. That's when I notice the fresh coffee grounds sprinkled all over the bush and now on me. Oh, that's just great. I'll smell like a walking espresso.

All of a sudden someone knocks on the window right behind me. My heart zips to my throat. Lily and Walter turn around.

"Does that lady want us?" Lily asks.

"I don't know. Did you leave your purse in there?"

"No, I have it here."

I slink further into the bush. "Go away," I mouth to Miss Concerned Citizen. She looks puzzled. "Shoo, go away," I say again, and brush my hand at the glass.

I hear a car door open and peek through the branches to see Gordon coming my way. Oh no. He'll ruin everything if Lily sees him.

"We had better see what she wants," Lily says.

"Yeah, I guess." Walter follows her back to the shop.

I slip deeper, causing limbs to prick and scratch underneath my jacket.

Gordon comes toward the shop. "Go back," I whisper as loudly as possible.

Gordon looks around.

"I'm over here. In the bush."

Gordon steps closer and looks very much like Moses as he peers into the bush. "Maggie, what in the world are you doing?"

"Bird watching," I snap, while trying to hide the fact I'm shivering. "What does it look like?" I shift between the branches, causing something to snap. I can only hope it's not me. "Go back to the car before they see you."

"Who?"

"Lily and Walter."

"They're in there?"

"Yes, now please go back to the car."

"Good grief, Maggie, this is ridiculous." Gordon turns toward the car, and victory is just in sight.

The door jangles once more. "I wonder where that lady went," Lily is saying to Walter as they step outside.

"Who knows? Maybe she went into the bathroom. Oh well, at least we didn't leave anything."

"Gordon Hayden, is that you?" Lily calls out.

Gordon turns around. "Uh, yeah. Hi, Lily, Walter," Gordon says, waving. "Good to see you again." He walks toward them.

"So where's Maggie?" Lily wants to know.

I'm so dead.

"Maggie?"

"Yeah, you know, the lady that hangs around your house, bore your children, cooks and cleans for you, does the laundry?"

I wince. Gordon never lies. Not even a teensy-weensy white lie at Christmas. I want to bang my head on the window.

His eyebrows raise. "Oh, *that* Maggie."

My arm is throbbing now, and I'm sure it's twice its normal size, though I can't tell since my jacket is covering it.

"She's around here, isn't she?" Lily takes her inquisition stance, crosses her arms, and taps her foot. "I know she's around here, Gordon. Don't try to deny it."

Gordon just stands there looking guilty. One would think a lawyer could do better than that.

I'm cold; my arm is throbbing and bruised. Sticks are jabbing into my side and pricking my face. I'm shivering and don't know why. I decide to forget the whole thing. Lily's like a hound dog on a scent. She won't give up until she finds me.

"Doggone it, Lily." I stumble from the bush and try to stretch my back to its normal position.

Lily turns to me wide-eyed, mouth gaping. "Maggie Lynn, what are you doing in that bush?"

"Looking for Easter eggs."

"I knew it! You just can't stop. You're addicted to snooping." She turns to Walter. "What did I tell you?"

"Okay, whatever." It doesn't help to know she's confiding in Walter about me.

"What? Just like that, it's over? No fight? Nothing?" she says, obviously up for a good scrap. Her nose sniffs the air, her eyes widen.

"Yes, I'm a walking coffee bean. Let's go home, Gordon."

They all look at me with disbelief.

"I'm sorry, okay? I want to go home."

"Maggie, did you hurt yourself? You're shivering." Gordon says with concern in his eyes.

"I hurt my arm."

Lily's eyes soften. "You did? Let me see." She reaches for my arm, and I shrink back.

"Don't touch it!"

"We're getting you to the emergency room," Gordon says after I gingerly slip my jacket off, and we take a look at my forearm that could rival Popeye's.

"I've got to go with them," Lily says to Walter.

"I hope you're okay, Maggie," Walter says. "I'll call you later, Lily, after Mother goes to her sister's."

That seemed such a perfect opportunity to comment, but I let it go because I'm in too much pain.

"I'll follow you," Lily says to Gordon.

"You don't need to come, Lily. I feel stupid, and I shouldn't have been checking on you." Checking sounds so much better than *snooping* or *stalking*.

"I'm sorry, Maggie. You must really be worried about me to risk hurting yourself to protect me."

We both get teary-eyed, and then we start to chuckle.

We stop at our car, and Gordon looks at both of us. "I think I'm taking you to the wrong hospital. They have another kind for people like you."

"I know, I know, where they wear custom-made white coats."

Lily jumps in her car, and the three of us head off for the nearest hospital—where they have loose-fitting paper gowns.

17

The next morning, groggy from my late night in the ER, I make a beeline for The New Brew. I maneuver my car down the road as best I can with my arm in a sling and spot Jade on the side of the road. Swerving over to the edge of the road, I get out of my car.

"Jade, you okay?" She looks weary and frustrated.

"Hi, Maggie," her voice sags. "My car broke down a couple of blocks back, and I have to get to work. She sees my arm. "What happened to you?"

"I had a run-in with a bush, and, well, the bush won," I say with a laugh. No need to go into details. Though the fact the doctor told me I had an allergic reaction to the black cohosh and that's why I was shivering and feeling all giddy does make me feel considerably better.

"Hop in the car, and I'll take you. I was just going there myself."

"Thanks."

Jade climbs into the car, and she quickly straps on her seatbelt. She's probably worried because I'm driving one-handed. Probably a legitimate concern since some days my driving suffers when I use two hands. "So what are you going to do about your car?" I ask with motherly concern.

She rakes her fingers through her hair. "I don't know. Dad doesn't need to hear this. He has enough on him right now." Her head jerks to me, and she looks as though she's said more than she had intended to say.

"Hmm, well, why don't you call me when you get off work tonight, and I'll see that we get you home? Maybe we can come up with a solution in the meantime." She stares at me. "What is it?"

"Why are you doing this?"

"Doing what?"

"Helping me? You've been extra kind to me since the day we met."

I shrug. "That's what Christians do."

Her eyes grow wide, but she says nothing.

"Besides, you're easy to be nice to." I smile.

"Thanks, Maggie."

Who would have thought I could bond with a girl wearing a nose ring? Further down the road, we pass a couple of Amish buggies. They are hardworking people, the Amish. They don't share in many of our modern conveniences. Funny how we have all that stuff, yet life is as complicated as ever.

Once we arrive at the parking lot, worry shadows Jade's youthful face. She's much too young to carry such a load. "You know, my husband works with cars. He's really busy right now at work, so I'd have to clear it with him, but maybe he would have time to look at your car and let you know what's wrong with it."

Jade smiles, but the look in her eyes says she doesn't want to get her hopes up. We step toward the shop, and Jade stops. "I really appreciate all that you're trying to do for me, Maggie." I reach over to give her a hug, and my heart sticks in my throat. Jade has on a thin jacket, sweat shirt, and pants. When we hug, I'm shocked at her frail body. She is much thinner than she looks. The TV special comes to mind, but maybe I'm overreacting again. Just knowing she's upset with her mom, the divorce, and everything is what's making me worry. Still, it's obvious she needs to eat better. Jade quickly pulls away, and things get awkward for a minute.

"Jade?" I whisper, not knowing what to say next.

Her cheeks flush.

"You take care of yourself, okay?"

She nods. "I'd better get busy." She opens the door, walks across the room, and disappears into a room behind the counter. I step into The New Brew behind her, wondering if Jade is in deeper trouble than I had suspected.

• • •

The New Brew bustles with activity, and Jade tells me a coworker is taking her home after work. So after my coffee and a little journaling, I decide to leave and go home to think and pray about her some more.

I pull in our driveway just as Elvira is shuffling to her mailbox. Her housedress hangs below her coat. The skin beneath her dress and above her bobby socks looks as though it hasn't seen the light of day since 1972. A groan escapes me. That is *so* me in thirty years. Okay, maybe twenty.

"Hello, Maggie," she calls out with a chipper smile and a wave. She shoots a quick glance at her mail, then heads my way.

Be nice, Maggie. She's old and she's lonely. Take time for her. You may need someone to do that for you someday.

"Hi, Elvira. How are you?" I reach over to give her a hug, and I am shocked at the thin build beneath the oversized cotton. She's not exactly Twiggy, but she certainly gives the appearance of being bigger than she is. At least she's not as skinny as Jade.

"Can't complain."

And she never does. Though I suspect today her arthritis is bothering her. "How's your arthritis?"

"Oh, you know, it flares up now and then. Comes with the age package. But then you're too young to know about that."

Excuse me while I linger in my delusion for just a moment.

"Did you know the Nelsons' daughter is going through some medical testing?" Elvira asks, referring to the nine-year-old daughter of a family who lives across the street.

"No, I didn't."

"Poor kid. She's been having blurred vision, headaches, that kind of thing." Water fills Elvira's eyes. "They already lost a son to cancer before they moved here, you know."

The news slams into my heart. The Nelsons have lived in our neighborhood for a couple of years now. How did I not know that?

"I suppose they fear the worst. She's such a young thing. I pray she's all right, bless her heart. And I pray that the parents don't have to endure another tragedy."

How can I live close to a family like that and not know they're hurting so deeply? It's true that we rarely see our neighbors. Everyone pretty much goes his or her own way. Maybe I'm justifying things here, but I suppose when one is older, like Elvira, there is more time to get involved with others. The thought that I have lots of time on my hands zings me, but I ignore it.

"I had no idea. I'll be praying for her too." I'll need to write it in my journal. "Do you know the little girl's name?" I'm pathetic for not knowing.

"Katie," she says with no judgment whatsoever in her voice. "Well, I'd best get back to work," Elvira says, as though she has a million other things to do—though I can't imagine what they would be. Her house is always clean, with no one but her to mess it up. What does she do with all of her time?

"Nice talking to you, Elvira." She has already turned and can't read my lips.

"Huh?" She swings back around.

I smile. "I said it's nice talking to you." I form my words slowly and with emphasis.

She grins, "You too, dearie."

Something tells me there's more to Elvira than meets the eye.

• • •

My afternoon is spent in the closet—not the attic. I sort my clothes into three stacks: clothes that I can wear but that have all the fashion statement of a tent, clothes that I can't wear but I keep because I'm in denial, and clothes that I adore but that would take a miracle tantamount to the feeding of the five-thousand to ever get into again.

Thoughts of Curves and exercise DVDs come to mind, but the phone rings, and I am, once again, saved by the bell. "Hello?"

"Hi, Mom." Heather's voice sounds almost back to normal.

"Boy, you sure sound better," I say, feeling relieved.

"I feel tons better. Though I still have the sniffles, I'm on the mend. I'm allowing myself time to rest."

"Sounds like a good idea. Guess you won't be needing my chicken noodle soup after all, huh?"

"Well, not this time," she says with a laugh. "Josh's mom was a great help while I was sick."

And you're telling me this, why?

"She brought dinner over every day. She is just so amazing."

Well la-dee-dah. Okay, so I'm not in the running for the Proverbs 31 Woman-of-the-Year Award.

"And get this, Mom: she talked to me about helping her out on a part-time basis with ideas for decorating some of their spec homes!"

I want to be happy for Heather, I really do, but I'm struggling.

Why am I struggling with jealousy at my age? It's such a juvenile thing, but here it is. "Well, how nice, Heather," I say for her benefit.

"Isn't it? She loves the way I have decorated our home and seems to think I have talent for it."

"I couldn't agree more. You are gifted in that way." Every word has to crawl over the boulder in my throat. "I suppose you'll have to be careful to not let it get in the way of your teaching?" I try to say this with as much nonchalance as possible. Heather does not like being told what to do. She must get that from her father.

"No, Mom, I'm not letting go of my teaching position just yet," she says dryly.

Doggone it, nothing gets past her. It bugs me a little that she says "just yet," but I let it pass.

"So how are things going with Aunt Lily?" she asks. Oh great, I have to tell her about my fiasco after she just rambled on about the perfect mother-in-law.

"Well—" I hesitate.

"Uh-oh. Come on, Mom, spill it. What did you do this time?"

I wince. She knows me well. "Why does everyone think it's always me? I mean, who said anything about me? We were talking about Lily, remember?"

Heather chuckles. "Yes, I remember. And anything to do with Aunt Lily always involves you, and vice versa. I know how you feel about her dating, so I have to assume you've gotten yourself into trouble."

Okay, who's the mother and who's the daughter here? *Hello? I'm not ready for this.*

"Mom? Spill it."

She has absolutely no finesse about her whatsoever today. I'm not liking this one little bit. I lift my chin. "There's nothing to spill," I say like a rebellious child.

"Oh, all right. I've been meaning to call Aunt Lily lately. I'll just give her a ring and see how things are going."

My daughter always was too big for her britches.

I blow out a defeated sigh and tell her about getting stuck in the bush, hurting my arm, the whole thing.

"Oh, I'm sorry you hurt your arm, Mom," she says in between giggles, "but I can just imagine that whole scene—" she stops and erupts into a fit of laughter.

"I really don't see anything funny about this, Heather," I say defensively, still trying to maintain my dignity.

She takes a minute to catch her breath and calm down. "All right, I'm sorry, but you have to admit, Mom, you do get a little, well, extreme, in your protection of the people you love."

"I have a past. So, sue me."

"Uh-oh, I see that Minnie has joined us in the conversation," she says, referring to her nickname for me when my dark side surfaces: Minnie Pause.

For the life of me I don't want to, but I chuckle and Heather joins me. "I'm a little extreme?"

"Uh-huh. But it's part of your charm, and we love you for it."

Okay, now I'm feeling better. The *kind* mother side of me slips back in, shoving Minnie out. Hmm, even the nice person in me has attitude. I like that. I had no idea schizophrenia was part of the whole menopause thing. Why didn't somebody warn me?

"Do you really think I've changed a lot, Heather?"

"Well, maybe a little," she says cautiously. Translation: *You've changed big-time, Mom, but I still love you.* "Are you taking any hormone meds or anything?"

"No. Just some supplements, herbs, that type of thing." I resent just a little that she's telling me I need medication for my *problem.* "You think I need to take medication for my attitude?"

She hesitates here. "No, I'm not saying that. I just think you're a little different these days, and I can tell your body is going through some changes."

I gasp. "You mean, by the looks of it?"

"No, no, just, well, your, um"—she's treading carefully, weighing each word, and I'm thinking this can't be good—"whole outlook these days."

"You're trying to tell me I'm not Pollyanna anymore?"

"Your Pollyanna days are over, Mom."

"June Cleaver?"

"Um, no."

"Carolyn Ingalls, *Little House on the Prairie*?" I say with measured hope.

"Nope."

"Ma Walton?"

"Don't think so."

I resign myself to the facts. "Granny on *The Beverly Hillbillies*," I say with defeat.

"You know, I always liked her. Lots of spunk."

"Okay, I brought you into this world, and I can take you out."

"Oh, hi, Minnie. When did you get back?"

We both laugh. Although hers is harder and much longer. I'm thinking I'll rewrite my will.

The phone beeps. "Oh, dear, I've got another call, honey. It might be your dad."

"Okay, I'll talk to you soon, Granny," she says, still laughing.

"I'll remember this come your birthday." With that, I push flash and click to the next call. "Hello?"

"Hey, babe." At least Gordon still loves me. "How's it going today?"

"Pretty good," I say, my perk back in place. "Hey, while I've got you on the phone, I've been meaning to ask you something. My friend Jade from the coffeehouse is having some problems with her car, and I was wondering if you could look it over one night soon? I know you're busy, but the poor girl has no money and she needs transportation for work." I appeal to his compassionate side.

"Sure, be glad to," he says without hesitation. That's my Gordon, always willing to help another. "Now for the reason I called."

"Yes?"

"Oh, wait. I wanted to tell you, too, that one of my partners is interested in buying the Corvair," he says all excited-like. "I may get that Mustang yet."

My spirits sink. "That's great, Gordon," I say, trying to act like I mean it.

"Now for the real reason I called. Remember I told you Bobby Vinton was coming to Rosetown to do a concert?"

My insides feel all blue-velvety. Well, except for the Mustang thing. "Yeah, I remember."

"You want to go?"

I squeal. "Really?" I can't remember the last time we went to a concert. And Bobby Vinton is one of my favorites! I haven't seen or heard about him in years.

"Yep. One of the guys in the office just told me where I could order tickets, but he said we'd better get on it because they were selling fast."

"Must be a lot of baby boomers in Rosetown." I laugh. "I would love to hear him. I'll cancel anything in my way."

"Great. I'll order the tickets for next Friday night."

I'm remembering how Gordon isn't all that into Bobby Vinton and think how lucky I am to have a man who cares so much about my feelings. How could I possibly suspect him of an affair? He treats me far too well. 'Course, a guilty conscious could make him that way too . . .

"Gordon, you're the best."

"Well, I wouldn't go so far as to say that, but if you want to, that's fine with me." He chuckles. "It's a date then?"

"It's a date."

"Great. I'll get right on it. Plan on dinner out, a concert, maybe even stop for coffee afterwards. I'll plan a big night out on the town with my best girl."

I love everything he says except for the "best girl" part. "Well, I'd better be your *only* girl," I say with a laugh that could easily turn into a growl.

"I've got my hands full with you. Why would I want anyone else?"

"My sentiments exactly."

"You crazy woman. I love you. I'd better get those tickets ordered. I'll talk to you later." He clicks off.

Crazy woman? He called me crazy woman! My daughter thinks I'm Granny Clampett.

My Pollyanna-June Cleaver-Carolyn Ingalls-Olivia Walton days are over. Granny Clampett rules! And you know what's really scary? I'm okay with that.

18

Yippee! Tonight is the Bobby Vinton concert! I splash on some perfume and primp a bit in front of my mirror. It's been a busy week—actually made some headway in the attic—and I'm so ready for this evening. Gordon was able to fix Jade's car and meet her dad. I even hum a little as I touch up my lipstick. No Granny Clampett tonight!

Lily's love life has calmed down a bit, so I can finally relax. I lay my watch across my wrist and push the clasp together.

My hot flashes are at a minimum tonight, so that's good. I'm thinking the exercise and herbs might really be helping. But if I tell Dr. Lily, there will be no living with her.

I roll my shoulders a few times and feel thankful my arm is out of that sling. It was so bothersome and wouldn't have looked nice at all with the silk navy dress I'm wearing to the concert.

Upon hearing the garage door, I grab my dainty navy purse, the kind you can only fit a tube of lipstick in, and head for the kitchen to greet my man.

When he steps through the door, he takes one look at me and whistles. I feel myself blush clear through.

"Be still, my heart," he says, sliding the laptop strap from his shoulder and lowering the machine to the floor, never once taking his gaze from me. He walks over and touches me as though I might break. In a flash I am transformed from Fairy Godmother into Cinderella. "Okay if I mess up your lipstick?"

I nod and stifle the giggle at the edge of my throat. He kisses me, long and hard. I feel breathless and lightheaded when we part and marvel that we still have that chemistry-thing going on after all these years.

"You look wonderful, Maggie Hayden," he whispers into my ear. His voice sounds gravelly and soft, like a cool stream running down the rough side of a mountain.

When he pulls away, his eyes look all dreamy and tender. "I guess we have to go, huh?" His lips curve in a teasing grin.

I grin back. "Afraid so."

"You're no fun." He goes over to his laptop and picks it up. "I'll put this away and change clothes real quick. Then we'll head out." He stops at the counter and starts to dump a pile of change from his pocket, but my frown stops him midair.

"No stacks?" he asks.

"No stacks."

He shrugs and heads for the bedroom.

"I'm glad you were able to make it home early tonight," I say, following him down the hall.

"I left a ton of work, but I figured it would have to wait tonight. I'm taking out my best girl." He turns around and gives me a quick wink.

There he goes with that *best girl* business again. Oh, well, we're going to a Bobby Vinton concert!

I feel so alive tonight.

• • •

Gordon and I settle into our seats at the restaurant and soon place our orders with the server, who is dressed with simple elegance in a crisp white blouse with a dainty bowtie at the collar and a wispy black skirt. Flickering candlelight casts shadows across the linen tablecloth.

I'm Cinderella, and Gordon is my Prince Charming. My Prince Charming from Charming. What could be better than that? I glance at my watch. There's still plenty of time until midnight. Letting out a pleasurable sigh, I lean back into my chair.

A soft chatter wafts through the air amid the sounds of tinkling silverware, swirling ice cubes, and the smells of pasta sauce, rich with garlic and oregano. The people around us are dressed in evening wear, enjoying romantic dinners. A fireplace crackles from one wall, filling the room with warmth, and I want the night to last forever.

"You enjoying yourself?" Gordon asks.

"Very much." I toss him a smile across the soft glow of candlelight.

"I know you love Italian food, so I figured I couldn't lose by bringing you here."

"It's wonderful." A thought hits me. "Oh, but what about your low-carb diet?"

He shrugs. "It won't hurt me to indulge every now and then. I just can't go overboard."

He's very disciplined with his diet, so it means a lot to me for him to sacrifice like this. "Thank you, Gordon."

"You know, Maggie, we should do this more often."

"Could I get that in writing?"

Gordon lifts an eyebrow.

"Being an attorney and all, you should know the importance of documenting such a statement," I tease.

"Point taken," he says, leaning into the table. "I mean it. I've missed doing things like this."

"Excuse me, but need I mention that you're the one who is working all the time?"

Gordon makes a face. "I know. I don't like it, either, but it will calm down soon."

Even though he says that all the time, hearing him say it tonight makes me feel better. I was silly to think he had anything going on with anyone else. Those crazy hormones make me think things I never would have considered before.

My attention is deterred only a moment as a group of friends gather at a nearby table, laughing and enjoying one another's company.

"You know, I really like it here," I say.

"Yeah, it's a nice restaurant."

"No, I mean here in Rosetown. It's a nice community. Lots to do, things to see, places to go."

Gordon nods.

"Why have we never thought of moving here?"

Surprise lights Gordon's eyes. "Well, we grew up in Charming, for one thing. For another, we thought it was a great place to raise our kids." He studies me.

"Yeah." I toy with the handle of my fork.

"What are you saying, Maggie. Are you wanting to move?"

I look up at him. "Well, you do work here, after all."

"True. What about Lily. Wouldn't you miss her?"

"Yeah, I would miss Lil. But we wouldn't be that far away."

"It wouldn't be like you are now, though. You're practically in each other's backyards."

I shrug. "Looks to me like she's got other interests anyway."

"She had Bob in her life, too, but that didn't stop you from getting together with her."

I bite my lip.

"What's up?"

"Charming is a nice place to live. I loved raising our kids there. But, well, can we talk candidly here? Charming is a tourist town for old people."

"Maggie—"

"I'm not trying to act all pious and young or anything, Gordon.

We're old, plain and simple. But I don't *feel* old, do you? And I'm not ready to *act* old. I'm not saying I want to play hopscotch; I'm just saying there's still life in me. We can hold off on the rocking chair and knitting needles for now."

"You're saying you have to be old and act old to live in Charming?"

"I'm saying it has a sort of retirement feel to it."

"That's odd that you would say that after living there all your life."

"I've never been this close to retirement age before."

"Then I would think you'd like it better."

"I said 'close' to retirement age. As in not there yet."

Gordon reaches across the table and takes my hand. "Look, Maggie, if you want to look for houses in Rosetown, that's fine, but I don't think that's really what you want."

"You don't?"

"No. I know you're caught up in this age thing right now, but when it passes, you'll wish you were back in Charming."

"When it passes or when I pass?"

"Not funny."

"Okay, so maybe I don't want to move. Still, I could stand a little more excitement in my world besides crafts and quilting."

He sits back. "Hey, you got a coffeehouse. What more do you want?"

"Definite improvement, I agree. Still, do I see Cheesecake Factory on the horizon? No. A chocolate specialty shop? Krispy Kreme?"

"I'm seeing a pattern here."

"What?"

"Food."

"Well, duh. What else is there at our age?"

"A few things come to mind, but I'll leave it alone for now."

The server interrupts our fascinating talk and spreads our meal before us. I stare in awe at the carbs on our table. The South Beach Diet is calling my name—again. Thankfully, I have ear plugs.

With the spicy scents tickling my nose, I struggle to listen to Gordon's prayer for our meal. By the time he's finished, I'm ready to dig into my lasagna.

"This concert will be so great, Gordon. I've been playing Bobby's CDs all week." I cut a dainty piece of lasagna noodles with filling and slip it into my mouth. This meal requires patience. If I were at home, I'd eat a bite three times this size.

"I saw the CDs on the entertainment center and figured you were listening to them. It's a sold-out crowd tonight, you know."

"Sold out. Wow. Shows you Bobby's still got what it takes."

Gordon nods while chewing his fettuccini.

I look at him and think how wonderful he is to set up such a special night for me. The thought hits me, too, that though I wanted to buy him that Nova, the car thing isn't about what I want. It's about what he wants. I decide to check into getting the Mustang. If it's a Mustang Gordon wants, a Mustang he shall have!

After sharing a wonderful meal, we head for the Rosetown Theater for the concert. Gordon has managed to get tickets near the front, which means we will get to see Bobby Vinton up close and personal. I can hardly wait to see those blue eyes sparkling from center stage.

We walk into the foyer of the theater and the surroundings are plush on every side. Elegant crystal chandeliers dangle like clustered diamonds from the ceiling. Women in evening wear and men in black suits and ties talk in hushed whispers as they stroll along the hallway, their footsteps muted by thick carpets.

Gordon leads the way to our seats down near the front. We talk a little about the velvety curtains hiding the stage, the ornate ceiling and walls, the thick cushioned seats, the lavish balcony, and fine lighting. Soon the orchestra rises from the pit and strains of "Red

Roses" fill the air with remembrance and anticipation. The thick velvet curtains pull apart, revealing a barren stage. The audience seems to collectively hold its breath. The music swells. We're practically on the edges of our seats when out on the stage steps a man with wavy, sand-colored hair, a bright smile, and twinkling blue eyes. He raises his arms in greeting, and the crowd goes wild with applause.

When the throng finally calms to a whisper, Bobby Vinton's soft, lilting voice fills the air with love songs from another time, another place. I close my eyes and relive the days of my youth. My days with Gordon. As the performer sings song after song, I relive our first kiss, our tender moments, our engagement, and, finally, our wedding. By the time we break for an intermission, my heart is so full of romance, I'm ready to burst.

"How about a breath of air?" Gordon asks.

"Great," I say, almost dreamily.

He takes my hand in his and ushers me from our seats, and we spill into the foyer with countless others. As we step out of the theater building into the cool night air, the breeze hits my face. My eyes are opened as if I've tasted the apple in the Garden of Eden—as though someone has fixed my internal antenna and the picture is suddenly clear. I wish they had left it alone. I was happy in my temporary oblivion.

I look around at the people huddled together, and I see them, truly see them, for the first time. And what do they all have in common?

Try gray hair, no hair, borrowed teeth, and leathery skin (some lined, some folded) all pale and freckled with age spots.

Now, call me pessimistic, but I'm thinking this can't be good. Cinderella tries to slink away. I want to shout, "You get back here."

"What?" Gordon asks.

Did I say that out loud? "Oh, nothing."

"Having a good time?"

He's taken great pains to make this night perfect, and I'm not about to spoil it with my age paranoia. "I'm having a wonderful time, Gordon. Thank you." I put my arm in his and snuggle up next to him. One day I'll do this just so he can hold me up.

"It's kind of chilly out here. You ready to go inside?" he asks.

"Sounds good."

We shuffle through the crowds and pass the snack area. I'm afraid to look. There just might be antacids, hot water bottles, and muscle creams bearing large print encased behind the glass counter. It's better not knowing. We pass a crowd of slow-moving people, and the movie *On Golden Pond* comes to mind. By the time we finally make it back to our seats, I'm just thankful I can breathe without life support.

I'm half-afraid to look when Bobby steps back onto the stage. Bobby starts singing, and I squint, peeking only a little through tiny slits. Looking at him this way, I can live in my delusion and keep Bobby in his twenties. But the reality is, the muscles in my eyes hurt already, and if I continue this for another hour, it might do permanent damage.

Slowly, I lift my eyelids, looking first at the stage floor at Bobby's patent shoes. I stay here for a good thirty seconds or so, then work my way up straight into Bobby's face. The truth of the matter is that though Bobby is still quite handsome, he is not twenty anymore.

News flash. Neither am I.

The rest of the concert is a blur.

"You're awfully quiet," Gordon says as we're driving home. "You feeling okay?"

"I'm fine." I turn to him with a smile. I don't want to dampen his spirits. He has been perfect the entire night, and he put so much thought into this. I'm thankful, I really am.

"What was with that lady in front of us?"

My spirit quickens. "What lady?"

"The blue-haired lady. She was chompin' her gum like nobody's business."

I laugh. "She was? I missed that."

"How did you miss that? I thought Bobby would stop the show, she was causing such a racket."

"Did you notice her husband? He had seven hairs on his head, and they had to be at least two feet long to stretch from one side to the other like that." I chuckle.

Gordon chuckles too. "Shoot me if I ever do that."

"I will," I say with no hesitation whatsoever.

He laughs harder.

I stretch toward him, hard to do with bucket seats. "Oh, Gordon, you feel my pain?"

"I feel it, baby." He puts his arm around me. "So we're not in our twenties anymore. Who cares? We've got each other, Maggie, and that's what's important."

"You're right. I don't know why I'm letting all of this get to me. I'm just not ready to be old."

"Do you think any of those other people felt ready when it hit them?"

"I don't even want to think about it."

"The way I understand it, age just sort of creeps up on us, so we don't really notice the changes all at once. It's kind of a gradual thing."

"I was oblivious to my changes until after Heather's wedding. Then I look in the mirror and yeowsa! I'm Grandma!"

Gordon chuckles again and squeezes my shoulder. "You will always be beautiful to me—"

"Yes, because your eyesight is going."

"Isn't that just like God?"

Oh, this should be good.

"I mean, our eyes grow dim, our hearing gets faint, so we see less and less the physical flaws in one another. I think the same is true of our hearts. The older we get, the less our hearts find faults with others. We find less enjoyment in criticizing others because we're just thankful to be alive."

He throws me a wink, and I lean into him. So according to Gordon, the older we get, the less critical we become. So if that's true, and I'm still critical—which obviously I am—then that must mean I'm still young! Okay, maybe that's flawed reverse psychology, but I figure if B plus A equals young, I'm all for it.

Once we're home and ready for bed, Gordon surprises me by putting Bobby Vinton's CD in our CD player. Strains of "Blue Velvet" float through the air. Gordon smiles and walks over to me. He takes me into his arms and slowly dances me around the room.

Nuzzling my face near his neck, I drink deeply of his Tommy scent and allow my heart to soar with the music. Crusher whines and scratches at the bedroom door, but we ignore him.

This night belongs to us.

19

"I can't believe it actually dipped down in the thirties last night. I was cold," Gordon says with a shiver as he dresses for another Saturday of work.

He obviously didn't notice my struggles after we went to bed last night, how I wrestled with the sheets and they won. I won't even bother to tell him that I was up at three thirty this morning with hot flashes, stumbling around the house as if I had something to do. Which reminds me, Elvira's lights were on, and I'm wondering why she was up that early. Hopefully, she isn't sick. Maybe I'll check on her later.

"I couldn't believe you," he continued. "Every time I woke up to pull the covers on me, you were completely out of the blankets. It was like you were hot or something."

The man is completely clueless.

"I thought maybe you were getting sick."

If age was contagious, I'd be quarantined.

"Are you?"

"Am I what?"

"Getting sick?"

Do I really have to have this discussion before my morning coffee? I'm cranky from lack of sleep, and I've been sweating through the night like a marathon runner. Hey, maybe I can skip my exercise routine. Okay, so I don't have a consistent one. Still, I manage to work out once every other week or so. It has to add up over time.

"No, I'm not getting sick."

Gordon walks over to me. "Just want to make sure you're all right, babe."

"I'm fine," I say, feeling a little guilty over my sharp attitude after all Gordon's hard work to make last night so nice. Of course, he didn't have hot flashes all night like I did.

He studies my face. "Are you sure you're all right?"

I squirm. Why does he look at me like that? I want him to look at me like last night, with eyes glazed over. That way he doesn't see all the wrinkles, all the age spots, all the flaws.

"Yes, why?" *Hello? Do I want to know this? I think not.*

"Well, you look kind of red and shiny, like you're hot or something."

"I *am* hot," I snap. "I could serve as a pot-bellied stove, okay? Just stand me in the middle of the living room, and I'll generate enough heat to obliterate our gas bill."

"Really? Can you do that?"

For the flash of an instant, Gordon looks as though he just might take me up on the idea, but one look at my face changes his mind. He raises his palms and backs away slowly like a character out of *Gunsmoke.* "Whoa, are we struggling this morning?"

"No, Gordon, *we* are not struggling. *I* am struggling." I follow him, poking his chest with my index finger. "I've had hot flashes all night. Hot flashes, Gordon, do you hear me? As in, I could start belching flames any minute. No sleep. Get the picture?" Poor Gordon, this is not his fault, but there is no one else I can vent to, except for Crusher, and we know how he handles stress.

We stop a moment. Gordon's wide eyes lower a bit and a teasing sparkle appears. "Oh, I get it. You want me to share in your pain, is that it?" He winks and turns toward his dresser.

"Oh, that's cute. Real cute." I'll wrap him in an electric blanket tonight and crank that puppy up while he's sleeping. Then he'll share my pain, all right.

I need an attitude adjustment. I need some air.

I need an igloo.

"I'll get our coffee," I say, figuring it's time to isolate myself before I hurt somebody.

By the time the coffee is ready, my internal temperature has cooled down a little. I'm feeling bad for snapping at Gordon. I just don't know what gets into me, besides that evil-twin thing.

We settle into our seats. Gordon takes a sip from his mug and looks over at me. "What are you drinking?"

"A latte, over ice." I'd rather have a mocha, but I don't know how to make a cold one, and I can't stand the thought of drinking something hot this morning.

He raises his palms again. "I'm not even going to touch that one."

"It's just better that way."

We have our devotions and pray. I do love these times we spend together before the Lord. It puts stability and calmness into my day. Goodness knows I need it.

Gordon finishes his coffee. "So what are you doing today?"

"Well, since you have to spend another Saturday at the office, maybe I'll spend another day slaving in the attic. First, I'm meeting with Jade this morning for breakfast, though."

He looks at me. "I've got to hand it to you, Maggie. It's pretty neat how you're trying to help that kid."

I shrug. "For whatever it's worth. By the way, thanks for fixing her car. I know it was a sacrifice for you to take the time, and she really appreciated that."

"I'm glad I could help her. Her dad seems nice enough. Ask her if she thinks he would mind if I gave him a call. I could invite him to a men's prayer breakfast or something."

"That sounds good."

He nods. "Well, I hope you two enjoy your time at breakfast." He rises to leave for work. On Saturday. Again.

I follow him to the door, all the while praying that my raging hormones don't scare Jade off. I'd better check into Dr. Lily's latest remedy. Up to now, nothing seems to get rid of all these symptoms. In fact, they might be getting worse.

Heaven help us all.

• • •

Before I meet Jade, I call the car place that has the Mustang for sale in Rosetown to make sure it's still available. The salesman tells me it still is. The price is more than the Nova, and I have no clue how to pay for it. But Gordon has his heart set on it, so I'll do what it takes to get it for him.

Then I place the dreaded call to Eric Galloway. I explain about the Mustang and tell Eric that I won't be getting the Nova. I tell him he can keep my deposit, but he refuses. He tells me the check will be ready on Monday to pick up. He's sorry it didn't work out, but he understands.

Eric is a great friend. I have to admit I'm a little disappointed we're not getting the Nova. After all, Gordon didn't drive a Mustang when we dated.

• • •

"I'm just tickled pink you could meet me for breakfast today, Jade," I say, spreading my paper napkin across my lap. When I look up, she's gaping at me.

"What?"

"I've never heard that expression before."

"What expression?" The light dawns. "Oh, the tickled-pink thing?"

She nods.

Why, thank you for reminding me that I'm outdated. Can we say 'Model T' here? By the way, you're buying breakfast. Down hormones. Down!

"Yeah, I guess that's an old expression." Especially for someone who is still cutting her molars.

The server comes to our table and takes our order. Of course, I don't let Jade know she's under scrutiny today. I've brought her to breakfast to see how she eats. That special on Oprah has me worried. If Jade eats like a horse today, then I won't worry about this whole anorexic deal anymore. And I know skinny girls can have big appetites. Heather had some high-school friends who could down a pizza before the delivery boy got paid.

"Hey, I really appreciate your husband fixing my car this week. I can't tell you how much that helped," Jade says.

"He was glad to do it. Says it didn't amount to much anyway; just needed a new battery. Gordon is really talented when it comes to cars. He can sniff out a problem like Yogi Bear after a lunch."

Jade smiles. "Well, I'm very thankful."

We pause a moment. "Hey, Tyler says you helped her with her boyfriend trouble." I smile. "That guy sounds like bad news. She deserves better."

"I think so too," she says. "Anyway, I'm glad you talked to her."

It makes me feel good that she says that.

"Everyone at the coffee shop likes you, you know." She smiles at me.

I'm surprised by her comment.

"Aaron says you helped him fill out some papers to get into college."

"I helped my son last year, so I remembered how to do it. They can be confusing sometimes."

"Still, you can relate to our age group better than most people your age."

My age? Okay, she could have gone all day without saying that. There's my cue to change the subject. "So how are things going for your friend?"

Jade looks puzzled. "My friend?" Her eyes grow wide. "Oh, my friend."

I smile and nod.

"Pretty much the same. It's going to be a while before her dad works through this, I think."

"Divorce is a hard thing to work through, I'm sure."

"How long have you and your husband been married?"

I sit up a little taller. "Almost thirty years."

"Wow. Thirty years with the same man," she says as if she's watching Neil Armstrong take his first steps on the moon.

I chuckle. "Well, it might be unusual these days, but not unheard of."

"I guess. I wouldn't know." She pauses. "The truth is . . . my friend is not really my friend."

My heart catches in my throat as I realize she's about to tell me the truth about her family. That's a good sign that she trusts me, and that makes me feel good.

Just then the server comes over with our food. Great. Jade probably won't tell me now. The server carefully places scrambled eggs, biscuits and gravy, and hash browns in front of me, along with coffee and orange juice. It's a wonder the table doesn't tip my way. Can we say portion control?

The server then places a bowl of fruit no bigger than a grapefruit in front of Jade. I eat more than that when I have the flu. I discreetly edge my bowl of gravy and the plate of biscuits toward her.

"That's not all you're eating, is it?"

She looks up, "Oh, I'm not much of a breakfast eater."

"I wish you had told me, Jade. We could have had lunch instead."

"That's no problem. I like fruit." She smiles, then picks up her fork.

"I'll pray for us," I say, immediately closing my eyes and offering a prayer for our food.

"Sorry," she says when I'm finished.

"Why?"

"I didn't know you were going to pray."

"Oh, that's no problem."

We share some small talk. She's been working a blueberry between her teeth for the past three minutes. That can't be good. It's like she can't swallow it or something.

My stomach churns with the possibility Jade might have a real problem here. I'm so ill-equipped to help, what can I do? Another quick prayer for direction, but the problem is I have no reserves upon which to draw. Still, I'm trying to change that by focusing more on my Bible reading and prayer time.

"So you were telling me about your friend?" I encourage, trying to steer the conversation back to what's important.

She finally swallows, then takes a drink of water as though to rid her mouth of the taste. "Oh, yeah. Well, the friend I told you about? She—uh, she—well, she really isn't my friend." Jade looks at me through haunted eyes.

I wait silently for her to press on.

"She's . . . " She clears her throat here. ". . . me." She studies me to see how the news affects me. I don't move, not even an eyelid.

"I figured as much."

"You did?"

"I'm sorry you're hurting, Jade. I want to help you."

"There's nothing anyone can do. Mom's made her decision, and we all get to enjoy the consequences." Distaste for her mom fills her voice. Chunks of fruit still line her bowl. She's had three blueberries, tops.

She shoves her filled bowl of fruit away from her.

"All this has to be really tough."

Tears pool in her eyes, and she nods then swallows. "We'll make it. We'll show her."

I have to help this girl. She'll grow bitter, and it will color the rest of her life. "You know, my husband could call and talk to your dad—"

"No." She cuts me off. "He wouldn't like that. He wouldn't want me discussing our personal lives with someone else. He's very private."

"Oh, Gordon wouldn't talk to him about any of that; he would just—"

"Thank you, but no, Maggie. We have to get through this alone."

Her words hold no hope. "We don't ever have to go through things alone, Jade."

"You're talking about God, right?"

I nod.

"It's easy to say that, but I haven't seen Him doing much to help us up to this point."

Her comment stings my heart.

"We can't always see what He's doing, but you can be sure He has your best interests at heart."

She doesn't say anything, so I let the matter drop. I finish my breakfast while Jade tells me about her life at the community college. She keeps the conversation on light, fluffy things. She's probably tired of dealing with the heavy issues. Not that I blame her. Some days even age spots are more than I can handle.

After paying the bill, we prepare to leave. I reach into my purse and dig around for my keys. "Well, that's strange," I say, feeling a sliver of panic.

"What's wrong?"

"I can't find my keys."

"Are they in your coat pocket?"

Oh, sure, that's probably it. I do put them there sometimes without thinking. I reach into my right pocket. Nothing. My left pocket holds two candy wrappers from my chocolate stash. Now panic washes clear through me. Jade must see it in my eyes.

"It's okay, we'll find them. If not, I'll take you home. Hey, maybe they're in your car."

That's hard to imagine. I've never left my keys in my car before. "I'll check the ladies restroom first since I went in there before our meal to wash my hands."

Jade nods, and I head for the ladies room. Looking all around, I find nothing. I even shuffle the wastebasket a little to listen for the jingle of keys. Nothing. Okay, full-blown panic here. Where could I have laid them? Could someone have taken them? What if my car is not out in the parking lot? My pace quickens. Things like this almost never happen in Charming.

"I'm going to check the car," I say to Jade at the door, practically running outside. Much to my relief, the car is still intact. I run over to it and it's locked. Just as I start to turn around, the light glistens on my keys in the middle of the seat. A sinking feeling hits my stomach. I left my keys in the car and locked the doors? How could I do that? Did I drop them? No, if I'd dropped them, they would have been on the floor or something. I always put them in my purse. This is so strange.

"Oh, they're on your seat," Jade says, pointing.

"Yeah, I see them. I'll have to call Gordon to bring me his set. He'll love me for this."

"From what you've told me of your husband, I don't think he'll mind. He sounds like a great guy."

"He is a great guy. But, well, I don't want to push my luck."

Jade chuckles. "I'd better get to work. Thanks for breakfast, Maggie. I really enjoyed talking with you."

"You're welcome." I want to add that she didn't eat a penny's worth. Without a thought, I reach over and hug her. She gives me a quick one in return, then pulls away. We both know why.

"See you at the coffeehouse."

"Thanks again, Maggie. I'm glad fate brought us together."

I want to jump on that fate comment and teach her about divine appointments, but now doesn't seem the time. Baby steps. Jade's silver nose ring glistens in the sunlight. I know that God has brought Jade into my life. Sure, I believe He wants me to reach out and help her, but I can't help thinking He's using her to teach me something too.

We wave good-bye, and I watch her pull away, when I remember the matter at hand. Reaching into my purse, I pull out my cell phone and call Gordon.

First he has to deal with me and the hot flashes, now this. What in the world will Gordon think of me? He works with Miss I've-Got-It-All-Together, and he's married to Miss Forgot-Where-I-Put-It.

I make my call, and Gordon is not thrilled; but he shows up minus a bad attitude, which is more than I would have done had the tables been turned.

He unlocks my door, reaches in, and gets my keys. He leans out of the car and turns to me. "So what are they worth to you?" Gordon asks with a teasing grin, holding my keys just out of reach.

I smile back, wondering how many men would be this sweet if they had to come and bail their wife out of a jam. "I'll fix your favorite dinner soon?"

He thinks a minute. "With homemade sugar-cream pie?"

I frown because he knows how I hate to make pie crust. If someone wanted to torture me, all they would have to do is hand me a rolling pin, flour, and shortening. Try as I might, I just can't make a good crust. I made a double-crusted pie one time for company, and they teased me that it looked like a flying saucer. I haven't tried one for company since.

Gordon is still dangling the keys out of reach. "Well, I'm waiting," he teases.

Doggone it, I hate it when he makes me commit. "What about the low-carb thing?" I raise my eyebrows.

He lifts his chin. "I've earned it."

"Okay, I'll do it." I say the words like he's pulling them out of me one by one. "But with frozen pie crust."

"Deal." He gets out of the car, gives me a peck on the cheek, and hands me the keys. "You make the best sugar-cream pie in town." He brushes the tip of my nose with his finger. "Well, I'd better get back to the office. Still have a lot to do."

"Are you all by yourself today?" I ask casually, trying to see if he is spending the day with Celine.

He shakes his head. "No, why?"

I shrug. "I just thought it must feel weird to be in the building by yourself."

"I'm a big boy, remember?" He turns to walk away.

"So the other attorneys work on the weekends too?" I press further.

"Sometimes. Ralph has been in and out today, but mainly it's just been me and Celine. I'll see you later, babe." He climbs in his car and pulls away with a wave.

A flush heats my face like a volcanic explosion as I get this image of a Paris Hilton-wannabe bending over my husband's shoulder to peer at legal files, and I sag behind the steering wheel.

20

Stay calm. Stay calm. Turning the air-conditioning on high, I maneuver the vent toward my face and drive home. I sure hope this is a menopause flush and not high blood pressure. Though goodness knows thoughts of Celine and Gordon alone in that office make my blood boil.

I know Gordon's a good man, and all the things Lily said made sense at the time, but he's still a man, and temptation is strutting in and out of his office all day in the form of one Celine Loveland. Doesn't the Bible say to shun the very appearance of evil? *Hello?* Does someone need to purchase a clue?

I pull my car into the garage, get out, and stomp into the house.

Should I grab my boxing gloves or knee pads? I'm thinking the Lord would suggest the knee pads. I have sissy knees. My grandmother never had sissy knees. Her knees were rough and calloused from years of prayer. My mother's knees are the same way. And then there's me. Mine used to bear battle scars when the kids were teenagers, but can we be frank? I'm afraid if I bend these joints now, there's not enough oil in Texas to get me back up.

Journaling is the prayer of choice for me these days.

Maybe deep down there's more to my prayer life than just the whole rusted joints thing. It's like I keep praying for direction in my life, the where-do-I-go-from-here kind of praying, and I'm just not getting the answers.

The best way I know how to fight this situation with Gordon and the fear of losing him is to get to work on me. Before Crusher can circle three times and collapse onto his chair, I'm dressed in my sweats and walking at a good pace on the treadmill.

I don't have the answer for all things, but I can get back into shape, take care of my skin and body, and wear nice clothes. Gordon can't help but notice me. If I stay beautiful—okay, well-groomed at least—he won't leave me for a younger woman. Right? I'm sure he won't leave me.

Gordon would never leave me.

After my workout, I drag myself into the shower and let the hot water ease over my aching muscles. I'll go to the library today and see if I can find any books on anorexia. Not that Jade has that, but it doesn't hurt to be prepared.

Elvira is outside as I pull the car out of the garage. She looks fine, so she must be feeling okay. I can't imagine that she has hot flashes in the night. I'm thinking she's way past that. Who knows why she was up so early this morning?

• • •

A musty smell mingles with the scent of book bindings and greets me when I enter the library. People mill around quietly, and I feel the need to tiptoe. Edging my way toward the book return slot, I see a sign posted that the library needs a storyteller for the children's story hour. How hard could that be?

Shoving my books into the slot, I head over to the information desk. A gray-haired lady is sitting behind the desk with her glasses perched on the end of her nose. She looks up. "May I help you?"

"Yes, I wanted to talk to someone about the storytelling position."

She gets up and walks over to the counter. "The position requires a commitment of three times a week—Monday, Wednesday, and Friday mornings from nine to ten o'clock." Her face looks a bit pinched; her words remind me of cold, crisp lettuce. She speaks with precision as though any slip of the tongue would be like spilling a cart of books all over a clean hardwood floor. "The job does not pay a lot of money," she continues, nose upward, lips pursed, "but it is a rewarding job to read to young children. At their age, they still appreciate books." I expect her to add a "humph" here, but she doesn't. "Once they hit their teen years, we lose them to wild music, sports, and video games. Too many distractions for children in today's world, I tell you." She surprises me by adding a *"Tsk, tsk."*

I nod and smile.

She looks at me over the rim of her glasses. "Do you live around here?"

"Yes," I say, basically giving her all my background information except for my Visa card number. Even I have my limits.

"I like you," she says matter-of-factly. "You will do just fine. Be here at eight forty-five sharp on Monday morning. Punctuality is a must."

I smile, agree to her requests, and walk away wondering what in the world just happened. Let's see, I ask about the job, Madame Librarian gets off on a speech regarding the trouble with today's youth, and the next thing I know, she's running a copy of my driver's license, social security card, and telling me I'm employed. Oh, well, at least this will give me a little extra money. I've got to make a down payment on the Mustang *now.*

After checking out some books on anorexia, I head for home. The phone is ringing as I push through the back door. "Hello?"

"Margaret, this is Celine."

My heart skips to my throat. "Yes?"

"Is Gordon home yet?"

"No."

"Okay, well, he's probably still at work, but I wasn't able to get him at the office. I have to go out of town, and I need to let him know I won't be at work on Monday. My mother-in-law has been rushed to the hospital. She may have had a stroke. If Gordon has any questions, he can call me."

"Okay, Celine, I'll let him know."

"Thanks."

I hesitate only a moment. "Celine?"

"Yes?"

"We'll be praying for your family."

"Thank you."

I hang up the phone and offer a prayer right where I'm standing. Regardless of my fears about Gordon and this woman, I cannot neglect to pray for her.

Normally, once I pray about a matter, it's pretty much forgotten. I'm not sure if that's a blessing or a curse, but it's a fact.

After Gordon gets home, I manage to refrain from asking him how his day was with Celine, and we go out for dinner. When we return, Lily's voice is on the answering machine. It seems she went to dinner with another Internet weirdo (my interpretation) last night, and since I was at the Bobby Vinton concert and not able to snoop, she's actually offering to meet us for coffee tonight so we can look him over.

Is that a true friend, or what?

Of course we will meet her. We head over to The New Brew before she can change her mind.

• • •

When we walk in the door, I wave to Tyler. Jade's shift must have ended earlier. Then I spot Lily and a man of about five feet eight inches, thinning hair, a paunchy middle, and a cheery smile. Speaking of that smile, I don't mean to cast stones here, but Mr. Ed, the talking horse, comes to mind.

I know. Sometimes I'm just ugly.

Lily makes the introductions, and the men go to the counter to order our coffees while Lily and I stay behind at the table. Seeing a napkin on the floor, I pick it up and throw it in the trash.

"You're always cleaning this place." Lily teases.

"Hey, I take pride in my coffeehouse."

She smiles.

"Thanks for inviting us, Lil."

"Well, I couldn't risk you jumping into the bush again."

"Thanks." I smile.

"The bush couldn't take it."

I stop smiling.

"Okay, I'm kidding. So what do you think?"

"Of the bush?"

"Dilbert."

Where does she find these guys? Oh yeah, on the Internet. "I've only known him for thirty seconds, Lil. That's hardly enough time to form an opinion."

"Didn't stop you with Walter."

"I don't know what you mean."

"You didn't like Walter from the start, until you found out he lived with his mother and he had been an Eagle Scout."

"Is it so wrong, Lil, that I want you with an Eagle Scout?"

"No, but do you really want me with Walter?" A grin escapes her.

"No."

"And Dilbert?"

"Come on, Lil, I mean, really, Dilbert? You're dating a Dilbert?" I start to laugh.

"Don't judge a person by his name, Maggie," she scolds.

"I know, I know. But *Dilbert*?" Putting my hand over my mouth, I attempt to choke back the giggles. Tears sting my eyes.

She's getting irritated, I can tell. Her nose lifts in the air. "Dilbert happens to be a very nice man."

"There's no doubt in my mind," I mumble behind the palm of my hand. I drop my hand from my mouth. "But those teeth, Lil! You've never liked large teeth."

She grimaces. "Do you honestly think I'm so superficial, Maggie, that I would not date someone because of his teeth?"

"Of course you are; you hate big teeth."

"I'm the slime of the earth." She slinks into her seat and covers her face.

I chuckle some more and pull her hands down. "You're not slime. You just don't like large teeth. I'm thinking you had a run-in with a beaver as a child."

Now we're both laughing. Gordon and Dilbert walk up behind us.

"What's so funny?" Gordon asks.

"Oh, nothing," I say. "Just girl stuff."

We spend the next hour getting to know Ed—I mean, Dilbert—and I have to admit he seems like a nice guy. He's a baker by trade, which would explain the plump cheeks and paunchy midsection, but who am I to talk? If he and Lily get serious, we could be talking discounts on doughnuts here. This relationship could have some potential.

We have a rather enjoyable evening, but by the time we go home, I'm convinced that Dilbert is destined to be a nice friend with big teeth, yet I suspect he will never make his way into the deepest part of Lily's heart.

Once inside our car, I pull the visor down and look in the mirror. I need a gallon of Spackle to cover the cracks in my face. I flip the visor back up with a sigh.

"Can we stop at the pharmacy on the way home so I can pick up something?"

"I guess."

"Can we go to the one on State Street? That's the only one carrying the product I need."

"What are you getting?"

I don't really like to share my beauty secrets with Gordon, but since he asked, I have no choice. "There's this stuff called 'Frownies,' and it's like a tape that you put on your wrinkles to kind of stretch your skin. I don't understand how it all works, but it's supposed to make your wrinkles less noticeable. I read about it in an article and looked it up on the Internet."

"Maggie, you don't have any wrinkles."

"Gordon, we've been through all that, and, yes, I do."

"I don't see any, but if it will make you feel better, we can stop."

"Thank you." He's a smart man to not argue the point tonight. I just don't feel like discussing my wrinkles.

The store is fairly quiet when we step inside. A sprinkling of customers amble around here and there. No one seems to be in a real hurry, though I know it's near closing time. Gordon goes to the beauty aisle with me, and we look for Frownies together. Not finding it, Gordon calls out to a young man behind the register counter, "Do you have any Frownies?"

Never mind that we're half a block away from this employee when Gordon asks the question. "Do we have to tell all of Charming that I need help with my wrinkles?" I whisper to Gordon.

"Sorry." We edge up to the counter. Gordon looks at the worker and repeats, "Do you have any Frownies?"

Counter Boy's brow furrows. I want to tell him not to make those faces or he'll need the product in another thirty years.

"What's that?" he asks.

"We're not sure, but some kind of strips for wrinkles," Gordon says.

Counter Boy looks at me a little too long. I'm guessing he's analyzing my need for the wrinkle cure. What's up with that? Why doesn't he think the product is for Gordon?

"Hey, Brittany, do we have any Frownies?" he calls out so that anyone within a twenty-five mile radius can hear him.

"What's that?" she shouts back.

"This lady needs some kind of tape for wrinkles," he yells. Humiliation brings my world to a standstill.

"Hmm, let me look," she says. The three of us follow her like she's the Pied Piper. She stops and scrunches down in front of a shelf, pulling out two different boxes. "Which kind do you want?"

Gordon picks up two boxes. She and Gordon read the labels while I claw through my purse to find my glasses. Before I can put them on, Gordon announces, "These are for the wrinkles between your brows, and this box is for the sides of your eyes and mouth." He points to the pictures on the boxes, then looks at me. "You want them both?"

Just call me a shar-pei.

I glare at him a moment and snatch the boxes from his hand. The worker seems to sense our need to be alone.

"You want *both*?" I sneer. "Thanks a lot!"

"What did I do?" Gordon asks in all innocence. Oh no, he's not getting out of this one.

"Why, hello, Gordon, Maggie."

I look up and see Debra Stiffler standing in front of us. "Hello, Debra."

"Good to see you both." She lifts a gorgeous smile. Gordon lights up like a Christmas bulb. I want to pull his plug.

She looks at the boxes in my hand and her eyebrows lift, barely making a ripple on her lovely forehead. I whisk my hands behind my back.

Just then her mother rounds the corner and approaches us. "Well, Maggie and Gordon, how are you kids doing?"

I haven't been called a kid since 1965.

We smile and exchange greetings. Mrs. Stiffler reminds me of Mrs. Claus: pretty, white hair; chubby, round cheeks; and sparkling eyes.

"You still living out there by Elvira Pepple?" Mrs. Stiffler asks.

We nod. "You know Elvira?" I ask.

"Sure do," Mrs. Stiffler says with a chuckle. "She's quite a lady. Goes to our church." She leans in as if not wanting to be overheard. "Her husband told my Darrell that she'd give away everything they owned if he didn't watch her. Too softhearted for her own good, he used to say. That's Elvira, all right, always thinking of other people. Why, do you know she gets up at four o'clock every morning to pray?"

I feel my eyes widen. So that's why her lights are on when I'm up with hot flashes.

Mrs. Stiffler evidently sees the flicker of interest in my eyes and pounces on it. "It's a fact. Fasts a couple of times a week too. Harold said she'd visit each of the neighbors once a week so she could keep up on their lives and know how to pray for them. I don't know if she still does that or not," she says, looking at me just a moment, but not stopping long enough for me to answer. "Harold told Darrell all about it—before Harold died, of course. God rest his soul." She pauses for the span of a heartbeat out of respect, I imagine, then continues. "She'd have a fit if she knew Harold had told. That whole Scripture about not letting the left hand know what the right hand is doing, you know." Her face turns serious. "She's real big into that. Doesn't want credit for anything, that Elvira."

I nod.

Debra smiles weakly and tugs at her mother's arm. "We'd better let these folks get back to their shopping, Mother."

Mrs. Stiffler blinks. "Oh, yes, yes. Well, it was nice talking with you."

It occurs to me that the only person really talking was Mrs. Stiffler, but that's okay. I've learned a great deal about my neighbor that I didn't know, even after all these years. Guess I should have been paying her more visits.

We edge our way out to the counter, pay for the two boxes of Frownies, and head for the car. I'm still stinging from the humiliation of my purchase, but then to run into Debra Stiffler is just more than I can handle. Even in my embarrassment, I attempt to keep my face expressionless to ward off any new wrinkles.

We get into the car, and Gordon is totally clueless. "They sure are nice folks," he says.

Looking at him sideways, I can still see the sparkle in his eyes, and it makes me downright mad. I know that sparkle is not for Debra's mom. He turns to me and smiles, then pulls the car onto the road like we're having the most pleasurable of evenings.

I'd like to whack him one; but since he's driving, I'll resist. For now.

21

Gordon walks toward the door to leave for work, but pauses at the kitchen counter. He picks up a bottle of the nutritional supplements I ordered online. "So, we had a pretty nice weekend. Do you think these are working?" he asks with a wink.

"They're big enough to choke a horse."

"Does that mean they're not working?"

"What good are healthy bones if I choke to death?"

Gordon shakes his head and disappears through the garage door.

I get ready for my first day on the job at the library. Afterwards, I make the bed and roam around the house picking up newspapers, stray socks, dusting, straightening stacks, that sort of thing.

At this rate, the attic will never get done.

One more swipe across the counter with my washcloth, and I notice a puddle on the floor. Another of Crusher's little offerings.

We are out of control, Crusher and I. Before I can make arrangements to have us committed, the phone rings.

"Hello?"

"I need you to say a prayer for me."

"Gordon, what's wrong?"

"I have a big project due today, and Celine hasn't shown up for work. I tried to call her at home, and she's not there. I'm worried about her, and I'm worried about getting my court document put together."

A wave of nausea hits me. "Oh, Gordon, I'm so sorry. Celine called on Saturday, and I forgot to tell you."

"What's wrong?"

"Her mother-in-law was taken to the hospital. They think she had a stroke. She said she would get in touch with you later but wanted you to know she would not be at work today."

His silence makes me feel worse.

"In all the rush of the weekend, I simply forgot."

"I've told you about writing things down, Maggie."

"I know. I'm sorry." How could I forget something so important? A bit of panic surges through me. What if I'm in the beginning stages of Alzheimer's?

"Well, I'll see if one of the other secretaries will help me out. Talk to you later."

I want him to assure me that everything is okay, that I'm forgiven. *Click.*

But he doesn't.

That's what I get for being so irresponsible. First, locking my keys in the car, and now this.

I'm mad at myself and feeling plenty horrible by the time I get to the library. Not the mood I was going for in my role as storyteller. The children gather in the story room, and I wave at Madame Librarian. Her lips are pursed as she charges up to me in her thick-soled shoes. "You're two minutes late," she quips.

"What? Do I have a target on my back today?" I say before I can stop myself.

She blinks but doesn't act like she heard me. "There's no time to lose. Here, put these on." She shoves a shawl, gray wig, and wire-rimmed glasses into my hands.

"Your props," she says when she sees my expression. "You'll be sitting in the rocking chair, front and center."

I gape at the chair and at the things in my hands.

"Bathroom is over there," she says, pointing. "Hurry up." She claps her hands like a teacher rounding up thirty students.

Patrons watch me as I scurry to the bathroom. Okay, I've suffered enough embarrassment in the last couple of days to last me a lifetime. With a groan, I pull the wig over my freshly shampooed, curled, styled, and sprayed hair. I stare at my reflection in the mirror. The very image I've been trying to run from since this whole age thing began.

Just call me Mother Goose.

With slow, deliberate steps, I walk past Madame Librarian—aka Gladiator Woman—and up to my rocker in the story room.

I'm thinking there has to be an easier way to get Gordon that car.

• • •

I'm feeling better when I finish the storytelling adventure, politely decline future employment in munchkin land with Gladiator Woman, and make my way home. Call me overly sensitive, but with so fragile a self-esteem these days, the last thing I need is gray hair, a shawl, and a rocker.

Elvira is raking leaves from her yard when I pull up. I stop and pull the envelopes from our mailbox, then walk over to see her.

"Well, how are you?" Elvira asks with her chipper voice.

"Fine, thanks. Could I rake those leaves for you?"

Elvira waves her hand. "Oh, my, no. Why, if I let everyone do my work for me, I'd lose my girlish figure," she says with a cackle. "Not that it matters, what with Harold gone and all." Her bright smile stays intact, but her comment jars me a little. Is that why she doesn't dress as nicely as she once did, because Harold is gone? Is she struggling with pain of her own, but refuses to look into it because she's too busy praying for others? My heart constricts with the knowledge that I have such a neighbor and that God would allow me the privilege of living by her.

"Have you heard how Katie is doing?"

Elvira shakes her head. "Still running tests on the poor thing. To make matters worse, her dad lost his job last week."

"Oh no."

"I'm afraid so."

"Does he have any new leads?"

"He's putting some feelers out there, but nothing yet."

I study Elvira's face and see how tired she looks. I remember what Mrs. Stiffler said and wonder if Elvira is taking on too much of the Nelsons' burden.

"Do you think they would mind if a few of the neighbors got together and took over some meals?"

Elvira brightens. "Say, that's a great idea."

"I'll get started on that this afternoon. It's the least we can do."

"Thank you, Maggie," Elvira says, her eyes warm and appreciative.

I feel uncomfortable, like a problem child under the gaze of Mother Teresa.

"Well, if you're sure you won't let me help you, I'll let you get back to work."

"I'm sure." Elvira smiles and scrapes the rake across the leaves once again, pulling them toward her growing pile.

Once inside the house, I drop the envelopes on the counter, pull off my jacket, and hang it up. Quickly, I make a list of neighbors who might be willing and able to help with the meals. I decide to call the Nelsons to see if they would mind, first off, so we don't offend them in any way.

I make the call, express my apologies for their recent trials, and

Mrs. Nelson agrees to accept dinners for a few days. No doubt they are reeling from the turn of events.

I reach one neighbor, but the others are gone. Maybe most of them work outside the home. Why don't I know that? I had no idea how out of touch I was with those around me. I feel ashamed but reason it's hard to be involved with people these days. Everyone is on the go. Busy working, playing, whatever.

Still, I can't help feeling neglectful.

The phone rings, and it's Lily.

"Hi! How did your date go with *Dilbert*?" I ask, with emphasis on his name.

"Now, don't start."

"Okay, okay," I say with a giggle. "I'll behave." I set my iced tea on a coaster on the stand next to the sofa.

"Oh, I'm sorry. I must have called the wrong number."

"Ha, ha. So tell me about Dilbert."

"Dilbert is nice."

"Um-hum."

"Dilbert is sweet."

"Yes, he is."

"Dilbert has large teeth."

"Good-bye, Dilbert."

"Honestly, it's more than the teeth. He's just not quite—oh, I don't know—what I'm looking for."

"I know. You want a man with shorter teeth, more gums."

"Now, cut that out."

I laugh. "So now what? Back to the Internet?"

"Yep, I have two prospects left."

"I don't know if I can take much more, Lil."

"Oh, come on, Maggie. If I can do it, so can you."

I take a sip of tea. "Well, I confess they've all been harmless enough. Makes me feel a little better."

"And I'm careful, taking them only to public places."

"True."

"And I can always count on you to stalk from the bushes."

"Need I remind you of the pain I endured for you?"

"I am sorry you were hurt. But you shouldn't be hanging out with bushes. I mean, after all, you're not exactly Moses."

"Hey, what do you mean by that?" Something tells me I should be offended.

Lily laughs. "You're such a great friend, Maggie. A little weird, but great."

"Okay, so we're even."

"Yeah, I guess."

"So, when is the next date taking place?"

"Don't know yet. But I'll be sure to call you."

"Yeah, *after* the date."

"Would I do that?"

"Just remember, if you get caught up in some diabolical plan, I tried to warn you."

"I'll remember."

I explain to Lily about the Nelsons and tell her that I need to get started on a meal for them.

"Okay, well, you have a nice afternoon. Oh, yeah, and take your supplements."

"Why did you say that?"

"Because I noticed your face was flushed when we were together."

"Dr. Lily is back."

"You'd feel better if you listened to me."

"Talk to you soon—"

"Maggie?"

"Yeah?"

"I'm glad you're my best friend. Thanks for caring about me."

My heart warms. There's no better friend than Lily. "You're welcome, Lil."

We hang up, and I smile to myself. No doubt she thinks I'm forgetting fully that she'll be having another date with an Internet weirdo. But such is not the case. I'm marking my calendar, and I will follow up.

That's just what best friends do for one another.

• • •

I stop by to pick up my deposit check from Galloway's Auto Sales. I am thankful Eric left the check with the receptionist. Feeling awful about this whole thing, I don't really want to see him.

After leaving there, I head over to Rosetown to put money down on the Mustang and fill out the paperwork to finance the rest. I can hardly wait to give it to Gordon, but Lily says I can keep it at her house until our anniversary.

Upon arriving at the car lot, I find that though they had told me the Mustang was still available, since I hadn't put any money on it to reserve it yet, they couldn't hold it for me. They sold it thirty minutes before I got there.

Tears sting my eyes. I go to all this trouble, and now I have to go back and grovel in front of Eric to see if he'll still let me buy the Nova—if he hasn't already sold it.

I head back over to Galloway's, and Rhonda tells me Eric is still out. I see the Nova still in the back, so I figure I'm good until tomorrow. I tell Rhonda to have Eric give me a call when he gets back.

So help me, Gordon better appreciate this . . .

• • •

While the stuffed pasta shells are in the oven, I click on the computer to check my e-mail. Thankfully, the Internet is working again. As it boots up, I refill Crusher's food and water bowls. He approaches it with as much enthusiasm as I tackle a carrot. Maybe I need to change his food. After all, eating the same thing for twelve years could get old.

I click into my e-mail. There's a note from Heather, and my heart leaps.

"Hi, Mom! Thought I'd check in and see how things are going. We are doing fine. My class is going great. Those little second graders are the sweetest. I love kids!"

With a catch in my throat, I stop reading here. She loves kids. As in, *I'm ready to have one of my own, or as in, I love teaching the second grade?* When she has a baby, my grandchild will be hours away. I never once thought of that possibility when my kids were growing up. It was a given that we'd all hang out together like the Waltons. I think it's Gordon's fault for not buying that house I wanted with the big dining room back when the kids were little. Everyone knows you need a table the size of a freight train to be the Waltons.

> Mom, I'm having such fun with Josh's mom. I can't believe she's including me so much in these decorating adventures. I wish you were here to enjoy it with us, but I know you don't get into it like we do. She's given me lots of wonderful ideas for our house too. Can't wait for you to see it. And guess what, Mom. She has asked me to go with her for a weekend to Chicago! We're going up Friday night, staying at some fancy hotel, then spending all day at market—this is where she buys things for her decorating business—then we'll spend the night Saturday and drive home Sunday. Can you believe it? We're going to have such fun! I wish you were here, and we could all go together.

I hear myself gulp out loud. Chicago is where *we* went together. It is so juvenile, but I can't help feeling replaced. I finish the rest of Heather's note, but it's pretty much a blur. I can't seem to get past her weekend with Josh's mom. I love special days with Heather, and I ache for them now. So when will she come home for the weekend again? If she's having so much fun with Marilyn "just-call-me-Martha" Stewart, I'll never see my daughter again.

This is ridiculous. My daughter still loves me. It's good that she gets along with her mother-in-law. It's what I want, really. Especially since I can't be there for her. But being replaced? That's another matter. I don't mind her making room for Marilyn, but please, Heather, don't replace me.

I whisper a prayer that the Lord will make me strong and help me not to give in to these foolish notions that are plaguing my heart just now. Once again I scan the note Nick sent to me the other day after we talked on the phone about his new job.

I take a deep breath and determine it's time to go tanning. I called the other day for prices and then just put it off. It's time to take action. I can do this. Marching to the phone, I call Charming Skin to schedule an appointment. They can take me in an hour. That gives me enough time to finish the Nelsons' meal, drop it off, and get to my appointment.

On my way to Charming Skin, I can hardly believe I'm doing this. I've talked my kids out of it how many times? I've droned on about the dangers of skin cancer and the leathery skin when they're older. Every argument I could think of, I shared with them. So what am I doing?

Well, I'm not going overboard here. These things aren't so wrong if you maintain balance.

Besides, I believe someone called this "midlife mentality." Well, okay, in my case it's post-midlife mentality.

• • •

As I browse through a magazine, awaiting my turn, I'm feeling more and more ridiculous at being here. Not one patron looks a day over sixteen.

The magazines flashing flawless twenty-year-olds and Hollywood marriages splitting over infidelity isn't helping matters.

I'm surprised the management hasn't made me leave. I look like an advertisement for what not to do to skin. The thought occurs to me that this can actually increase the visibility of my age spots. Closing my magazine, I'm ready to bolt, when they call my name.

The sixteen-year-olds look at me. If they can do it, I can do it, right? I mean, I'm not exactly ancient.

"Hello, Mrs. Hayden," the worker says. "You'll need to take a pair of goggles with you into the room." She points to some weird-looking eye protectors in some kind of cleaning solvent. I fish some out and wipe them with a fresh cloth. "Okay, now take a clean towel with you," she says. I obey and follow her into my room.

Colorful vacation pictures are plastered all over the walls. The room smells of suntan lotions and oils. They're probably trying to make people think they're in the Bahamas or something. It's not doing it for me.

"You have a radio right there. The beds are cleaned after every use, so yours is ready to go. Just take off whatever clothes you want to remove and pull the lid toward you as far as you want. It will lock in place when you bring it down so low. Since this is your first time, I'll set the timer for ten minutes. This is not our hottest bed, so you'll be fine. Your skin is medium, so you won't burn. It's best to add a few minutes every time you come in and work up to a tan."

She smiles, and I notice how white her smile is, but then again, it could be because her skin is so dark. Obviously, she gets free run of the beds.

"Some girls come in here and try to start out at half an hour, and they get burned."

I nod.

"Well, that's it. Good luck. If you need anything, just let me know."

"Thank you." When she leaves the room, I quickly lock the door.

I scan the room for any hidden cameras. You can't tell about a place like this. I've heard about perverts who look through hidden cameras and watch people undress. Checking the posters for holes, I do the test on the mirror. You know the one. If there's a space between my finger's reflection, then it's a true mirror. If there's no space, it's a two-way glass. I can almost hear a drum roll as I put my finger up to its reflection. I look. Ah, it's a mirror. Nothing there but a smudge where my finger has been. It's probably a totally bogus test, especially since I learned it in grade school, but it makes me feel better.

Now that I've determined that the room is "clean," I disrobe down to my skivvies.

I feel positively scandalous doing this. My mother would have a hissy fit, as she calls it. Isn't it funny that I'm fifty years old and still worrying about what my mother would think? How come my kids don't do that?

I turn the radio to the Christian station and then smear the tanning lotion all over my body, compliments of the establishment. Marinade sauce.

Finally, I slide onto the glass bed with all the grace of a hippo. Visible bulbs lie dormant underneath. I'm not one to like enclosed spaces, so this is really a stretch for me. Still, I figure if Lily can stretch, so can I.

My skin flops and squeaks around on the bed until I scoot into position. I place the goggles over my eyes and push the on button to start the lights. Quickly, I reach up to pull the lid toward me. Now, call me morbid, but this just reminds me of a coffin. Hey, maybe this is what my coffin will be like when I wake up in glory! It will light up, and I'll rise out of the bed with my hallelujah body. I'm feeling better already. Well, a little anyway. My heart is still beating faster than a scared rabbit's, but the warmth of the bulbs soon lulls me into a sense of peace.

I can't help wondering if this is how the lobster in the boiling pot feels . . .

22

It's four o'clock in the morning, and I'm whipping off the covers again. The tanning bed turned my skin pink, and the sunburn combined with the hot flashes is enough to drive me crazy. I would strip down to my skivvies, but what if we had a fire? If I ran into the front yard with nothing on but my underwear, I'd scare Elvira's teeth right out of her head.

Instead, I slide into my slippers, leave my robe hanging in the closet, and trudge down the hallway. I wonder about Elvira and make my way upstairs to the guestroom. When I look out the window, Elvira's light is on in her bedroom again. Her blinds are pulled, but I'm sure she's praying after what Mrs. Stiffler said. I wonder if Elvira prays for me.

I'll have to tell her about the hot flashes.

Edging out of the bedroom, I close the door behind me, determined to be more dedicated to prayer. As old as Elvira is, she is still making a difference. Oh, people may not know that she is making a difference, but heaven knows. Elvira is a behind-the-scenes kind of person. She doesn't want applause from men. She seems to truly love people.

I used to think I loved people until my evil twin moved in. Now I hunger for isolation.

This menopause thing has affected every area of my life. It's like I'm being held prisoner by some cantankerous old woman. I fear a total takeover. At this rate, by the time I'm in a nursing home, she'll have me smoking cigars and swearing a blue streak.

I suppose that's why it's so important to keep on track spiritually. What goes in must come out, right? So if I'm putting the Word into my heart, hopefully, that will override my evil twin.

As Gordon would say, "The jury's still out on that one."

Elvira gives me hope. She has aged well. Wait. What am I saying? Aged well? Elvira? How many times have I mentioned I don't want to be like her when I'm old? It's too early for me to analyze that just now. I need my coffee. My hot flash is easing up, so I'll try a cup. I edge down the stairway and head for the kitchen when the door to our bedroom opens behind me. I turn around. Gordon is standing there in his robe, disheveled hair, a shadowy beard covering his jaw. He looks kind of cute.

His eyes crack open in little slits, and he blinks a lot. "Maggie, you okay?" His fists reach up to rub his eyes, and he reminds me of Nick when he was little. I want to hug him.

"I'm fine, honey. Just heading for the coffee."

"Can you make me some?"

"It's early, Gordon. Why don't you go back to sleep?"

"I want to get up with you," he says, and my heart turns soft like honey. I love him so much.

Once the coffee is ready, Gordon and I sit in the living room together. Crusher jumps up and curls onto my lap. I stroke his bald head a couple of times, take a drink, and look over at Gordon in his recliner. "How's work going?" I ask.

He shrugs. "I'll just be glad when we close out the Keller estate. We've had such a struggle with the family fighting us every step of the way on this." He sighs.

He has circles under his eyes. I've been so caught up in myself that I've neglected to see what Gordon has been going through. "I'm sorry, honey. Do you think you'll be finished soon?"

He takes a drink from his mug. "Hopefully, if we can get the siblings to cooperate. I just want to get it wrapped up." He runs his fingers through his already messy hair. The compulsive side of me—which, by the way, has subsided greatly since this whole menopause thing has kicked in—wants to fix it for him. He turns to me. "Why are you up so early?"

I don't really want to talk about menopause. Seems like a sign of weakness or something. All right, the truth is it's like admitting that I'm old. Do I want Gordon to know that I'm old? I guess that sounds pretty stupid. Gordon is not deaf, dumb, nor is he blind.

"Maggie?"

He's waiting on an answer. "Just can't sleep."

"Hot flashes?"

I don't respond.

"It's not like leprosy, Maggie. You don't have to hide and be all secretive about it. Women your age go through these things. It's all right."

"Okay, does the fact that I considered streaking through the neighborhood this morning mean anything to you?" I put my cup on the stand. I'm too hot to drink it anyway.

Gordon grabs his mug, gets up from the recliner, walks over to the sofa, and sits down beside me. Crusher lifts his head for a moment; then it falls back onto my leg. Gordon covers my hand with his free one. "Maggie, I love you. 'Til death do us part, remember?"

Gordon loves me. When will I learn to trust him?

"I remember."

"We're both getting older, so what?" He shrugs. "It happens to everyone. It doesn't change how I feel toward you. In my eyes you will always be 'My Maggie.'"

Before the hall clock ticks the next beat, out of nowhere tears fill my eyes and plunge down my cheeks. Gordon puts his mug on a nearby coaster, reaches over, and pulls me into his arms. Crusher tips a little, but stays fixed on my lap.

"Honey, it's all right." He holds me tight against him and strokes my hair. "What is it, Maggie? You're not sick, are you? I mean, something you're not telling me?"

"I don't know what it is, Gordon. I'm just not myself anymore. I used to be a nice person."

He squeezes me and chuckles. "You're still a nice person, Maggie."

"No, I'm not nice. I think mean things toward people. I'm sarcastic, rude, negative." I brush the tears from my face and look up at him. "I'm not exactly representing Christ in a positive way these days, you know?" Tears splatter upon Crusher, and he sleeps right through it. I grab a tissue from the box on the stand.

"Yes, you are, Maggie. You don't see the things you do. Why, you're the best friend Lily could ever hope to have. You are always there for her."

"She says I stalk her," I say, wiping my nose.

Gordon laughs. "You do. But if you didn't care about her, you wouldn't do that." He looks into my face. "Don't you see, Maggie? You put yourself out—even at physical risk—to make sure she is safe." He rests his chin on the top of my head. "That's a true friend."

I think about it a moment. Maybe it's okay that I do these things. Lily knows I love her. My motive is right in that, isn't it?

"You made a nice dinner for the Nelsons last night. I'm sure they appreciated it. The Lord sees those things, Maggie. He also sees your heart."

I groan. "That's what I'm worried about."

Gordon chuckles again and looks at me. "Maggie, physical changes affect us. As long as you're seeking God's help and doing all you know to do, what else is there?"

I nod. I suppose he's right. Still, I'm not liking myself these days.

"You're forgetting that bumper sticker we saw the other day, something about Christians not being perfect, just forgiven."

Well, I certainly qualify there. Okay, that makes me feel a little better.

"You worry too much, you know." He squeezes my arm.

I look up at him and smile. "By the way, did Celine call about her mother-in-law?"

"Yeah, looks like she suffered a slight stroke, but she should be okay."

"Oh, I'm glad." I snuggle back into his arms. "I'm sorry about forgetting the phone call."

Gordon pats my arm. "Those things happen. Next time, though, write it down, okay?"

"Yeah." I don't look at him. These days, reprimands and I don't get along. Still, I shouldn't have forgotten.

"Hey, I forgot to ask you," he says, picking up his mug. "How did your storytelling go at the library yesterday?"

I grimace.

"Oh no, that bad?"

"Gordon, they made me wear a gray wig, a shawl, and plunked me in a rocking chair!" I hear my voice rise with every word.

Gordon struggles to keep from laughing. I can see it in his eyes.

"Not exactly your dream job, huh?" He sips his coffee, then returns the mug to the stand.

"No," I say fervently. "I quit."

"Already?"

"They made me pretend to be everything I don't want to be. I'm not ready for the gray hair—okay, so I *have* gray hair, but I'm not ready to show it to the world. Why do you think stores carry hair dye, Gordon?"

He looks at me wide-eyed and shrugs, trying to smother a grin with his hand.

"For women in denial. Women like *me.* And a shawl? For crying out loud, Gordon, old people wear shawls! Sit in a rocking chair, in a gray wig and shawl? Just shoot me now." I think a moment. "Oh yeah, and the glasses—the glasses were as old as Grandma's." I'm near hysteria just thinking about it. "And I don't even want to think about Gladiator Woman." I drop my head against the back of the sofa and sigh.

"Who? Oh yeah, the five-foot-two gal that weighs, what, about ninety pounds, didn't you say?"

I look at him. "She might have been small, but her bark had the punch of a gladiator, believe me."

Gordon chuckles, and it makes me smile. He grabs me into his arms again. "You're an adventure, Maggie Hayden, and I love you for it." He kisses the top of my head.

We sit there for quite a while, just wrapped in each other's arms in the silence—well, except for a slight snoring coming from Crusher—and my anxieties melt away.

"Though I'd rather stay here like this all day, I had better get ready for work, or we won't be able to buy groceries. And we know how you are without your chocolate," Gordon says with a wink.

So much for the warm fuzzies. "No chocolate. We have enough in the cupboards, remember?"

He winces and heads for our room to get showered and dressed.

The cold reality is Gordon has to go to work, and I am left behind to seek comfort from a skinny, bald dog.

After Gordon leaves, I decide to make a batch of chocolate chip cookies for Jade and Tyler this morning. Might as well get rid of some of our chocolate.

• • •

Once the cookies cool down enough to put in a container, I grab my journal, purse, the container of cookies, and head for the coffee shop.

I enter The New Brew and wave to Tyler and Jade. The room is fairly quiet, only a patron or two.

"Hey, you've got a tan," Jade says, smiling.

"Yep." I'm feeling all proud and young here as I tell her about my trip to the tanning booth as though I do it every day. "By the way, these are for you and Tyler," I say, handing Jade the container. She probably won't eat any.

Tyler enters from the back room. "Hi, Maggie." Jade shows her the cookies. "Wow, thanks! You make, like, a great second mom," Tyler says with a grin.

Heather should hear this.

"Better than my first one," Jade mumbles. Before anyone can say anything, she hurries on. "You want the usual drink?"

I shake my head for her to wait a minute, take my things over, drop them on a table, then walk back to the counter.

"I want a mocha frappe."

Jade's eyebrows raise. "Oh, you're changing on us."

If she only knew. "I want something cold today," without offering an explanation.

Jade nods her head. "One mocha frappe coming up," she says with a wide grin. Kids today are so flexible.

"So, how are you girls?"

"Good," they reply. Jade takes my money while Tyler fixes the frappe.

Tyler makes my frappe to perfection, and I sit down at the table and pull open my journal. I write a little while; then Jade walks over to me.

"So, how are things going for you, Maggie?"

I close my book. "Pretty well. How about you?"

"By the way, I've been using my journal. I really like it."

"Good. It does help to write some things down."

She sits down in a chair across from me for a minute. "We're a little shorthanded, so it's kind of frustrating to get all the work done."

"Did someone leave?"

"Yeah, Chris left."

"Oh, that's too bad. He was a good worker."

"Yeah, he was. He's gonna work at the Starbucks in Rosetown."

"At least I might see him once in a while when we go there." I take a sip of my frappe. "So, do you have an ad in the paper?"

"It goes in tomorrow."

"Full-time?"

"Actually, it's only about twenty-five hours a week. Just five hours a day. The schedule rotates; sometimes it's mornings, afternoons, evenings, that kind of thing."

"Uh-huh."

"You know, Maggie, we all look forward to you coming in. It's like you're the coffeehouse mom," she says with a grin. "I don't suppose we could talk you into working here?" With one look at my face, she hurries on. "You could have free coffee."

Okay, that's just wrong to appeal to my coffee addiction. Me? Working at the coffee shop?

"Even if you only helped us temporarily, until we could find another employee, it would be great. You're always picking up around here anyway. Might as well get paid for it." Her eyes twinkle.

I think a minute. The money could help me pay for the Nova, if it's still available. I could agree to a temporary assignment, staying long enough for them to find someone else.

My pause energizes her. "Would you consider it, Maggie?" Her eyes widen. "That would be so cool if you worked in here. We would love it."

Tyler hears the commotion and walks over to my table. Jade turns to her.

"Maggie is thinking about applying for the job."

Tyler jumps on the bandwagon. "You are? That would be totally awesome!"

Now, I haven't said a word one way or the other, mind you, but these girls already have the paperwork finished and the W2s filled out before I can comment. Okay, maybe not, but you get the idea.

"I don't know, girls," I say with obvious hesitation.

"Why not, Maggie? You would be perfect. You could add the parental supervision and guidance we all need," Jade says, smiling.

She's appealing to my nurturing side here. It gets to me every time. "Well, I could work on a temporary basis, until you can find someone else." I grin.

Hey, my life is crazy right now, kind of topsy-turvy, never know what's going to happen from one day to the next. I'm living a roller-coaster kind of life. One minute my hormones take me to the top; the next minute I'm plunging downward, hair blowing straight back, fear in my eyes, heart pounding so hard I'm sure it will blow any minute. Then I bottom out and start the uphill climb all over again.

What a ride!

"You mean it?" Tyler claps her hands. "You're hired."

"What?" I'm shocked.

"I said, *you're hired.* I'm the one who, like, does the hiring since I've been here the longest," Tyler says with confidence. "The owner trusts my opinion. And there is no doubt in my mind we would, like, love to have you on board."

"Well, how do you like that? I come in to journal and sip my frappe, and the next thing I know, I have a job."

We all laugh.

"So does that mean you accept?" Tyler asks, anticipation in her eyes.

I look from her to Jade, whose eyes look hopeful, but something about her worries me. Then it hits me. They need me. These girls need me. My joy knows no bounds. *Somebody* needs me. And I need them. That's what I've been missing since the kids have left home.

No one needs me anymore, well, except for Crusher, and the skinny, bald guy just doesn't do it for me, you know?

"I accept."

Once those words leave my lips, the place becomes a commotion of activity. Customers start filing in and Tyler brings paperwork for me to fill out.

Tyler sits down with me, and we go through the schedule. I won't actually be "working" for a couple of days. I'm thinking this will be a fun job. After all, who better to sell coffee drinks than a coffee addict? Not to mention the fact that I could never pass up a free mocha—or a teen who needs me.

23

I spend all day at the coffeehouse, journaling and looking around the place with an "insider's" perspective. It feels great. I call Lily to tell her to come join me, and when she walks in the door, I am beaming—and flushed. And, oh no, starting to feel warm again.

"It's getting cold out there," Lily says with a shiver when she arrives at my table at The New Brew. "I'd better start with the Vitamin C."

"Cold? Did you say 'cold'? I want to shove snow down my blouse, and you say you're cold?" I rub the napkin across the back of my neck.

"You're still having hot flashes?"

I start fanning myself. "No, Lily, I always resemble a cook stove."

"You need some dong quai."

I stop fanning and look at her. "Now, that name just scares me."

Lily shrugs. "Suit yourself. It's good for hot flashes. Just thought you'd like to know."

Fanning again. "I'm going to the doctor to check into a natural hormone cream. If I don't get these hot flashes and flushes under control, I'll just incinerate." That word makes me fan all the harder.

"Bless your heart. Well, this, too, shall pass." Lily pulls off her jacket and slips it around her chair. "Glad I have my sweater on today." She tugs it closer to her, then looks at me. "Your face is really red—like you've got a fever."

I stare at her. "I have a little burn, and I'm having a hot flash."

"A burn?" She looks at me like I'm crazy when I explain the whole tanning experience.

"I'm not even going to go there. You ready to order?"

I nod and get up to follow her to the counter.

"Were you really here all day?"

"Yeah. This is practically my second home. And guess what? It's officially going to be my second home now. The New Brew hired me!"

"What! Are you kidding me? This is the perfect place for you, Maggie." She hugs me tight.

"Yeah, isn't that great?" Jade says, obviously overhearing Lily's comment as we approach the counter.

We both smile.

"We're gonna love having Maggie onboard. Free mochas, remember, Maggie," Jade says as if she needs to dangle the carrot in front of me. Why is that? Is there a hidden warning in there somewhere? Hmm, maybe I should reconsider this.

We place our orders, then step over to the waiting area where we pick up drinks.

"So what does Gordon think about this?" Lily asks while stuffing her change back in her purse.

I wait a moment to talk. They're blending my mocha into a frappe, and the machine makes too much noise. "Well, I haven't told him yet."

Her head shoots up. "You haven't told him? Why not?"

"Well, I just got the job this morning, and I haven't talked to him yet. He'll get home late. Probably won't get the chance to tell him until tomorrow morning."

Lily shakes her head. "You two need a vacation."

"Tell me about it. He works too much."

She nods. "Well, like you said, maybe once he gets through this latest estate matter, he can take a break."

Hopefully, that's the problem and not a certain paralegal, divorcee, or client. Every time I think I've worked through all that, my paranoia strikes again. It's silly, I know. I'm almost 100 percent sure it's caused from my hormones working overtime.

Almost.

Jade gives us our drinks. Mine looks like a chocolate shake with great swirls of whipped cream on top.

"That's a coffee?" Lily asks, staring in disbelief.

"Mocha frappe."

"How can you drink something cold on a day like this?" Lily asks with a shiver.

I frown.

"Oh, the hot flash."

"Yeah. I'm telling you, Lil, I'm gulping down ice cream when I should be chewing on carrots."

Lily shrugs. "Remember what someone told us, Maggie? If the ladies on the *Titanic* had known it was going down, they wouldn't have passed up the chocolate dessert the night before."

"True." Like I said, Lily always makes me feel better. I dive into my frappe, and soon I'm in chocolate bliss once again.

"So, are you going to tell me when your next date is?"

Lily looks up from her drink. "Nope." Her eyes twinkle. Sometimes she just irritates me.

"Okay, but I have ways of finding out."

"Don't I know it. And you have the battle scars to prove it."

I ignore her comment entirely. "What's this next guy like?"

"Seems really nice on e-mail. He owns a motorcycle." As soon as Lily says that, her hand covers her mouth.

I smile.

"Doggone it, Maggie. You tricked me into telling you that."

"I have no idea what you're talking about," I say before sucking more frappe up my straw.

"Now you'll be watching out for a motorcycle." She frowns at me.

"Great idea."

Her lips purse together. "Stalker."

"Am not."

"Are too."

"Peaches." I use the word like a secret weapon.

Lily shivers. "Okay, I give up."

It works every time. I flash a victory grin until I see the scowl on her face. I hide the smile, but inwardly I'm still celebrating.

"Oh, did I tell you about my whole fiasco with Gordon and the Frownies purchase?" I say to change the subject.

Lily shakes her head.

I tell her what happened up to the point where the worker hands Gordon the boxes and Gordon asks me if I want both—the comment he has since lived to regret.

"Anyway," I continue, "you will never believe who turns the corner right about then and sees me holding the wrinkle cover-ups."

Lily leans in like this is going to be good. And, of course, it is. "Who?"

I start to tell her, and my mind goes blank. Totally. Nothing there. Nada. Zip. Zilch. We're talking not so much as a blip on the computer screen.

"Well, who is it?"

"I'm thinking," I say a little too crossly.

"What's wrong?"

"I think I have Alzheimer's." I tell Lily.

Her eyes widen. "What? You are making no sense, Maggie." She goes back to her drink.

"Exactly. That's what I mean. I can't remember her name. I'm forgetting everything these days, Lil. Do you know, the other day I was telling Gordon about this ceramic nativity set I want to buy for Christmas, but I could not think of the word *nativity*?" Just remembering that makes me cringe. "I told him, 'You know, the barn scene, a bunch of people standing around the baby Jesus in a manger, farm animals, all that?' He just sort of dropped his jaw and looked at me. Finally, he said, 'Nativity?' I pounced on it as though I had just won the game of Clue. The butler, in the kitchen, with the knife! 'That's it!'"

Lily's laughing hysterically at my expense.

"It's not funny, Lil."

"Ginkgo biloba."

"Excuse me?"

"It helps with forgetfulness." Lily takes a sip of her drink. "You'd better write it down or you'll forget."

"Ha, ha." I stir the whipped cream into my frappe and replace the lid. "I have no counter space left."

Lily stares at me.

"There are so many herb bottles on my counter, I have no room left."

She leans in. "Well, when you forget Gordon's name, you'd better buy some." She smiles.

I don't.

She sits back in her seat. "Oh come on, Maggie. You worry too much."

"I do not. Why doesn't anybody take me seriously anymore? One of these days you're going to come up and talk to me, and I won't know you."

"Drama queen."

"Doggone it, Lil."

"Oh, okay. I'm trying to feel your pain here, Maggie, but honestly, everyone has memory lapses. It's no big deal. Just take a deep breath and think for a moment. It will come to you."

What will come to me? Oh yeah, the woman's name.

"You know her, the high-school beauty queen who just returned to Charming."

Lily thinks a moment.

"I told you I ran into her recently. She didn't remember me?"

"Serves her right that you've forgotten her name then," Lily says with encouragement, though it does little to make me feel better.

I can almost imagine the blinding spotlight aimed at me as I sit on a tattered chair with cracked upholstery in some dark, musty basement. Thugs are standing around waiting for me to spill the truth. Perspiration forms on my brow—whether from a hot flash or straining my brain, I'm not sure—when all of a sudden, it comes to me.

"Debra Stiffler," I finally blurt and fall back into my chair, totally exhausted. Feeling so relieved that I've remembered, I consider buying another frappe.

Lily's eyebrows lift appropriately. "She's the one who saw you with the wrinkle stuff?"

"The very one. With her mother too."

"How do you do it, Maggie?"

"Just lucky, I guess."

We moan together. Lily's such a good friend.

"Well, Debra was probably glad. I'm thinking she owns stock in the company." She chuckles.

"Did I ever tell you she and Greg got a divorce?"

Lily's expression turns serious. "Oh, I'm sorry to hear that."

"Yeah, me too."

"Just goes to show you can have everything, including beauty, but it doesn't guarantee happiness." Lily finishes the last bit of her latte.

Such an innocent statement, but it strikes deep in the heart of me. I mean, it's not something I haven't heard before, but for some reason it penetrates the layers of negative self-talk I have built up over the past months. It captures my undivided attention in a real way. I'm thinking God might be in this.

"You okay, Maggie?"

"What? Oh, yeah."

"Lily, Maggie, how are you?" A female voice calls to us.

We look up. My mind pauses a fraction of a second, then kicks into gear. *You remember her name. Louise Montgomery,* I say to myself as she walks toward our table. I'm a little embarrassed to see her, since I acted like such a goof at the restaurant.

"You two enjoying some time out on the town?" she asks with a sweet smile.

I smile back. *Louise Montgomery. Louise Montgomery.*

"Mind if I join you? Don had to go to the store across the street for a while, and I told him I would grab a coffee."

"Please do join us, Louise," Lily says while I continue to roll her name around in my mind so I won't forget it.

She settles into her seat. "So what's going on with you two?" Before we can answer she looks at me. "I know you've been busy, because I'm having an awful time getting you and Gordon to our house for dinner." I start to reply, but she continues. "By the way, we're having the Hattons, Hedricks, and Hussongs over this Friday. Any chance you and Gordon can join us?" As if not wanting to be rude, she turns to Lily. "Of course, you know you're welcome to come along, too, Lily."

Though we don't say anything, we all know Lily's last name being Newgent would throw off everything. An "N" showing up on an "H" night could set Louise back for weeks.

"I'm afraid Gordon is working late Friday night, Louise. Maybe one of these days we'll get there. I'm sorry."

"Oh, that's too bad. How about you, Lily?"

Lily fingers her cup, and I realize she's stalling. She glances at me.

"Well, I have a prior commitment," she says, practically in a whisper. I have to lean in, but it suddenly registers to me what she's said. Her cheeks fan pink.

Bingo. Biker Man will be here on Friday night. I lift an evil grin.

She glares back at me.

"Am I missing something here?" Louise asks, clearly seeing the facial communication between me and Lily.

I laugh. "No. Lily tries to hide things from me, but I always find out no matter how hard she tries to keep it from me."

Lily drops her chin into her palm like she may as well give up. I could have told her that a long time ago.

Louise takes the last drink from her cup. "Well, I guess I'd better go check on Don." She's up and out the door before we can blink.

"Guess she didn't want to get involved," I say.

"Can you blame her?"

Lily and I grab our purses and step into the evening, and I'm already making plans to meet Lily's biker man . . .

• • •

With fear and trembling, I make my way to Galloway's Auto Sales. Gordon owes me big time for all I'm going through for him. I step into the lobby area.

"Hi, Rhonda. Is Eric here?"

"Good afternoon, Mrs. Hayden. Yes, he's here. Go ahead and take a seat, and I'll let him know you're here."

"Thanks." She talks on the phone a few seconds while my hands get sweaty, and I walk toward the chairs.

I'm barely seated before Eric steps into the lobby.

"Maggie, how are you?"

"Great. Do you have a minute?"

"Always for my good friends."

"You still call us that after what I've put you through with the Nova?"

"Well, I've owed you all these years, you know. You did a favor for me by introducing me to my wife. You drop a car deal; I still call you friend. We're even." He laughs, but somehow I don't think he's teasing.

"Well, actually, that's why I'm here. Did you get my message?"

"No." He looks worried.

"Oh, well, I've decided I'd like the Nova after all."

His face sags, and my heart skips a beat. "What's wrong?"

"Someone else bought it, Maggie. I'm sorry."

"In just a couple of days?" I'm practically frantic here.

He shakes his head. "I'm sorry. That's the car business."

I sit there, stunned. Eric calls my name, asks me if I'm all right. I take a deep breath and lift the best smile I can muster under the circumstances. "I'm okay," I say, standing, "Thanks anyway, Eric." I reach out my hand to him.

He shakes it and apologizes again.

"Don't worry about it. It's my fault for trying to get the Mustang." I start to leave the room.

"I'll let you know if another Nova comes along, Maggie."

"Thanks." By now I'm wondering if Gordon would consider a cool bicycle.

24

I used to love Fridays because it meant more time with Gordon. Now I think I'm going to love them because of my job at The New Brew. It feels great to be needed again!

I'm learning that life is all about adjustments. Have I mentioned that? Not that I've conquered this whole thing yet, mind you, but I'm getting there.

After I shower, get dressed, make our bed, and straighten our room, I head down the hallway. It's about time for our mail, so I walk to the window and peek outside. The mailman's truck has just driven down the street. With something in her hand, Elvira crosses the street to the Nelsons' house. Bless her heart, always thinking of others. Just as I start to close the blinds, Elvira stops at the Nelsons' mailbox. She looks around as if doing something in secret. How odd. She takes whatever is in her hand and shoves it into their mailbox.

Probably has a card for them or something—though the envelope looked a little bulkier than that. She probably put some kind of trinket inside the envelope, along with words of encouragement.

"Well, that's just nice," I say to Crusher as I walk across the hardwood in our dining room. I grab my jacket. "I hope I'm that nice when I'm old."

Crusher looks at me as if to say, *You are old, and you're not that nice.*

I glower at him. "Oh, yeah? You're bald, skinny, and you have three teeth."

Wait. I'm getting mad at a dog that has merely looked at me. True, he could have been thinking those things, but I don't know that for sure.

Okay, I'm scaring myself.

I start to head outside when the phone rings. "Hello?"

"So what are you doing?" Lily's chipper voice says.

"Crusher is being mean to me," I say like a tattletale.

Lily gasps. "I just don't know what's gotten into that dog lately. He's ruthless, I tell you. Ruthless. What did he do this time?"

"He told me I was old, and I'm not nice."

"Honest, but ruthless."

"What?" I say, all aghast.

"I'm kidding."

I start to comment, but she cuts me off.

"I'm thinking a talking dog could bring in big money. Then we could travel the world—well, I guess we'd have to take Gordon along, but that's okay."

"That's nice of you." I play along. "Hmm, let's see, where shall we go?" It always amazes me how Lily and I entertain ourselves.

"Oh, I don't know, there's Hawaii, Bermuda, Caribbean cruises, Alaska—you want me to go on?"

I take the kitchen phone into the living room and sit on the sofa. Kicking off my shoes, I get comfortable. "I'm liking the sound of this so far. But where shall we go first?"

"The New Brew?"

"Wow! Now, there's an idea. Shall I start to pack now?"

"A couple of sweeteners, maybe a coffee stirrer or two wouldn't hurt."

"When are we going?"

"Would you believe tonight around seven o'clock?"

"Oh?" My interest is piqued.

"Harley will be there."

"Oh, Harley Biker Man will be there?" Now I am interested.

Lily gives a cautious laugh. "Listen, I'm giving you first dibs on our meeting, so you behave yourself. Although you knew I was meeting him tonight, I didn't have to let you know when and where, but that whole bush thing made me feel bad. I figure if you're that worried, I'll just let you meet these guys up front and get it over with."

"You know, you're smarter than you look," I tease.

"I like to think so."

"I start working there today, you know."

"Oh, I forgot. Then you might not want to go there tonight," Lily says, her voice sounding suspiciously hopeful.

"*Au contraire*, my dear friend. I wouldn't miss it."

Lily groans.

"So what do you think this guy looks like?" I probe. "I'm thinking sumo wrestler, long hair, chains, leather jacket?"

"No, no, his e-mails seem really—oh, I don't know—sweet. So I'm thinking big burly type who is nice to his mother."

I perk. "Do you think he still lives with her?"

"You just won't let that die, will you? Poor Walter."

"I think it's a real plus—that Walter still lives with his mother, I mean. You know they say you can tell how a man will treat his wife by the way he treats his mother."

"I don't *even* want to go there," Lily says, her voice as dry as forgotten toast.

"You're absolutely no fun at all."

"I know. Gotta run. My appointment is here. See you tonight at seven."

"Does it matter if I come alone? Gordon may still be at work."

"No problem. Just don't hide in the bush."

She clicks off. Lily's not going to let go of that whole bush deal—which isn't necessarily a bad thing. After all, now she's introducing me to these guys, saving me the trouble of sneaking around.

I have to think about what I was doing before she called. I look over and see my jacket beside me on the sofa. Oh yeah, the mail. I shrug into my jacket and head out the door. Rita Nelson is staring at her mail. She's probably discovered Elvira's note by now.

I start to turn, and Rita calls out to me. "Hey, Maggie."

"Hi, Rita."

She motions me over. I cross the street. "How are you all doing?"

"We're fine. We still don't know what Katie's problem is, but they're ruling out things. Rick has a small severance package. It won't last long, but at least it buys him a little time to find the next job. He's already been putting out résumés."

I nod and smile.

She looks at me with concern. "Are you feeling okay? Your face is sort of red, like you have a fever."

I touch my face. "Oh, I'm fine." So much for my trips to the tanning booth.

"We sure appreciate all the meals the neighbors have been bringing over. The kindness has meant as much to us as the food."

"We're glad we could help."

She looks at her mail. "Listen, I was wondering, have you seen anyone near our mailbox? I mean, I received an unmarked envelope, and it had to be delivered after the mail came or the mailman would have taken it. It's against the law to put things in the mailbox, you know."

"No, I didn't know."

"Anyway, I opened this envelope and it's stuffed full of twenty-dollar bills!"

I gulp. "You're kidding. As in *cash*?"

"The very same."

"Wow."

"My sentiments exactly."

Elvira. I can't snitch on Elvira. If she had wanted the Nelsons to know it was her, she would have told them. But I can't lie either. So I'll just have to avoid the question.

"I can't imagine someone giving us money like that."

"Pretty cool how God takes care of us, don't you think?"

Rita blinks, then smiles. "Yeah, it is."

I don't know what her relationship is with the Lord, but obviously, He's reaching out to this precious family in a real way through His people.

"Since there is no marking on the envelope, I wonder if the person or people who gave us this got us confused with someone else."

"I doubt it. Someone obviously cares very much for your family and wants to help you through this difficult time."

"The neighborhood didn't take up a collection, did they?"

"Not that I'm aware of," I say, though I'm feeling ashamed that we didn't think of that. Leave it to Elvira to handle everything. No wonder she doesn't buy new clothes.

Rita's face lights up. "Well, I guess I'll just take this in and show it to Terry. He won't believe it."

Without thinking, I reach over and give her a hug. "We're praying for Katie and for you and Terry," I say.

Tears fill her eyes. "Thank you, Maggie. It means more than you know."

We each go back into our own homes. Funny, I've rarely had a conversation with her since they've moved in. This concern is bringing neighbors together.

• • •

In no time at all, I have to get dressed and head off for my new job. Though it's not a huge corporate career move, I can't deny the excitement I feel driving toward the coffee shop. I think it's the idea of at least having something to do, a place to go where I'm depended upon, that makes the difference for me.

When I step into The New Brew, I'm not in my relaxed, journaling mode, but rather I'm a little nervous about learning how to make these drinks and waiting on customers. Adrenaline is at an all-time high.

"Hi, Maggie!" Tyler says. Her smile is huge, and her eyes sparkle. "Hey, are you tanning? You look good!"

My spirit lifts. "Yeah, I've tanned a little." Feeling *with it*, I stretch to my full height here and smile.

"I like it. Gives you a nice color."

My smile drops. "What? You don't like skin the color of muslin?"

Her eyebrows draw together.

"You know, the bland fabric?"

She still doesn't get it.

"Never mind."

She shrugs. "Why don't you, like, wash your hands in the bathroom, then come in here, and we'll start going over the drinks? Jade has to leave early to take a test for one of her classes."

I nod, wishing Jade could be around. Though I'm comfortable with all the kids, I just know Jade a little better. Pushing through the back room, I put my purse and things away where Tyler indicated and then head to the ladies room. I step inside just as Jade is pulling a blouse over her head. The sight of her skeletal frame leaves me speechless.

She pulls the oversized blouse the rest of the way over her head and looks at me. I'm certain the color has drained from my face.

"Oh, hi, Maggie," she says, obviously trying to ignore my shock.

"I have to go over to school and take a test, but Tyler will be here to train you for today. I'll be back to help tomorrow," she rambles on, stuffing her work clothes in a gym bag.

I step closer to her. "Listen, Jade, you're in trouble."

Her gaze meets mine, then quickly zips away. "I don't know what you mean. Hey, we'll have to talk later. I've got to scoot, or I'll be late for my test." She pushes out the door, leaving me gaping after her.

I have absolutely no idea what to do.

After Jade leaves, I walk blindly to my workstation behind the register. I'm taking the money, and Tyler will make the drinks, showing me how to do it as she goes along.

I hear the bell over the door, and it shakes me free from worrying about Jade. I look up to see my first customer.

It's Debra Stiffler.

I have to wonder if this is some kind of sick joke.

"Maggie?" She looks shocked to see me behind the counter.

"That's me," I say with a smile.

"You work here?"

"Just started."

"Your expensive tastes are catching up with you, huh?" She laughs.

Okay, do I need this my first day on the job? I'm thinking no.

"Well," she takes on the I'm-the-customer-you're-the-worker attitude. "I believe I'll have a decaf Americano."

"Whipped cream?" *Please, say yes.*

"No, thank you."

Of course not. That's why she's a size 6.

I take her money, and Tyler shows me how to make the Americano. I can hardly wait until my break. I plan on a mocha frappe with double the whipped cream . . .

• • •

After work I go home, take care of Crusher, down a sandwich, and get ready to meet Lily and Biker Man.

My brain had gone into freeze mode after I saw Jade's ribs poking out of her body. I knew she was thin, but I had no idea she was that thin. Has Jade's dad noticed her body lately?

I want to help Jade, but how? The books I read from the library told about different signs to watch for in girls who were suspected of anorexia. They also told of possible reasons that girls allow their bodies to get into that mess in the first place. But where can Jade get help around Charming, Indiana, for crying out loud? This isn't New York or California where they seem equipped to handle such things.

Well, this is definitely something I need to pray about because it is totally beyond my control. I send up a quick one, because I really don't have time to think about it now. Lily and Biker Man will be at the coffee shop any minute.

I grab my purse and head out the door. The night air is so brisk, I can see my breath as I make my way to the car. It's parked outside the garage since I wasn't going to be long. But of course I ended up taking longer than planned, and now I'm cold and wishing I had put it in the garage.

Hey! Mark it on the calendar, Maggie Hayden is *cold*!

The bell over the door jangles the moment I enter The New Brew, and I have no trouble whatsoever spotting Lily and Biker Man. He is everything I thought he would be and oh, so much more.

Stringy gray hair drapes around his shoulders and mingles with a long, unruly beard that has been left ungroomed since, oh, I don't know, maybe tenth grade? I'm thinking he's a frustrated guru or an over-the-hill remnant from the hippie culture. We're talking Alice Cooper meets Father Time here. Either way, I worry about that hair getting all tangled up in his motorcycle.

"Hello," I say to Lily as I approach the table.

She stands, and Biker Boy follows suit. My eyes dip to him as he is a head shorter. Tattoos cover arms the size of thick logs. I'm thinking the man bench presses cement trucks.

Oh, yes, this is Lily's soul mate. Uh-huh.

"Maggie, glad you made it." Her eyes implore me to stay. "This is Bi—," she stops herself from saying what I am sure was going to be Biker Boy and quickly inserts, "—Harley Jackson."

He shakes my hand heartily. "My name is really Howard, but with my love for cycles, my friends dubbed me Harley," he says with a laugh suspiciously similar to Gomer Pyle's. I'm telling you, being Lily's best friend is like taking a class on character study.

"Hello, Harley," I say, struggling with every fiber in me to behave as a mature adult.

"So, Lily here says you done got yourself a job in this here coffeehouse today." Though he doesn't say it, I can almost hear him add the word "Shazam" at the end of that sentence.

Stop it right now, Maggie.

I tell them a little about my experience of learning how to make new coffee drinks. Then Harley tells us that he lives down South but that he doesn't enjoy all that country-western music at all. I'm sure he's going to say something about preferring the heavy metal stuff, but he surprises me.

"I'm a Beach Boys fan, myself," he says, thumping back in his seat as if he'd just made a brilliant announcement.

Lily's eyes lock with mine. We dare not utter nary a word. Lily swallows hard. I see the lines on her neck move slightly.

"Harley, what do you do for a living?" I ask.

"This will probably surprise you," he says. I'm practically on the edge of my seat. "It's the very reason Lily's name caught my attention on e-mail. I own a floral shop."

A gasp lodges in my throat. The man looks like a sixty-year-old hippie, but he owns a floral shop and grooves to the Beach Boys?

"I've got to get coffee. I'll be right back," I blurt.

I'm just sure I hear Lily mutter "Chicken" as I leave, but I don't care. I can't risk sitting there another minute.

Once I get my coffee and feel I have regained my composure, I rejoin Lily and Harley. Before the evening is over, we have learned just about everything there is to know about good old Harley—and probably more than Lily wants to know. But I can see this is one date about which I won't have to worry.

Lily's eyes are glazed over, and she sags lower into her seat with every jangle of the door bell. She's all too agreeable to call it a night when I say I have to leave.

"Oh, I'll just pick up that dress tonight, Maggie, if it's okay, because I'll need it tomorrow," she says with wild eyes that pin me to my chair.

"Uh, oh, okay, that's fine."

She turns to Biker Man. "Harley, it was so nice to meet you. I thank you for taking the time to come here tonight."

We all scoot our chairs under the table and head for the door. Harley walks in between us, while Lily and I communicate nonverbally over his head. We step into the cool night air, and Harley climbs onto his, um, Harley.

"I'll have to take you for a ride sometime, Lily."

"Uh, yeah," she says, clearly having no intention whatsoever of getting on that bike with him.

He kickstarts his manly machine, and it's then that I notice he's wearing cowboy boots with three-inch heels. No wonder he's a biker man. It's kind of like that "Boy Named Sue" syndrome. A man has to do what a man has to do just to get a little respect these days. No doubt he's had a difficult childhood. Still, it's clear that Harley is an overcomer. He obviously lifts weights, wears tall shoes, and drives a motorcycle for a reason. Well, okay, that whole floral shop deal kind of throws everything off, but I'm thinking his mother was a florist.

Harley peels out of the parking lot like a junior high show-off, and I want to holler, "Citizens Arrest," with a Gomer Pyle twang, but I behave. When I turn to Lily, I'm thinking she is considering the same thing because we both burst into laughter.

"Have you learned anything at all about this whole Internet adventure, Lil?" I ask as we make our way to our cars. I'm almost certain she's going to say that her Internet dating days are over.

"Yes, I've learned there's a lot of 'different' people out there." She laughs.

"Ugh."

"What?"

"You just wear me out."

"Look, Mom, you don't have to get involved."

"Like I have a choice." I click my key remote, and the car door unlocks. "Just give me a chance to rest up before the next one, okay?"

"Monday."

Our eyes lock.

"My next date." She smiles sweetly and bats her eyelashes. Then, without so much as waiting for a response, she gets in her car, gives a happy little wave good-bye, and drives away while I stand gaping.

I might have to tell the man with the white beard and flying reindeers that she's forgotten that whole naughty-and-nice thing.

Call me a party pooper, but I am not happy about this.

25

The next week or so passes in a blur. I keep busy at the coffee shop, working more than my normal hours as I train and get a handle on things. It's great to be busy again, although hot coffee and hot flashes are not always fun together.

My conversations with Jade have been brief and purely professional. She avoids me at all costs. Maybe I should have Gordon contact her dad. I've called the counseling agencies in town for help with anorexia, but have come up dry. Maybe Rosetown has someone. I don't know where else to turn. Still, I keep praying.

"You take a break, Maggie," Tyler encourages, once the customer onslaught calms to a trickle. "You've been at it nonstop for the last hour and a half. Grab a mocha and, like, sit at one of the tables."

"You know, I never thought I'd see the day where I'd turn down a mocha, but after working around it all the time, it does kind of lose its appeal."

"I tried to tell you," Tyler says with a laugh.

"A frappe sounds pretty good, though." I wiggle my eyebrows and she laughs.

"I'll get you one. You go ahead and take a break."

"Thanks, Tyler." I turn to Jade. "You want to join me?" I ask, ever hopeful.

"Thanks, Maggie, but no, I need to study," she says.

Tyler and I share a knowing glance. Excuses. Always excuses. This girl needs help. She never eats anything, and she is definitely in the starvation mode. I know this is none of my business, but Jade is in trouble. Deep trouble. There must be something someone can do to help her.

Jade goes in the back room to study—or so she says—and I say nonchalantly to Tyler, "Do you know where Jade's dad works?"

She thinks a moment. "Let's see, I think he works at, like, Owen Corporation at the edge of town. Lately, his hours have been, like, cut back, so he should be home."

I don't say anymore. I don't really want to share with Tyler my concerns about Jade. I know Tyler cares about Jade and worries about her, but I don't think it's wise to talk with one employee about another.

Tyler sets to making my frappe, and I head to a table for a much-needed break. My legs ache from standing so long, and my shoulders are tense from worrying about Jade.

Settling into my chair, I stretch my legs. I look at the newspaper on the table for a little bit, but feeling too tired to read it for long, I shove it aside.

I get to go home in an hour. Hopefully, Gordon will be there when I arrive. I miss him. Seems we hardly see each other anymore. I wonder if he misses me. He has to remember me. I'm thinking my clothes in the closet might give him a clue.

"Here you go." Tyler places the frappe in front of me.

"Oh, that looks too good to drink," I say, admiring Tyler's chocolate creation."

"Enjoy." Tyler smiles and walks back toward the counter.

It seems I've tried every herbal supplement and medication known to mankind, but my hot flashes still come and go. My emotions continue to take me to extremes, and I'm wondering if I'll ever be normal again.

I'm not exactly winning the war on aging, either. I've tried every antiwrinkle remedy on the market, and nothing seems to help. I go to bed every night slathered up like a pie with whipped cream. Gordon can hardly give me a meaningful kiss without his lips sliding off my face.

We're a mess, Gordon and me. Between his snoring and me thrashing around in a blanket war, it's a wonder we get any sleep at all. And sleeping is all we're doing lately. Let's just say we ain't what we used to be, that's for sure.

I can still remember when we were a young family, sleeping peacefully through the night without any medicinal help whatsoever. We had a watch dog with a youthful bladder and a mouth full of teeth, and there were two kids who filled our home with laughter and constant commotion. Back then I couldn't hear myself think. Now, I hear every tick of our clock . . .

"Can I talk to you a minute?"

I look up to see Jade standing by my table. "Sure. Have a seat."

She licks her lips. Her hands are clasped and on the table in front of her. She stares at them. "I've not been very nice to you. I haven't been mean, I don't think, but, well, I'm sure you've noticed that I've ignored you."

"A little," I say, appreciating her bravery to talk to me at all.

"I'm sorry, Maggie. It's just that, well, I'm okay. I don't need another parent to freak out on me all the time."

I want to interject my concerns, but something tells me she needs to vent; she just needs someone to listen and not give her advice this time.

She looks up at me. "Can you understand that?"

"Yes," I say carefully, "but—"

Jade purses her lips.

"—if you had a friend you cared about very much, would you sit back and let her hurt herself, without ever trying to stop her?"

"I'm not hurting myself. I'm fine. I eat what I want. I'm just not that hungry. America way overeats, you know."

"I don't doubt that, Jade. But let's be honest here: you haven't overeaten since you were two." I attempt to keep things light, and Jade smiles. She gets my drift.

"I'm trying, I really am."

"Prove it."

She looks at me in surprise.

"Eat something in front of me." A stubborn spark flashes in her eyes. "Oh, you don't have to prove anything to me. I'm just someone who cares for you. You don't owe me anything. But if you really mean what you say—and I believe you do—then show me. Do it because you know I care about you, and you want to put my mind at ease."

"Listen, Maggie, I want to, but I ate just an hour ago."

"What did you eat?"

"I ate"—she hesitates like she's trying to think of something in a hurry—"a piece of pizza."

"What else?"

"A glass of pop."

"Anymore food?"

"No, but that was plenty."

When was the last time I sat down to pizza and ate only one piece? Try 1959. I was five.

"Okay, then tell me you'll let me take you to lunch tomorrow." I press.

"I have classes."

"Dinner?" I'm hoping Gordon is working late since I offered.

She hesitates. "All right."

I reach over and put my hand on hers. "Thank you," I say. She gives a halfhearted smile and walks away.

At least it's a start, right, God? Please show me how to help her.

• • •

As I dress for choir practice, my thoughts are filled with Lily. I've hardly seen her lately, and I'm hoping she'll be at church tonight. I glance in the mirror. Yes, we exchange occasional glances, the mirror and I, but no loitering is allowed, so I make it quick. After I'm satisfied with the clothes I've chosen for choir practice, I spray on some perfume.

Lily seems consumed with her latest Internet friend, and I'm feeling a little jealous. I know that sounds really weird at my age, but still. Between work and cars, Gordon's busy all the time, the kids are gone, and now Lily's unavailable. Crusher can fill the void only so long, and then I need breathing, walking human beings. Of course, I've been busy with the new job too. But still—where's the loyalty here, people?

I met Lily's latest date when they stopped in The New Brew, and he's the first normal guy in the bunch. Ron Albert. All right, I admit the fact that the man has two first names bugs me a little, but Gordon says I'm just looking for a reason not to like him. What does Gordon know?

Lily hasn't invited him to her house yet because she's still getting to know him; but she says he lives about an hour away, which is kind of scary. He can zip in and out as he pleases with no problem. And he's been around plenty. I'm glad Lily is still keeping this public, not revealing intimate details such as address and phone number, but I can tell she's about to cave. She likes this one.

One last spritz of hairspray and I turn away from the mirror. I can only handle so much.

Gordon says I have to let this whole dating thing with Lily go. After all, I can't control what she does; she's fifty.

With ten minutes to spare before I have to leave for church, I sit down on the sofa, turn on the television, and stare blindly at one station and then another.

Who am I kidding? I can't control anything in my life these days. If I could just fix one thing, I would feel encouraged, but I seem to be losing the battle on all fronts.

I'm beginning to wonder if Gordon will even remember our anniversary. He's been so busy at work. He's not talked much about Celine lately, which makes me feel better. On the other hand, I've seen him so little, we've hardly talked about anything. But I'm sure things will get better soon.

I've never approached Gordon about that note from Celine. I wanted to, especially on my insecure days, but Lily's wisdom prevailed. There comes a time when we have to learn to trust people, and I'm choosing to trust Gordon. Well, okay, I'm trying to trust him, anyway. It's that doggone nagging in the back of my mind that's driving me crazy. You know, the thought of him working with such a gorgeous woman and that a man can only stand so much temptation.

But then I remember that Celine is married too. She has a young husband, no doubt, so why would she be interested in my husband? It's a foolish notion. Hormones talking.

Nothing is on the TV, and it's time to go. I grab my purse and get in my car. As I back out of the garage, Elvira waves. A thought hits me. I pull over into her driveway, and she hobbles up to the car.

"Well, hello there, neighbor," she says, her dentures slightly askew. She clicks them back into place.

Bless her heart. "Elvira, I know you are faithful in prayer, and I wanted to ask you to pray for someone."

Her eyes light up like a birthday candle. A true prayer warrior. I smile. "I work with a young woman named Jade, and I'm concerned about her health. She's had some emotional turmoil in her life, and she just isn't eating right."

"Oh, dear. She's not anorexic, is she?"

Elvira's question shocks me to the core. Why, never in a million years would I imagine Elvira would be up on such things. She must see the question in my expression.

"I learned it all on Oprah here a little while back."

I smile and nod. Most likely we saw the same special.

She clicks her tongue. "It's nothing to take lightly, that's for sure. These poor kids nowadays sure carry a lot on their shoulders. It's a different world, I tell you." She looks in the distance. "Yes, indeed, a different world."

I would love to chat with her, but I need to get to choir practice and don't have the time to get into the world's woes. "If you could just add Jade to your prayer list, I would greatly appreciate it."

Elvira turns back to me and smiles. "I sure will, honey. I'll add you too."

I'm wondering why she says that. Do I look like I need prayer?

"I figure if you're working with her, you're going to need wisdom on how to handle things."

That woman is wise beyond her years, and we know how old she is.

"Thank you, Elvira. I really appreciate it."

She smiles. "Glad to do it, Maggie."

"Guess I'd better get to choir practice before I'm late," I say.

Elvira nods and waves.

I pull out of her driveway and feel great comfort in knowing Elvira's light will be burning tomorrow morning at four o'clock for Jade.

• • •

Choir practice goes all right, though I miss Lily and Gordon. I climb into my VW and start the engine and the heater. Winter's chill is definitely upon us. I wouldn't be surprised if it started to snow soon.

Try as I might, I just can't get used to going to church alone. Still, I've been doing that very thing for the past several weeks. Gordon is consumed with work, and I'm thinking we have to make some changes. When I pull the car into the garage, Gordon's car is there, and I decide we need to talk tonight. No amount of money is worth never seeing each other and him not being able to go to church with me. I feel like even if there is no competition with another woman—and I'm not totally convinced of that just yet—his job is certainly coming between us, and it's time we talked about it.

I grab my purse and get out of my car. Stepping into the house, I take a deep breath. I have no idea what to say. I don't want to argue. Gordon and I rarely have a disagreement. Of course, it's kind of hard to argue by yourself. And since he's never home . . .

Sounds from the television echo into the kitchen as I head toward the living room. Good. Gordon is up. This will be a good time. I stop in the kitchen long enough to drop my keys on the counter and then walk into the living room. I start to open my mouth and greet my husband, but when I look at him in his recliner, I see that his mouth is dropped open, and he is sound asleep. A snore escapes him and rattles our windows.

So much for meaningful talk tonight.

"Gordon." I shake his shoulder lightly. "Gordon, wake up."

It takes a few seconds but finally his eyelids flutter open and his mouth snaps shut. "What?" He looks disoriented for a moment; then his eyes focus on me. "Oh hi, Maggie. Must have fallen asleep," he says, rubbing his face.

"Yeah, I guess you did."

"How did choir practice go?" he asks as we make our way to the bedroom.

"It went fine. We missed you."

Gordon goes to his dresser and pulls out his pajamas. "Yeah, I know. Hopefully, things will calm down soon at work."

How many times is he going to say that? When will it happen? I want to talk to him. I need to talk to him. But the way his feet drag on the floor and the tired look in his face both tell me tonight is not a good time. Gordon goes into the bathroom and closes the door behind him.

The door looms before me, a huge barrier between us. It shuts off possible conversation. I can't see him. I can't talk to him. I feel Gordon has shut me from his life.

And I have never felt so lonely in all my life.

26

I muddle through the next couple of days, and by the time I get off work Saturday afternoon, I'm pretty beat. Still, knowing Gordon and I are going to dinner with Lily and Ron makes me feel better. We have met him only briefly, so this will be the first time we will actually have a chance to talk with him. Lily says she's proud of me because I haven't "stalked" them, though I still insist I don't stalk.

The truth of the matter is I've been too busy at work to do much of anything else. They've had a couple of people start and quit unexpectedly, which pretty much has left Jade, Tyler, and me to hold down the fort.

I still haven't talked with Jade's dad, and when I approach Jade about it, she says her dad has been busy. Doing what, I have no idea.

Of course, Gordon has been busy at work, so I still haven't had a chance to have that "talk" with him yet.

Why is everyone so busy these days? Sometimes I wish I were living in the fifties or sixties right now. People seemed to have more time for each other then. Might be that whole Ozzie and Harriett influence, I don't know. Now our television entertainment consists of sitcoms where young people laugh about bodily functions. And this is funny, why?

I pull into the garage, shut off the engine, and head for the house. Gordon isn't home yet. With him working so much and me losing my memory, it's a wonder I recognize him when he comes home at night.

The phone rings. "Hello?"

"Hey, babe. I'm going to be a little longer. I hate to do this, but would you mind driving to Rosetown tonight?"

"Oh Gordon, do I have to?" My voice has a nasal sound to it and definitely a whine. The very thing that husbands hate in a wife. I wish I could take it back.

"If it really bothers you, I'll come on home. I'm just putting the finishing touches on a document and wanted to finish it while it was fresh on my mind."

I suck in my grumpy retort. I'm competing with a legal document, and it is winning. How sad is that? "Never mind, Gordon, you go ahead and work. We can meet in Rosetown." I try to replace my whine with the right amount of cheer without sounding as though I'm forcing it. Though we both know that I am.

"You're the greatest, Maggie. See you all at Angus Steakhouse at six thirty." He clicks off.

Surely Gordon is doing the best he can. "A little understanding would be good here, right, Crusher?" I say, scooping wonder dog into my arms. I nuzzle him a moment and actually feel a little proud of myself for keeping positive in spite of my disappointment.

One glance in the mirror, and I frown at the wrinkle between my brows. Then I remember frowning is what put it there, so I smile at my reflection. The rut between my brows might have a fighting chance if I'd quit taking the Frownies off during my sleep. It's like my evil twin is working against me in the night.

After dressing, I head out to meet Lily, her date, and the man whose clothes hang in our bedroom closet. *Stay positive, Maggie.*

On my way to Rosetown, I pass the usual amount of Amish buggies. It's been a fairly warm day despite the approach of winter. Dreadfully exposed maple trees and large oaks huddle in distant forests attesting to winter's soon arrival. Fragmented leaves scatter here and there as evidence of autumn's departure.

Time passes so quickly.

I crack the window open, turn off the radio, and listen to the clip-clop of horses' hooves and the rattle of an approaching buggy. Burning wood scents the evening air, and smoke spirals from chimney tops. The soft glow of lamplight spills from Amish homes as dusk settles upon our town. Sometimes I get frustrated here, wanting more to do. But Gordon is right; I could never leave Charming. These sights and smells are home to me.

Charming is the one constant in my ever-changing world.

I consider going to Gordon's office, but I figure he's already headed toward the restaurant anyway. I wish we didn't have to drive separately. It hardly feels like a night out together when we have to do it this way.

By the time I arrive at the restaurant, the place is booming with business. I see Lily, her date, and Gordon walking toward the entrance together. They remind me of The Mod Squad. Well, sort of.

I sit in my car for a minute and mentally prepare myself to meet Lily's new date. I really need to stop worrying about her. I switch the news off my Christian radio station to a station that plays '70s music. Three Dog Night starts singing, "Mama Told Me Not to Come," and I have to wonder if it's a sign. At least I don't have to hide in the bushes tonight. I click off the station, grab my purse, and climb out of the car.

I'd like to catch up with them. I would yell their names, but I am trying to appear somewhat dignified, after all. Though Lily would laugh if I said so. Have I mentioned that Lily can be harsh at times?

Once I step inside, Gordon is the first to spot me. He walks over, gives me a kiss on the head, puts his arm around me, and guides me toward the others. "Sorry you had to drive, Maggie," he whispers in my ear.

"Hey, Maggie," Lily says, her face all rosy, her eyes sparkly. She has a goofy smile on her face. I haven't seen that look in a very long time. She's definitely smitten.

Ron extends his hand. "Good to see you again, Maggie." He's got that same goofy look. I wonder if I'm losing my friend.

We exchange greetings and share a little small talk while we wait on our table. Once we're finally seated in our places, we give our orders and settle in for a friendly evening together.

I watch the way Ron and Lily interact, and I have to admit it's nice to see Lily happy again. And she is happy. I can tell—not only by the look on her face, but in the way she moves her hands, how she laughs, her voice, everything. I'm watching them with interest when a thought hits me like a two-by-four. She'll probably have to move when they get married. He lives in Indiana somewhere, an hour away. And to think I worried about moving here to Rosetown twelve miles away. What will I do? How will I survive?

I'm losing my best friend.

"Maggie, did you hear me?" Lily says.

Everyone is staring at me. "I'm sorry?"

"I said, 'Are you doing all right?'"

"Sure, I'm fine."

Gordon scoots closer to me, putting his arm around me over the back of the booth. "You seem a little preoccupied. Is everything okay?"

"Yes. Why does everyone keep asking me that?"

"Just wondering, Maggie."

His kindness makes me feel badly. I didn't mean to sound so harsh. I give myself a pep talk and force myself to get into this conversation.

Lily has made it a point to bring us all together, so obviously, it's important to her that we like the man with two first names.

"So Ron, tell us about yourself," I say. He and Gordon share a glance. What's up with that? It's as if they share a little joke or something. But of course that's ridiculous because Gordon has hardly spent any time with this man. Lily throws me a look that says she knows exactly what I'm up to. So everyone at the table is aware that I'm digging for information. What do I care? Still, I dig.

"Well, I'm a financial advisor. Sold my business a year ago, and I now work as a consultant from my home. I also have a business on the side."

My eyebrows hike. "Oh? What kind of business?"

"I sell herbal supplements."

My gaze collides with Lily's. She smiles. I hear the bridal march in the distance.

I sigh. Well, at least if they get married, they'll never be sick. Sounds like he might have a little money, too, so he can take care of Lily. He's obviously not after her money. No, wait. He could have lost his business and "working out of his home" could be his pretense for having a job.

I want to ask him where he lives in Indiana, but I'm afraid that will lead to him asking Lily where she lives, and I don't want to endanger her.

"Do you live alone?" I ask.

Gordon's knee nudges me underneath the table.

Lily's eyes get expressive. Think Janet Leigh, shower scene, in *Psycho*.

"Uh, yes," Ron answers.

"Oh, I didn't mean anything by that," I say, flipping out the end of my napkin and laying it on my lap. "I just wondered if you lived with your mother or anything." I stop smoothing the linen and look up.

Okay, here Lily's expression turns dark. Think Anthony Perkins, aka psycho man, in the same movie.

Ron lifts a good-natured smile. "I haven't lived with Mom since I left for college," he says with a wink at Lily.

A wink? They're at the winking stage already? I mentally calculate how long they've been dating, and, to me, it just doesn't add up to the winking stage. I think he's moving too fast. She'd better be careful.

Gordon talks to Ron a bit about his job, and Lily shoots fierce glances my way. As I said, harsh. I try to be nice, and what do I get? Heartache.

Ron is not bad to look at, really. All right, so he does remind me of Captain Kangaroo, but then that's just me. Besides, who didn't love that man? At least he's not Mr. Green Jeans. I could not have handled Lily dating Mr. Green Jeans. I have my limits.

We enjoy a great meal over friendly chatter. In fact, we have such fun, we carry the party over to The New Brew. Good thing I don't get tired of that place.

We arrive at the coffeehouse about the same time. Lily gets to the door first, with Ron right behind her. He quickly steps forward to open the door for her. I like that. He treats my friend well. That's a good sign.

I get to the door, with Gordon right on my heels. Approaching it with confidence, I plow ahead, sure that my man will open it for me as is his custom. I stop short of falling through the glass. In a huff, I turn to see why Gordon hasn't opened the door for me and see that he's fidgeting with the zipper on his jacket. I guess that's what you get after thirty years. He looks up.

"Oh, sorry, honey. It got stuck," he says, pointing to the offensive zipper. He reaches over and opens the door. Somehow the gesture has lost its charm.

Despite Gordon's *faux pas*, we have a pleasant evening and learn a great deal about Ron with two first names, and, okay, I like him. Well, as much as I could like anyone who threatens to take away my best friend.

We finally say our good-byes and head to our cars. I watch as Ron walks Lily over to her car and opens the door for her.

This time, Gordon does the same for me.

"Do you like him?" Gordon asks.

"Yeah, I do. Do you like him?"

"He's a great guy. I think he's good for Lily." Gordon looks kind of ashen.

"Are you feeling okay?" I ask.

"Hey, you got mad at me for asking you that."

"This is different. You're pale."

His hand reaches for his face. "Uh, Maggie, when we get home, I need to talk to you about something, okay?"

My heart drops to my toes. Fear grips my throat. "You want to tell me here?"

He looks around. "No, I think this would be best at home, okay?"

"All right." With all the grace of Ma Kettle, I fumble into my car, fearing the worst.

"I'll follow you," he says.

I nod, saying nothing. The ten-minute drive home seems more like three hours. My throat is so dry, it feels wooden. He's going to give me "the speech." I know he is. He's going to tell me he's tried to fight this thing between him and Celine—or him and Debra or him and Sparkle Toes—but he can do it no longer. He's in love with someone else, and he's leaving me.

I'm not only losing Lily, but also I'm losing Gordon.

I've tried so hard to make myself more presentable. I've spent too much money on cosmetics, endless hours exercising—well, maybe not hours, but certainly minutes. I've tried new shampoos, clothes, everything I can think of to improve my image. But let's face it, I'm limited by what I've got to work with here.

Still, have I changed that drastically from the day we got married? I mean, Gordon is older, too, but I still love him. Now I see why he's been so nice to me, so loving to me—the whole bit. He wants to let me down gently. Say what you will about Gordon; one thing he is, he's compassionate. He will not intentionally hurt someone. Probably knowing his love was changing, he was preparing me for this day.

Try as I might, I can't stop the tears from falling. I've lost the love of my life.

Gordon Hayden doesn't love me anymore.

My kids are gone, and my husband will be gone. I have nothing left. Buggies pass me in the night, and I don't bother to lower my window. The sound will not soothe me tonight. I cannot be soothed. I hurt all over. A deep pain, the kind that takes your breath away. My lungs refuse to work. My throat feels like it's closing. My heart feels deflated, as though all the love has been squeezed from it.

Once I pull into the garage, I've managed to dry my face, but there's nothing I can do about my red, puffy eyes. I avoid Gordon at first. Maybe if I get him sidetracked, he'll forget about this nonsense, and we'll go on as if nothing has ever happened.

Don't leave me, Gordon. Please, don't leave me. I love you with every fiber in me. If you leave me, my heart will shrivel.

"I'll take care of Crusher," I call over my shoulder as Gordon stumbles in through the back door.

"Okay."

I hear him stop at the kitchen sink and pour himself a glass of water. His throat is dry too. He's probably wondering how he will break this to me. Gordon can't stand to see me cry. No doubt, right this minute he's mentally going over how he can say what he has to say without me losing it.

How can he do this to me? How can one woman do this to another woman? Crusher comes back in the house and I unlatch his leash. The moment of truth has come.

Quickly, I slip into the bedroom and retouch my makeup. I will not look like an old hag when he tells me he's leaving me for another woman. I will not collapse into a heap of tears. With the Lord's help, I will be strong—at least until Gordon is gone. I wonder if he'll leave tonight or wait until morning.

He won't wait. He'll leave tonight so he won't prolong my agony. With any luck he'll come into the bedroom, put on his pajamas, and show me I'm wrong. But instead he stays in the living room.

"Maggie?" his voice calls out. "Can you come here, please?"

A glance in the mirror. "I could use your help tonight. Tell me I'm okay, just this once?" One look at the red eyes and puffy lids tells me all I need to know.

I suck in my breath and head out the door to an unknown future. A future that could rock my world forever.

27

The living room feels cold. Shadows streak across the walls, and I stop to turn on another light. The hall clock ticks away the minutes of happiness I have left. Crusher watches me walk across the room as if he knows what's going on.

One glance at Gordon confirms my greatest fears. His expression tells me he doesn't want to do this, but he has no other choice.

I have a yucky taste in my mouth. It's the same taste I had when I found out Lily's husband died.

"Please, Maggie, sit down," he says, pointing to the sofa.

He sits on the edge of his chair and stares at his fingers clasped in front of him. "First off, I want to apologize for what I have to tell you. I should not have kept it from you. It was wrong."

I swallow hard past the growing lump in my throat. "I'm listening," I whisper, without looking up.

Gordon rises from his chair and comes over to the sofa to sit beside me. I wish he wouldn't do that. His Tommy scent fills my senses. The smell of his clothes and the touch of his warm hand upon my own, and I think the next few minutes will suck the very life from me.

"Maggie, please don't get mad at me," he begins.

Oh, right. I won't get mad. Turn my world upside down; I have no problem with that. I'll make it easy on you.

"I know I should have told you, but knowing how protective you are of Lily, I figured you would put your foot down and tell me not to do this, but I just knew it was right, you know?"

Wait. Lily? Did he say Lily? What does she have to do with this? Did she know all this time about Celine and not tell me? She tried to encourage me. Why would she do that if she knew Gordon and Celine were—

"Maggie, are you listening to me?"

I still refuse to look at him. I nod.

"No doubt you and Lily both are going to be plenty mad when I tell you this, but doggone it, Maggie, I think it's better for everyone involved."

What is he babbling about? What does Lily have to do with this? Would she be mad because she doesn't know about Gordon and Celine? I can't stand it any longer. I look at him.

He sees my face, my eyes. "Uh-oh, do you already know?" He squeezes my hand. Before I can answer, he continues. "I didn't mean to upset you, Maggie. Our firm handled Ron's wife's estate when she died four years ago. He's a great guy. I thought if I had him join that dating service he could meet Lily and choose whether he wanted to pursue this relationship or not. I knew they were perfect for each other. I could see their personality types blending well together. And that's what those dating services are all about. I knew if they were matched, it was meant to be, and I could vouch for what a great guy he is. I wasn't sure how you would feel about me trying to get them together because, well, I know you're afraid of losing Lily. But I also know you love her enough to let her go."

I blink. What did he just say? Did he say what I just think he said? I start to cry. I mean, *really* cry.

"Aw, Maggie, now I've really upset you," he says.

I shake my head furiously. "You wanted to tell me that you actually set this up with Ron and Lily by having Ron go to the Internet dating site where Lily is meeting these guys? *That's* what you wanted to tell me?"

Gordon looks uncertain whether he should answer. "Y-Yeah."

"Oh, Gordon!" I should strangle him, but instead I throw my arms around him and shove into him so hard that he falls sideways, and we both spill onto the floor in a heap.

"Maggie, are you okay?" he asks, totally clueless as to what's going on.

"I'm great, Gordon. I'm doing just great."

"Then you're not mad at me?"

"Mad at you?" I kiss his cheeks, his forehead, and his lips. "No, I'm not mad at you, Gordon Hayden. I love you fiercely; do you know that?" I kiss him again. "I love you." Another kiss. "I love you." One more. "I love you."

His glasses are cockeyed, and his hair is all crumpled. He looks a mess, and I've never seen him look more wonderful in all our days together.

"Maggie, are you all right?"

"I'm delirious, but I'm fine," I say, my energy and emotions fully spent.

Then, as if the thought hits him that all is forgiven and everything is okay, he pulls me back into his arms and stops me right in front of his face. "Maggie Hayden, you're a wonder. I never know what life will be like with you from one day to the next, but I wouldn't have it any other way."

He kisses me full on the lips, and all at once my world is right again. We head for the bedroom, and I decide to keep my fears and suspicions to myself. After all, we have better things to do.

• • •

Monday morning, once I'm dressed and ready to start my day, I make plans to go shopping. It's my day off, and I haven't treated myself in a while. I've been setting aside money for Gordon's car, even though I haven't found one for him yet, but I've saved a nice sum so far.

I look at my vintage jewelry collection. I've been collecting old pins and necklaces from flea markets for years. I'm quite proud of my collection, but as I pick a silver pin that resembles the shape of the sun, I'm wondering if these pins make me look too old. I noticed vintage jewelry sells well on eBay. It seems to be all the rage these days—though I thought of it first—but somehow it just doesn't do it for me this morning. I put the pin back in its place. Maybe another time.

Once I'm ready to go, I stop long enough to eat a bowl of cereal. While pouring my flakes into the bowl, I notice Elvira putting something in her mailbox when it dawns on me that maybe she would like to go shopping with me. I go to my back door, walk around the side, and call her name loud enough for her to hear just before she slips back into her house.

Surprised, she turns around. "Yes, Maggie?"

"I'm going to do a little clothes shopping this morning, and I wondered if you would like to go with me?" I feel a little silly now that I've asked her. She probably isn't into shopping and would just as soon stay home.

She brightens. "Well, wouldn't that be nice," she says loud enough for the neighborhood to hear.

"Great! You get ready, and I'll swing by, say, in ten minutes and pick you up. Will that be all right?"

"Sure, I'll be ready," she says, kicking her knee in the air and snapping her fingers like an excited old-timer. We laugh together.

I'm feeling a little more lighthearted today. It feels good. Seems my thoughts have grown so heavy lately, I can use a light day now and then.

After eating my cereal, I head over to Elvira's house. I walk up to the door to get her, and she's ready to go. She turns to lock her door, then heads toward the car. Her purse resembles a small suitcase rather than a handbag, but to each her own. I'm afraid to ask what she's storing in there, so I don't.

"How's Katie Nelson doing? Do you know, Elvira?" Of course, she does. Elvira knows everything.

"Don't you know that girl is doing wonderful?"

I'm shocked. "Really?"

"Yes, ma'am. They never did find anything wrong with her, so they chalked it up to some kind of viral infection. They always call it that when they can't put a name on it. I know the Lord's been working, though, and they can't convince me otherwise."

I smile and nod. My heart warms to Elvira. Such a godly woman, so sincere and loving. Funny, I hadn't noticed all that before. I couldn't seem to get past her physical attributes, or lack thereof. But she seems different to me now, somehow. It's interesting to know she hasn't changed since I've known her, so I can only assume one thing.

I must be changing.

"Glory be!" As Grandma would say, "Strike up the band, and shout it from the rooftops, there's hope for that girl yet." Grandma would tease me and say that when I'd come out of a headstrong situation and surrender my rebellious spirit. I miss Grandma.

"That is great news," I say, offering a prayer of thankfulness for Katie's recovery.

"Any news about Jade?" Elvira asks.

I'd forgotten I had asked her to pray, but she certainly hasn't forgotten.

"She's pretty much the same. Gordon and I have been trying to reach her dad, but he's never home. I don't know if he's too busy to call us, or if Jade isn't delivering the messages. I've considered calling him at work, but just haven't wanted to bother him there."

Elvira rubs her jaw. "You might have to take matters into your own hands."

"How's that?"

"You might *have* to call him at work."

That was a last resort for me, but I'm thinking Elvira's right. That's what I need to do to make sure Jade isn't intercepting the phone calls. I make a mental note to check into that.

Shortly thereafter, we arrive at the shopping center and commence to some serious shopping. I find a cute pair of black pants with an elastic waist and a matching top and show it to Elvira. "Try this on."

"Oh, posh," she says with a wave of her hands. "I wouldn't look good in that get-up. I'm better off in my housedress."

"But would you try it on for me? Just for fun?" I encourage.

She wavers. I can tell she could go either way on this, so I press further, encouraging her to do it, appealing to her friendship side, and she finally concedes.

When she steps out of the dressing room, I am so totally unprepared for what I see that I almost fall off my shoes. It reminds me of when Patty Campbell wore clogs at our high-school graduation and clunked across the stage before falling off of them on her way down the steps.

"Why, Elvira, you look positively beautiful."

"Oh, go on," she says, waving her hand dramatically.

It's obvious she likes the clothes, though she's trying not to. We discuss the wisdom of such a purchase, and she goes back in to change. I've already made up my mind to buy them for her. I want to contribute to the "new" Elvira. I look around the area for a matching purse and shoes. She'll choose, of course, but I can at least make some suggestions.

"Well, I must say that was fun," Elvira says, straightening her hair.

I take the clothes from her and put them in the cart.

"Oh, I'm not going to buy those, Maggie. I have perfectly fine dresses to wear around the house. Besides, there's nobody to see me in them anyways." There's something sad in the way she says that. It causes my heart to constrict.

"Well, I'm going to get these for you, Elvira." Her eyes widen, and she puts her hands on her hips. "And I'll tell you right now before you get all stirred up, it's not right for you to deny me a blessing when you are blessed all over the place for the good that you do."

My comment takes the fight right out of her. She stares at me and swallows her words. I can almost hear her thoughts rattle about in her head as she tries to figure a way out of this.

I smile and push the cart forward, not looking back at her.

We soon head for home. By that time Elvira has a new pair of glasses that I bought at the pharmacy. They're cheap, but they help her see better—which should improve that whole lipstick thing—and that's what matters. She has a new pant suit, purse, and pair of shoes. We had a wonderful time.

After saying our good-byes, I pull the car into the garage. It's only after I grab my purse that I realize I don't have any packages to take inside. I'd only bought for Elvira today, and it felt wonderful.

My heart couldn't feel any better.

• • •

After putting the baked chicken in the oven, I head for the sofa to rest a moment. I'm pretty tired from shopping all morning, and I spent the afternoon cleaning the house. I lay my head back on the sofa and close my eyes. Just then the phone rings. Crusher yips wildly—probably the most excitement he's had all day. Relaxing in the quiet, the loud jangle causes my heart to race like a woman on a treadmill.

"Hello?"

"Hi, Mom!"

"Heather, honey, how are you?"

"I'm doing great. Listen, Mom, I won't keep you because I know you're fixing dinner right about now, but I just wanted to thank you and Dad for understanding about the Thanksgiving thing."

My stomach clenches. "The Thanksgiving thing?"

"Didn't Dad tell you? We were planning to have Thanksgiving with Josh's family this year? I called to make sure you were okay with that, and Dad said it was fine. Josh's extended family, including cousins he hasn't seen in a couple of years, will be here, and Josh really wanted to see them." She hesitates. "Do you mind?"

Of course I mind, I want to shout, but how selfish would that be? I'm an adult, and I have to learn to share. I should have already had that lesson down.

"Oh, honey, that's just fine," I say through clenched teeth. Gordon could have at least warned me. "We can see you at Christmas?" I'm trying very hard not to make it sound like we *will* see you at Christmas—as in a controlling manner—but that we are hopeful.

"Oh, sure. We'll be home. Thanks for understanding about this, Mom. You're the greatest," she says with obvious relief. "Well, I have to go. Give my love to Dad."

I stare at the phone. I'm thinking that phone call cost me some wrinkles. I get up from the sofa and run into the bedroom to slather on cream. I'll tackle the gray hairs in the next washing. I can get through this. True, it's our first Thanksgiving, actually, our first holiday, without Heather, but we still have Nick.

I wonder if Nick is even aware that Thanksgiving is coming up.

28

If I were a car, I'd be showing rust right about now. Hey, but at least my engine's still working.

This is only the middle of the week, but for some reason it feels like I've put in a full week already.

I go to the back of the coffee shop and gather my things so I can leave. There are a couple of hours yet before choir practice—for me anyway. I doubt Gordon is going. He tells me this Keller estate he's working on is coming to an end soon. I'll believe it when I see it.

After I retrieve my purse and coat, I turn to leave.

"Maggie, can I talk to you a minute?" Jade's eyes are red and swollen, but that's the only color in her face. She looks pale, almost gaunt.

"Sure, Jade. What's up?" I sag into a chair and put my purse beside me on the floor.

She sits across from me and, with glazed eyes, stares at my purse. "I don't know if I told you about my friend who has the same problem as me, you know, with the eating and everything?"

Good, she finally admits there's a problem. I shake my head, "I don't think you did."

"Well, she, uh, she—" Jade drops her face in her hands and starts crying. I get up and go over to her. Scrunching down beside her, I put my arm on her back.

"Jade, what is it?"

She waits a moment to regain her composure. "She got sick, awful sick this week. She's in the hospital. They told her if she didn't start eating right again, she could die. Her heart could give out." Tears trickle down her cheeks. "I just had no idea. I mean, I thought—" she says as she raises her hands. "I don't know what I thought."

"Well, honey, the important thing is that you see the problem now. What are they going to do for your friend?"

"They're hooking her up with a counselor, a nutritionist kind of person."

"Is there someone in town?"

"I think this lady is over in Rosetown."

"I see."

"I don't know how to eat right anymore. I've done this too long. When I try to eat anything, I get sick." Jade looks at me. "I don't want to die, Maggie." Tears fill her eyes again. I squeeze her close to me.

"I'll get you help, Jade."

"But Dad doesn't have the money to help me. I don't think his insurance would cover this."

"There are ways, Jade. God will make a way. He loves you, and I love you. He'll show us what to do."

"I don't know why He would help me. I've never done anything for Him."

"He loves you, period. We all mess up, but still He loves us. His love is unconditional."

She cries some more. We talk about the mercy and love of God reaching out to us in our unworthiness. I can see He is working in her heart.

"I'd better go wash my face," Jade says, turning to leave. She looks to me once more. "I'm so thankful you came here." Before I can respond, she walks out of the room.

I stare after her. Tyler still hasn't picked a replacement for me. Maybe the Lord could use me right here at The New Brew. I feel sort of like a frat mom, helping direct the kids along the way. Why not? If the Lord wants to use me in a place where I get free coffee, who am I to complain?

On the way to my car, I pray God will show me where He wants me to serve, and I pray that He will grow the seed planted in Jade's heart and give me wisdom to know how to help her.

I start the engine. And to think when I first met Jade I had assumed her biggest problem was not having a date for a Saturday night.

• • •

I grab a quick sandwich when I get home. There's not enough time to make a decent meal before choir practice. It feels like someone is inside my head pounding to get out. I swallow two migraine pain reliever tablets and sit on the sofa to rest a moment. The phone rings, and I answer.

"Hey, Mom. What's up?"

My heart warms at the sound of our son's voice. Just hearing from him lifts my spirits.

"Not much. How are you doing?"

He tells me how classes are going, how the basketball team is doing, and the latest college news.

"So, are you still seeing Melody?" I ask, figuring his latest crush is long since gone by now.

"Well, that's the reason I called—"

My heart freezes in place. "Time to schedule the restaurant for the rehearsal dinner?" I ask in a teasing voice, though I'm half-afraid to hear his answer.

"Not there yet, no."

I relax.

"But she wanted to know if I could come home with her for Thanksgiving and meet her family. Dad said it was okay, but I wanted to make sure you wouldn't freak out or anything."

Oh sure, Gordon, make me look like the selfish parent. Do you want to have Thanksgiving without Nick and Heather? Meet the family? This must be getting serious.

"You like her that much, Nick?"

He hesitates. "Yeah, Mom, I really do."

"Then it's time you brought her home so we can meet her too."

"Yeah, I know. I plan to do that at Christmas break, if that's all right with you and Dad."

This *is* serious. He's got my attention.

"So, what do you think, will it be okay if I go there for Thanksgiving?"

Nick is nineteen years old. Most guys his age are doing pretty much what they want without worrying about what their parents think or say. I am touched by Nick's thoughtfulness. Pushing my own wishes aside, I answer him. "Of course it's okay, honey. If that's what you want to do."

"Thanks, Mom."

"Just as long as we get you next year," I quickly add.

"You got it."

We talk a while longer about Melody, and then we hang up. My head is really pounding now. Looks like I'll have to skip choir practice. I go to our bedroom and lie down for a short nap.

• • •

The alarm wakes me from my deep sleep. I glance at the clock. It's six o'clock . . . in the morning. Gordon is already up. I must have slept through the first alarm. Sitting up in bed, I rub my eyes. At least my headache is gone.

"Good morning, sleepyhead," Gordon says when he steps into the room.

"I'm sorry I slept so long. I had a bad headache and just planned to take a quick nap last night."

"I know. I saw the pain reliever on the counter. You're sure these headaches are hormone-related?"

"Yeah, the doctor said so." I pull off the covers and prepare for my day while Gordon gets our coffee.

Once I shower and dress, I join him in the living room. "Heather and Nick called last night," I say, settling onto the sofa.

"Oh?"

I tell him about my conversations, and Gordon listens intently. "I hope you don't mind, Maggie, but they are grown up now, and we have to let them go. You okay with that?"

I look at him. "Like I have a choice?"

"Good point."

"We'll still have Elvira over for Thanksgiving." Elvira and her husband have celebrated Thanksgiving with us for as long as we've all lived here.

"Well, we'll make the most of it. I suppose this is just the way it gets once the kids are grown. We no longer have them to ourselves," Gordon says, taking a sip of coffee.

"I guess."

"Well, I've got to get to work," Gordon announces. He reads a short devotional and says a quick prayer. Fast-food mentality is what I call it. Life seems to squeeze even God from our busy days.

Gordon kisses me good-bye, then disappears behind the door.

"Another day, another dollar, huh, Crusher?" I turn to make my way back to the kitchen, rinse out my coffee mug, and dry my hands. I walk into the bedroom and straighten things. Gordon left his suit coat on the back of the chair, so I hang it up. I notice some papers in the inside pocket and figure I'll put those on his dresser, in case he needs them and forgets where he put them—which, I might add, happens from time to time.

I pull out a couple of bank receipts and a note. Memories of the note from Celine makes my stomach knot, and I open the paper. It reads, "Burnette." I shrug. It must be a client's name or something. I put everything on his dresser.

The phone rings.

"Maggie, this is Eric. You won't believe this, but the Nova is for sale once again."

"You are kidding me. Is something wrong with it?"

"No, the buyer just ran into some financial problems, so here we go again." He laughs. Eric's so easygoing about things. I don't know how he does it.

"Don't you dare let it get away. I'll be there in five minutes, and I want to bring it home with me. I've been saving my money, and I'll finance the rest."

He laughs. "Good girl. Glad it's working out for you. Tell you what, I've got a few minutes to spare. I'll come pick you up and bring you here so you can drive the Nova home."

"Sounds great! Thanks, Eric."

As soon as Eric shows up, I rush out the door. We no sooner get to his lot than I shove my money his way and grab the keys to the Nova before he can change his mind. I move the Corvair to a nearby neighbor's house so it won't spoil the surprise, and I park the Nova in Gordon's work space and close the door. I'll figure out how to handle it later.

Right now, I have to get to the senior water-aerobics class in Rosetown that I saw advertised in the paper. I figure I'm so newly senior—Is fifty really a senior?—that I am bound to look pretty good against my other, uh, classmates.

After arriving in Rosetown, I drive into a store parking lot to read through the directions once more that I had pulled off the Internet. Once the route is fixed in my mind, I ease back into traffic. Further down the road, I get stopped by a red light. A fairly busy intersection, I look around at the various businesses. The light turns green just as I spot a large white sign in front of a brown brick building. The sign reads "Burnette Travel Agency."

Might be the same Burnette from Gordon's note. It wouldn't surprise me to find that he represents the travel agency. He has built up quite a list of clientele in his many years at the law firm. He's well respected in the community.

Arriving at the YWCA shortly afterwards, I have little time to dwell on the matter. Much to my dismay, I find that I have the wrong time for the water-aerobics class. It doesn't start for another two hours. I decide to drive over to Gordon's office, pop in, and say hello. Then I'll come back to the class.

"Hi, Emma," I say, upon entering the reception area of Yates, Comstock & Hayden.

A wide smile brightens her face. "Hi, Mrs. Hayden. He's free if you want to go on in."

"Thanks." I round the corner and walk down the narrow hallway to Gordon's office. His office is on the right, just ahead of me. His door is closed, but the top half is glass, and when I peek in, I see the back of Celine. Gordon's face is down, so he hasn't noticed me. I jerk back from their view and wait for them to finish whatever it is they're doing.

The door opens, and I hear Gordon's voice. "Did you order the plane tickets from Burnette's Travel Agency?"

"Yes, I did." I can see Celine's lips curved up on the end. "What a wonderful trip that will be. I can hardly wait—"

"Well, Maggie Hayden, how are you?" Roger Yates's booming voice is loud enough for everyone in the building to hear.

"Hi, Roger."

He talks to me for a minute about his wife and children, but my mind is swirling from Gordon's discussion with Celine..

She turns to me. "Hi, Margaret. You can go on in."

Why, thank you so much for your permission, I want to snap, but I don't. *Stay calm, Maggie. Stay calm.*

"Well, nice talking with you, Maggie. You take care." Roger trudges on down the hallway.

"Hey, babe. What brings you to Rosetown?" Gordon looks uncomfortable, caught in the act. I just know it. He stands up, walks over to the door, and closes it. Then he turns and gives me a peck on the cheek.

"So, what are you doing here?" he asks.

"So, where are you going?" I retort.

He looks up, acting puzzled. "What do you mean?"

"I heard you talk about airline tickets. You going somewhere?"

"Oh, that." He seems to stall for a little time here. "Well, actually, I do need to talk to you about that." He proceeds to tell me about a business trip he just found out that he has to take over Thanksgiving weekend.

Life just keeps getting better.

I have my arms folded across my chest, my lips are pursed, and I am downright mad.

"Now, before you get too upset, Maggie, just let me tell you things aren't as bad as they seem. I—"

"Is she going?"

He blinks. "What?"

"I want to know if she's going." I nod my head toward the door.

"Celine?"

"Yes." I tap my toe on the floor.

"Why, no, she's not going."

"Who, then?"

"What are you talking about?"

I don't care if I'm sounding like a jealous wife, because I am one. "I distinctly heard you ask her if she ordered the tickets, as in plural. More than one."

He looks as though a judge has just cited him for contempt.

Celine walks in. I'm facing her as she stands in front of the door. Gordon is behind me.

"How many tickets did you order for Gordon, Celine? Airline tickets?" I ask sweetly so she will have no clue why I'm asking.

"Tickets?" Her eyes are wide as she fidgets with the file in her hand.

"Yes, for the trip Gordon just asked you about."

"Oh, that." She smiles, her gaze flitting past me to Gordon. I see his reflection through the glass in the door. He's holding up one finger.

"I ordered one."

Something is definitely wrong here.

Without saying another word, she places a file on his desk and leaves the room. I turn to Gordon, who simply smiles, walks back to his chair, and sits down.

"You haven't explained why you have to go over Thanksgiving weekend." There is no way he's getting off the hook this time.

"It's a personal injury case on which I've been working. I'm co-counsel with a couple of Florida attorneys for the defendants. I represent Casper Trucking from here in Rosetown. Trial starts the following week. Florida counsel wanted to meet with insurance representatives on the weekend to finalize things before trial. I figured it would be okay if I promise to make it up to you. And I will, you know."

"Whatever. I have to go."

"Maggie, I'm really sorry to disappoint you, honey."

I turn to him. I can almost feel smoke coming from my ears. "And you told the kids it was okay not to come home, not once thinking about the fact I would be home alone over Thanksgiving weekend." I choke back my tears. I want to be mad, not sad.

Gordon gets up, his face full of concern.

I don't want to see that, not now. I back away.

"Listen honey, I can't explain it all right now, but—"

"It doesn't matter. I have to go." I spin around and head out the door before I lose my resolve not to cry.

29

I need answers, but all I have is an ache in my heart.

What are Gordon and Celine hiding from me?

With a heavy weight in my chest, I enter the pool area where I see five senior women wearing swim caps—complete with bright red flowers on the side—bobbing in the water, sheer joy on their faces.

I don't want them to smile when I'm grumpy.

The teacher immediately introduces us to one another, explains what they do in the class, and I settle in to watch. They perform various exercises, trying for all they're worth to resemble Esther Williams, but it just isn't happening. The movie *Fantasia* comes to mind, but I refuse to dwell there.

Afterwards, they giggle and talk their way into the locker room like schoolgirls. The teacher asks me to wait for her in the locker room while she talks to someone.

"You gonna join our class?" A lady with a broad smile and a size twenty swimsuit holds the door open for me. I like this group. I really do.

"It's a way to get exercise without hurting your joints," says another.

Pretty soon they're all crowded around me with welcoming smiles. I like them.

They chatter about all the advantages of the class and how it has helped them to grow close as friends. They tell me they go out together on a regular basis. Sometimes they even drag their husbands along.

I settle onto a side bench while they finish getting dressed and chatter on like friends do.

"Are you going with us to the mall, Mabel?" a bony woman with blue hair shouts.

"For goodness' sakes, Ruby Lee, I'm right beside you, and I'm not deaf," Mabel says matter-of-factly. "Yes, I'm going." She shrugs on a bright new pair of Nike tennis shoes.

"Irene, you going?" A plump woman with a straw hat wants to know.

"I'm going home, Carol, and taking a nap," Irene answers.

"Oh, come on. You can sleep when you're dead. Get your shoes on and go with us," Mabel says.

Mabel turns to me. "I suppose we sound a little loony." She chuckles. "We may not have a lot of years left—"

Years? Did she say years? I'm thinking someone is in denial here.

"—so we plan to squeeze the life out of every minute."

They're living life for all they're worth, while my life is falling apart.

"We sure do that, don't we, gals?" A woman with leathery skin and a hoarse voice pipes up. She looks at me. "Don't waste your days, sweetie. Make 'em count. That's the key." She tips her head and clucks her tongue like she's telling a horse to giddy-up.

What kind of days do I have left if Gordon leaves me? I feel a knot forming in my throat. How will I live without him? *God, please, help me.* Before I can move my feet, tears stream down my face.

"Oh, honey, it's all right," Mabel says, wrapping her damp, wrinkled arm around me.

The others gather around.

"What is it, dear?" the woman they call Ruth asks.

I keep my head down, saying nothing.

I feel a bony hand upon my own. "You know, we don't have all the answers, but God does. Talk to Him about it."

"Can we pray with you, honey?" Irene asks.

I nod.

This special group surrounds me, lays their hands upon me, and leads me into a prayer so beautiful that when I open my eyes, I'm sure I'll see Jesus.

"Thank you." My words are barely a whisper. I get up from the bench and look to them once more. "Thank you so much. Will you tell the teacher that I'll call her later?"

"Sure thing," Mabel says.

They all smile and offer more words of encouragement. Before I leave, they promise to pray for me in the days ahead.

I go to my car. In a matter of minutes, these ladies have touched my life in a profound way. They are the catalyst God has used to get my full attention.

With the afternoon to myself, I drive to an area park, reach for the extra Bible I leave in my glove compartment, and find an isolated bench.

Tucked in the whisper of the trees, I seek God's guidance for dealing with Jade and this thing with Gordon. My husband has never given me reason to doubt him before. I want to trust him now and live out all my days here with him.

I open my Bible to 2 Corinthians 4:16–18. The words reach to the core of me.

"Therefore we do not lose heart. Even though our outward man is perishing, yet the inward man is being renewed day by day. For our light affliction, which is but for a moment, is working for us a far more exceeding and eternal weight of glory, while we do not look at the things

which are seen, but at the things which are not seen. For the things which are seen are temporary, but the things which are not seen are eternal."

I glance at the age spots on my hands. "That's me. My outward self is perishing." Elvira Pepple comes to mind. She's perishing, too, but her inner beauty grows with every breath and shines from her life.

To my utter amazement, I realize I want to be like Elvira Pepple. Elvira Pepple with the clacking teeth, oversized housedresses, limited hearing, sloppy lipstick? Yes, she's the one. Okay, maybe I don't want to be like her on the outside, I still want to do my best to take care of this body. But you know what? I realize I have only so much say in what I look like on the outside. The age thing is the fate of all humanity. But I do have a say on the inner me. I can choose to grow bitter or better.

I choose better.

I choose life.

I choose Gordon.

• • •

The water-aerobics experience has left me with renewed strength and some answers. I'm determined to show Gordon that though the flames may be sputtering, the fire is not out of this marriage yet.

Once I get home, the answering machine light is blinking. It's Louise Montgomery. She's having the Hatfields, Hensleys, and Hansens over for dinner two weeks from Friday. She wants us to join them. It's awful that we've messed up her dinner plans all this time.

Before I can think of what to do, the phone rings. I hope it's not Louise. Decisions are not my forte today. My mind is pudding.

"Hello?" Crusher hobbles over to me and jumps on my lap. I run my hand along his back and his right leg quivers in sheer delight.

"How was your water aerobics class?" Lily asks.

I fill her in on my day with sketchy details.

"I still don't believe you have anything to worry about, Maggie. That just doesn't sound like Gordon. There is no doubt in my mind that he loves you and only you."

"Well, time will tell, I guess. Either way, I'm determined to do all that I can to make our marriage work. Let's just pray he cooperates."

"Have you decided how you're going to pay for Jade's counseling?"

"Yes, I think I've found my answer. You're familiar with my vintage jewelry collection?"

I hear her gasp. "You're not going to sell that, are you?"

"That's exactly what I'm going to do. You wouldn't believe how that stuff sells on eBay!"

"I know, but how can you do that? You love that jewelry."

"It may sound crazy. I do love that jewelry—or at least I *did* love it. But you know what, Lil? It's old. Why would I want to wear old jewelry? It's like wearing a flashing neon sign that says, 'Oh, yoo-hoo, look at me, I'm old.' I'm thinking no."

Lily laughs. "Only you would think of that."

"Besides, I feel kind of like I'm shedding the past or, I don't know, starting a new life. You know what I mean?"

"I think so."

"Plus, it feels good to give away something that I love to help someone I love more. Somehow it means more to me that it's costing me something. It's like I'm finally at peace with myself. I've been mourning the fact that my body is changing and I'm growing old, and then all this stuff with Jade. Well, I finally realized we both had the same problem."

"How do you mean?"

"We didn't appreciate the bodies given us. Jade was abusing her body, and I despised mine. She tried to control her life through her eating habits. I tried to control the aging process with endless products. So I have wrinkles." I shrug. "They prove that I've lived. I've had a wonderful life, and it's okay that I'm not twenty anymore. I'm enjoying the journey, you know?"

Lily gets quiet.

"You still there?"

"I'm here. I'm really proud of you, Maggie."

"Trust me, it has nothing to do with me."

"Oh, I believe you."

"Well, you don't have to be *so* agreeable."

We laugh.

Before we end our conversation, we talk about Lily's growing feelings for Ron with two first names, and Gordon arranging the Internet thing. Lily thinks it's neat that Gordon went to the trouble. Love could be in the air for Lily and Ron. I pray my future will be as happy as Lily's.

30

Now comes the hard part. Calling Gordon.

"Hello?"

"Hi, Gordon," I say, feeling a bit shy for some reason.

"Maggie. I can't tell you how good it is to hear your voice," he says with obvious relief. My heart warms to him. "Do you want me to come home so we can talk?" he asks.

My mind swirls with all that I want to accomplish before he gets home. "No, actually, I'd like you to stay at work 'til, say, about seven o'clock." I can't believe I'm actually saying that.

"Really?" He sounds stunned.

"Will that work?"

"Yeah, but do you want to talk at all, Maggie?"

"Not now. We'll talk tonight, okay?"

"If that's what you want."

"It's what I want. Oh, I almost forgot. Park your car in the driveway. Don't come in through the garage. Use the side door, okay?"

"Did the garage door opener stop working?"

"I'll talk to you about it later. I've got to go. Bye." I click off.

The timing has to be perfect. Now is not the time to say anything to him.

We hang up, and the phone rings again. It's Jade's dad returning my call. I explain to him who I am and how I've gotten to know Jade. I tell him what Jade has shared with me about her friend.

"I know she's not quite right," he says in a voice thick with pain. "I want to help her, but—" He chokes on the words. Jade had mentioned he's a proud man, so I tread easy here.

"I have prayed about Jade's situation and would consider it a real blessing if you would allow me to pay for her counseling." I practically hold my breath, afraid he won't let me help.

"I want to tell you no, that I'll take care of my baby myself, but the truth is, I can't. I don't know how to get help, and I know my insurance won't cover it. Work has been down. Way down. I'm not even sure how much longer I'll have a job."

"God has put people in our lives who have helped us over the years, and it's time we gave back. You are helping us by allowing us that opportunity." I figure after the money from my jewelry runs out, I should have the car paid off. And now that Tyler has asked me, and I've agreed, to stay on permanently at the coffeehouse, my earnings there will be able to help Jade.

"I can't thank you enough for helping my baby girl. I don't know what I'd do without her."

I tell him I will mail him checks for the counseling sessions.

"Ma'am?"

"Yes?"

"Where do you go to church?"

His question surprises and excites me all at the same time. I give him the name.

"We've never attended church much. Just on the holidays, but I think it's time we changed that."

After talking a little longer about the church and giving him the times and directions, we say good-bye.

I hang up the phone and glance toward the heavens. "Thank you."

• • •

I head to the grocery to pick up the things I need for dinner. I stroll down the beauty aisle and spot a jar of cold cream, of all things. Expensive products have done little more than the tried and true, so I plunk it from the shelf and put it in my cart. I can't help smiling. It feels wonderful to accept myself as I am. It takes a lot of pressure off me.

Once I get home, I set to work in the kitchen preparing Gordon's favorite meal of filet mignon, roasted red potatoes, sautéed mixed vegetables, and salad. Two tapered candles flicker from the middle of the table laden with a white linen cloth and china bowls filled with steaming entrées.

"Wow, what's this?" Gordon asks, walking through the door, sniffing the air in appreciation.

"Go wash up for dinner, and I'll tell you," I say.

"I have to do this first," he says, stepping over to me. He drops his briefcase and pulls me into his arms. "I love you, Maggie Hayden, just in case you didn't know."

My stomach turns to mush, and I feel all my resolve melting away. This man could not be planning a rendezvous with another woman. He just couldn't. Still, he has some explaining to do.

We eat our meal and enter into simple chitchat. I want to save our discussion for afterwards, and have told Gordon so. He agrees, though I notice his appetite has waned a bit. Mine too.

We clear the table and rinse off the dishes. Drying my hands on a towel, I turn to him. "I have something to show you." Grabbing his hand, I lead him to the door that opens to the garage. "Now, close your eyes," I say. He complies. I open the door and lead him by the hand to his work area so that we're directly in front of the Nova. "Okay, now you can look."

Gordon opens his eyes. "Maggie, what? Where? When?"

I laugh. "A 1971 Chevrolet Nova, from Galloway's Cars, picked it up today."

He runs his fingers along the driver's door.

"I know you had your heart set on the Mustang. I tried to get it, but it was already sold by the time I got there." I explain what had happened with the Nova and how kind Eric was to let me drop it and then buy it again.

Gordon starts laughing. I mean, *really* laughing. I'm not sure I like it.

"What's so funny?"

"I was the one."

"You were the one what?"

"I was the one who put the money down on the Nova and tried to buy it when you let it go."

"You're kidding."

He shakes his head. "I wanted to get it, but I thought we were going to get paid on the Keller estate sooner, and as soon as I got the news that the money wasn't coming for a while, I didn't feel it was fair to Eric to keep it on hold, so I let it go. I had other plans for the money, and my coworker wasn't able to buy the Corvair yet."

Gordon pins me with his gaze. "I love this car, Maggie," he says like an excited high schooler. He picks me up, lifts me in the air, and squeezes me. I'm thinking I'll have to call 9-1-1 for him if he doesn't put me down quick.

He eases my feet to the floor and continues around the car, checking out the interior, the engine, all the parts, the trunk space, and the outer body. "Boy, this takes me back thirty years."

"Doesn't it?" It feels good to see him so happy. I'm glad he likes it.

"But how could you afford it?"

I tell him how I've managed to pay for it up to now and how I plan to finish off the payments. He hugs me again.

We talk about all the things he wants to do to the car, and I see that Gordon's free time is pretty much taken for the next six to eight months. But I'm okay with that. At least he'll be home. Who knows? Maybe I'll even come out in the garage and help him.

After the excitement dies down, we settle in the living room.

He sits beside me on the sofa. "Okay, Maggie, I can't take this anymore. I don't know what's going on with you, but I have to tell you, I'm sorry for all the time I've been away from home. Work has been crazy, and I've told you that, but I also want you to know our efforts have culminated into a couple of huge settlements for the firm. The work is finally finished, but we won't get paid for a little bit yet."

"I don't care about that," I say.

He smiles. "Now, what's going on with you?"

I explain all the fears that have bottled up inside me. Debra Stiffler, Sparkle Toes, Celine.

He takes my hand and shakes his head. "Maggie, after all this time, how could you doubt me? First off, Debra came to my office with some matters pertaining to her ex-husband. I went into the restaurant to grab a sandwich, and she spotted me. She insisted on buying me lunch for helping her with the legal matter. What could I say?"

"'No,' comes to mind, especially after you turned me down when I asked if we could go to lunch."

He peers at me over the rim of his glasses.

I shrug.

"As far as, Sparkle Toes, er, uh, Brenda is concerned, what you overheard had nothing to do with me and her. It had everything to do with her trying to make her husband jealous. He was in the hallway flirting with one of the secretaries. She was trying to get back at him."

I keep listening.

"Okay, that leaves us with Celine." He runs his fingers through his hair, then looks at me. "I wish you would have come to me about Celine's note, Maggie. It could have saved you a lot of grief. One of the girls in the office told me that Celine and her husband were going through some financial difficulties. She only told me because Celine went home early one day in tears. I had no idea what it was about, and Celine didn't tell me. This coworker did." He blew out a sigh. "Anyway, I gave Celine and Jared a couple hundred dollars to help them out. I had meant to ask you about it, but when I called you that day, you were gone. I didn't really want to leave a message like that on the answering machine, so I didn't. Then I got so busy here at work, I totally forgot about it. You know how I struggle with being a softy. They were in need. I had to do something."

"But what about that line?" I ask, pointing to the part that says: "What we share is special even through the obstacles."

"She was talking about herself and her husband, what they share and their financial obstacles."

I try to process all that he's saying. He pulls me into his arms, and I just stay there for a moment. Then I remember the unfinished business. I pull away and look at him. "There's something else."

He searches my face, worry in his expression.

"The tickets. What about the airline tickets? I know there were two. When I asked Celine, I saw you through the glass in your office door raise one finger so she would answer accordingly."

He groans and lays his head back against the sofa, confirming my fears. Finally he says, "It's not what you think, Maggie."

Tears prick my eyes. "Then please explain it to me, Gordon."

"Okay, but you're going to wish I hadn't once I'm finished."

"Let me be the judge of that."

He blows out a sigh. "It was supposed to be a surprise."

I'm totally confused now.

Suddenly, he kneels down on the floor in front of me, takes my hands in his, and says, "Maggie Hayden, I love you. I have loved you from the moment I first saw you, and that love has grown more with every passing year. I want to grow old with you. I don't care what comes our way; I will never leave you or forsake you. I told you that almost thirty years ago, and it's still true today. Will you marry me again?"

Tears are all over my face now. Gordon is a blur, and I feel so foolish. "Lily was right. I never should have doubted you."

"The kids are coming on Saturday—"

I gasp. "The kids? But I thought—"

"You thought they wouldn't be home Thanksgiving weekend because we wanted you to think that. I told them to spend Thanksgiving Day with whomever they wanted, as long as we got them on Saturday. They will stand with us when we renew our vows in front of a few friends and family members this weekend. It's all arranged. Heather and Nick are singing 'We've Only Just Begun,' just like the lady from your church did thirty years ago."

The comment takes me back to our wedding day, to the Carpenters' song that had been one of our favorites while we were dating.

"I couldn't have done it without Heather's help," Gordon continues. "She's made phone calls, picked out a dress for you, made silk flower arrangements, everything. She has been swamped helping me because I was too consumed with work to take care of things myself."

Heather loves us. More tears.

"The reason I couldn't buy the Nova? The airline tickets. One for me, one for you."

I stare at him, gaping. "So you're not going to Florida on a case Thanksgiving weekend?"

He shakes his head. "It was just the first thing I could think of when you asked me on the spot like that. I figured if I said it was over

Thanksgiving weekend, I could start packing my things so at least one of us would be ready to go before you had to know the truth."

"Then the tickets are for—"

"Our anniversary. But I guess it's all for nothing until you answer me."

None of this is registering. My brain feels fuzzy. "What do you mean?"

"Maggie Hayden, I *still* love you with all my heart. Will you marry me?"

With all his heart? As in every part of it, with nothing left over for Celine Loveland or Debra Stiffler, or— "Yes, Gordon, I will marry you."

"Then you had better get packed, because after the ceremony on the twenty-seventh, we'll be using the tickets when we head to Maui for a week!"

His words hit me like a hot flash. I scream. "Hawaii!" I lean in to kiss him and pull him toward me. Gordon shifts forward then instantly stiffens. He winces in pain and his hand grabs his lower back. He rolls over to his side, bringing me crashing to the floor with him. Pillows fall from the sofa and scatter around us. The commotion scares Crusher, who scampers away, leaving a liquid trail behind him. I see it and groan. Despite his pain, Gordon laughs.

I look over at him. "Are you all right?"

"Yeah," he says between chuckles. "Back spasm. It's easing up a little now." He gently pulls me into his arms. I snuggle in close to his chest. I can hear his heartbeat, and I think of the ladies at the water aerobics class. I'm thankful for life.

"I will always love you, wife of my youth," he whispers into my ear, squeezing me tight. "And I can't wait to see how crazy our lives will be when we're old."

We chuckle together.

When we finally quiet down, we just lie there and stare at the ceiling. I'm wondering how we'll get up. "Is your back okay?"

"Yeah," he says, but it's not convincing.

"You want some muscle ointment?"

"Yeah."

I laugh. "Come on, old man," I say, grunting as I attempt to carefully pull him up, while struggling with some muscle pain of my own.

"Hey, you watch it, Mrs. Hayden."

We finally stand to our feet. "Here, lean on me." I pull his arm around my shoulders. We step over Crusher's mishap and hobble off toward the bedroom in search of ointment.

I think I've finally learned that life is more than hot flashes and cold cream. It's about keeping focused on my relationship with the Lord, keeping Him first in my life. That leaves no more room for self-pity.

Life is digging in my heels with stubborn determination when needed. It's letting go of the people I love and trusting them to make the right decisions. It's about believing in the man I married and making peace with my body. It's about getting rid of my mirror.

So that's my plan from this day forward.

I will live this life that God has given me with gusto, not wasting a single moment but using it as He intended. And when my journey here is over, I plan to skid into Glory with a smile on my face, a Bible in one hand, a chocolate truffle in the other, and I will yell at the top of my lungs:

"Daddy, I'm home!"

Reading Group Guide Available at

www.westbowpress.com

Special thanks to:

My readers for taking the journey through this book with me. You make my mother proud.

My husband, Jim, who constantly feeds my creativity. We've been on an awesome adventure for the past thirty years, and we're just getting revved up! I love you, honey!

My daughter, aka PR Woman, Amber Zimmerman, and her husband, Kyle, for actually reading my books and still telling others about them.

My son, Aaron Hunt, and his wife, Megan, for their ongoing encouragement. I love you all!

My friends, Colleen Coble, Kristin Billerbeck, and Denise Hunter. You have answered my endless questions, challenged me to grow, encouraged me to believe in myself, and offered laughs over lattes! This book wouldn't be here without you!

My prayer partners, Donna Cass and Nan Forrest. Your ministry gives mine meaning. Thank you, girlfriends.

My awesome agent, Karen Solem, who refuses to settle for mediocre. Thank you for making me rise to the challenge.

My in-house WestBow editor, Ami McConnell, for believing in me before I became an AARP member. Your editing expertise boggles my mind. Because of you I want to reach for the stars—or chocolate, depending on what you're teaching me at the time. Truly, I'm forever indebted to you.

Editor Natalie Gillespie, whose sharp eye for grammar and technique makes my words and punctuation fall into all the right places.

The creative team at WestBow Press: book cover creators, copy-editors, and marketing personnel. You've made *Hot Flashes & Cold Cream* a dream come true.

My church family at Grace Point Church of the Nazarene for loving and supporting me through the wrinkles of life.

All my "boomer" girlfriends—you know who you are! Thanks for making me laugh and giving me writing material. I couldn't do it without you!